Sometime before ni~~ne joe rose and went to the bathroom~~ to take a shower. When he came back into the bedroom, Samantha lay in a tangle of pillows and sheets offering glimpses of skin smoother than the fine silky cotton sheet that covered her. The cloud of black hair he would never tire of touching seemed to reach out and ensnare his fingers. He kept his eyes averted as he finished dressing.

"This is never going to happen between us again, is it?"

He sat down to put on his shoes.

"Don't you give me that goddamn silent Indian treatment, Joe Ferris!" She leaped out of bed and came to him. "Look at me!" He kept his eyes downcast. "I said look at me!"

He looked at her and smiled a rueful smile. That tone of voice. He could still hear the imperious tone of the ten-year-old commanding him to teach her how to ride bareback like he did. Tough, cynical Joe Ferris had images of wind blowing through black hair and golden skin glowing under clear water, of a man and woman walking hand-in-hand through wildflowers and wrestling like young cubs in a fresh snowfal!. His mind led him down all the clichéd romantic paths. "I know," he whispered. "But, Sam, it's not going to work. It's wrong for you."

"You mean for you." She pulled away from him, suddenly aware that she was naked. She was about to cover herself with a sheet. Instead she stood up and said, "The hell with it. I'll never forgive you." She sounded like a small child who has just been refused an extra hour of television.

"I don't blame you." He took her reluctant hands in his and kissed the palm of one, then the other.

Aspen

LORAYNE ASHTON

LYNX BOOKS
New York

ASPEN

ISBN: 1-55802-023-3

First Printing/October 1988

This is a work of fiction. Names, characters, places, and incidents are either the product of the author's imagination or are used fictitiously. Any resemblance to actual events, locales, or persons, living or dead, is entirely coincidental.

This book is published by Lynx Books, a division of Lynx Communications, Inc., 41 Madison Avenue, New York, New York, 10010. The name "Lynx" together with the logotype consisting of a stylized head of a lynx is a trademark of Lynx Communications, Inc.

Printed in the United States of America

0 9 8 7 6 5 4 3 2 1

To MHS who, as always, makes it possible.

ACKNOWLEDGMENTS

There are many people who have helped with this book. Some of them are: Kay Clarke, Connie, Maureen Bell, and Mary Eshbaugh Hayes at the *Aspen Times*, Peggy Clifford for her memories of Aspen, the ladies of the Pitkin County Library, Kearen Matsoukas in the City Manager's Office, Peggy Stevens at the Aspen Historical Society, Robert Ritchie of Coates, Reid and Waldron, Susan Gurrentz, and all those others who have contributed knowingly and unknowingly to my Aspen impressions and memories over the years.

AUTHOR'S NOTE

The Wheelers, the Browns, the Hopkins, the Hymans, the Webbers, the Cowenhovens, the Pabsts, and the Paepckes are the names that define Aspen's past. They existed, they excelled, they dreamed, and thus put their stamp on a small silver town in the West. The Mallorys are the fictional inheritors of these extraordinary adventurers. The Hotel Jerome is one of the town's great landmarks, but the Silver Leaf Inn exists only on paper. The theme of this book, the overdevelopment and destruction of a fragile landscape, are real concerns in the Roaring Fork Valley, as they are all over the country.

The history of the Roaring Fork Valley, though brief in this book, is accurate and based on the writings of many experts of the period. If any inaccuracies have slipped in, the author takes full responsibility for them.

I have taken liberties with history and assigned to my characters certain aspects of the lives of those real and vital people who turned Aspen into the social and cultural phenomenon it is. May their ghosts rest easy.

CHAPTER ONE

A LOW-LYING SUN GLINTED OFF THE HIGH PEAKS THAT pierced the brilliant blue sky and sent long shadows soaring like eagles down the Roaring Fork Valley. It was lovely weather for April, but rotten for Aspen's slopes in mid-November. As the United Express jet turned toward Sardy Field it was clear that Aspen was suffering from a lack of snow.

Suddenly the plane veered off its course, sending beverages in plastic cups sloshing over passengers and onto the floor.

"Jesus . . . what in hell is going on? Did you see that?" The Woody Creek rancher with the sheepskin jacket and the big Stetson jammed on his head turned to his seatmate. "The crazy bastard coulda killed us." The man took off his hat and wiped his face with a red bandanna.

Samantha Mallory frowned and wisely held her tongue. She was used to it. The sleek *Conquest II,* which had just subtracted several years from the

United pilot's life by dipping its wings in the jet's path, was her brother's plane, and this was his customary way of welcoming her home. Every time she returned to Aspen from somewhere, Patrick rolled out a kind of symbolic red carpet in the air for her.

Tom Landon, the ops manager at Sardy, would, as usual, ream Pat out for twenty minutes and then the two of them would meet later for a beer at The Red Onion where Pat would swear once again to keep out of the way of commercial jetliners' flight paths. Sam wondered how Pat managed to hold on to his pilot's license, especially with the brouhaha that was going on over air safety.

She peered out the window of the plane. The last seven years had brought inevitable changes to the valley. On her left she could see Starwood, with its huge houses, massive security gates, and lush landscaping. It was home to John Denver, Rupert Murdoch, Bill Ziff, Ted Field, and other privacy-loving celebrities. Just west of the airport was Pitkin Green, a development of million-dollar homes and the source of vociferous protest against the Roaring Fork Railroad, whose proposed tracks into Aspen threatened to run right under their expensive landscaping. Farther up valley would be Red Mountain, the oldest of the three superluxury areas, where the latest and grandest house in the area, reputed to be 28,000 square feet, was going up.

She sighed and leaned back in her seat. Sam had always carried an idealized picture of Aspen in her mind: snow-capped mountains and unchanging views; icy, rushing streams, and snowbirds hovering overhead as she hiked the trails in splendid solitude. Yet all the things that were meant to tie her to the land had been too weak to still the siren call of New York. After Sam's first visit to the big city, she knew she had to live there. She had felt the pulse of the city congruent with her own, loved even the dirt and noise and danger, the anarchy and freedom from family ties. For a while. And then it had all changed. She had struck out to conquer a world, and in turn had been struck down by it.

She had always remembered the high mountains, yearned for them even when she couldn't wait to get away from them. And so she was returning to the place that gave her breathing space, that had the power to heal her.

Despite the huge homes and trendy boutiques, the celebrity-choked slopes and fancy parties, Aspen continued to be—in her mind, at least—so very special. Winters were white and silent with black mornings turning to pale cornflower by midday. Spring came in softly, then was over in the blink of an eye. During the summer the air was cool and piney at first, with crisp, winter breezes, before it turned warm and caressing. But it was autumn she loved best; when the tourists had gone, and the light was pure and clear, when the aspens shimmered like gold coins in the sparse air, and the ducks chattered all day as they made ready for their flights south. In the fall, nights were crisp and cold, but the days were still blissfully warm, bathed in a light as limpid as a Chopin étude. And there was always time to stand on a corner and talk and breathe.

In winter where else could you find that happy combination of brilliant sunshine, perfect snow, and challenging slopes? No sooner had the snow receded than everyone was off fishing and biking or hiking to the high peaks through meadows of magnificent alpine flowers. Aspen, with its timeless, unchanging mountains! She'd been away too long. Well, she was back now. For good.

As the plane taxied to a stop, Sam grabbed her bags and—in an unaccustomed burst of impatience—stepped into the aisle and onto the foot of a package-laden woman who squealed, "Ouch! Why don't you watch—" The voice changed from an unpleasant whine to a rich drawl. "My God, Samantha Mallory! You were on this plane all this time and I didn't know it? I can't believe it."

Sam stared curiously at the other woman.

"It's Melanie! Don't tell me you don't recognize me?"

"Melanie! Of course."

Melanie Rogers was considered the most beautiful woman in Aspen. She had grown up there, but along with her outrageous sense of style, she had somehow picked up an accent from her four years of school in Mississippi. She was now a classic southern belle from her drawl to her magnolia skin.

Vivienne Rogers, Melanie's mother, and Sophie Mallory, Sam's mother, had served on numerous committees together and there had been genuine closeness between the two husbands, so the two girls had been thrown together since childhood. Sam had been forced to drag Melanie, four years younger, around like a bratty little sister for longer than she cared to remember, constantly reminded to share her toys, and later her friends and boyfriends.

At first Melanie had been in awe of her older friend, then jealous. When Sam had gone away to school in Denver, Melanie had thrown a screaming fit and obtained permission to go there, too. When Sam went to New York to live, Melanie had ended up going off to ole Miss.

"I heard you were coming home. Sophie told me at the Herberts' party last week. She's so excited having you back. So tell me, did you get tired of the big city? God, I envy you. New York! I'd kill to be living there." Her voice dropped. "You wouldn't believe what's been happening here. Why, it's like a feeding frenzy in the piranha tank. Everyone tryin' to outdo the other. I swear I am in a constant state of exhaustion trying to keep up."

Melanie's mind was like a hummingbird in flight. It

was difficult to keep up with her thought processes, but Sam could see that she hadn't changed a bit.

Until she was eighteen, Sam had dutifully suffered all the frills and pretensions of being the daughter of the first citizen of Aspen. Not that her parents ever insisted she attend every function, but Sophie and Big Sam, as her father was always called, had been part of the continuing movement to make Aspen a center of culture dating back to the days of the silver barons and old B. Clark Wheeler, and which reached full flower under Walter Paepcke after the Second World War.

It was the social life that had gotten to Sam, the very same things that were as mother's milk to Melanie Rogers. It was the endless parties and luncheons and dances, the hour-long phone calls back and forth to arrange the day's calendar, the buzzing off to Denver or San Francisco for a shopping spree, the gossip and jealousy and underlying nastiness that had finally driven Sam away. In New York she could wallow in the anonymity she craved and be unique among all the other unique ones. Or so she had thought . . .

"So tell me, did you meet any great men there? Or are they all workaholics like I hear." Melanie was still at her elbow, sniffing around with the persistence of a bird dog. "What's the real reason you're home? Off the record."

"I'm going to paint," Sam said as she walked down the steps and hurried across the tarmac.

Melanie called to her retreating back, "You mean paint pictures? We'll have lunch. I'll call you. I'm dying to talk to you."

Sam smiled grimly. The real reason, Melanie asks. Gregory Francis is the real reason. New York's most eligible bachelor, who shared my heart and my bed for the last two years, who betrayed me by trying to make me less than I could be.

She had first met Greg Francis when he'd personally interviewed her for a job with the prestigious Museum of Indian Art. He was not only, along with his wealthy family, the curator, but the guiding force behind the gallery as well. She remembered how quietly approving he'd been as she spouted her encyclopedic knowledge of southwestern art, easily identifying everything he set in front of her: the black Martinez pottery from San Idelfonso and the Tafoyas of Santa Clara, the black and ivory Acoma. She had explained the difference between Zuni and Hopi kachina dolls, pointed out the meaning of forms in the glowing Navaho rugs. She told of the digs she'd been on at Chaca and Canyon de Chelly, of the lost cities of the Anasazi, of her love for the raw materials of the great southwestern Indian master craftsmen. He'd been impressed, telling her later that he'd hired her not only for her knowledge but for her fierce passion.

It was the same intensity of feeling that she'd brought to their relationship and which had finally frightened him away.

"Your desires overwhelm," he had said. "Not just your physical ones. Everything. I never knew anyone who had such an appetite to see and hear and touch and taste. Too much for me to cope with."

And so they had stopped seeing each other. But there was still the museum and their daily contact there. Once they had worked in exquisite harmony, two minds with but one sensibility. After the breakup they had taken to squabbling over everything: acquisitions, shows, how to hang and display their treasures. Everything became a confrontation, from the toilet paper for the staff bathrooms to what color ink to use on the invitation to their first gala fund-raiser. It was then that Sam realized the time had come to say good-bye.

As she walked through the busy terminal, she was amazed to see that it was no longer the little country airport she had remembered. Glancing out the window to see if Pat had landed yet, she suddenly felt herself caught up in a bear hug that threatened to crack her arms. As she was kissed noisily on both cheeks, her feet dangled off the ground, then set down.

"Samantha MacNeal Mallory! Let me look at you," Pat Mallory held his sister at arm's length and stared. "Well?"

He nodded approvingly. She was still as dark skinned as an Indian, and her straight black hair still fell about her face severely. She was small boned with wrists and ankles that looked as if they could be snapped like chicken wings. But Pat knew her fragile appearance was as false as the persistent rumors that she was the product of her mother's liaison with a mysterious Navaho. On the other hand, he could understand why they refused to die. Not only did she look like an Indian, she rode like one. Thanks to Joe Ferris, he thought wryly. Sam, bareback on an Indian pony, was sister to the wind. She was the same on a pair of skis. Set her on top of Aztec and she'd leave you standing in a cloud of powder. She was like the aspen tree; slender and supple and unbreakable.

"You look good, sis. A few dark circles under the eyes from all that high living, but we'll straighten you out. C'mon, Sophie's walking holes in the floor."

At his words, she pulled back. Despite her love for her mother, Sam wasn't quite ready to meet that indomitable woman. They'd had some pretty knock-down drag-outs over the years about Sam's willful behavior. Once Sam had given all her new school clothes to a rancher's child who had come to class in hand-me-downs. And she had defied her mother about Joe Ferris, the half-breed, her best friend and the boy who'd taught her to ride Indian style. She had gone off to New York knowing her mother disapproved of the city and continued to see Greg Francis after her mother warned it would end in disaster. How could you stand a mother that was always right?

"How's Liz?" she swiftly changed the subject. She

didn't much care for her sister-in-law, so the question asked out of duty was perfunctory in tone.

Pat grimaced. "Let's not spoil your homecoming."

Pat Mallory's wife, Liz, stretched her arms over her head and yawned deliciously. Her breasts tilted up, and the dark-skinned man beside her cupped one in his hand before lowering his sleek head to cover the hard nipple with his mouth.

She squirmed against a thigh that was as hard as Colorado granite. Her lover, Joe Ferris, was a daily habitué at her mother-in-law's Silver Leaf Spa, and his body was the living proof of it. Lean and fit, elegant as a bullfighter, yet with powerful shoulders and legs, he seemed to be chipped from stone; all sharp edges and ridges. A long, slightly flat nose divided his narrow fox face into symmetrical halves, each shadowed by high cheekbones. Although his mouth seemed to curve in a chronic smile, upon closer scrutiny its amused mockery was readily apparent.

Liz put a slender white hand against the dark, beard-shadowed face. "Are you going to do me again?"

The smile turned cruel. With a graceful turn, he rolled off her body, a cloud of her Tiffany scent clinging to his chest. "No," he said. He had a soft twilight voice full of vaporous shadows skulking through a forest and ready to spring at your throat at the slightest provocation. Even a monosyllabic yes or no had danger in it.

To a woman like Elizabeth Lloyd Mallory, there were many words in the English language, but *no* was not one of them. She couldn't remember the last time she'd taken no for an answer when she wanted something badly enough.

Liz looked at her lover with narrowed eyes, trying to figure out what she really liked about him besides the way he made love. His voice was too soft for her taste, definitely wrong for his physique. She wondered if she could teach him how to change its timbre. And of course, he was much too dark skinned. It irritated her that people took him for a Chicano, or worse, an Indian. She laughed mirthlessly to herself.

Endicott Lloyd had never denied his daughter a thing except for a heritage and a position of social significance. Consequently they were the only things she'd ever really wanted. As if to make up for these abysmal lacks and to expiate the guilt he felt, he'd lavished a great deal of the questionable money he'd made during the war on her. Finally he'd lived to see her marry the man she couldn't live without, Patrick Mallory, the *crème de la crème* of Colorado bachelors.

But like the furs that languished in her closet and the jewels tossed carelessly in a box, she had tired of Pat, too. Joe Ferris, on the other hand, was endlessly fascinating. She loved the idea of an illicit romance, the way her blood raced when the phone rang and he suggested a meeting, the heady fear of imminent discovery. She found their secret coupling wildly exciting. Although his Spanish-Indian background was *un peu dégoutant,* he made love like a dream: he was passionate, inventive, violent.

"I don't like it when you say no."

"I know. That's why I say it."

She made a sound of annoyance and kicked the sheet off the bed to reveal a body as white and rich as cream. She shook her head angrily, and blond hair the color of moonlight flowed over the pillow.

He threw his head back and laughed, then leaned on his elbow to stare down at her with wet, dark eyes.

She reached out a finger and touched his lashes. "It's not fair that a man should have such ridiculously long lashes," she pouted, "nor skin that feels softer than mine." The finger continued its way down.

"Nor this, either, eh, *carita*?" He pulled the sheet down and took his swollen penis in his hand and shook it at her. "But this you can have anytime. You know it, don't you? You want it, eh? Say pretty please."

A throaty growl was her answer. Her finger continued its journey and touched the head of his penis. Suddenly her mouth was on him, devouring him.

His breath caught in his throat, and he squeezed his eyes tightly shut. With his two hands he forced her deeper until he felt himself touch the back of her throat, then he moved rapidly in her mouth, all the time holding her head in a viselike grip.

With a burst of strength, she wrenched herself away from him. "You crazy spick bastard, what are you trying to do? Strangle me?" She flung herself from the bed and across the room where she stood looking at him furiously. "That's what I get for . . ."

"For what?" His voice was quiet, controlled, unlike the blood-hot fury that raced through him. "For what, *mi corazon*?" He got off the bed in one fluid motion and stalked over to where she stood. She watched him with smoky gray eyes, the vein in her throat beating visibly.

He caught her to him with a grip of steel. Flexing his knees, he circled her body with his, grinding against her until she felt him harden again. With a cry she reached for him and brought him into her. He attacked her like a jackhammer, his hands all over her body, his mouth devouring her breasts until she screamed with desire. Her body began a tattoo against him, and slowly they sank to the floor where he shuddered once, then twice while a low, keening wail flowed from her mouth.

Their labored breathing filled the room, finally returning to normal. He began to shake with silent laughter which grew into an audible laugh. "What's so funny?" she asked, looking at his fox face with the long, feminine eyelashes shadowing his cheekbones.

Every time Joe Ferris fucked Pat Mallory's wife, he felt he'd triumphed over an old enemy. Liz Mallory meant nothing more to him than a means to an end. Whether Pat Mallory knew it or not didn't matter as long as Joe knew.

"Why are you laughing?" she insisted.

"I was just wondering what Rosie Sukert would say if she could see us now."

Liz Mallory flung her lover from her. "That's not remotely funny."

Rosie Sukert, her head swiveling up and down and from side to side, bore a somewhat human resemblance to ET. The gossip columnist for the *Aspen Times* was at Sardy Field to pick up her friend, Sunshine Campbell, and at the same time check out the arriving celebrities.

She waved to Sam and Pat Mallory who were waiting for the luggage to arrive and ignored that bitch, Melanie Rogers, just back from somebody's warm bed, she was sure.

Rosie was dying to get out of Aspen. After twenty-five years, she'd made a lot of enemies and lost a lot of friends, but she couldn't afford to go, unlike Melanie, who was so loaded she could go anywhere. And did, using that new boutique of hers as an excuse to chase over to Paris or San Francisco or Shanghai whenever she wanted. Everyone knew Melanie slept with anything in pants as long as he was good looking.

There was a new face in the crowd: a woman, attractive in a quiet way, wearing a suede skirt, expensive boots, and a city-styled sheepskin jacket. Rosie wondered if she was "someone," then decided she was just a tourist even if she did carry a briefcase. Maybe she'd arrived for one of the zillions of conferences held annually in Aspen or Snowmass.

Aha! Pay dirt! A divine man followed Sunshine and young Alex Breton into the baggage room. Late forties, Rosie guessed, even though he looked younger. Tall, elegant, with straight, almost pompadoured dark hair with distinguished wings of silver at the temples.

And those black eyes, so soulful, so sad. He had the familiar look of a celebrity, but she couldn't place him.

She waved impatiently at Sunshine Campbell, not even waiting for her friend to approach before she asked, "Did you see him? Who is that gorgeous hunk?"

"Which hunk?" asked Sunshine lazily, not bothering to look around, as they walked through to pick up baggage.

"The one who got off the plane with you! Didn't you see him?"

"I saw Sam Mallory and Melanie Rogers and Lem Sharpless."

"No, no, I don't mean Lem Sharpless. Who cares about him? I mean that gorgeous guy over there." She pointed to the man who had just fitted a cigarette into an ivory holder as he waited for his baggage. He wore his overcoat over his shoulders, a pair of pigskin gloves tucked into the breast pocket. "Very European."

"He is," interrupted Alex Breton with a sly smile. "Rosie, I'm surprised at you. Don't you know who that is?"

"Would I ask if I did? Who the hell is he?" Spying the stewardess making her way into the waiting room, Rosie, ignoring Alex, went to ask her. The girl glanced at the tall man standing quietly in a corner and shook her head.

Rosie came back dejectedly. "Alex," she said at last, "who the hell is he?"

Alex looked around, then bent down and whispered in her ear. "It's Marcello Mastroianni's brother. He's an internationally famous plastic surgeon and he's here for a seminar and some skiing." He glanced out at the flawless day. "Unfortunately, by the looks of it, he's not going to have any."

"How do you know so much?" asked Rosie, eternally suspicious.

Alex ran his hands through his touseled dirty blond

hair and grinned. "I sat next to him and he told me. See you around, Rosie."

"Do you believe him?" Sunshine asked.

"Sure, why not? He looks Italian."

"That kid," she said, referring to Alex, "is so tanked up most of the time, I don't think he even knows his own name."

The doors slid open, and the baggage wagon was pulled up to the waiting platform. The system was a little primitive, but the airport was undergoing a major renovation so it could handle jet traffic on direct flights from the major gateway cities.

"Hurry up!" prodded Rosie. "He's about to leave."

"So what?"

"I want to follow him."

"Why?"

"Sunshine, don't ask questions. Just get your stuff and let's get out of here. For Christ's sake, I'm a reporter."

"And I'm Ginger Rogers," Sunshine said under her breath, grabbing the well-wrapped fishing rod she'd brought back for her father.

Rachel Fulton watched the several scenes playing out in the baggage room with the practiced eye of the writer. She, too, had noticed the handsome Italian, had even sat next to him on the short flight up from Denver. They had exchanged a few pleasantries regarding the scenery but nothing more. Not even when Rachel had taken out her manuscript to work had he expressed any curiosity about her.

Despite his obvious good looks and expensive attire, there was something unsettling about the man. Waves of nervous energy emanated from him, heavy as the smell of his after-shave lotion. During the brief flight his fingertips played a restless tattoo, growing more impatient as they came closer to landing. She had already decided she didn't trust him. David, her ex-husband, would have told her she was doing her "mumbo jumbo" stuff again. Nothing had infuriated him more. In the rational, logical, computerized mind of David Fulton there was no room for the irrational or the magical. Why they had ever married in the first place was still a source of surprise to her even after the last five years of solitary living.

Still, she had her ex-husband to thank for her writing. True, she had begun out of desperation and a desire to close him out of her life, but the need and the desire to write had always lurked beneath the surface.

For years, as an editor, she had played nursemaid to a bunch of petted and indulged writers who made huge quantities of money even though they couldn't write a coherent line. The knowledge that she could write rings around them and that her marriage was a total failure arrived at about the same time.

Two novels and a National Book Award later, she was free of her marital and editorial bonds and on her own, comfortably well off and looking forward to the research and writing of her third book which, if she was lucky, would be written in Aspen.

She looked around at her fellow passengers. The striking girl with the Indian black hair interested her. She could be an actress, a model, or even a housewife. But not an ordinary one. By her clothes, Rachel figured her to be a local returning from a day in Denver. From her years of research on the region's Indians, she recognized that the concha belt the young woman wore was both antique and rare. The turquoise was an exquisite robin's-egg blue with a dense matrix of gold shot through it. The buckskin jacket, with its intricate beading and deep fringe, might have been worn by a Sioux over a hundred years ago.

Of even greater interest was the man she clung to in the baggage area. Too handsome for his own good, thought Rachel, even with the almost imperceptible fan of white scars. His smile was too wide, too white, and the eyes, ah, the eyes. They were a piercing black and clung to the girl with affection and . . . was that pain she saw? A little haunted perhaps. His well-worn flight jacket had obviously earned its rends and tears, and he wore it with the style of an old-time flying ace.

Rachel wondered what his story was. Where had the scars come from? He was probably . . . She stopped. This habit of observing people as if they were characters in a book, of weaving fanciful histories for them after a brief glance, was becoming an occupational hazard. Well, one thing was perfectly clear, she decided, they are not lovers. Then she wondered why she was so sure.

The arrival of their luggage stopped Rachel from further conjecture. Picking up her bags, she followed the couple to the curb. His Jeep was in a no-parking zone. She watched him help his companion into the car and ride away, still wondering who they were, knowing that she would no doubt find out sooner or later. Aspen was a small town.

Pat turned onto Highway 82, called Killer 82 by the locals because there were too many accidents caused by too many drunk drivers heading home after too many beers on the tortuously twisting road which was the main route into town. Driving while intoxicated was a serious offense in Pitkin County; so was speeding, Pat explained when Sam remarked that he had become a more sensible driver in his old age.

"So what's been happening since I've been in New York?" asked Sam, pushing Pat's golden retriever aside and settling into the sheepskin-covered seat. The dog edged back against her and dropped its big soft head into her lap. Idly she fingered the silky ears.

Pat swung the pickup into a narrow opening between an old beat-up Ford and a Cherokee to a cacophony of protesting horns.

"I was wrong. You still drive like you own the roads," she said, clutching the seat and the dog to her.

"It's the only way." He grinned. "What's been going on, you ask? A man from El Jebel got picked up for assaulting two schoolkids, some guy committed suicide at the Airport Business Center, the town's fighting about how high the new houses in the West End should be, some disgruntled help torched a house in Woody Creek, then there's the . . ."

"That's not what I mean. What's happening at home?"

"Mother's so excited about seeing you, I don't think she's slept for a week. You don't know how happy it makes her that you're coming back."

A frown creased her face. "I bet. She's just waiting to take over my life again. Pat, you've got to help me. I want to get my own place."

"Uh-oh."

"Damn it, Pat. I'm twenty-eight years old."

"Hey, don't take it out on me." Pat raised his hands in surrender. "You know how she is about you. You're her darling baby," he said with poorly disguised bitterness.

Sam turned away abruptly and stared out the window. It was always the same. She and Pat always started out happy to see each other, and then came his mother-never-loved me crap. It had been going on for years. From the moment she was born, Pat had felt pushed out of the limelight. He should be glad. It was far worse being Sophie's daughter than Sophie's son.

Pat bit his lip. Why did he put Sam through this each time they saw each other? It wasn't her fault that their parents preferred her to him. Pat had vague memories of his mother feeding the squealy, squirmy thing, bathing it, cooing and kissing every rosy toe and finger as Pat watched gravely from a distance. When he tried to kiss the baby, he was driven away as though he was a murdering stranger. Even though there was a nurse to take care of her, his mother seemed to consider Sam her exclusive property. And Big Sam's love for the baby was mixed with reverence.

Even this, however, did not stop Pat from loving the little scrap of humanity in the handmade dresses.

When Pat had started first grade the baby had started to talk, and from that point on all he remembered was that the entire house revolved around this small entity as he grew lonelier and lonelier. His loneliness finally drove him to develop his own strengths. He caught his first trout when he was seven (accidentally, it was true), killed his first deer at ten. At twelve he could outski any kid on the mountain. Then they had sent him away to school. Oddly enough, the person he missed most was his sister. She had turned into a pretty little thing with a heavy cap of black hair and the odd turquoise-colored eyes. He remembered coming home from school to stare at her and tell her stories that made her laugh and coo and giggle.

As she grew into cherubic toddlerhood, it was obvious that she adored her big brother. The minute she saw him, she would race to him and hug him, saying his name over and over again. And no one ever had to tell him to watch her or take care of her. He liked nothing better than to give her rides on his bike or attach her wagon to its tail and wheel her all over town. He was the one who introduced her to skiing. She adored it, sharing his love of danger and adventure.

Sam had never judged him and found him wanting. To her, he was big brother, all-knowing, all-seeing, fighter of her battles, adoring knight in shining armor.

Big Sam treated his son with deference and respect. Pat remembered his father tramping through the woods with him on one of his wild-bird hunts. When Pat saw his first soaring hawk, he was awestruck by the beauty and freedom of its flight and raised his gun. There was an old Indian myth that said he who killed would take on the qualities of the thing killed. But Sam Mallory had pushed the gun down and explained to him why he shouldn't hunt, how precious all life was, and how all was interdependent in the wild. Because he loved his father with a pure, brilliant love that craved only his approval, Pat never hunted with a gun again.

His mother was something else entirely. He couldn't remember her ever touching him with love—not even as a baby. She would take his hand when they crossed a street but immediately drop it when they reached the other side. Her good-night kisses were dry, almost absentminded, while his sister was drowned in affection, covered with kisses and hugs. Pat grew up thinking that was the way parents were with sons, a myth immediately dispelled when he held his own son for the first time. Neither Tooey nor Mandy ever knew anything but affection from their father.

"You keep avoiding any mention of Liz," Sam's voice cut in on his memories.

Pat shrugged.

"Still together?"

"In a manner of speaking."

"Still using the kids as an excuse?"

Pat smacked his hand against the wheel. "Damn it, Sam, don't start with me." The fan of white scars seemed to swell and grow livid against his tanned skin. "There's never been a divorce in the family," he said sullenly.

"That's the most idiotic thing I ever heard of. So what? It's the nineteen-eighties. What a family we are! You've got a wife that you never see. I keep looking for a man that mother will approve of, and end up having one disastrous relationship after another. Mom won't remarry because she's still mourning Daddy's death. I flit from career to career and you look for new and improved ways to kill yourself."

Pat was taken aback by his sister's outburst. Ordinarily, she was the gentlest of creatures, soft-spoken, kind, able to see both sides of the question, and rarely taking sides. "What's gotten into you? I've never heard you talk like that before. What's made you so cynical?"

"A few years with Greg Francis and too many years trying to survive in New York." Sam clamped her mouth shut obstinately. She didn't want to tell him about her fruitless attempts to become a painter, nor the means Greg had used to discourage her.

"I'm not so sure I like this new you."

"Neither am I." Sam smiled. "I'm hoping a few months home will get me back to my old self. I need to breathe some fresh Rocky Mountain air."

"Which is not so fresh anymore. Well, we finally have something Vail doesn't."

"So prohibit cars."

He laughed. "That's only a small part of it. It's the romantic wood fire that does it."

"Simple, just pass an ordinance."

"And what do we do with good ole boys like Hank Campbell? He still won't put in electricity, let alone gas. And a lot of those ranches out by Woody Creek and beyond can't afford to heat or cook with anything but wood. And of course, the tourists expect a roaring fire in their condo fireplaces after skiing."

"Aspen's rich. Let them make the necessary adjustments. There can't be too many poor people left in the valley at this point. The developers have made sure of that."

He colored. "Let me remind you that I am a developer, and you are one of the rich ones."

"Not me, hero. You're rich. Mom's rich. I'm a poor, struggling artist."

"With a significant trust fund, I might add. Just because you let it lie in a bank accumulating interest doesn't mean it's not there."

"I forgot." She broke the tension with a laugh. It was a deep, creamy sound and it came right from her toes. It was one of the things Pat really liked about his sister. When she was at her most obnoxious self-righteous worst she was still able to laugh at herself.

She changed the subject. "How're my niece and nephew?"

His face softened at the thought. "Oh, Sam, they're great kids. I took Tooey up in the plane for the first time. Ten minutes in the air and he was ready to learn how to fly. And you should see him on skis. He's absolutely fearless. This summer he took tennis lessons from Jaime Fillol at The Grand Champions Club, and Jaime thinks he's good enough to encourage."

"Sounds like a chip off the old block. What about Mandy?"

"I'm afraid she's already picking up some bad habits from her mother. Imagine, she's only five and a clothes horse already. Do you know she refuses to wear anything that doesn't have the right label? I hope you can rescue her before she becomes totally obnoxious."

"Hey, I'm only the aunt." Sam had never learned to hate, but if she had, it would be all spent on Liz Mallory, her sister-in-law. What annoyed her even more was that Pat had met Liz because of her. They had been classmates at the Denver School. When Sam had gone off to Rhode Island School of Design, Liz, who lived in Denver, had pleaded with her father to let her go, too. Endicott Lloyd could deny her nothing, so Liz and she packed away their western togs and filled suitcases with preppy college clothes, only to find that jeans, heavy sweaters, down vests, and flannel shirts were de rigueur.

School away from Colorado had been scary, but fun, too. Before long Sam found herself at the center of an avant-garde group of artistic and creative people. As Sam's attention turned more and more toward her new friends, Liz felt more and more left out. Despite the fact that she refused to socialize with the Jews and blacks in Sam's crowd, Liz accused Sam of trading her in just to be popular. Out of a peculiar sense of guilt Sam invited Liz home to Aspen for Christmas where she met Pat Mallory and ostensibly fell in love with him.

Liz had eventually dropped out of RISD and returned to Denver, going to interior-design school and finally marrying Pat. Liz opened an interior-design business in Aspen and, as Sophie Mallory's daughter-in-law and Pat's wife, had become quite successful. Sam wondered what Liz had done to trap her handsome, popular brother. For the longest time, Sam felt Liz had married Pat just to spite her. Certainly the marriage was in trouble almost from the start. Even the two kids had not helped.

When Sam came back to Aspen on brief vacations, it was usually to see her little niece. All the child-hunger she'd managed to hold at bay during her relationship with Greg Francis manifested itself with Miranda, Mandy. She simply adored the child with her tangle of dark curls, her heart-shaped face, and sturdy legs.

"I hope it's not too late," she said after a long silence. "I mean, to rescue Mandy from the dragon. You know what the Catholic church says: 'Give me a child before it's three and he is mine forever.'"

"You got to her earlier than that. She still talks about Aunt Sam." He laughed. It was a happy sound. "One day she's going to find out just how funny that sounds. Aunt Sam." He took his hand off the wheel and gave her hand a squeeze. "Lord, it's good to have you back."

Sam forgot about family problems for a moment as Pat, in his usual nonstop, exuberant fashion, gave her a tour of the town she hadn't really looked at in several years.

"Let's swing by the West End. I want to show you what's going on there."

"Good. Maybe there's a small house I can buy that doesn't cost more than a million and a half." She laughed. She might not have lived in Aspen for a few years, but she certainly knew what was happening to real estate. But with her brother as owner of Silver Mountain Real Estate, the biggest, most profitable office in town, she was sure he could find her something. "I remember there was an adorable little Victorian on North Street, or was it Smuggler? I don't remember. It was always painted in the most wonderful colors. I don't suppose it's for sale, is it?"

He didn't answer. Instead he drove down Smuggler and showed her her dream house.

Sam looked at it blankly. "Is this it? I don't remember it being this big."

"It's been renovated."

"I hardly recognize it."

"Wait until you see what we're doing out here." In his enthusiasm, Pat had failed to register Sam's shock.

Aspen's West End, famous for its elegant Victorians, had survived busts and booms, depressions and wars, only to fall into the hands of developers, who—under the guise of improvement—were subtly altering the character and look of the neighborhood.

He pulled to the curb. "These are our new houses. We got permission to tear down a couple of really decrepit places that happened to be on good-sized building lots. We call them neo-Victorian. What do you think?"

Sam was speechless. Aside from cupolas, fish-scale gingerbread, and wraparound verandas, they bore no more resemblance to Victorian than a sparrow to a peacock.

"I hate them! They're ugly." How could he think these monstrous buildings were wonderful? Even combining two or more building lots wouldn't make the lots big enough for these behemoths, which seemed to crouch behind the cottonwood trees ready to spring.

"Thank heaven everyone doesn't share your sentiments. I sold them right from the plans. One million four and one million six."

"That doesn't surprise me. Everyone wants to live in the West End. But if you insist on building these kinds of houses, sooner or later no one will want to live here. If you ask me, you've developed some kind of edifice complex."

Pat, sensing her anger for the first time, hoped to mollify her. "At least look at them. Maybe you'll change your mind."

Sam followed her brother through the two houses as he proudly pointed out the gray stone fireplaces and wide-pegged floors, the floor-to-ceiling windows with their mullioned glass panes, the modern Poggenpohl kitchens, and sexy marble bathrooms with their Jacuzzis and steam rooms. As he babbled on happily about the great development plans afoot, he was unaware of the anger building in his sister. This was not the Aspen of her pure vision. This was what was happening to every charming resort town all over the country.

Sam turned on him. "Why don't you build on Red Mountain or Pitkin Green? Why do you have to muck up the West End? Can't you see what you're doing? Before you know it, you'll be pulling down Bullion Row and putting up skyscrapers," she said.

"Don't get hysterical, Sam." Pat was growing angry, but he tried to control his temper. "You know that can never happen. They're protected by the Historical Preservation Committee, and the Planning Commission is really conscientious about what gets built here."

"You're a Mallory. When could the Planning Commission ever stop a Mallory?" Sam turned on her heel, leaving him with an angry rejoinder frozen on his lips.

By the time they pulled up to the Silver Leaf Inn, they were barely speaking. She was aware of his shock over her reaction, but she was convinced that Pat would do whatever he wanted in Aspen. He was rich and powerful. He was a Mallory.

"Look, he's getting off at the Silver Leaf Inn." Rosie Sukert slammed on the brakes of her Saab 900 and got ready to jockey into a parking space about to be vacated by a faded blue pickup with a Texas plate.

"Does that surprise you?" asked Sunshine.

"Some people stay at the Jerome."

Sunshine shook her head. "The Jerome's for tourists."

"What about the Lenado?" Rosie mentioned a charming small hotel on South Aspen Street famous for its comfort and elegance. "That's a pretty place."

"Too small, too intimate. A man like that wants dazzle, people, impeccable service. You know. The Silver Leaf Inn."

Rosie pulled into the space, neatly cutting off a Ford Escort that had been patiently waiting for the spot, and got out of her car. Sunshine grabbed her arm. "What are you going to do?"

"Go in and check things out. Are you coming?"

"You're crazy. What's the big deal?"

"He is. And I want to find out all about him."

"Can't you take me home first? I want to see Hank before he goes to sleep."

"I'll get you home in plenty of time to see him. Don't worry. C'mon, be a pal. This is important."

Sunshine was not one to make waves. With few definite thoughts of her own, she found it easier to go along with someone who had them. Rosie made life easy for her. Rosie decided when they would go skiing and where, what parties they would go to, where they would dine. Not since the days when she was part of the Sunyassen community in Oregon had she been so well taken care of. Although Rosie was not quite as spiritual as the Rajneesh, she did have nerve and spirit.

Rosie pulled Sunshine into the elegant lobby of the

Silver Leaf. In a town famous for its Victorian ambiance, the interior of the Silver Leaf was a surprise. Outside it might be a collection of bays, porches, gables, towers, turrets, and fish-scale gingerbread, but inside it owed more to Vincent Fourcade. It positively dazzled with luxury. There were marble floors covered in rare Orientals. Polished oak and applewood cabinets gleamed under soaring beams while crackling fires blazed in the river-stone fireplaces. A vast glass roof revealed the night sky above. Instead of stiff Victorian pouffs and settees, there were inviting clusters of couches in pale pigskin, Indonesian cotton, and English linen. A veritable paradise of tropical plants and flowers climbed a gently trickling wall of water that cascaded from the top of the three-story ceiling to a bubbling pool below.

Rosie pulled Sunshine into a loveseat where they were able to see without being seen. "Who's that woman he's talking to?" Rosie whispered.

Sunshine looked at Rachel Fulton. "I think she was on the plane. Yes, she was. They were sitting next to each other."

"Alex said he was."

"And you believed him?"

"They look very cozy."

"Rosie, I think you're going through some early change or something. They're just talking. I mean, if a good-looking man was standing next to you while you were waiting to check in, wouldn't you talk to him?"

"I wonder what they're saying."

"Why don't you just go over and listen?"

"I think I will."

Sunshine shook her head in disbelief as her friend got up and strolled over to the reception desk.

CHAPTER TWO

WHEN SOPHIE MALLORY'S GREAT-GRANDFATHER GERALD MacNeal first entered the Roaring Fork Valley with Charles E. Bennett's prospecting party in 1879, he wasted little time looking at the spectacular mountain scenery spread before him. Instead his eyes turned to the surrounding rock formations where marauding Utes might be hiding, while he contemplated the mineral wealth hidden in the lower altitudes.

Following the rushing water for twenty miles, the party came to a lovely mountain park filled with meadows and clear pools. Again they wasted no time in admiring nature's glory. As they proceeded through a gap in the ridge, the valley floor and four mountain landmarks spread out before them. On the left, tumbled with the remains of snowslides, was Aspen Mountain. Just beyond was Shadow Mountain. Behind them Smuggler guarded the entrance to the upper Roaring Fork Valley and farther down on the right loomed the red clay spine of Red Mountain.

Skirting Aspen Mountain, they negotiated the swiftly running Castle and Maroon creeks and ran into another prospecting party who, using the Hayden surveys of 1873, had left the booming silver town of Leadville to open new virgin terrain to the miner's pickax. Instead of resentment at finding others there, the two parties felt relief. Their increased numbers could only give them added strength against the Utes. Around a campfire the Pratt party spun dazzling tales of riches to be found and exploited in the valley. MacNeal, who balanced the soul of an adventurer with the canny foresight of his Scottish ancestors, was caught up in the fever of discovery.

Over the next five days, the parties crisscrossed the valley, finally laying out the claims that would splash across the consciousness of the country, bringing great wealth, then great tragedy, and finally becoming merely the names of ski trails, streets, inns, and restaurants.

Before the end of the summer of 1879, the town builders had arrived, and Ute City was born. They passed a winter that was long and lonely, as six feet of snow fell and the mountains seemed to grow taller and taller. Many sleepless nights were spent awaiting a rumored Ute uprising that never materialized. Finally the spring snows melted and the hordes, who'd heard of the untold wealth to be had, set out from Leadville and points east and west to start the nucleus of a mining camp at the junction of the Roaring Fork River and Castle Creek. By 1893, Aspen, as the town came to be known, was the third largest city in Colorado after Denver and Leadville. The city had paved streets, gas streetlights, a municipal streetcar system two miles long, two electric-light and power companies, a municipal water system, three banks, a post office, an opera house, a courthouse, a city hall, a jail, a luxury hotel, a hospital, three daily newspapers, an effective and stable city government, and a thriving though well-concealed collection of *filles des joies*, ready to satisfy the whims and desires of the powerful and rich new mining tycoons.

In the early days, the girls had come in with the prospectors from all over the country: St. Louis, New Orleans, Philadelphia, Charleston, even as far away as Maine. Here they had plied their trade in "cribs" that clung to the railroad tracks along Shadow Mountain. These were tiny, windowless boxes with barely enough room for a bed and a washstand, but lonely, desperate miners did not stop to survey their surroundings. They had spent hours in dark tunnels; what did it matter if they spent another dark hour or two above ground? At least, there was a soft body to fill the darkness. Even if she hadn't bathed in a week and stunk to high heaven, who noticed?

As the town prospered, Durant Avenue, close to the mines and the railroad, developed a "red light" district that could hold its own for elegance and delicacy with any city of the gaslight era and that included Denver, Leadville, and San Francisco.

In the early days Gerald Patrick MacNeal, like many of his fellows, thought nothing of seeking ease and satisfaction with one of these "soiled doves."

Once MacNeal's wealth was assured and the town had taken on the moral convictions of the God-fearing, Bible-reading women who were arriving to be with their husbands, Gerald joined the hue and cry against these houses of sin, not overlooking the fact that their geographical location was among the choicest of future prime real estate.

With the country on the silver standard, these good men saw silver mining as an endless source of riches. They believed in gentility, religion, good manners, and good works. Even when they had lived in tents, hadn't they had a Sunday school and a literary society? So finally they drove the girls out of town, tore down the hovels, and began to build the grand Victorian houses that were to give Aspen its special charm.

By 1890 the Sherman Silver Act had been passed,

requiring the Treasury to nearly double its silver purchases. While temporarily very bullish for the silver industry, it led to silver's becoming the scapegoat for the ensuing inflation and undermining of the nation's gold reserves. A few clever men saw the handwriting on the wall. Silver's days were numbered.

As far back as 1880, B. Clark Wheeler had sung the praises of Aspen as a paradise for sportsmen and artists. When fear drove mine owners to sell their rights, Gerald MacNeal bought them. He and DRC Brown invested in power and water, goods and services, thinking to a future that didn't require silver to survive. Very few of the pioneer silver men had that kind of foresight. Even when the signs were evident, it never occurred to them that silver would collapse.

In April of 1892 the price of silver fell two cents in twenty-four hours. Radical reformers and conservative businessmen with silver interests forgot their political differences and fought to keep silver queen. But the situation steadily worsened, and Aspen could do nothing about it because the problems were international. The failure of two Philadelphia companies early in 1893 triggered an economic crisis, leading President Cleveland to blame the drop in gold reserves on the Sherman Act and inflation of currency by silver money. By 1893 the economic depression rolled west. Within thirty days, every mine in the state had closed. There was panic as the work force dropped from 2,250 men to 150. There was a run on the banks. When the Wheeler Bank of Aspen suspended operations it was almost as great a shock as the closing of the mines. Many took their last few dollars and set out for Cripple Creek, where the gold mines were producing around the clock. In 1894 the largest silver nugget ever coined was found 800 feet below the surface of Smuggler Mine. It was 93 percent silver and weighed 2,060 pounds. But the repeal of the Sherman Silver Purchase Act was already a fact and the price of silver was only sixty cents an ounce.

Independence and Ashcroft, once thriving silver towns, became deserted shells as the high winds and plentiful snows reduced them to board and batten. Only Aspen hunkered down and waited.

By 1900 the great Victorian mansion that Gerald MacNeal had built was converted into a hotel by Sophie MacNeal Mallory's grandfather, James. Despite the staggering blow delivered to the town by the demise of silver, there were those who refused to give up. Silver was still in those seams, and the tunnels that crisscrossed the mountain had not yet filled up with water. The mines started to work again, the workers glad to accept the offered wage—two dollars a day. Dividends—tiny in comparison to what they once had been—were once more paid. Entertainments were scheduled every night at the Wheeler Opera House.

Mrs. DRC Brown held a reception at her palatial residence on Hallam Street to which came the cream of Aspen society. Mollie and James MacNeal gave the first of several balls to introduce Aspen to the Crystal Ballroom of their new Silver Leaf Inn. The Aspen *Sun* gushed, "surely not even the pleasure palaces of San Francisco and New York can boast of such a rich array of fabled decorations. The great crystal chandelier, made in Venice, is reputed to have over 500,000 hand-cut crystal prisms, the walls and draperies required 5000 yards of scarlet silk brocade imported from France. Queen Victoria's favorite rugmaker has produced the glowing Axminster that adorns the anterooms, and it is reputed that the Sèvres porcelain objects once resided with Marie Antoinette in Versailles." (It was not recorded, but James had been particularly taken by the handblown glass called Favrille by a young artist he found interesting and gifted. Despite his wife's disapproval, he filled his rooms with some of Louis Comfort Tiffany's examples.) "Mrs. MacNeal received in a striking black satin dress by the famous Worth of Paris whilst her suite of diamonds veritably outdazzled the chandelier." When Sophie MacNeal had read this account of her grandmother's first major party, she always wondered if that last statement did not have a bit of a sharp, jealous claw in it.

By 1912, only the Mollie Gibson and the Smuggler mines kept Aspen alive as a mining town. The legendary entrepreneurs that had given their names and their energies to Aspen's amazing growth had moved on to new endeavors or died.

Henry B. Gillespie, who had literally created the town of Aspen, failed at other schemes, contracted malaria, and died after a brief illness. Jerome Wheeler, who had seen his name on the city's most prominent buildings, who had been lauded as the "rich uncle" who brought elegance and culture to the mining town, failed at both mining and banking after the crash of 1893. The last eighteen years of his life were spent trying to put his tangled affairs in order.

Only David Hyman, whose name adorned both a street and a mall; David R. Brown, referred to as the Landlord of Aspen because he owned most of the light company and the waterworks; and James Patrick MacNeal, the golden Scotsman, continued to enjoy success.

The MacNeal fortunes grew apace, each succeeding son having learned from his father not to put all his eggs in one basket. Clever investments had protected the family through panics, wars, and depressions. Some sons went downvalley to giant spreads and found ranching hard but satisfying work. Daughters married the scions of other early families and drew into the protective confines of marriage and motherhood. By the time Sophie MacNeal was born, Aspen was on the verge of discovering a new natural resource: snow. The Silver Leaf Inn expanded with its growing clientele and was the first in Aspen to put telephones in every room, as well as radios, reading lights, hot-and-cold running water, heated towel bars and, after a trip to Paris, Turkish toweling robes in every bathroom.

Despite the constant renovations and changes, the Silver Leaf remained essentially what it had always been, one of the finest and most beautiful examples of Victorian art and architecture, until Sophie MacNeal Mallory decided to make a few changes.

Sophie Mallory strode through the lobby of her inn, peeling off her riding gloves. She was a tall, slender woman with short silver hair and the tanned skin of an outdoorswoman. She had a broad Roman nose which gave her a magnificent profile even though it seemed wrong on her otherwise delicate face. At first glance, there was something daunting about her, a regality that suggested strangers keep their distance. Patrician was the word often used to describe her looks as well as her demeanor. But when Sophie smiled that image was soon dispelled, for her smile was impish and warm.

Despite what could be considered an imperfect beauty, she had the ability to overwhelm a room the moment she entered it, which she was doing at this moment. All eyes immediately focused on her. She exuded a humming energy that seemed to infuse everyone it touched with a heightened sense of reality.

She nodded absently to several employees on her way to her own suite of rooms attached to the inn by a glassed-in walkway. Despite her apparent distraction, her professional eye did not overlook the ashes that had spilled from an overflowing ashtray on one of the many mahogany tables, nor the discarded newspaper stuffed into the side cushion of one of the couches.

As soon as she entered her suite, she called house-keeping and gently but firmly suggested someone be sent to straighten the mess. That accomplished, Sophie got out of her riding clothes and went to her bathroom. Though she was faithful to the inn's Victorian heritage, she saw no reason to live in the

overheated, overdecorated atmosphere of her ante-
cedents. In her private quarters, the clean earth and
sky colors of the Southwest prevailed. Here were
whitewashed walls and dark-stained beams, corners
that curved and undulated like gentle sculpture, rich
natural woods, huge hunks of raw larch which held
lamps, an exquisitely carved Spanish colonial table
that filled her dining room. Bright blue wool, the color
of autumn skies in the high desert, covered deep
comfortable couches and pillows. The rooms were
literal treasure houses of Indian art: kachinas, the
spirit dolls of the Hopi and Zuni, fetish dolls and
animals which were hundreds of years old and displayed the simple, direct lines of the most contemporary of sculpture, exquisite Navaho rugs and baskets,
a string of brilliant dried red peppers, a collection of
Maria Martinez's legendary St. Idelfonso black pottery as well as a museum collection of fine old Acoma
pieces, their colors muted by time.

Only the bathroom, with its large Victorian tub and
gilded claw feet, bore a resemblance to the inn's
heritage. But in place of the florid cabbage rose
wallpaper in the hotel's bathrooms, she had had the
walls painted a rosy adobe brick color to match the
quarry tile floors which were kept warm in winter by
hot water pipes. She drew a tub and lowered herself
into it, luxuriating in the delicately scented water as it
slowly rose to her chin.

She ached in every bone. She was a fine rider, but
that didn't prevent her from feeling stiff and old once
she stopped. "Don't ride when it's so cold," her son
said every time she mentioned her latest ache. Pat's
wife, Liz, would smile sweetly, a smile that had the
same effect on her as chalk on a blackboard, and say,
"Really, Sophie, you're not a youngster anymore."

How well she knew that. Liz was really a bitch. As
hard as she tried for Pat's sake, she could not like her
daughter-in-law. Why Pat had married her was beyond her. But that was Pat. Ever since he was a little

boy, he had done just the opposite of what he was told. Once, in despair, Sophie had gone to a psychiatrist who told her bluntly that it was Pat's way of seeking attention and that if she were more cognizant of his emotional needs, he would come around. But try as she might, she could not generate feelings for this strange son who watched her with such hunger and waited for a love that never came.

Still and all, he had been a bright, quick child and, despite everything, Sam Mallory had gone out of his way to be a good father. Sam. Even after all these years thoughts of him still made the ache as fresh as yesterday. She had married Sam without loving him. Married him because she was carrying another man's child and abortion was out of the question. She had waited for him to grow tired of her, but his sweetness and gentleness had remained constant. Finally, his great love for her and the sacrifice of his own ambitions to hers had won her completely. When had she discovered she loved him? It had come over her slowly, subtly. And then one night she went to sleep and the next morning, she awoke in love with her husband.

"Sam!" she had cried with a sense of wonder. "I love you!"

"I know," had been his answer as he scooped her up in his arms. That morning they had conceived Samantha, the child they had both loved with a terrifying single-mindedness. And now she was coming home. Her twenty-eight-year-old daughter, devastated by a most unhappy love affair, was coming home to lick her wounds. God, she hoped Sam wasn't pregnant.

Sophie Mallory's secret was known to only one other person, and now he was dead. That Big Sam was not Pat's father was a fact she was determined to take to her grave. Cruel as it seemed, it would be crueler still—after such a long time—to let Pat know that Big Sam, his beloved and revered father, had not sired him, that he had been conceived in anguished passion one night when a young girl, desperately in love and afraid of losing the young man, had thrown caution to the winds, then learning of her pregnancy, had gone to the young man and been roughly rejected by him. No, rejected was not even the word. He had said without blinking an eye, "How do I know it's mine?"

She had wanted to die, to cut out this unwanted child from her own belly. But Sam Mallory, loving her silently, always there for her when she needed him, guessing what had happened when he'd seen the young man with her best friend, had pried the truth from her and married her.

Her family had been surprised, then annoyed because she had been so willful and precipitous in marrying while she was still in school. Her mother had been particularly furious, cheated out of the society wedding she had dreamed of for her only daughter.

Two years later her father was dead at fifty-three, and Sam and Sophie were returning west with their husky one-year-old son. Sophie took over the inn, and Sam gave up a promising law career to assist her.

With her guilt as a spur, Sophie MacNeal Mallory discovered she had a gift for organization. Her innovations turned a charming sleepy Aspen hostelry into a world-class establishment. She thought nothing of taking ideas from the world's great hotels: welcoming bowls of fruit, down pillows and comforters, fresh flowers and fresh orange juice delivered every morning. She redecorated the fussy interiors, added a state-of-the-art spa, hired three-star chefs for her restaurants, spared no expense.

Soon Sophie Mallory was the *grande dame* of Aspen; loved, hated, feared, envied, but always respected for her energy, her brilliance, and her stubbornness. Aspen had its new silver queen, a human one!

It seemed there was nothing she couldn't do—from

breaking a horse to shaking up the complacent powers that be. She got rid of a venal sheriff when no one else could. She decided too much charity was going to the arts and not enough to the poor and forgotten, and got the allotments changed! She turned the town on its ear and herself into a powerhouse.

After Big Sam died, Sophie grew to rely on her son to manage the other Mallory affairs, and as a result a cautious affection sprung up between them. They were like old lovers who had somehow remained friends.

Now her daughter was returning. Her beautiful, adored child—not a child anymore—but a woman of twenty-eight years. Pat had found his life's work, but his sister was still looking for herself and a place to be that self.

It was hard for Sophie to understand her daughter. By now she should be settled in marriage, a career, anything that might bring her some measure of peace.

Had they been too indulgent with her, allowed her to believe she could succeed at anything? Whatever Sam had wanted to try, Sophie, if not always approving, had tried to be encouraging.

She shook her head. Dilettantism was not something the Mallorys approved of. And lately it seemed that was what Sam was in danger of embracing. She had flitted from one job to another those first years in New York. When she finally settled happily into the Indian-museum job, Sophie had breathed easier. Then came Greg Francis. What disturbed her now was the way Sam was reacting to her breakup with Greg.

Sophie toweled herself dry and hastily stroked on body lotion. She had been exposed to the high desert sun for many years, but her skin was still remarkably good. Only her face carried a few deep lines, lines which she referred to as her "service stripes." She was lucky. Pooh! Luck had nothing to do with it. It was money. There was something to be said for having the money to take care of one's body.

She slipped into a faded blue chambray shirt,

washed so many times it felt like silk, and tucked it into a well-worn lambskin skirt. Slipping her feet into beaded Indian moccasins, she padded to the living room and lit a fragrant fire of resinated piñon logs in the fireplace. Then she sat down to wait.

The meeting between mother and daughter had been awkward at first. Each year the time between visits had grown longer and longer. They had lost the knack of easy exchange. Neither was quite sure of how to cross the chasm that time had placed between them.

"Do you want to talk, Sam?" her mother now prompted softly. She was curled in a corner of a comfortable sofa. Sam, knees tucked under her, sat in the other. She folded and refolded the hem of an ancient quilt which hung over the back of the couch. Ice tinkled as Sophie swirled a stiff double bourbon around in her glass.

Sam looked up. "I don't know what to say." She eyed the series of niches molded in the wall. In them was a collection of kachina dolls from the Hopi and Zuni, Acoma Pueblo owls, and a delightful ceramic Nativity scene from Cochiti Pueblo. How she loved this room! Here was where her fascination with Indian art had started. Encouraged by her parents to touch and hold and carry, she had become endlessly fascinated by this culture long before she even knew what the word meant.

She stroked a sinuously carved snake, enjoying the roughness of its raised scales. "Why does everything seem so much simpler here?" She sighed.

"Does it?" Sophie drained her glass and splashed another inch of Jim Beam in it. Again there was silence, broken only by the sound of ice cubes plopping into the glass and the sizzle and snap of burning wood. The aromatic scent of piñon filled the room. "You just got home. Have you forgotten how claustrophobic you used to feel here?"

"I guess I'd forgotten." I'm a total fraud, Sam thought. I'm a child whistling on a dark street to keep the goblins away, a citadel of shifting sand that collapses at the first breath of wind. I am not brave and independent and certain. I am just the opposite. Someone has cut the ropes of my confidence, and I'm drifting without direction in a menacing sea of doubt. Suddenly she crawled over to her mother and put her arms around her waist. "Oh, Mummy!"

Sophie's heart contracted at the child's cry of old. Her arms tightened around her daughter. Memory filled her eyes with tears.

"God, I can't believe how I fuck things up."

"Stop it! I don't like that word in your mouth, especially when it's not true. You aren't the first woman to suffer from a bad love affair, and you probably won't be the last."

"Damn it! It's not just the love affair. It's everything I've touched or tried to do. You told me I could do anything I wanted to, but I can't. Mother, I want to paint. I've been trying for years. You remember when you used to put up my pictures on the refrigerator door?"

"I do. They were charming."

"Charming wasn't enough."

"Why are you being so hard on yourself?"

"Because I'm Sophie Mallory's daughter, and I can't live up to that image. No one can. Not even Pat, who's certainly been more successful with his life than I have. No, Mother," she put her face in her hands, "Mallorys are not permitted to fail."

"That's utter nonsense. Besides, what were you doing all those years when you were in New York?"

"What does it matter?"

Sophie recognized the emotion of defeat. She had seen it in Big Sam before he died. The frustration that he had kept under wraps for so long had finally surfaced in a burst of rare anger. He, too, saw his life as a series of not quites, of incompletes, blaming his failure on an inability to rise above the ordinary. But Sophie knew it was all her fault. He'd married not only her but her larger-than-life legends. They filled every corner of his life with their ghostly presences and whispers. He lived in their home, on their land, and off their largesse, pretending to be a prince in their empire while all the time he felt like an interloper. In all their years of marriage, she'd had no inkling that he felt that way until illness made him honest. Crying bitterly, she had apologized over and over. But she felt that he had died without forgiving her. Had she unwittingly shunted her obsessive need for perfection onto her daughter's shoulders?

"What exactly have you tried that's been such a failure? You were a fine curator. Everyone says so. No one knows the Indian culture or art better than you. Why are you letting this affair color everything in your life?"

"I know I was a good curator. But it was the painting I wanted to succeed at. Not for fame and fortune," she smiled wryly, "but to prove to you and Greg, too, that I was worth something in my own right."

"Surely you always knew that?"

Sam took her mother's glass and swallowed a healthy belt of the sweetish alcohol, made a face, and wiped her mouth with the back of her hand, bringing a smile to Sophie's face. There were so many little things about Sam that hadn't changed.

"I trusted Greg. He came to mean many things to me. I never told you this before. Greg was the first relationship I ever had with a man that lasted more than a few months. Oh, I could catch a man, but I couldn't hold on to him. Really," she emphasized when she saw the look of disbelief on her mother's face.

"Out of some perverse gratitude, I handed myself

over to him on a silver platter. My thoughts, my body, my so-called talent. Tell me how good I am, make me feel special. That's what I wanted from Greg."

Sophie frowned. Wrong, wrong, she wanted to cry out. Instead, she said softly, "Then it's our fault. We thought we'd brought you up to be more independent."

"I thought I was. Until I got to New York. I was so frightened. The city crawls with talented people. And there are others, critics, teachers, other artists, who will be happy to shred you to pieces. Then I met Greg. He was the kind of man who went out with the smartest, most successful women in the city. Do you know that both *Cosmo* and *Vanity Fair* named him the most eligible bachelor in the country? He knew everything—food, wine, books, music, spoke four languages fluently. I'd been knocking my head against a wall, working in a small SoHo gallery, painting, trying to get some recognition, and there was Greg. He knew everyone, he could open doors, push buttons, and he was interested in me—a small-town girl from Colorado."

"You must have had something."

"Yeah, I made great *huevos rancheros* and sat a horse well."

"I think there was more to it than that."

"Maybe. Anyway, I went to work with a vengeance. I was like a crazy person, like Van Gogh in Arles. Everything I saw I wanted to paint. I worked all day and painted half the night. I dragged him to every gallery, challenged his every opinion, forced him to communicate with me, woke up in the middle of the night to tell him my ideas." The excited haste with which she spoke slowed to a dull whisper. "He said I frightened him. Can you believe that? Me? Frightening someone? Is that a laugh?"

No, said Sophie to herself. It's not. It's probably the truth. She looked at her daughter's face, a gentler replica of hers. She was so much like Big Sam. Under that quiet demeanor lay a powerful presence still not acknowledged, an intensity that burned, a hunger to learn, to feel, to experience. Sam's problem was that she wanted too much. She asked uncomfortable questions. She demanded perfect honesty. She could not settle for sloppy anything. Yes, she could make a man uncomfortable. She had. A man like Greg Francis would never be able to take the fervent heat of a Samantha Mallory in pursuit of her real identity.

Sam continued. "I think Greg really wanted a simpler woman. A complement to himself. Already formed, not too pushy, not too emotionally needy. He hadn't the time or the emotion to deal with someone like me. I think what first attracted him to me finally repelled him. He couldn't have made it clearer when he said, 'You want too much. I can't give it to you. I don't even intend to try. The prospect is too exhausting.'"

"Just as I suspected. I know it's painful for you to accept, but he was a weak, selfish man."

"The worst part," Sam continued, not hearing her mother, "was that he absolutely trivialized my work. I met so many influential art people through him, but when I asked him to intercede on my behalf, he laughed and called me a gifted amateur, said I should give my work to the family for Christmas presents. I was absolutely crushed. This from a man who had been telling me how clever and delightful and hard-working I was. I couldn't believe it. I was better than that. At least, I thought I was . . . but Greg was the expert. Maybe he knew better." She was unaware of the clenched hands in her lap, but Sophie could see her knuckles gleaming white from the pressure.

"How cruel of him."

But Samantha couldn't tell her the cruelest blow of all. She remembered it as though it were yesterday: the Christmas party at their high-ceilinged old Central Park West apartment. She had been experimenting with the naïf—the colors and figurative representations of the American Primitive school transmuted to her western consciousness. Greg, treating her with a kind of parental indulgence, had permitted her to hang some in the den.

The party had been an unqualified success. The tree was hung with her collection of southwestern Indian ornaments; she had designed an elaborate feast centered around roast suckling pig with all sorts of authentic Indian and Spanish side dishes.

Hours later, in search of Greg, she'd heard voices coming from the den. Greg, in company with two well-known art critics and a famous collector, was standing in front of one of her paintings. They were laughing.

"I hope she's better in bed than in front of an easel," said the number-one art critic.

"Oh, she's good at many things," Greg had equivocated.

"But not painting," insisted the first.

"Oh, I don't know," said the famous collector. "She has a certain fauvelike flair. I'd rather have one of these hanging in the bathroom than my wife's flower studies. Poor darling thinks she's Winston Churchill. Tell your lovely friend I'll buy one from her. How about that one?" He pointed to a solitary warrior sitting on a tired old horse, his shoulders slumped, his bow dragging, heading into a vivid lavender void. It was one of Sam's favorites.

"How much?" asked Greg.

"A hundred?"

"Make it two and she can take me to Lutece for lunch." Greg laughed.

Her cheeks aflame, Sam had grabbed her coat and fled into the cold indifferent New York night, not returning until she was certain everyone had gone and Greg would be asleep.

The incident had never been mentioned although she was sure he knew she had overheard the conversation. Shortly afterward she had moved out, continuing to work at the museum until that, too, had become impossible. Before she left, she had tried to bring up the incident, but he had cleverly avoided her by interrupting and changing the subject.

"Believe me, in six months you'll have forgotten all about him. In the meantime, there are all sorts of things going on. I took the liberty of accepting . . . ," Sophie's voice cut in.

"No! No! Don't accept anything for me. I'm not a child you have to chauffeur around, Mother. Haven't you learned anything yet?"

The words came out harsher than Sam had intended them. But it was true. She wanted to tell her mother she loved her unequivocally. But she couldn't. All her life she'd been fighting to free herself from her mother's monumental shadow. Maybe her father had not minded being referred to as Sophie's husband. But she was Samantha Mallory. Not just Sophie's daughter.

"Mother, do you have any idea how difficult it is being your daughter? You've never made a serious mistake in your life. Whatever you wanted to do, you did, and brilliantly. Everyone expects me to be another you. I don't want to be you. I want to be me, whoever that is."

"Then be her. You want to be a painter? Fine. Then do it. But if you fail, it's your responsibility. Not mine. Not Greg's. Besides, you've been out of my"— she grimaced distastefully—"orbit for a long time now. Your successes and failures are your own now." Sophie tried to conceal her hurt. Reason told her that there was much truth in what her daughter said. And right now Sam needed to strike out at someone, anyone. Sophie was convenient. She took a deep breath to steady herself, then spoke in a calm neutral voice. "I can't understand you. You think you've failed, and as far as I'm concerned you haven't even gotten started."

"Because that's the way it feels, Mother, it feels that

way. And damn it, I can't fight the feeling." She pounded her fists into a pillow helplessly. "Damn it, why can't I be more like you? You've always been able to take charge of your life. You're a natural at it."

"Is that what you think?" Sophie shook her head. It never failed to amaze her. Big Sam had said essentially the same thing. It was his excuse for putting their lives in her hands. She'd heard it from Pat, too. But strangely, it had been spoken in admiration, not as an accusation. Now it came from her daughter. And it was so far from the truth. "If you only knew . . ."

"I don't care what you say. You're a strong woman. Whether you believe it or not, you have the kind of power that makes it easy to resent you."

"I didn't know that." Sophie's voice sounded tired, without emotion. Where had it all gone wrong? Her daughter whom she loved more than anything was talking like an angry stranger. "I'm sorry. I had no idea you felt that way." The tears came to her eyes unbidden.

Sam reached for a tissue in her pocket and wiped her mother's eyes. "Oh, Mother, I didn't mean that to sound so cruel. I don't resent you. Maybe a little, sometimes. But that's natural, isn't it? Oh, darling, Mother!" Sam threw her arms around Sophie's shoulders. "My God, I can't believe I'm behaving so horribly. I do love you, Mother. I just wish I could be more like you. Forgive me for being such a brat. I guess I'm still straining at the maternal leash."

"There hasn't been one on you for years." Sophie sat quietly for a moment. Then she straightened up and looked directly at her daughter. What she was about to say would not make her happy, but it was necessary for her daughter's happiness. "You know there's nothing I would like more than to have you stay here with me. But under the circumstances, I think it's better for our relationship if you get your own place."

Sam smiled widely. "You must be a mind reader.

It's what I had in mind, but I didn't know how to bring it up without hurting you."

Sophie was surprised to find that she wasn't hurt at all, that in fact she felt vastly relieved. Over the last few years she had gotten quite used to the quiet of her own home and her own company. And Sam would be better off not having her mother looking over her shoulder.

"I've already discussed it with Pat. On the way in I had him take me through the West End. I thought I might find a small Victorian to buy."

"And did you?"

A shadow crossed her face. "Mother, we had a horrible fight over what he's doing there. You can't hear yourself think above the banging of nails and the whine of saws. There are all these awful houses going up, and Pat is gloating, reveling, bragging about his part in the carnage."

"He's one of the prime movers," her mother said tightly.

"I take it you're not exactly pleased."

"I would say that that was the understatement of the century. I'm going to fight him tooth and nail on this idea of progress he has. Unfortunately the town would like nothing more than to see the Mallorys go at each other. But let's save any discussions on Pat for another time. You'll be around for a while yet, I hope."

"After all the things I said, am I welcome?"

Sophie hugged her daughter. "Just barely. Let's go have some dinner. There are loads of things I want to discuss with you."

"Not too fancy, please. Remember, I've come back to simplify my life."

"Good luck. We'll go to the Touchstone. It's one of our new grille rooms and very good, if I do say so myself."

"Promise me I won't run into Melanie Rogers there."

"Oh, no, Melanie prefers much grander things. Of course, if she discovers you like it . . ."

"Mother! So you finally got wise to dear Mel."

"Oh, dear, I've always been wise to her."

Though their words were light and bantering, their attitude affectionate, there was still the lingering sting of words spoken too quickly, too harshly. It would take some time to bury them. But at least they were now on the right path.

CHAPTER THREE

AS HIS SON CHATTERED HAPPILY, PATRICK MALLORY scraped the shaving cream from his face. He was still smarting from Sam's hurtful words even though there was a great deal of truth in what she'd said. She had probably told Sophie about their fight, and Sophie, as usual, would side with Sam. Even though what he was trying to do was as much for the family as for himself.

As custodian of the family fortune, he was merely following in the MacNeal-Mallory footsteps of increasing the family wealth by well-considered acquisitions, investments, and diversification. He'd been brought up hearing about his forebearers' accomplishments and had always wanted nothing more than to have his mother include him in that galaxy. And despite his mother's distaste for his latest ventures, he knew what he was doing made sense for the future of the Mallorys. If the Mallorys were to continue to increase their power and their wealth, and since Pat was certain that development would continue with or without them, they would be fools to give up the opportunities now in front of them.

So occupied was he with his own thoughts, he was barely aware of his son's flutey voice, answering the boy with "un huhs" until Tooey, giving up in disgust, left the bathroom.

The face emerging from the razor's stroke was deeply tanned from years of exposure to the high western sun. Pat ran his fingers through the waves of dark heavy hair and frowned at the silver strands. He needed a haircut. He needed a lot of things, but as he heard his wife slamming doors, the one thing he was sure he didn't need was her sardonic tongue.

As he washed the remains of white foam from his face, she appeared in the doorway. "Your mother called yesterday to ask if I'd chair the Valentine Ball," she said without preamble.

"Are you seeing her today?"

"Why?"

"Just answer the question. Please?" he asked wearily.

The negligent pose she affected showed a body that still had the ability to arouse him. She was a remarkably beautiful woman. A heavy coil of moonlight blond hair trailed over the shoulder of her white satin robe. The modest neckline could not hide the provocative swell of her heavy breasts. Helplessly he reached out to touch the pearly glow of her skin. "Liz?" His voice was smoky.

She pulled away as if his touch could burn her. "Don't. You promised."

"What did I promise? Only that we didn't need to have any more children if you didn't want to. I'm still your husband. We haven't made love in weeks."

She started to walk away. His anger exploded like a sudden summer storm. "Don't you turn your back on me when I'm talking to you." He seized her arm in a painful grip. "I know you're sleeping around, Liz. Anyone will do but your husband, is that it?"

Her laugh was infuriating and provocative.

"Why did you marry me?"

"You must be joking. Do you want me to enumerate the reasons?"

"I presume they're the same reasons why you won't divorce me."

"Bingo!"

His face turned mean and cold, and she knew he wanted to hit her. "It's ridiculous living this way." He threw her arm from him in disgust.

"I think it's just fine. In public I am your adoring wife. I give marvelous dinner parties, try to raise your children properly even though you insist on indulging them."

"You never hug them or play with them."

"Are you afraid they'll grow up to be like you?" In a moment of weakness he had once told her how he had always longed for the approval and uncomplicated love of his parents and how, many years later, he realized they simply were not capable of giving him what he wanted. He had sworn his children would not grow up loveless, attended by nannies.

"Goddamn you," he exploded.

"Darling, what you need is a good fuck." The harsh word sounded out of place on those sensuous lips. "But you're not getting it from me. I know there are any number of ladies out there—your secretary, for instance—who would be thrilled to oblige. You have my permission. After all, we're Mallorys. Gossip can't hurt us."

"If you hate us so, why do you hang around?"

"And give up the name and all that lovely money? Don't be silly. Besides, my father went to so much trouble to marry me into your family."

Pat's broad shoulder slumped in weariness. "What about the Valentine Ball?"

Liz ran her fingers through her hair. It was a sexy move, maliciously done to taunt him. "Tell Sophie I'm simply too busy with work to be able to spend much time on it."

"Why can't you tell her yourself?"

"I'm tired of her hassling me."

"Mother doesn't hassle."

"No, she doesn't. She just fixes those steely gray eyes on me and makes me feel like shit."

Pat still couldn't get used to his wife's truck-driver language. That a woman who looked like a Christmas-tree angel could talk like that boggled his mind.

He turned away, despising himself for still craving her body.

"Oh, by the way, remember we're going to the Hellers for dinner tonight. Try to be home on time."

He slammed the door in her face, but not before he heard her chuckle.

He gave his children more attention at breakfast, promising to take them flying as soon as he had a free Saturday. To them it was an adventure with Daddy. To him flying meant total freedom. In the sky his mind emptied itself, exulting only in the silence and speed.

His frustrated quest for approval had turned him into a daredevil, forever courting danger. When he was seventeen and a promising ski racer, his craving for speed had landed him in the hospital for months and lost him a possible berth on the Olympic ski team.

Hang-gliding was his next obsession. That produced only a broken arm. But when he discovered flying, he knew he had found his metier. All his young life he'd had daydreams of becoming a flying ace, but when he grew up there were no "clean" wars to fight in. When he wanted to quit college to go to test-pilot school, his horrified mother had pulled strings and he was turned down. In frustrated fury, he had flown his light plane into a mountain and miraculously survived even though his face was torn to pieces as a result. The best plastic surgery that money could buy left him with a few charismatic scars on his Smiling Jack face and a great deal of time to read. He became an expert on the exploits of the fighter pilots of World War II, stories his children never tired of hearing.

Along with his name and fortune, it was Pat's reckless devil-may-care attitude that had fascinated Liz Lloyd. She had come home from school with Sam. She'd been, as she was now, a woman of lush proportions, full breasted and narrow waisted with melting curves and ivory skin that drew men to her like iron filings to a magnet. He usually preferred more athletic-looking women, and he'd never been attracted to blondes. Liz was definitely blond with dark chocolate bedroom eyes and a sulky mouth. A woman to bed and forget. But her feined indifference had piqued his manhood. When introduced, she'd given him a limp handshake and immediately turned to continue her conversation with Morris Stanton, an architect friend of his mother.

Liz had ignored him the entire evening even though he managed to stay within an arm's length of her. Her little game worked. If it hadn't been so well played, he probably wouldn't have given her more than an instant's thought. But Pat was not accustomed to being ignored by women.

By the end of the week, he'd taken her to bed, and six months later they'd had a huge wedding and two years later, two children. On their wedding night, Pat knew that Liz's indifference had been part of a deliberate plan to ensnare him and the Mallory name, a fact that was made abundantly clear to him when a Denver friend, who'd been one of her earliest lovers, had gotten very drunk one night and told him a few stories about her.

After the two children were born, she told him she had had her tubes tied and there would be no more children. Before they were married she'd been a voracious lover. Two years later, she was practically yawning in his face with boredom. And protected by the mantle of Mallory clout, Liz was going out of her way to make a fool out of him. For a man of Pat's ego and self-esteem, it produced a highly undesirable state, and periodically he would bed someone, anyone, to find out if he was still potent. If he was, he never saw the woman again. If he wasn't, he definitely didn't want to see her again.

"Why is Mommy always mad?" Mandy broke in on his thoughts.

"Is she?"

"She yelled at me a little while ago and told me to get out of her goddamned way."

Pat's jaw tightened. He had made his bed and had to lie in it. But the children didn't have to be subjected to Liz's dislike of him. He should talk to Bradley Hotaling, his lawyer, and find out what he could do to get her out of his hair. Even if it took his entire fortune, it would be worth it. His entire fortune . . . that was a laugh, he thought. After today's lunch with Richard Farwell, that could be a paper tiger.

If New York had its "21" and Four Seasons, San Francisco its Banker's Club, and Washington the Senate Dining Room, in Aspen, the power lunch of note was the Silver Queen Room of the Silver Leaf Inn. Here the power brokers met every day to decide the fate of the Roaring Fork Valley and even the state of Colorado and the world.

The rich mahogany walls and authentic brass sconces and spitoons gave it the elegant atmosphere of a gentlemen's club. A blazing fire crackled in the vast fireplace over which lorded Remington's portrait of Gerald MacNeal in buckskins and moccasins, looking more like Buffalo Bill than the patriarch of the magnificent MacNeals.

The only thing separating this western outpost

from its mates on either coast was its diners' style. Whereas the movers and shakers of those empires wore bankers' gray and pinstripes, the Rocky Mountain variety tended to a more casual dress. Many an easterner doing business had been fooled by the high-heeled boots and jeans, unaware that the hand-tooled boots probably cost at least 750 dollars, the Levis might be faded, but the shirt and blazer were made to order at Saville Row's best tailor, Gieves & Hawk.

The menu did not cater to the health concerns of the day, offering vast slabs of beef, baked potatoes dripping with butter and sour cream, and Caesar salads with freshly grated Parmesan cheese. Desserts, both in size and creativity, were on the heroic side as well.

Pat Mallory paused to say hello to Gladys Welch, the hostess, and received in turn one of those fatuous smiles that men of money and looks are always receiving. He looked around the room for his luncheon date and found him sitting at his favorite table overlooking the garden.

Richard Farwell was sixty-two years old and looked forty-five. He looked like a successful rancher who had achieved his success only after years of back-breaking work, which was not so far from the truth. However, he was the CEO of Silver Mountain Industries, a far-reaching Denver conglomerate that controlled all aspects of the resort from downhill ski facilities and restaurants to a considerable financial interest in many of the subsidiary businesses such as ski shops, real estate, and the Silver Mountain Ski Manufacturing Company. A towering man with a Gregory Peck kind of monumentality, his dark red hair had faded to the color of a ginger snap, the crisp waves blending in with a face the same color. He was a wintery-looking man with eyes the color of a December sky. Joviality did not come easily to him, but lurking amongst the natural lines of his face were a surprising set of dimples, visible only when he smiled broadly, an infrequent habit.

Pat had that easy elegance that came from money, lots of it. He wore his faded khakis and old suede jacket with natural panache. His wide-brimmed felt hat could have made the trip from Oklahoma's dust bowl to California during the Depression. He hung it on one of the brass hooks that lined the walls and held other similar head gear.

After giving the waitress his drink order, wasting no time on pleasantries, he got straight to the point. "My spies tell me that the whole block over by Shadow Mountain is going to default soon. Richard, we have got to get our hands on those properties before someone else does."

Richard Farwell frowned, and with the patience usually reserved for a small recalcitrant child, tried to explain. "Pat, we just can't commit that kind of money this year. You know what kind of shape the corporation is in. Three below-average years, snow-wise, plus all the new resorts opening up so much closer to Denver have really cut into our skier days. And we lost a ton of commissions from our central reservations office. We won't even be able to make our usual big donations to the Springfest or the Children's Christmas Festival. And don't forget you want to increase the marketing budget."

"That only makes sense," Pat insisted. "You forget we've got to keep reminding people that there's no place like Aspen. We've got to make them want to come the extra two hundred miles."

"If we don't get some decent snow soon, the whole subject will be academic."

Pat's Corona beer came at the same time as his roast beef. He hated being that predictable, but he was a true Coloradan and loved red meat. As he thought over Richard's last statement, he sliced off a hunk of the beef and held it on his fork, staring at it as if it hid magic signs and portents within its bloody flesh. In his enthusiasm to rush things along on his grand development scheme, he had forgotten that little aspect. The weather, usually so predictable in the High Rockies, had been, as it had all over the country, unusually tricky. By Thanksgiving, there was usually enough snow to open the mountain. With normal below-freezing temperatures, snow-making machines could make up for any lack of natural snow. But after a cold snap in October, a protracted Indian summer had arrived and night temperatures were so benign that gardens of annuals all over town continued to bloom. The array of petunias, impatiens, pansies, and geraniums planted under the trees of the Mill Street Mall had a spectacular midsummer brilliance even now.

Richard Farwell had learned long ago to avoid alarming his minions by his tone of voice. He tended to speak with soft neutrality even to Pat Mallory, the man he felt closest to on his board and the one he trusted implicitly. "This dry spell is playing havoc with all ski-related business, you know." He couldn't blame the younger man for wanting to move forward on what he euphemistically called Aspen's Tomorrow Plan.

Both Pat and Richard knew Aspen would need more than its mystique to carry on into the new century. It was crying for beds. The older condominiums which had been around for years were dark, dingy affairs with tiny rooms and decaying services. What Pat wanted to do was demolish practically everything close to the mountain but the Aspen Alps and build an exciting cluster of inns, lodges, and hotels that would stretch along the mountain's instep and continue around Shadow Mountain. It was a plan that would take all of Pat's charm and clout to get by the Planning Commission. And it was a plan that was nothing but a dream on paper unless he could raise the money.

As if he were reading Pat's mind, Richard said,

"We're talking hundreds of millions of dollars. And improved lift facilities will add more millions. Remember, the Silver Queen gondola cost six million dollars two years ago."

"The problem is that everything has to happen at once. And that airport renovation is a joke. By the time Sardy Field's expansion is finished, the airport will probably be too small again."

"Pat, this is not Chicago. Where are you going to go to get more space? Sardy Field is limited by the mountains. I suppose you think we should flatten one of those?" He offered a rare smile.

"There must be some way to go out toward Owl Creek Road."

Richard shook his head. "Do you think somewhere back in your genealogy there was an Egyptian pharaoh?"

Pat's face reddened. "My sister said I had an edifice complex."

"Don't we all in this business?" Farwell gave a gloomy look at the brilliant blue cloudless skies.

The truth was that Richard Farwell was frustrated as well as furious. It seemed the gods were all conspiring against him, punishing him for his hubris. For generations the Denver Farwells had been successfully turning ranch and farm lands into commercial and residential developments. Farwell had tried to pattern himself along the lines of Walter Paepcke, who had come to Aspen in 1945 and fallen in love with the dead, poor town. He came, he saw, and dreams of glory danced in his head. Aspen's apparent drawbacks: the fact that it was remote and poor were actually—in his eyes—synonyms for serenity and purity as Peggy Clifford, an Aspen journalist, had quoted in her history of Aspen.

But Paepcke made his dreams come true, organizing the Aspen Company with plans to lease and restore the old Hotel Jerome, the opera house, and a number of old houses. He took over the work that Andre Roch had begun on the trails and lifts. He established the Aspen Institute for Humanistic Studies to give a boost to the summer economy. He was considered the father of modern Aspen.

Richard wanted to be considered the father of the Aspen of the future.

Like Paepcke, Richard was a man who attracted people to him like satellites around a magnetic planet. The best came to work for him: lawyers, architects, engineers, all attracted by the lure of the climate and the sports, the glamour and the money, the lush life-style which offered luxury and adventure side by side. When Richard was eager to hire someone, he often used Pat Mallory as the perfect example of the meshing of the two life-styles.

There was one major difference, however. Paepcke was not interested in money but an ideal. With Herbert Bayer, a Bauhaus master, he laid out the pattern that would keep Aspen small in scale and Victorian in character. He fought against pseudo-Victorians and shoddy modern, hated the Swiss chalets and characterless motels springing up despite his urgings against them.

Richard Farwell hated them, too. That's why he wanted to tear them down. But not for an ideal. His ideals were wrapped in the brown paper of pragmatism. If Aspen didn't grow and expand, it would wither and die. Its growth would naturally and eventually be slowed by the immovable mountains that rose on all sides. Blended into the dream was the smell of financial success. Constantly upgrading the town, its lifts, and its services would produce the green stuff. Richard was not necessarily interested in the ski-week package business. Real profits come from a healthy influx of moneyed people who wanted the best of everything. So growth was essential. And it would be expensive. Farwell had been pumping substantial amounts of his own considerable fortune into Silver Mountain as he awaited the approval of a line of credit from the banks.

Pat had been talking steadily for several minutes before Farwell's attention returned to the matters at hand. "I'm meeting with a couple of heavy hitters from Texas and California who are interested in putting a great deal of money into my project."

"Which project?"

"Jesus, Richard, haven't you heard a word I've said?"

"Sorry. My mind must have wandered for a moment. You were saying you have the promise of some fresh money?"

"Right. But you're my friend as well as my associate, and I want your input."

"Do they want to do this as part of Silver Mountain?"

"That depends." Pat averted his gaze.

"On what?"

"What kind of deal you'd be willing to make."

"What does that mean?"

"C'mon, Richard, you know what I'm talking about. These guys are not philanthropists. If they go in on a Silver Mountain deal, they want assurance of stock and a seat on the board."

"Forget it. The board is full."

Pat understood the unspoken fear behind Richard's unequivocal refusal. He, too, had heard the grumbling of the board over Richard's stewardship, knew there was talk of replacing him, knew that he, Pat, was really the swing vote that could maintain or unseat Richard. Pat also knew how much of his private fortune Farwell had already invested. It was only a question of time before Farwell would be forced to listen to deals he'd have turned his back on ten years ago. He, too, had his own sweeping expansion plans, plans that Pat enthusiastically favored, but which were now on the back burner due to the negative cash flow.

"What do you want to do, Pat?"

"You know as well as I do. Build more luxury hotels and rental apartments. Buy up that East End property as it becomes available." He pushed his plate away and poured himself a cup of coffee from the silver urn at his elbow. Leaning forward, he said softly, "I'm convinced the Institute is going to pull out. It's absolutely crucial that we develop a new plan to keep summer business from drifting away to places like Taos and Santa Fe or even Vail and Telluride. I want to move up Castle Creek or take over the highlands. Let's develop the best facilities for hiking, hunting, and fishing. Let's have a film festival, a music festival of our own. Christ, we have enough movie stars in residence here during the year to make it as big as Cannes."

Richard put his hand on Pat's arm to stop the stream of excited words. "You don't have enough to deal with? You want to take on the environmentalists as well? They are dead set against gentrifying the Castle Creek area. Your own mother is on their side."

Pat wrenched his arm away. "Forget about my mother, she's not the issue. Besides, my group has spent over one hundred thousand dollars already on impact and feasibility studies. Trygve Lindstrom has done a brilliant plan for the area. The model is in my office if you want to see it."

"Of course I'd love to see it. Not that I can do anything about it, but I'm always interested in your concepts."

"I think the Planning Commission and the Zoning Board are eventually going to give me a go-ahead. I've complied with every requirement of the growth management plan. There are no historical monuments that need permission to be torn down. I've complied with the PUDs, the MIAs. The plan includes provision for employee housing and parking. There are detailed cash-flow projections. I can't imagine what could go wrong."

Richard laughed. "Sometimes you amaze me, Pat. For one of the most successful real-estate men in Pitkin County, if not the state of Colorado, you are either an idiot savant or hopelessly naive. Everything could go wrong. How many terrific ideas have gone to hell in a handbasket because a group of protestors, no matter how small, raise a hue and cry about digging up an acre of Indian paintbrush or destroying the habitat of the Rocky Mountain newt?"

Pat gave him a rueful smile. "I have to admit I do get carried away. But seriously, I'm going to need a great deal of cash from these guys before I can get my own line of credit. I want you to be a part of this deal, Richard. I think it's important for both of us as well as for Aspen."

"Your timing is rotten, you know that?"

The waitress wheeled up a cart filled with desserts, smiling expectantly at Richard but really looking at Pat Mallory, hoping he'd flash her one of his dangerously teasing smiles.

"Something sweet?" she asked innocently. She gave her dark blond hair a toss.

Richard gave Pat a wink and a leer. Pat cocked an eyebrow. "Two helpings of double entendre."

"That's not on the menu today, Mr. Mallory. At least, I don't think so. Maybe I don't recognize it? What is it?"

"Make it apple pie a la mode and another pot of coffee," said Richard. As the girl rolled the cart and her luxurious fanny away, he turned to Pat. "You're going to get in trouble one of these days."

"I'm planning to."

"Don't tell me—"

"I got permission from home," Pat said with a bitter smile. "Sauce for the goose? . . ." He left the statement unfinished.

Richard tried to conceal his surprise. Everyone knew Liz Mallory slept around, but most thought Pat either didn't know or didn't care. Apparently he did.

"Let's not talk about Liz. What about the deal?"

Richard spread his big hands wide and made a noise that was half snort, half grunt. "Give me some more time to think about it, not that I think it'll do a whole lot of good. My hands are just plain tied."

The waitress brought their desserts, hovering about Pat just long enough to irritate him. He gestured her away with his head. She turned on her heel, then shot a hurt look over her shoulder at the man who only last week had smiled so invitingly and made her tingle like a live wire. She had thought about him constantly, dreaming of them together in the big house Pat lived in on Red Mountain. Pat would have been amazed to know that a mere smile had started such an avalanche of hope in motion. "Listen, let's forget everything for a while. Mother's giving Sam a homecoming party Saturday. Why don't you come? Or are you going home to Denver?"

"I'm not going to Denver," he said curtly. "So how is Sam?"

"A little bent around the edges. And furious with me for what I'm doing to the West End. Her words, not mine. We're barely talking. But I'm sure all will be forgiven soon. She's talking about opening a gallery."

"Just what we need, eh? Another gallery."

"Could be worse. Could be a jewelry store."

They laughed. For a moment they had forgotten the reasons that had brought them together and which still lingered unresolved. As they parted company, each carried his unspoken thoughts along with the batch of memos in his attaché case.

Richard Farwell, despite the corporation's cash-flow problems, was not about to admit to failure. He'd never failed at a single thing in his life. That was not quite accurate. He had failed at marriage and at fatherhood. His handsome, aristocratic wife was a hopeless alcoholic and pill addict. She checked into posh drying-out establishments with the same frequency with which she went to the hairdresser, only with less success. His daughter was working on her second divorce and she wasn't even thirty yet. There were no Farwell sons, so he was the end of the line as far as the Farwells were concerned. He had a stepbrother, but he wasn't a Farwell.

Pat, on the other hand, was torn between his loyalty and genuine feelings for Richard and the opportunity of a lifetime. Richard was more than a friend. He was the father he'd always wanted. Richard's affection and praise were unstinting. Their relationship spilled over into a rich life of the soul that included trips to the Canadian Rockies for heli-skiing or a weekend of theater in New York.

Richard Farwell had tried to give Pat Mallory a true sense of his own worth. But a childhood of neglect had set the younger man's character indelibly. There was little Richard could do to change him, and Pat Mallory was a man with an almost obsessive appetite. His sense of adventure, his appetite for danger, came from a deep-seated feeling of unworthiness. He placed little value on his life, so it meant nothing to risk it. Fast planes and cars, high-goal polo and high-stakes poker, a willingness to try every new sport that came along so long as it offered a challenge. The first in the valley to go free-falling, soaring, hot-air ballooning. A year out of college and he'd decided to sail alone from Los Angeles to Perth, Australia. He would have, too, if he hadn't broken his arm in an avalanche on Highlands Bowl. Once again only his catlike reactions and pure luck had saved him from certain death when the entire slope cracked above him and thundered down the steep grade leaving a rubble of boulders and aspen trees in its wake.

Now Sam was home, and Pat didn't know whether to be happy or depressed. He couldn't help loving his kid sister, but he had enough problems dealing with his mother. Even though Sam's absence had created the first closeness he and Sophie had ever shared, he knew it was temporary. Awkward at first because they were both unaccustomed to showing their affection for one another, it had ripened slowly through need. After Big Sam's death, he'd felt—what could he call it?—a kind of accusation in her eyes, almost as though she were holding him responsible. That insight had terrified and confused him. After a while he was convinced it was his own mind and his almost obsessive need to have his mother's love and approval that was playing tricks on him.

Just as he was allowing himself to feel comfortable about the relationship, two things happened: Sophie's decision to take a rigid stance against development, and Sam's decision to come home. Now they would be bonded, not only by their love for each other, but by their mutual horror at his role in what they perceived as the destruction of Aspen.

Sam, he cried out silently, why does it always have to be you?

Sam woke the next morning from the best sleep she'd had in months. The dread of meeting her mother again had dissipated after the first confrontation. She really did adore her mother and appreciate just how unique she was. But she had been serious about how difficult it was to be her daughter.

She couldn't remember one thing her mother had failed at. Sophie hadn't even had the opportunity to fail at marriage; Big Sam had died too soon. And, in a town filled with divorcées and widows constantly on the prowl, often taking young drifters as lovers or getting themselves involved with married men in town for a vacation with the "boys" or a "freebee" seminar, Sophie was a gossiped-about exception.

Not once had Sam been aware of Sophie's going out with someone she couldn't introduce to her children, nor was there ever a time when she had not come home to sleep. Sam realized that didn't necessarily mean her mother was celibate but, if she had a lover, she was keeping it very much to herself. On the other hand, Sophie's circle of friends and acquaintances was vast and deep. All year long, interesting and successful men found themselves at the Silver Leaf Inn for one reason or another. Sophie was a gracious hostess, a perfect companion for the many functions about town, a good listener, and an intelligent conversationalist.

As Sam came out of the bustling lobby of the Silver Leaf Inn into the crisp, winy November air, she looked up at the towering peaks with a renewed sense of awe. A ribbon of cloud coiled lovingly around a blue sky that always seemed as vast as a sea to her. Downvalley the high cirrus indicated a change in the weather, but it would be many hours before the clouds would arrive in Aspen. The low-hanging winter sun etched sharp shadows on the brightly painted false fronts of the Victorian shops. Real cowboys in jeans with a week's growth of beard parked their battered pickups at Clark's Market to pick up the week's provisions.

Ordinary-looking girls in short denim skirts, opaque stockings, and long, bouncing hair twitched their fannies down the street, giggling and waving at the boys who honked and called from their pickups. With a kind of benign desperation, they hoped that today would be the day they might meet Mr. Right and give up their jobs as hotel maids or waitresses, get married, and buy a condo at Centennial and hang drapes and line shelves with pretty contac paper and buy fancy ruffled sheets and pillowcases from Sears to adorn the nuptial bed.

Sam strolled the familiar streets, stopping to look at the old Victorian buildings that had existed since the beginning of the town and whose histories she'd known from the dozens of tours her mother had taken her on as president of the Aspen Historical Society.

Sophie was a fierce conservationist when it came to the town's heritage, an emotion obviously not quite shared by her own son, who by the looks of things was—in the name of progress—ready to turn it into a Hollywood version of Victoriana.

She passed the bright blue Aspen Drug building, once the home of the old Ford drugstore which specialized in cures for hysteria, dizziness, and nervous prostration caused by alcohol or tobacco, and which now sold nothing more exotic than pink-striped condoms. She went in for some toothpaste and shampoo. No one even recognized her, a fact that both pleased her and made her realize how long she'd been gone.

Outside The Paragon, a young man who could hardly wait to exchange his current job for that of a ski instructor was sweeping the sidewalk. Decades before, the building had housed the town's first silent-picture house. Then it had become the best restaurant in the city, with a world-famous wine list and small private dining rooms. Now it was a vast plant-filled meeting place and disco with a huge movie-sized television screen that showed sports events. Often the local rugby team made up of the transplanted Aussies, Welsh, and Scots who had come to ski and then stayed on, came in after their games, videotapes in hand to cluster around their Foster's lagers and vociferously relive every delicious moment of violence.

She walked up Galena to Cooper. On the corner stood the Crossroads Drugstore and the Independence Hotel. In 1890, the hotel's popularity had been due to its proximity to the red-light district of Durant Street and its fame came from the third floor run by Mrs. Winnie, the famous madam.

Continuing her walk, Sam saw the signs of growth and change all over town. Elli's, the place where she'd bought her first boiled wool jacket, was undergoing renovation and expansion. Shops that she thought would go on forever had passed into oblivion. The

Shaft, where tourists and locals alike had stood in line for cornbread, cole slaw, and the best barbecued ribs in the world, was gone, as was the whole block. In its place rose some red brick and gables, some architect's solution to updating the Victorian notion, a solution which in her mind succeeded in being faithless to both old and new. Gone, too, was the old gas station at Cooper and Galena. In its place a fancy bakery, a jewelry shop, and several T-shirt shops.

She was trying hard to battle her feelings of nostalgia. Reason and cynicism honed from her years in New York, where buildings rose and fell in what seemed like minutes, where friendships were numbered in months—not years, where people who said they were looking for commitment disappeared after one or two dates because they were afraid of finding what they were looking for, told her that nothing could remain the same, nor should it.

At least one thing hadn't changed. The mountains were still there. Once, on a trip home, a friend from the East had stood at the foot of Little Nell, looked up, and said with disappointment, "Is that all there is? It doesn't look like much."

Silently she had led him onto the Nell lift, then to the Bell Mountain lift. As they rose, it was like a curtain slowly opening to reveal a vast panorama of mountains that seemed to stretch out forever. So high, so far, it was a world of glorious silence and terrifying grandeur.

The memory flooded her with desire. She looked downvalley at the slowly moving clouds laden with moisture. She wanted nothing more than to experience that first run on the season's first powder. To hear the almost silent whisper of her skis through the dry fluff that made Aspen so different from every other ski resort in the West. That first day of skiing always made her feel like a child again, with no responsibilities, no fears, no pain. She needed that feeling right now.

Back on the Cooper Street Mall, she noticed a new

shop had opened with the witty name of Twentieth Century Fox. In the window an arrogant blond mannequin stood in lean profile. She had marceled hair and wore a white satin bias cut dress from the thirties, and a clutch cape of fox-trimmed white-panne velvet. Sam went in.

The shop was all mirrors, shiny black floors and white satin pouffed chairs and divans. Kleig lights focused on mirrors and T-stands where a few special pieces were displayed.

Sam browsed around, peeking into glass cases housing some unusual art deco marquisite pins and evening bags. She definitely should buy something for the party Sophie was planning for her homecoming. None of her New York clothes seemed quite right and, although she would have been content to wear one of her suede outfits, she thought it might be more appropriate to wear something a little more glittery.

"Is someone helping . . . my heavens, Sam, imagine finding you here!"

Sam swung around at the sound of the familiar voice. "Melanie! The surprise is mutual. Are you shopping, too?"

"Heavens, no! You didn't . . . of course, how could you? I own this place. Of course, I'm hardly ever here. One of the lovely things about owning a boutique is that it gives you a good excuse to go shopping all over the world. Why, you would be astounded at the places you can get into by just showing them a business card with your name on it. But you didn't come in to hear me natter on about world travel." She gave Sam a quick all-inclusive look. "What *are* you here for? I hope you're planning to buy some clothes. I see that whatever all those years in New York did, they didn't teach you about fashion. I declare you still dress like Annie Oakley." She shook her head in despair and smoothed down the jacket of her own Calvin Klein suit.

Nothing had changed. Melanie's conversations

were still monologues of her stream of consciousness. She still asked questions which needed no answers, made observations that required no comment, and pronouncements that brooked no contradiction. From long experience Sam knew that whatever Melanie had on her mind would be immediately translated to her mouth.

Melanie tucked her arm through Sam's elbow and led her to a pouff. Once seated, she poured a cup of coffee. "Blue Hill, Jamaica," she added as she handed it to her. Then, leaning forward, she asked in a friendly tone, "Now, tell me why you're really back. Did you get fired? Pat seemed to think there was something about a man. Really, Sam, was it a man? You never change, do you? You always had the knack of attracting the most attractive men. But you never seemed to be able to hang on to them. Now why is that, I wonder? It never was my problem. My problem was finding them interesting enough to go out with more than once. Thank heaven I don't have to spend all my time in this town. It's so dull now. Of course, next week everyone will be charging in for Thanksgiving, even if there isn't any snow. By the way, are you going to Lita's big bash?"

Melanie paused, and Sam, who'd been on the verge of interrupting several times, was trying to frame an answer when Melanie started to talk again. Listening to her was like reading the *LA Flyer* and the *Hollywood Reporter* at the same time. A barrage of names flew at Sam.

"Cut, Melanie. Time out. I'm really not interested."

"No, you wouldn't be." Melanie stood to her full height, which was several inches below Sam's. Grudgingly, Sam had to admit, she was a gorgeous pain in the ass. Pausing to admire herself in one of the mirrors, Melanie said petulantly, "I forgot, your interests lie along more intellectual paths. I thought you might be curious about what's been happening with some of your old friends."

"I suppose I am, but I thought perhaps I'd just kind of find out for myself. Look, enough of this nonsense. Mother's giving a party for me, and I thought it might be nice to have something new."

"Your mother's giving a party? Am I invited?"

Sam bit her tongue. Why did she have to mention the party? On the other hand, if Melanie wasn't invited, she would never hear the end of it. Talk around town would be vicious. The one thing that Sam could not bear was being talked about. And she knew Melanie. Gossip was the keystone of Melanie's conversational life.

"I think it just occurred to her last night when I came in. She's probably on the phone right now."

"I suppose Pat and Liz will be coming?"

"I assume so. He's my brother. Why would you think otherwise?"

A knowing smile crossed Melanie's lovely lips. "Then you haven't heard the gossip?"

"I just got back. You're the first person I've seen. So no, I haven't heard it. And I'm not sure I want to."

Melanie shrugged. "Up to you. It's pretty juicy."

Sam frowned. "Then I definitely don't want to hear it."

"Do you want to try on some clothes?" Melanie asked abruptly. Sam hadn't changed. She still had those airs. Still thought she was smarter and prettier and better than anyone else just because she was a Mallory. As it was she had raged at a god that gave Samantha Mallory a lean body and straight black hair (Melanie maliciously called it "squaw hair") while she had to suffer with curls and baby fat. When Sam got her first horse, Melanie had tormented her parents for one, too. She had taken two riding lessons and hated it. The horse grew fat and lazy in a rented stable while Joe Ferris took Sam out into the backcountry and showed her how to ride bareback. Then Joe had disappeared. When he came back, Melanie was fourteen and thought he was the most gorgeous thing she'd ever seen. Her parents would have sent her packing to her grandmother if she'd ever mentioned that half-breed's name in their presence. Well, the laugh was on her now that Sam's uppity sister-in-law was shacked up with him. She was furious that Sam wouldn't even listen.

The rivalry that existed between the two women was strictly one sided. Sam, being older by three years, had been the first with everything, thus setting the stage for Melanie's longing to have what Sam had, be what Sam was. Sam had naturally been the first with breasts and then with boyfriends. When Melanie got her first period and tried to discuss it with her mother, she had turned white and sent her to the doctor. It was Sam to whom Melanie turned when she entered fearful adolescence. It was Sam who helped with math and French, Sam who advised what to do and not do on her first date, and Sam who yelled at her when she had coldly dropped her best friend for a very rich young girl who'd come to town with her divorced mother and wore a real mink coat, even though she was only fifteen.

While Sam had hated every minute of her coming-out year, Melanie had relished hers. And while Melanie would have been thrilled to dance at Cotillion coming-out parties in every city, it was Sam who had been presented in Kansas City, Denver, and New York. Melanie was so angry, she didn't speak to her mother for weeks.

And then Melanie had fallen in love with Pat Mallory. Really and truly in love. She was sure that it would just be a question of time before Pat proposed. Then Sam had come home from school, bringing Elizabeth Lloyd with her. Everyone in Denver knew that Liz was a climber. Her father Endicott Lloyd, a Denver rancher with no manners at all, had been trying to buy his way into society for years. Despite all his holdings and philanthropic largesse, the huge house in Starwood and the villa in Antibes, it seemed that he was always on the outside looking in.

What he never accomplished for himself, he accomplished for his daughter, living to see her marry into one of the best families in Colorado, a family that Melanie felt she herself had every right to. Endicott couldn't have been happier if Liz had married a Rockefeller or a Vanderbilt.

She remembered that Christmas party when Pat Mallory saw Liz Lloyd for the first time. He'd gone to her side and never left it. What could he possibly see in her? She looked like some kind of actress with that messy blond hair and big made-up brown eyes. She had worn some tacky black velvet thing. Strapless, of course, with her big breasts practically falling out of the dress as she and Pat danced. And Pat couldn't take his eyes away from that cleavage! When they had announced their engagement, Melanie wanted to tear the flesh from Sam's face. It was all her fault for having brought Liz to Aspen in the first place. Sam would soon discover what a mistake she'd made.

Now she was having the last laugh. Liz Mallory was cheating on Pat. And even if Pat got down on his knees and begged her for a date, Melanie would laugh right in his face. In the last seven years, Melanie had had dozens of lovers; she didn't need Pat Mallory.

Melanie emerged from the back room with an armful of clothes which she treated as if they were children, introducing each by name as she hung them one by one on the T-stand.

"Ferre," she said, holding up black cashmere leggings and sweater, then tossing a full-length quilted suede coat over it.

"Ralph Lauren." A bright purple cashmere sweater went up, followed by a chrome-yellow suede mini-skirt.

"Claude Montana." A ribbed dress in acid-green wool looked about doll size on the hanger. At Sam's raised eyebrows, Melanie said, "It stretches," and demonstrated, pulling it out like a rubber band.

The clothes got more and more outrageous. They were flamboyant funk at couture prices. Sam had never stinted on herself, but since her interest in clothes was in the same league as her love of tea parties, she paid little attention to what she wore and still managed to look unique.

"Enough!" she finally cried. "Melanie, I don't want to make a statement. These clothes are not for me. They're very exciting," she said placatingly as she watched the thunder clouds gather on the other woman's face, "but really."

"Everyone's dressing for parties," said Melanie, making a chilly defense.

Finally Sam selected a pair of gray flannel pants and a deep purple satin western-style shirt. Melanie insisted she take the velvet bomber jacket to wear over it. She also took a swingy taupe suede skirt and pale heather cashmere sweater.

"Honestly, Samantha. You are too boring. And so predictable! What is it with you and leather? I swear all those rumors I used to hear about you are true."

"What rumors?"

"That you're part Indian."

Sam chuckled. "Things are duller than I thought, if that one is still making the rounds. Okay, Melanie, now that I have what I like, what would you suggest? What would you wear if you were me?"

With a cry of triumph, Melanie whipped out a lamé-trimmed white crepe dress with long gold straps and a slit to the waist. "Now, this is really stunning."

"Then I think you should buy it." And with a wide grin Sam handed her credit card to Melanie. "And wear it to my party. I'll pretend I never saw it."

CHAPTER FOUR

"OH, GOD, LOOK AT THIS BODY. I ASK YOU, IS IT FAIR?" moaned Rosie Sukert to the four other women changing into their leotards in the mirrored dressing room of the sunny Silver Leaf Spa.

"Must I answer?" asked Liz Mallory. "I haven't had breakfast yet."

"Very funny." Rosie grimaced, mouthing "bitch" behind her back.

"You asked for it, honey," Sunshine Campbell said.

Undaunted, Rosie continued with the familiar diatribe against her parents and their lousy gene pool. "The worst part is that my mother was pretty decent in the body division. It was my father that was weird looking. So naturally, my brother got my mother's looks and I got my father's. Bah! Humbug!"

"Fortunately, God compensated by giving you a big mouth," Melanie commented, pulling on a pair of vivid violet tights. She stood in front of the bank of mirrors and appraised herself. "Do my boobs look droopy to you?" She turned to Sam, who was braiding her long dark hair. It was a rhetorical question.

Sam was surprised to find Melanie and Liz at the early-morning exercise class. Both professed a public distaste for anything that produced sweat. But physical fitness was an obsession in the mountain town. Even before skiing season was over, the mountain bikes were dusted off, running gear was unpacked, sailboards were cleaned off, and anyone who could was out to whip already superb bodies into even better shape. Aspen was probably the most sports-intensive five square miles in the Western world. Alcoholism was more permissible than blubber. Some wag had suggested founding a new help group for the "aerobically insane."

Accustomed to other obsessions from her years in New York, Sam had almost forgotten how Aspenites venerated their bodies. But the magnificently tuned bodies that filled the pool, the weight rooms, and the aerobic classes soon reminded her. The town was loaded with spas and health clubs, trainers and masseurs who spread the gospel of fitness and the religion of nutrition to all their congregation. That's what drove Rosie crazy. No one paid more attention to her body with less reward. Her basic contours never changed. Rosie would always look like an egg on stilts.

"Maybe I'll have my face lifted?" Rosie squinted into the mirror and looked at herself through blood-hound eyes. Despite all her moaning, she was not an unattractive woman. True, her eyes did droop a bit, but she had a ready smile and perfect teeth, a good nose and decent skin despite its constant exposure to the elements: Rosie was an avid and extremely fine skier, a decent tennis player, and a tireless hiker.

"Rosie," said Melanie, "you're in great shape." Before Rosie could thank her for the unexpected compliment, she added with a malicious smile, "It's just that your shape isn't much to begin with."

"Ask them to do something about your mouth

while they're at it," Liz Mallory snapped, tying a scarf around her small waist and yanking down the top of her baby-blue-and-pink-striped leotard until a great deal of creamy breast was exposed.

"Liz! Melanie!" Sam scolded. "What rotten things to say."

"Sorry. I forgot she was your favorite charity," said Liz Mallory.

"Really, Liz . . . don't you? . . ."

"It's all right, Sam. What can you expect from a cunt?" Rosie's smile was etched in acid.

Liz tossed Sam a superior look that seemed to say, see what I mean? Then she snarled at Rosie, "That vile mouth of yours is going to get you in trouble one day."

Sunshine put an arm around Rosie and pushed her toward the exercise room. "Why do you always have to say things like that?" Sunshine was Rosie's closest friend, and it really upset her that Rosie always found it necessary to go on the attack when she felt insecure. Sunshine, a follower of every self-improvement discipline known to man, a practicing pacifist, a peacemaker, and a promoter of laid-backness and coolness, followed the motto, Go with the flow. She was a flower child of the sixties still blooming in the eighties.

"I have to," Rosie retorted. Turning to Sam, she added, "And I don't care if she is your sister-in-law."

Sam shrugged. "It's your fight, not mine. C'mon, Rosie, lighten up. Liz isn't worth it."

Rosie smiled. For a moment she looked almost pretty. "You're right." Then, referring to her New York upbringing in a tough neighborhood on the West Side, she said, "I guess you can take the kid out of the streets, but you can't take the streets out of the kid." She threw her arm around Sam's shoulder. "C'mon, nurse, let's go."

As they walked down the busy corridor, she let out a yelp. "Ohmigod, it's him! It's him. He's here. Don't let him see me."

"Who, him? What are you talking about?" Sam looked around as Rosie tried to hide herself behind her friend.

"The gorgeous Italian that flew in with you. The one that . . . If I ever get my hands on Alex Breton, I'm going to strangle him. He made me look like a schmuck." Rosie was fond of Yiddish expressions because they gave her anger such color.

"You should have checked your facts," accused Sunshine. "What kind of newspaperwoman—?"

"Yeah, yeah, you're right. But who ever said I was a newspaperwoman? I wonder what he's doing here."

"Obviously the same thing we are."

"He's really gorgeous, isn't he?" Rosie watched as he asked directions to the squash courts. He wore a Fila warm-up that did little to hide his apparently good body.

"I don't know. I think he's got a long way to go to beat Roger." Sunshine Campbell, to her own amazement, was a favorite dinner companion of Roger Standish, the famous and ageless Hollywood leading man who spent his winters in Aspen. Roger and George Hamilton, the other Hollywood personality with whom he was frequently compared, were friends and sparring partners. Pledged to secrecy, they swore never to reveal the diabolical pacts they had made to appear eternally ageless.

Pausing before the door of the sun-filled aerobics studio, Gianfranco di Lucca temporarily forgotten, Rosie turned to Sam. "You have a real treat in store."

"Really? What?"

"Not a what, a who."

"Paul Emerson," Sunshine confirmed.

"That macho Australian?" Melanie looked bored. "The only thing he cares about are his pecs and deltoids."

"You're just jealous because he doesn't care about yours." Rosie, head held high in triumph, marched into the room and began her stretches at the barre.

If the polished oak and glowing brass of the previous century dominated the intricate network of winding hallways, stairways, dining rooms, and lobbies of the Silver Leaf Inn, the fitness facilities were as sleek and streamlined as the next century's. Discreetly hidden from the street, the huge complex boasted a glassed-in Olympic-sized swimming pool surrounded by tall palm trees and huge terra-cotta containers of tropic flowers. The Pool House caught the last dying rays of the sun in winter, making it an ideal après-ski rendezvous. Most people came to swim a few laps or take a sauna before going on to the Ute City Banque or Hotel Jerome bar.

Visible from the pool was the glass semicircle housing the fitness facility with its tennis and squash courts, Universal and Nautilus equipment, aerobic studio, sauna, indoor track, hydrotherapy, and massage rooms. Over the years the spa had developed such a reputation that Sophie Mallory became convinced that nonskiers as well as skiers would flock to it if she developed a program such as the ones which existed at La Costa and The Golden Door. She had consciously put a high price tag on the week-long program, making it the most expensive in the country, thus the most desirable. She had a waiting list for every week in the year.

"Who's this Paul Emerson?" Sam asked.

"I forgot you were gone when all the Aussies hit Aspen," said Rosie. "It happened a couple of years ago, right, Sunshine? They descended on us for the ski season. About twenty of the most gorgeous hunks you've ever seen. I guess there was something about town that reminded them of home. So they kind of stayed on. At least the ones that could did."

"They must all have trust funds," observed Sam. "It's pretty hard to live in Aspen without money."

"Tell me," said Rosie. She was constantly reminded that her friends all had more money than she had. Still, her lack of it hadn't stopped her from being welcomed into that rarefied social set. She was a living example of democracy in action. "They managed to find jobs of sorts."

"Until the Feds started snooping around looking for wetback labor," reminded Sunshine.

"It was your brother who discovered that Paul was a terrific physical therapist when he took care of him after a ski accident. So he got Sophie to pull a few strings and hire Paul to run the sports training center," Rosie said.

"Lucky him," said Sam as they entered the studio.

One wall of the studio overlooked the pool; the others were mirrored. A ballet barre encircled the room, and an elaborate sound system and screen were set up in the corner. When they came in a man in white gymnast's tights and a tank top was doing chin-ups on a bar which hung, along with rings and trapezes, from the ceiling. At the sound of their chatter, Paul Emerson lowered himself to the floor and flashed an easygoing smile. He looked like a man who took his sports seriously. He had a superb, deeply muscled body, and a nose that had apparently been broken several times and pushed back into place so haphazardly it looked like a pair of quick bends in a road. His smile was raffish and open, his blue eyes deeply set under beetling brows. There was a sharp cleft in his chin that gave the otherwise tough face a deceptive boyishness.

Rosie dragged Sam over to meet Paul. He gave her a huge wink. "Ah, I know who you are. You're the boss's daughter. I'd better be on my best behavior." He took Sam's hand and gave her a brisk handshake.

He was like a big friendly dog, and she found herself immediately responding to him. She could certainly see what Pat would like about him. He was unquestionably a man's man.

As he moved to the center of the floor, he whistled for attention. "All right, mates, no more talking. Stand up and take your punishment."

Sam smothered a grin. She liked his breezy technique. Accustomed to the heavy come-ons in New York health clubs, she found his technique more like a camp counselor's.

"Sam, honey, you stick close by me until you learn the routines. Okay? We start off pretty easy, but these sheilas are rough and tough and when they get going, they'll run right over you. I'm taking it for granted you are not a beginner at this stuff?"

She smiled and nodded. Paul Emerson might have a jock's mentality, but he wasn't stupid. He had obviously learned that the spoiled rich of Aspen loved to have love affairs with their instructors.

The next hour was more than she bargained for. Paul Emerson was a slave driver once they got started. He apparently felt that if a person was in one of his classes, she was a superwoman. But with her he was kind, telling her when to slow down or stop, taking great pains to correct her when he caught her doing something wrong. "Don't want you to pull one of those gorgeous calf muscles," he might say, or "You're going to feel this in that sweet rump of yours tonight." In the cool-down, he came to her and showed her how to stretch properly. His hands were warm and gentle, but there was nothing in his manner to suggest that he was doing anything more than he should.

Sam caught Melanie looking at them with suspicion. Sam recognized that appraising glance. Melanie rarely expressed interest in anything—and that included a man—until she discovered that someone else wanted it. Then she went after it—especially if she thought Sam wanted it. Melanie's techniques were almost foolproof and had proven remarkably inventive over the years.

Sam wondered how long it would take Melanie to work out a plan to capture Paul's attention. She looked up at the wall clock; Melanie didn't have much time before the class ended.

Suddenly, Melanie uttered a small cry and collapsed on the floor, rubbing her right ankle. Paul, the consummate professional, immediately ran to her side.

"What happened, Melanie? Are you hurting? Can you stand?"

"I don't know," she said in a small, quavery voice. "Could you help me?" She put her arms up and he gathered her into his. She held him tightly, unshed tears making her eyes glitter like blue ice. "If you hold me, I'll try."

Bravo, Sam silently applauded. The trick was obvious but effective.

Melanie slid down the length of Paul's body and with an arm still around his neck, gingerly put her weight on her left foot, then remembering, swiftly switched to her right. Only Sam, used to Melanie's tricks, saw the switch.

"Oh, no. That hurts too much." Clinging to Paul's neck, she forced a few tears to splash on his bare shoulder.

"Okay, just take it easy." Again he swept her up in his arms. She nestled her head against his chest and choked back a sob. It was an Academy Award performance.

"You finish the cool-down while I take Melanie into the dressing room and call the doctor. If I'm not back in a few minutes, I'll tack on the extra time tomorrow. Okay?"

As he spoke, Sam saw Melanie's smug look of satisfaction. Sam had to hand it to her, but she'd gone to all that trouble for nothing. Sam hadn't the slightest interest in Paul Emerson except as a sports trainer.

Rosie shook her head in disbelief as Paul carried Melanie from the room. "Do you believe her? Yesterday she thought Paul Emerson was a macho pain in the ass, now she's sticking to him like fast-drying glue."

"A bit heavy in the metaphor department, but essentially accurate, I'd say," Liz continued with her cool-down, speaking between deep inhales and noisy exhales.

"What was that all about?" Sunshine, ever the innocent in sexual chess games, had missed the significance. "Are you telling me she did that deliberately? I know she's not great shakes as an athlete, but she's no beginner."

"My guess is that she wanted equal time." Rosie gave Sam a broad wink.

"Would someone please tell me what's going on?" Sunshine insisted.

"Paul was giving Sam a little too much attention," Rosie explained, pulling off her headband and wiping her dripping face. Looking up at the wall clock, she chortled. "Poor bastard hasn't come back yet. I bet she's got him by the balls."

"There you go again," warned Sunshine.

"There *she* goes again." Rosie turned to Sam. "Your old buddy is going to get the golden cunt award this year."

"Rosie, she's not my buddy. And do me a favor. Sunshine's right. Lay off the four-letter words. They sound awful."

Rosie shrugged. "I'm an awful person. Love me or leave me."

Sunshine gave Sam a long-suffering look. It wasn't easy being Rosie's friend. No one was sure of Rosie's age; somewhere between thirty-five and fifty, and no one knew much about her past. As dedicated as she was to everyone else's business, she was equally dedicated to keeping her own private. She was prickly, like a fighting cock, ready to go for the eyes of anyone who challenged her or criticized her. Smart enough to know that her acid tongue and tough manner drove many people she wanted to attract away, Rosie was nevertheless helpless to stop herself. Over the years she had developed thick skin and a quick retort as her defense. These crucibles tested the depth of friendship. If you were still with her after she had done or said the unforgivable, you passed. Those who no longer cared wondered why there were still those who did.

Sunshine, who knew her best, had put it best. "She's a fiercely loyal friend, needy for an equally loyal friend. It's not you she's testing for worthiness, it's herself."

Sam had met Rosie just before she'd gone to New York. They had shared a great love for the outdoors. They needed few words when they went riding and skiing together. The exhilaration of speed and the bliss of action were more than enough. What Sam liked best about the odd little woman was her honesty and her self-deprecating humor. There was something else, too. When help was needed, Rosie was the first one there, offering everything she had without thinking twice about it, even if it meant she'd have to do some fancy financial juggling to meet her monthly expenses.

"You think it's safe to go back in there? I've got to get back to the newspaper office."

"I'm going to the weight room," said Sam. "You're on your own."

Sam put the thick silver-colored monogrammed towel around her neck and dried her face as she went in search of the weight room. Adjacent to the Nautilus center, it was filled with grunting male bodies working on various parts of their anatomy. Despite scrupulous housekeeping, the room was filled with the pervasive smell of overheated masculine bodies and the beauty of skin glowing under the sweating patina of effort.

No one paid the slightest attention to Sam as she came in. In New York the health clubs were like singles bars. Men lined up on the treadmills and bicycles to watch the women come in for their aerobic classes, scrutinizing their breasts, ankles, and hips as if they were horses at an auction. The women referred to the few feet of corridor which separated them as the "meat rack" and learned to give tit for tat. The AIDS scare had made them all wary, so the scrutiny was as much to determine physical health as beauty. But Aspen was different: Body-building was serious religion, and the health club was its church.

As Sam looked about for some light barbells, she noticed a man hoisting a steel bar to which were attached several hundred pounds. With the fascination of a painter for the human body, she watched the play of lean, hard muscles articulating and swelling with effort. It was a perfect anatomy lesson and he was a perfect specimen, sleek as a dolphin, smooth *café au lait* skin shining with effort. He paused at the top of his lift, suddenly aware that he was being watched. His back changed shape and the muscles rose across his shoulders like rocks from the sea as he slowly replaced the weight to its rack and turned to stare at her. She saw admiration, then something else flickering in his dark liquid eyes, something that made her cheeks flame as he looked her up and down with the insolence peculiar to Latin men.

Pinned, held motionless by his stare, she trembled. His brows, dense smudges across the high smooth forehead, lifted, and he tossed back a lock of straight jet hair which fell across one eye. Suddenly his entire expression changed from one of dangerous invitation to surprise.

"Sam Mallory?"

She recognized that soft voice. Drawing closer, she peered at him. "Joe? Joe Ferris. I hardly recognized you."

"I shaved off my beard."

"You had a beard? I don't remember."

"Well, it's been a long time since we've seen each other." That wasn't quite true. They had seen one another occasionally on the street or on the slopes since his return to Aspen seven years before. Once at a large party they had spoken briefly, but before they were able to break through the barriers, Sam had been reclaimed by her date. Then she had gone away, coming home for a few days once or twice a year. He would hear of her visits through the grapevine, but they had not spoken in the last few years. It was better not to.

Against her will, Sam's eyes were drawn to his bare chest. His skin looked as smooth and hard as a piece of onyx. A faint smell of lemon and musk rose from it. She mumbled some inanity and brought her eyes to his face.

"I heard you were coming back. How long this time?"

"I'm here for good."

"And?" His heart thudded against his chest.

She shrugged. "We'll see. I hear you've come up in the world." She winced. What a stupid thing to say.

"I've done well for a poor 'half-breed.' A couple of pieces of property, a decent job, and a rather nice place to live. Not like the teepee, but not bad." His smile was mocking.

She flinched at his words. Joe Ferris had gone to the local high school with her brother. The summer before he mysteriously disappeared, he was seventeen and working horses on Richard Farwell's ranch where she and Pat had often gone to ride. She had been ten years old the first time she saw him; a skinny boy bared to the waist, his skin so tanned it was difficult to see where boy ended and horse began, his shoulder-length black hair held back by a rawhide thong. He was riding down the meadow without a saddle, feet bare, knees holding lightly. He seemed to float on air, horse and boy one fluid motion. She had never seen anything like it in her life. "He's a half-breed. That's why he rides so well," her brother had remarked. She didn't understand what the words meant then.

Then the boy reined in so tightly the horse reared on its hind legs in protest. When at last he cantered over to them, he was unsmiling, suspicious, full of tension. Without understanding why, she felt his unspoken enmity. He leaped from the horse in one bound as Pat approached him and peremptorily commanded him to saddle up the horses so he and his sister could ride.

"Jose," he pronounced it Joe-zay, "this is my baby sister, Samantha."

"I'm not a baby." Her protest had brought a fleeting smile to the boy's fierce face. Ignoring her brother, she seized him by the arm and shaking it for emphasis said, "I want to ride like that. Please teach me to ride like that."

"Like what, Miss Samantha?"

No one had ever called her Miss Samantha before. She didn't like the way it sounded. She frowned. "Like you do. Without a saddle."

"Only Indians ride without saddles. And not because they like to, but because they can't afford to own one."

"I don't care. I want to ride like that."

"Like what? What is so special?"

"I don't know. But it makes your hair fly straight back. So you must be riding very fast. And you look like you're swimming on it . . . the wind, I mean . . . swimming on the wind." Her words tumbled out on top of each other. How could she make him understand? She turned away in frustration, groping.

Sometimes when her dad let her ride in the open bed of the pickup with Toffee, the old red lab, and the wind whipped against her face, she pretended that she was flying. It was the most wonderful feeling in the world.

"No, Sam, you can't. If Mother ever found out I let you ride without a saddle, she'd kill us both. Joe, too."

"You don't have to tell her. Please, pretty please, with sugar on it?"

Finally Sam had gotten her way. And Joe had indeed taught her to ride bareback. She learned quickly. He used to tease her, "I think you must be part Indian." She had swelled with pride and one day even repeated his words to her mother, a statement that was to have distasteful consequences.

It was obvious now they were both remembering that first meeting when the willful ten-year-old and the skinny seventeen-year-old half-breed had become friends. They had formed a silent bond, aware of their similarities. Like him, she was as brown as Cordovan saddle leather, with the same Indian black hair. They looked more like brother and sister than she and Pat.

"Remember what you said to me that first time?" she asked.

"It was a long time ago." She saw a look of pain pass fleetingly across his face.

"You said, 'I think you must be part Indian.'"

"Did I say that?" It was true her appearance had come as a shock. Only when he had heard the rumors that her father had been an Indian had it really struck him how alike he and Sam were. But he knew that the stories were ridiculous. If they weren't, would the Mallory family still be looked on with such respect? But those very words, that gossip repeated to Sophie Mallory so many times, had been the reason for his being sent away.

Sam had changed very little in all those years. She was still as dark as saddle leather and her hair was still long and shiny black as a crow's wing. The ten-year-old child had given no indication that she would grow into such a beautiful woman. The years in New York had not put an ounce of extra flesh on the fine-boned body.

What had not been there before was the gloss and sophistication that living in a city like New York produced. Where once the brilliant eyes the color of old turquoise had looked upon everything so clearly, they now seemed hidden behind a veil of too much knowing. There were lines of dissatisfaction—permanent, he realized—around her eyes. The regally proud carriage was still apparent, but there was defeat in the set of the shoulders.

"Are you married?" she asked.

"No."

"Oh." She blushed, feeling foolishly happy. "You never told me why you went away so suddenly."

He shrugged, trying to show no emotion. His disappearance had fostered some nasty talk. "Apparently you didn't keep up with local news." His voice contained an edge of bitterness; unspoken was the question: Do you really want to know, do. you really care what happened to the half-breed?

"I had other things on my mind," she said tightly. "Well?" she asked imperiously.

He bridled. The very rich had this impatient edge to their voices when you kept them waiting. That she hadn't lost.

"My grandmother needed me in Los Angeles," he lied. "I received a scholarship to Stanford. I graduated. Went to work. Came back." He left a lot of gaps on purpose.

"I'm impressed."

"Are you?" He turned abruptly and set a new pair of weights on the end of the rod. Joe Ferris was in turmoil. Sam's unexpected appearance had triggered unwanted memories. He found himself being inexplicably drawn to her, realizing that the tender feelings she had evoked in him when she was a child were in danger of fanning into something deeper now that she was a woman. It took a prodigious act of will to remember a pledge he had made to a dying man when he was still a small boy.

The icy curtain she remembered so well came down around him. "But, Joe . . . that's really what I'm—"

"Excuse me." He glanced at his watch. "I'm due at the office, and I still have a lot to do." He made a formal little bow and lay down on the bench. Without looking at her again he proceeded to bench-press 400 pounds.

"Joe! Joe?" She stamped her foot angrily. "I wanted to ask you to come to my homecoming party Saturday, but under the circumstances I can see you're not interested." She fought the angry tears that were threatening to overrun her eyes. What had she said to turn him off? They'd barely exchanged more than a dozen words. She gave him a puzzled, hurt look, then stormed from the room, clutching the five-pound weights. She was in the dressing room before she realized they were still in her hands.

The minute she was gone, Joe Ferris sat up abruptly and stared thoughtfully at the spot where Sam had been standing. He had seen the hurt, confused look on her face. For a moment he'd forgotten their differences. He hadn't seen her in a long time; his guard was down. They were about to start talking like two long-lost friends before he caught himself. That was just too bad, but he couldn't be troubled by his lack of manners or worry about her hurt feelings. He hadn't survived this long by behaving like a perfect gentleman.

As he pumped up the heavy weights, he wondered why she'd come back. He'd heard about a man, a breakup, but Liz had no desire to talk about her sister-in-law. He couldn't help but remember the adorable ten-year-old who had plucked at his arm and pleaded with enormous blue eyes to be taught to ride like an Indian.

Over that summer, she had grown as dear to him as a sister. During their rides, he had given her lessons in Indian lore, showing her how to read tracks, find mushrooms and berries that were not poisonous, how to read clouds and wind shifts. He had taught her how to make a shelter in the woods if she ever got lost, how to evoke the Indian spirits when she was troubled, how to speak a few words in the language of the old ones. Then all of a sudden she had stopped coming. He'd been caught in a fool's paradise, then forced to leave. From then on the bad things had started happening to him. No way that was going to happen to him again.

CHAPTER FIVE

SHORTLY AFTER MIDNIGHT IT BEGAN TO SNOW. THICK flakes built up rapidly into inches. When dawn came, every tree and shrub, every street and path was transfigured and now lay sparkling in the early-morning sun.

Joe Ferris, whose apartment overlooked the mountain, awakened with a start at the insistent ring of his phone. He groaned as the dazzling mist-light of a snowy morning hit him forcefully in the eyes.

"Yeah," he struggled with the phone, "Ferris here. What's up? Yeah, I can see how much snow there is. Sure . . . start up the gondola. Tell the snowcats to start packing Copper and Ruthie's. How much do we have up there? That much? Terrific! Call the ski patrol, I'm sure they'll be glad to go to work. I'll be there in a half hour." As manager of the Silver Mountain Resort, he was relieved that it had snowed overnight. Plain Joe Ferris would have preferred another hour wrapped in the pleasant dream he was having.

A foot of new snow on top of the modest hard base would have every powder freak in Aspen clamoring to get up the mountain. Joe would have preferred to keep the mountain closed until the official Thanksgiving Day opening, as he prayed for a few more judicious snowfalls to give him a great opening weekend, but he knew the local hotshots would find a way to ski no matter what he did. One way to keep them off the main trails was to pack them. The Black and Double Black trails would need more than twelve inches to be skiable, although that crazy Breton kid would ski anything that had a bit of white on it. Even Main Street with a roll of toilet paper on it!

There was no question that Alex Breton was a phenomenal skier. He was also a kid who believed in excess. Before he was twenty, he'd experimented with every drug in the book. Now he was strictly a cokehead. Joe knew that for a fact; he'd been his source.

It was not something he liked remembering. Those early years had been the worst and the best in Joe's young life. Had it been worth it? Yes, he was forced to admit. Ironically, if he hadn't dealt drugs he would never have been able to go to Stanford. And without Stanford he would never have been able to return to Aspen. That he was forced to continue his drug dealing when he returned had made him painfully aware that only a miracle could save him from a life he despised. Then drug dealing in Aspen got dangerous. Dealers started to disappear. Cars blew up moments after suspects started them. Houses mysteriously burned. Deliveries were hijacked. The drug wars had been declared. Fear of the Feds turned big-time dealing in Aspen into a trickle, taking the pressure off Joe, allowing him to get out from under the onerous fear that pursued him even in his sleep. Joe had no stomach for the life anymore, if indeed he'd ever had.

Joe was not so naive as to believe that Alex had stopped using just because Joe had stopped selling. He didn't really care what Alex did with his life as long as he showed up for work. And if he knew what was good for him, he would at this very moment be opening the Silver Mountain ski shop for business.

There was nothing like the first big dump to make people think of clothes and equipment. Hot new skis and boots, so advanced in design and styling that they made last year's obsolete, packed the spacious shop. And Joe knew Aspen. No one would be caught dead with last year's equipment!

Opening the drapes of his bedroom window, Joe looked at the slopes of Ajax Mountain. Bright colorful figures, skis over their shoulder, were already milling around the lift. In town the snow-clogged streets waited for the plows to do their jobs.

People might think Aspen was only out for the quick buck, but the truth was, skiing came first . . . if the weather was perfect. And today was a classic Aspen day: After a big dump of snow at night came deep blue sky and a bright sun that sent diamond flares of brilliance off the pristine crystals. It was what locals called a bluebird day. Joe decided he'd better stop and make sure that Alex was on the job. He might be the son of one of the town's wealthiest men, but he still worked for Joe Ferris.

Alex Breton loved skiing and anything to do with it, which made him one of the savviest equipment experts in town. Not only did he run the shop with complete authority to buy what he felt was necessary, he got a personal "bonus" from manufacturers when his sales figures were higher than projected. In a town where thousands of dollars were dropped in minutes for skis, boots, and bindings, he did well. And of course, he got to demo all the newest equipment.

With his reputation and ability, ski manufacturers realized that having Alex Breton on their equipment team was practically a guarantee of hefty business.

Alex had only to appear on the mountain with a new pair of Dynastars or Atomics, wearing the newest, most expensive ski suit, and the shop would be jammed with buyers. When Alex decided that zigzag racing poles were for the birds, hundreds of zigzag poles hit the dump. When Alex switched from his Nordica yellow zonkers to sleek, white Salomons, the shop couldn't keep white boots in stock.

He was the expert's expert. Aspen was filled with wealthy middle-aged men who spent the winter skiing on Bell and Ajax and quickly got bored with equipment and mountains. When conditions were not optimum they'd saddle up their jets and fly off to Jackson Hole or Snowbird for a weekend or go heli-skiing in the untracked powder fields of the Monashees, the Bugaboos, and the Selkirks in the Canadian Rockies. Deep powder heli-skiing was the ultimate thrill, and they were only interested in ultimates.

As equipment freaks, many owned eight or nine pairs of skis for (as they rationalized) wet snow, packed snow, deep powder, moguls, ice, hard pack, wind slab, cruising, turning, etc. With few exceptions they were solid skiers and probably knew as much about equipment as Alex. Highly successful, charged with nervous energy, impatient with waiting on lines or for answers, they thought nothing of spending their precious hours with Alex arguing over the intricacies of proper ski tuning or the esoteric merits of one ski over another. Even the pro and World Cup racers, despite their coaching staffs and the hordes of technicians supplied by the equipment manufacturers, consulted with Alex about tuning and waxing for local conditions.

Ordinarily Alex Breton would have caught a couple of powder runs in the morning and arrived to open the shop around eleven. But he'd spent the summer skiing in Chile, so he didn't have too much to complain about. Chile had been great; he'd come in second in the downhill speed trials at Portillo. Clocking 110 miles an hour in a straight schuss hadn't been enough to win, but winning wasn't everything. He'd had a lot of fun with a gorgeous young Chilean named Mercedes and scored some incredible stuff while he was there. Besides, there'd be plenty of good skiing this winter.

Alex unlocked the doors of the shop. It was big and handsome with plenty of room, good lighting, and luxurious dressing rooms. He had Joe Ferris to thank for that, for it was Joe who had convinced Richard Farwell to redo the place. He bet there wasn't a ski shop in the country that looked classier or more high tech. And when it came to equipment, they were the best.

Alex, tuned in loudly to his Walkman, didn't hear Samantha Mallory come in. He boogied down the line of skis, made a Michael Jackson pirouette, then stopped short, his mouth open in surprise.

"Sam!" he cried. "I was just thinking of you. Are you gonna be hanging around for a while?"

"I guess so." Sam kissed Alex on both cheeks and gave him a hug. Although Alex was four years younger, she'd always been fond of him. He was a happy-go-lucky kid, sweet-natured and fun, a kind of Peter Pan to her Wendy. One of the most irresistible of all the young men in town with his mop of dark gold hair, amber cat's eyes, and a nose that always seemed to be peeling, he was privileged, amiable, and lazy about most things with the exception of fishing, hunting, and skiing. Sam loved skiing with him. Like her he was absolutely fearless and would try anything. How many times had they gone out-of-bounds to ski some bottomless powder? Knowing it was forbidden only sweetened the experience.

She remembered one illicit excursion that had almost ended in tragedy when Alex, caught in a small slide, lost his footing and was carried down a steep and narrow couloir. Skiing as though the hounds of hell were behind her, she'd raced to summon the ski patrol, waited while they got him out. A bad liar, she'd admitted their folly and had her special Aspen Foundation pass revoked. It was the last time. She finally decided the thrill wasn't worth it. From then on, she stuck to the marked trails. But not Alex. Next year, he was at it again, defying the warnings, breaking the rules, and generally doing things his way. No one seemed to care what he did because he wasn't hurting anyone but himself.

"So what can I do for you today?"

"The works, Alex. I haven't bought any ski equipment in a couple of years."

"You didn't do any skiing at all back east? Even Stowe?" Alex had the westerner's healthy respect for the Mt. Manfield skier. Although he'd never skied there, he heard how tough the mountain was with its icy moguls, steep, narrow slopes, and frigid temperatures. When those guys came out to Aspen for the first time, they went ape-shit in the sun and the snow.

She shrugged. "A couple of times. I didn't like the trip. It was too long." Which wasn't true at all. It was Greg Francis who hated the trip, who hated the entire sport, in fact. Greg found all sports but polo and squash boring. And he considered exercise useful only for men with small brains and large muscles. She had a sudden flash of Joe Ferris lifting weights, his brown body gleaming like silk, his muscles long and sleek. With a touch of masochistic loyalty, she remembered how wonderfully Greg, the relentless clothes horse, wore his Paul Stuart clothes. Paul Stuart, he claimed with the authority of gospel, was worth twice every tailor in Saville Row.

Bastard! He had almost had her believing that muscles were embarrassing! "I'm much more interested in seeing you develop that lovely mind, my darling. I find that much more sexy than your quads, or whatever you call them," he'd once said to her after they'd made love.

With the exception of her artistic ability, he considered Samantha a tabula rasa, waiting to be filled with the glories of the intellect. Every concert, opera, play, ballet, or trip was preceded and followed by a fascinating lecture delivered by the master himself. Greg seemed to be a bottomless pit of knowledge. Sometimes when he became excruciatingly boring, she'd let her thoughts drift off to skiing or riding. But he always knew, pulling her back with that cello throb in his voice, chiding her for not paying attention, making her feel guilty and unworthy of his attention. His distaste for things athletic was so much greater than her love for them that she had, in her adoration and wish to please him, simply canceled them from her life.

But adoration had finally bored him. Somewhere along the line she had sublimated those things about herself that had made her unique and passionate. After a while she even bored herself with her dull perfection. And when her fascination wore thin, he started to philander and lie about it. When she found out and accused him, he demonstrated his cleverness by making her apologize for not trusting him.

She shook off his lingering presence. "The works, Alex. I want the whole kit and kaboodle."

"What color skis and boots?"

"Color?" She laughed. "What's color got to do with it? What happened to height, weight, ability?"

"Later. Man, we're into color these days. Pick your skis and boots and then we can color-coordinate your whole wardrobe."

"You're joking."

"Nope. Look." He pushed a pair of pink Elan Comprex G's at her and showed her the name of the glamorous film star on the ticket. "And you know she can ski."

"I don't think I'm the pink type," she said, shaking her head. "How about something fast in white?"

For the next twenty minutes Alex rattled on about

deep-waists and narrow sidecuts, hardwood cores, carbon and Kevlar, wet-wrapped fiberglass torsion boxes, and skis that were light and lively or mean and lean.

"It all sounds like diet food." She looked bewildered.

"Trust me?"

"If it has to do with skiing? Of course. I'm in your capable hands."

He chose a pair of Dynastar Course for her, then had her slip on a pair of white Salomon SX91 rear-entry boots with red throats to which he fitted a red-and-white Salomon S747 binding with an inclined-pivot toe piece. "State-of-the-art equipment," he proclaimed.

While she was clumping around in the new boots, the door opened and a tall man in an elegant Italian down coat walked in. He wore his straight black hair combed back from his forehead in—as she would describe it later—a Robert Taylor pompadour. Despite his square jaw and firm chin there was something in the face that spoke of indulgence and boredom. He looked like a man to whom there were no more surprises.

"Hello." He smiled. His nod included both of them, but his dark eyes lingered on Sam, whose faded jeans outlined her trim body. Struggling to remove the new ski boots, she would have fallen over if he had not extended an arm to steady her.

"I say, didn't we both arrive here on the same plane? Forgive me if I seem overly familiar, but I feel as though I know you."

His voice was oddly accented. Definitely Italian but broadly English. Obviously educated there, thought Sam before she answered. "Yes, I believe we did."

"I knew I could never forget such a lovely face. Permit me to introduce myself. I am Count Gianfranco di Lucca." He spoke his name with a fanfare of flourishes.

"Howdy, Count." Alex put out his hand and gave a lopsided smile. He wasn't very familiar with titles, and he cared very little for protocol, so he addressed him as if Count were his first name. "Alex Breton's the name. And the lovely lady here is my friend, Sam Mallory." Sam stifled a smile. Alex could do a presentable John Wayne when the spirit moved him.

"Mallory? Mallory?" He groped. "I know that name. I have only recently met a most lovely and elegant woman by that name. Sophie Mallory who owns the Silver Leaf Inn where I am a guest. What a coincidence."

"She's my mother."

"But it's not possible." And then he tilted her chin with his hand and stared down at her. "But, of course. Now I see the resemblance. You and your mother look like sisters. Amazing."

"She'd be pleased to hear you say that."

Alex rolled his eyes at the count's flowery words. Sam gave him a quick jab in the ribs. "Are you here for the skiing?"

"That among other things. Such a wonderful place, Aspen. So charming. An old silver town, I understand. So Victorian, yet so chic. You know in the Alps there are many new *stations de ski*. Unfortunately, the need for "—he rubbed his fingers together in the universal gesture for cash and raised his eyebrows—"has created such ugliness. And I am afraid it was my own country most at fault. Yes, in Italy we have such beautiful mountains and such ugly aesthetics. Except for Cortina, of course. That is a miracle. Such beauty. My family has long had a ski lodge high in the Dolomites. And I pay you the ultimate compliment when I say your Aspen is equally beautiful."

"I'm sure the Chamber of Commerce will be most appreciative, Count di Lucca," said Sam, amused by his florid speech.

"No, no." He put a carefully manicured hand on

her arm. "You must not call me Count. You must call me Gianni."

Alex, who was standing behind the count during the long disconnected speech and elaborately miming the last two statements, wet his little finger and drew it over his eyebrow. "Gimme a break," he whispered.

"Ah, yes. How homesick I am for the Dolomites. Like a gorgeous stage set they are. So jagged, so majestic. At sunrise, there is a rosy ring around the village. And at Christmas, whole families descend for the skiing and the festivities. To spend a week there is to rub shoulders with Italy's *bella gente*." He shrugged and said reverently, "You could share a gondola or a chair lift with the Pirellis, the Buitonis, the Agnellis, even Mastroianni and Gassman."

"We do pretty well here, too," said Alex, only no one was listening.

"By the way, do you know this person, Rosie? She has written the most amusing thing in your local newspaper. Apparently someone has told the social editor that I am Marcello's brother. Is that not amusing?"

Alex burst into a fit of coughing. The red-faced young man looked as if he were about to choke to death. As Gianni pounded Alex on the back, he turned worriedly to ask Sam. "Do you think he will be all right?" Alex broke away and hurried off. By this time his choking had turned to hilarity.

"Oh, Alex just swallowed his tongue. He does that a lot."

"But it must be quite painful. Is it something he was born with? Some problem?"

"You might say that." Sam grinned.

A few minutes later Alex returned, his lips twitching with ill-concealed mirth.

"So now, my friend, I see that you have recovered. I need to buy a few things."

"If you're only staying a short while, you might be better off renting."

Gianni shrugged. "On the other hand, I may stay for the winter. I like your Aspen greatly." He offered a broad smile to Sam. "A town such as this must have many lovely people in it. I find it so warm and friendly already."

"If you plan to stay, then you must come to my homecoming party, Saturday. I'm sure Mother would be pleased."

At Gianni's look of surprise, Sam blinked. She couldn't believe she'd asked him!

Secretly, Gianni was delighted. Americans were so predictable. Here he was a complete stranger and just a few minutes of conversation produced an invitation to what he was sure was an important party. Of course, he wouldn't know a soul there. On the other hand, it would be a good way to meet the most interesting people in Aspen. He had not planned on having such good luck so quickly. He flashed her his most humble and grateful smile. "That is most gracious of you. I accept with pleasure."

Alex looked disgusted. It never failed. Why did women roll over for European accents? Couldn't they see that their charm was about as deep as a winter tan?

"Now, young man," Gianni interrupted Alex's uncharitable thought, "let me tell you what I need."

As Sam looked through the new ski clothes, Alex outfitted Gianni. His original scorn had turned to quasi-respect, for the man obviously knew what he was talking about.

Sam returned with a handful of bright things. "Put these on my tab. If someone can mount the bindings, I think I'll change and try a couple of runs. I'll pick my stuff up after. Okay, Allie?" He smiled fatuously at the use of the old nickname.

"You bet. Wish I could join you." He summoned a young man from the back room to get Sam's skis.

"There'll be loads of time for us." As an afterthought, she turned to the Italian. "By the way, Gianni, have you ever skied here?"

"My first time, alas. I will need some kind of map to get around."

"Why don't you make a few runs with me? I'll show you the ropes."

"The ropes?" He looked puzzled. "I thought you had only the most modern of ski lifts. The rope tow is no longer used even in Europe."

Sam laughed. "It's an American expression. It sort of means the inside track."

Gianni still looked puzzled. "Ropes? Tracks? We are skiing, are we not?"

"Right. And I'm going to show you where to go on the mountain. That's what I've been trying to say."

Sam disappeared into the fitting room and emerged transformed. She wore a tight one-piece suit in bright jade green with a shocking pink bodywarmer vest, bright yellow gloves, and headband. Her long black hair streamed loosely down her back.

"Dynamite, Sam," said Alex. "You look great."

"You better hope I still know how to ski," she teased.

"Piece of cake," reminded Alex.

Sam left the shop with Gianni, who carried her skis along with his demos. At the Silver Leaf Inn, he excused himself to change into ski clothes. As Sam poked about the lobby waiting for Gianni, her mother, dressed in jodhpurs and a turtleneck, walked through.

"Mother!" Sam called. "Over here."

"Hi, darling. Don't you look bright. Just buy them?"

Sam nodded. "I'm going skiing. With one of your guests."

"Oh? Do I know him?"

"Count di Lucca."

Sophie had trouble placing the name. Then she remembered. He'd checked in at the same time as the writer—what was her name?—oh, yes, Rachel Fulton. She frowned. He had to be twenty years older than Sam. And he was just a little too slick for her taste.

Sam spotted the frown. "Mother, don't be nervous. I'm just going to show him the mountain. He's never been up before."

"That's nice of you."

"And, Mother, I've invited him to my party."

"Oh, dear. Why did you do that? He won't know anyone. It will be boring for him."

"No, it won't. Besides, he seemed delighted. I'll introduce him to Rosie. She's dying to meet him."

"That ought to get her out of your hair," Sophie said dryly. She didn't share her daughter's affection for Rosie Sukert. In fact, she couldn't understand why everybody made excuses for a woman who was so obviously malicious and manipulative. Sophie didn't like gossip, and every nasty piece of gossip shunted around town could be laid at Rosie's doorstep.

Sam frowned as she felt her mother's mind marshal the familiar arguments against Rosie. "Mother!" she warned.

Sophie Mallory was still an anomaly to her daughter. She was one of the most philanthropically-minded women she'd ever known. She could turn a lost cause into an overnight success, would give unstintingly of her time and money to every organization that needed it, yet she was still an infuriating social snob.

Sophie had tried to discourage Sam's relationship with the twice-divorced Rosie and with Sunshine Campbell, whom she referred to as an overaged flower child. And it had been Sophie who put a stop to the rides with Joe Ferris after discovering them together at Indian Lake when Sam was supposed to be having a riding lesson.

When Sam had once accused her mother of being an imperialist and told her that her charities were elitist, with sweet reason, which only served to infuriate Sam more, Sophie had replied—and Sam remembered the words as if it were yesterday—"Darling, you needn't feel guilty about having money or position. Your great-great-grandfather worked very hard to put us where we are. There's no crime in having money. And if you choose to contribute to what you feel are more worthy causes than mine, go right ahead. But I don't believe you have to marry an Indian or make a pecunious—this said with the slightest curl of lip—divorcée and a hippie your best friends. Even if she can be a bit tiresome at times, Melanie is much more . . ."

On that occasion Sam had cut her mother short with a four-letter word and stormed from her presence.

She loved her mother, but it was that narrow kind of thinking that had been one of the reasons she had had to get away. It wasn't until she got to New York that she realized she had not gotten away at all. The faces and addresses had changed, the style had not. There were still the same balls and charity functions, the benefits and fund-raisers that she had grown so tired of in Aspen. The celebrity names had become the society names: Buckley, Trump, Whitney, Kempner, Bass. Everyone gave money. Very few put on an apron or rubber gloves and pitched in to help. The causes were high profile and glamorous. No one cared about women whose husbands were abusing them and the children unless it happened within their own social set and then the punishment meted out was not jail but the absence of an invitation to a coveted party.

Samantha Mallory, like many second- and third-generation offspring, was embarrassed by her inherited wealth. It was difficult for her to be comfortable with money she had not earned. Unlike Alex Breton, she just couldn't blithely squander away every cent she'd inherited, then try to borrow from friends and forget to pay them back.

In the sixties, with a young president reminding

them of their responsibilities, people such as she had joined the Peace Corps, and Vista, had gone where the need was great, and worked side by side with the poor and disenfranchised. Sam, in her zeal to follow in their footsteps in the eighties and not willing to endanger her life in places like Nicaragua and Haiti, had turned instead to the soup kitchens that fed the homeless, the church groups that sponsored reading programs for the determined children of the ghettoes, and the Gay Task Force trying to bring a measure of comfort to those afflicted with AIDS. She had found some satisfaction in these good works, but her relationship with Greg had forced her back into making those empty philanthropic gestures she'd so despised.

"Darling," he'd pleaded so rationally, "there is no reason why you must break your back washing dishes and slinging soup. Other people can do it. When it comes to the ills of society, your money is of greater value than yourself."

And now she was back home in the clean air and towering mountains where she knew she really belonged, and she was determined finally to do things her way.

Despite their truce, Sam knew her mother would not be able to give up managing her life, a fact that made it urgent that she find a house. Bestowing a kiss on Sophie's cheek, she went out to meet Gianni, having already decided to talk to Pat that afternoon about showing her some property.

Gianni made a rather theatrical appearance in Bogner's spectacular white-and-silver one-piece suit, which she knew cost at least $1,700. She was about to feel embarrassed when she remembered where she was. This was Aspen. Never-Never Land. You could ski in sable if you wanted to.

The Silver Leaf was only a minute's walk from the Silver Queen Gondola.

"I am very much looking forward to this," he said, stepping into his skis.

She smiled. "You have to carry them." She pointed to the skis. "We're going to take the gondola up."

"Of course, of course. I wasn't sure."

On the trip up to the top of the mountain, Sam told him a little of the history of the area.

When they reached the top, she asked him how well he skied.

"Well enough," he said.

She wasn't sure what that meant, so she took him over to Ruthie's Run, a good challenging intermediate trail which she knew would be well groomed.

She started off carefully. It had been several years since she had been on skis, and she wasn't sure how well she still skied. But someone had once said it was like riding a bicycle. You never forget. And it was true. Her muscles remembered. Finding her rhythm returning, she increased her speed, stopping periodically to wait for Gianni to catch up before continuing on. At the top of Roch's Run she paused.

When he caught up she continued with her history lesson. "This is named for the man who laid out the first ski trail on the mountain: Andre Roch. You used to have to drive up the Midnight Mine Road on the backside of the mountain to where The Sundeck Restaurant is now. Then the WPA helped build the boat tow, which I understand was two sleds, two mine hoists, some cable, and a gas motor. They could carry up ten people at a clip."

"Interesting," he commented, although he was not interested at all. What he wanted to talk about was her brother. He knew that the brother was an influential businessman as well as a member of the board of Silver Mountain Enterprises and a close friend of Richard Farwell.

"They built the first ski lodge up where Castle Creek and Conundrum Valley meet." She gestured with her pole over her shoulder in the direction of Aspen Highlands. "Then, in nineteen forty-one, they offered the lodge and the Ashcroft area nearby to the U.S.

Army Ski Troops for one dollar."

"I hope they made a great deal of money afterward." Gianni smiled. The Americans were just as fond of the grandiose gesture as the Italians, only the Italians were not quite so cavalier with their money.

"Afterward, when the war was over, Friedl Pfeifer, who'd come to teach skiing in Sun Valley in the thirties and been in the famous Tenth Mountain Division here, came back and started the Aspen Ski School. And Fritz Benedict, who also served with the division, came back, sold his car, and bought Red Mountain." With her ski pole she pointed south to the adobe red mountain with its necklace of large, imposing houses.

"He must have done very well." Gianni's eyes glittered.

"Very well, indeed. You see, he was an architect, one of Frank Lloyd Wright's pupils. Originally he designed some buildings for Walter Paepcke, our local Caesar. Then he found a barn on Red Mountain and turned it into a house, sold it, and with the money he made he bought the Bowman Block in town with his brother-in-law, a man named Herbert Bayer. It was a crumbling old Victorian that probably would have gone the way of so many other old buildings in town if he hadn't restored it and turned it into office buildings."

"And these two men, Bayer and Benedict, met in mortal conflict one day?"

Sam laughed. "In an Italian opera, maybe. They had different styles, but no, I'm afraid they just got rich and famous. Benedict is the man who really kept the town looking Victorian. He liked native materials. Bayer liked glass, metal, and brick. I frankly prefer the Benedict style. It's more authentic.

"Now, of course, everyone's coming to Aspen. I guess because they love our life-style and want to be a part of it. The problem is that once they get here, they all try to change it."

"And get rich." Gianni's soft mutter went undetected. "And you, what do you think of all this?" He swung his pole in an arc that encompassed the town beneath them, which lay in a pattern of neat grids, the wide Main Street cutting the town in half from west to east.

With surprise Sam realized she had never really thought about it before. The years she'd been away had unquestionably changed the small town. It wasn't just the renovations she'd seen. Once neat and confined, it now stretched down the valley like a snake. Behind Red Butte lay Starwood while Pitkin Green ran parallel to the Roaring Fork River. Up toward Independence, an arm of houses and subdivisions grew, and she realized that all the vast, lonely stretches she'd once loved were gradually being filled with houses.

She pulled her sunglasses off and planted them on her head. "You know, no one has ever asked me that question before. I remember a different Aspen. A sleepier one. I used to think we lived on the edge of the world and that no matter what happened out there," she made a vague gesture, "it would never affect us. The skiers came and went. In the summer the intellectuals came for the Aspen Institute programs and the music. There were a lot of celebrities, but I never paid much attention to that. Mother told me that Gary Cooper used to be the goalie for the weekly broomball games they played between the ski school and patrol. And that he used to come in the summer for the music. I didn't even know who he was until I saw his movies on the Late Show.

"A lot of strange people started to come in the sixties. No one paid a whole lot of attention to them. We were always a live-and-let-live kind of town until the drugs started coming in. Then Aspen got to be like anyplace else." She did not elaborate and Gianni did not ask. He knew that if he listened quietly without undue curiosity, he would learn everything he wanted to know about this town from her or, better yet, her brother. All he needed was patience.

Sam shrugged. "That's enough philosophizing. We came to ski. So let's ski."

As they waited for the lift, she said, "You haven't told me a single thing about yourself other than how lovely Cortina is."

"Oh, it is nothing much. I was born after the war and lived in Lucca, a very old town in Tuscany. We live in a beautiful villa which was very run down because of the war." Gianni was a firm believer in staying as close to the truth as possible. It was true he lived in Lucca, but he had been born in Naples, the son of a minor Mafioso and a well-born Neapolitan who was thrown out of the family when they learned of her pregnancy. It had been easy enough for her to say that the child's father had been a victim of the war. It had been another thing for her to find work when she had not been raised to be anything more than a wife. In a Florence still rebuilding after almost total destruction, she had met a woman who had told her of the di Lucca family and their search for a housekeeper for their palazzo in Lucca.

"The family produced fine olive oil. The best in Italy. After school I went into the family business." That was true. What he left out was that the real di Lucca son, the one who wanted to be a priest, who could not be bothered with commerce, gave him a fistful of lire, big as napkins, if he would serve in his place. And to Gianni's surprise, the old count had been pleased, had officially adopted him, and sent him to London to learn English and business. Gianni had fallen in love with London, and by the advent of the swinging sixties, he had discovered the gambling clubs of Belgravia and Mayfair and forgotten all about olive oil.

It was there that he became a very efficient cog in an international network that controlled prostitution, drugs, and gambling. He had what very few of the group had: impeccable manners, a command of the English language, courtly airs, an ability to do whatever was asked of him, and unquestioning loyalty. He was the perfect front man.

"Are you still in the olive-oil business?"

"Oh, the family is involved in many things," he said without going into further explanation.

"How long do you expect to be here?"

He shrugged. "That depends."

"On what?"

"On how long it takes to find myself."

He gave her such a forlorn look, she believed she had trespassed on some private world.

"I'm sorry," she said softly.

He patted her hand and tried not to let her see him gloat. She had taken the bait like a foolish fish and believed what he wanted her to believe.

They made a few more runs. He proved to be a quite decent skier. What he lacked in speed, he more than made up in form. "You're a pretty skier, Gianni," she said.

He winced at the word. "I should have preferred the word graceful."

"Okay. It wasn't meant to be a sexist remark."

He smiled. Suddenly he passed his hand over his eyes and frowned.

"Something wrong?"

"A sudden very intense headache." Looking at his watch, he said, "I see I am still on Italian time. If you will forgive me, I will leave you. I feel very tired."

"It's the altitude. You have to get used to it. You know we're at over eleven thousand feet up here at the Sundeck and the air's pretty thin. Tends to make you feel lethargic. You'll be fine in a few days."

"I am sure you are right. I hope you will let me join you again?" His eyebrows arched as he brought her hand to his lips and kissed it gallantly.

"Of course, although I don't know how much skiing I'll be doing this winter."

"If you will show me the best way down?"

She took out a trail map and showed him where he was and how to find his way down. When he was safely off, she headed toward Bonnie's Restaurant, hoping to find it open.

It wasn't, but Rosie, Sunshine, Sally Burke, and Gretel Schiller were sharing a picnic lunch on the bare sundeck. The weather had turned warm and the morning's snow was melting in puddles from the peaked roof. The women had removed their jackets and were now stretched out on them, their faces turned like sunflowers to the overhead sun.

"Aha," squealed Rosie, rising to a sitting position. "There she is. Where's Marcello?" She peered around. "C'mon, give, we saw you skiing with him."

"There's nothing to give," said Sam.

"Do you believe her?" Rosie turned to her companions. "Who is he, what's he doing here, is he married?"

"I don't know. I didn't ask him."

"You didn't ask him?" Rosie echoed. "What did you talk about?"

"I got a few vital statistics. Otherwise, nothing much."

"You're infuriating, you know."

"Leave her alone, Rosie," interjected Sunshine. "Not everyone is as curious as you." She turned to Sam in explanation. "You know how she is."

"Yeah," said Sally Burke, a dark, striking female ski instructor. "She's like the housemother in a dorm. Has to know what all her little charges are up to every minute of the day."

"C'mon, you guys, I saw him first. It isn't fair that everyone gets a crack at him before me," whined Rosie.

"Who said life was fair?" said Sunshine. "Besides, with a town full of gorgeous young things, why would he look at an old bag like you?"

"Some friend," muttered Rosie, turning to Sam

again. "Did he say anything about the thing in the paper?"

"He mentioned something, but he wasn't angry. More amused, I'd say."

"Oh, God, I could kill Alex. How could he do this to me?"

"You say that every time he does," reminded Sunshine.

"Doesn't mean I like it any better. So what's your feeling about Signor . . . Signor . . ." Rosie stopped, realizing she didn't even know his name.

"Gianfranco di Lucca. Count Gianfranco di Lucca, known to his friends as Gianni." Sam bent down and took a bite of Sunshine's sandwich.

"A count?" Rosie almost choked. "A real count?"

"How would I know? That's what he said. I didn't check him in the Almanach de Gotha," she apologized.

"What's the Almanach de Gotha?" asked Sunshine.

"It's an international Who's Who of royalty and aristocrats," explained Rosie. "Oh, well, who cares?"

"Right," agreed Sam. "He's charming, attractive, and by the looks of his equipment, wealthy. In Aspen, that's usually enough."

But the more offhanded Sam tried to be, the more uneasy she felt. There was nothing specific to make her feel that way. Still there it was, that feeling of dread, of bad things in the offing. She remembered one day when Joe Ferris had looked at her strangely after she had described a dream and its chillingly real aftermath. "I think you have the Indian gift of second sight. Are you sure you're not part Navaho or Ute?" Her laughter had been slightly strained.

She skied a couple of runs with her friends, hoping the sheer exhilaration of activity would drive away her misgivings. But every time she thought she'd banished her suspicions, they returned like angry, swarming bees to plague her. If she were to mention them to her friends, they would burst into laughter and jokingly suggest she see a shrink. Only Joe Ferris would understand, she told herself wistfully. That is, the old Joe Ferris would. This new one with the smooth face and icy exterior had lost a lot more than his beard. She wasn't sure she even liked him much anymore.

Sam returned to the Silver Leaf Inn, more determined than ever to find a house and quickly take charge of her life, normalize it, if there was such a possibility. She wanted to settle down and really start painting.

The first cracks in her relationship with Greg had sent her scurrying to the Art Students League where the students' intensity had made her feel like a dilettante. On the nights that she waited for him to come home, when she had been too upset to call a friend, too restless to see a show or a movie, she had turned—as she had since she was little—to sketching. Often when she and Sophie got trapped in one of their impasses, she would gather up her paintbox, get on her bicycle, and ride up Castle Creek Road, stopping only when she reached a gurgling pool formed by the river as it narrowed to a trickle. There she would lie on her stomach and watch insects work or pick flowers or stare at the ceaselessly moving patterns of the water. Then when a sense of calm filled her, she would paint her impressions, her feelings. These were her secret sketch books. No one had ever seen them.

She was in turmoil again. Only this time it came from knowing she was almost thirty, and that once again she was starting over. Life would be so much simpler if she could accept the fact she was a wealthy woman living in a sybarite's town, that there were dozens of ways of amusing herself, that she could fly off to New York or San Francisco or even Hong Kong if she got bored.

She thought of Melanie, blithely sliding out from under the satin sheets of Beverly Hills one week and into the antique linens of Paris the next. In between her "trips," there was a nonstop parade of lawyers, investment bankers, directors, entrepreneurs, racing-car drivers, and football players.

Painting is safer, she decided.

Or was it? Her dabblings on canvas had given her satisfaction as long as no one else knew. But when Greg had chided her about keeping secrets from him, she had shyly revealed her work to him. The paintings she had shown him had an O'Keeffe quality about them, only more diffuse, impressionistic, softer.

When she had pressed him for an opinion, he seemed loath to speak.

"Tell me," she insisted.

"Darling, you are so wonderful at what you do, why do you insist on putting yourself in the line of fire?"

"You mean I'm not good enough?"

"I didn't say that exactly. You have a small talent. But . . ."

"If you saw one of my things in a gallery, you'd walk past it."

He shrugged in embarrassment. "I'm only trying to keep you from the wolves."

His voice was soothing, but she'd caught a look in his eye that was disturbing. Was it fear, anger, jealousy?

"I'm not giving up," she'd said stubbornly.

From that point on, his criticism had taken on a new subtlety. Never outwardly hostile, it became charmingly patronizing. He would force her to show her work to guests with the blind insistence of a parent forcing a recalcitrant and not-too-gifted child to perform.

Once again she was put in the position of living up to someone else's expectations.

She took a quick shower and changed into a pair of jeans and a buckskin shirt. Slipping on her sheepskin jacket, she let herself out the rear door and walked to the garage where her Jeep was parked.

The piles of dirty, drifted snow were beginning to melt in the late-afternoon sun, sluicing down the streets in muddy rivulets to the storm drains. She climbed in her jeep and pulled into Durant Street, her heart beating with excitement at the thought of owning a house of her own.

At the Hotel Jerome, she took a right to Bleeker and slowly crisscrossed the streets of the West End, stopping to look at any house that looked interesting. Without Pat to rush her about, she had an opportunity to move at her own pace. With a shock she realized that many houses had either disappeared or been so completely renovated she could barely recognize them. And the new Victorians that Pat had so proudly pointed out offended her not only by their pretensions but by their size. Trying to look like the best of several worlds, they managed to look like the worst, and at a cost of only one or two million dollars!

Those that remained were lovingly and defiantly cared for. The bright coats of paint, the carefully planned landscaping, the attention to human-size detail, all paid tribute to the efforts of the Historic Preservation Committee, Planning Commission, and City Council to save as much of the town's Victorian heritage as possible. Unfortunately there were developers—and it appeared that her brother, Pat, might be one of them—who knew the tricks to use to bypass the rigid codes.

On Hallam Street she parked in front of a For Sale sign. Though it said Coates, Reid and Waldron Real Estate, she was sure that they would be glad to co-broke with Pat. The house looked perfect. Small, on a corner lot with two big cottonwood trees, a screen of junipers, and a handkerchief-sized garden peeping out from the melting snow, it was painted in shades of gray with accents of cerulean and garnet. She knew it was the house for her. It might not make it to the Great House tour, but that was all right. She didn't want a lot of strange people tramping about her house anyway. Her house! The decision was made.

Desire lent wings to her feet. Main Street traffic was

normally heavy at that hour, and with the slush starting to freeze, traffic was crawling. She willed patience upon herself. When she could, she kicked the Jeep into gear and, ignoring the posted speed, made it to Pat's office in a minute flat.

She burst into the office and past Pat's secretary, Betty, who tried to stop her.

"Pat—" She stopped in midsentence. He was deeply involved in a phone conversation that she was obviously not meant to hear. He turned a bright red when he saw her and covered the mouthpiece.

"What is it, Sam? I'm on the phone."

When she was about to throw herself in a chair, he added, not too politely, "It's private."

"Sorry." She bit her lip. With a look that was meant to express apology but came out irritated, she returned to the outer office to pace back and forth until Pat was ready to give her audience.

Pat's secretary looked up from her computer to stare. Just because Pat was Sam's brother gave her no cause to just burst in like that. Even his mother was polite enough to knock.

A few minutes later the door opened and Pat stuck his head out. "Okay, Sam." Once inside, he seated her, then threw his long body onto the couch. He rubbed his eyes and then said wearily, "Now, what was so damned important that you had to come bursting into my office like that?"

"I'm sorry, I didn't think—"

"No, you never do. Sometimes I could put Sophie over my knee and spank her for not teaching you better manners."

"Hold on a second! Don't blame Mother. You know damn well she taught us both good manners."

"Then why do you think you have some special dispensation to forget them? How would you feel if I went charging into your bedroom without knocking?"

"Your office is hardly a bedroom. Besides, I've already said I was sorry." She stood up, quivering with angry tears. "You'd think I interrupted a conversation you were having with your girl friend. . . ."

From his reaction she knew she'd touched a tender nerve. "Is that what I did? Were you talking to a woman?"

"Cut it out, Sam. I'm busy. What do you want?"

"Yes, I can see how busy you are." She walked to the door. With a cold, hurt voice she said, "Never mind, I'll just go over to Coates, Reid."

"What are you talking about?" His tone altered dramatically.

"There, that's better." She came over and laid a tentative hand on his arm. "Brother, dearest, I've found a house I want to buy. It's the one on the corner of Hallam, in shades of gray. You know it, I'm sure. When can I look at it, and how much is it?"

"There isn't a Victorian, a good Victorian, in the West End for under five hundred thousand dollars."

"Really?"

"Really. Even the crap is selling in the fours and fives."

"Call Coates, Reid and find out. I really want that house. I can afford it. This is Aspen. Tomorrow it'll be worth a million, won't it?" Her smile was mocking. The look that Pat gave her was puzzled and a little wary.

CHAPTER SIX

OUTSIDE THE STARS DUSTED A MIDNIGHT VELVET SKY, AND the snow-covered slopes gleamed ghostly in the moonlight. It was near zero, cold enough to turn warm breath to white mist.

Inside Sophie Mallory's solarium it was warm and tropical. A huge glass-enclosed dome brought the night within touching distance. Trees usually seen in hot climates flourished in the unexpected warmth. The room held a profusion of oversized white linen couches covered with brilliant Indonesian pillows arranged for conversational groupings around a vast river-stone fireplace. Along the opposite wall, the buffet table groaned with the unique foods of Larry McIntyre, Aspen's acknowledged catering genius. The scene was a typical example of the casual but expensive Aspen life-style.

Sophie Mallory, ever gracious, roamed about her room, spending a moment or two to chat with each group. She was a skilled party giver, but she felt nervous about this one. Sam had been home barely a week, and she and Pat were already speaking in the hostile tones of people who really love and hurt one another.

Pat and Liz were something else altogether. Their problems accompanied them wherever they went. Upon arrival they had each gone their separate ways: Pat to huddle with Richard, Liz to the bar where she could watch each new arrival behind the protective curtain of a glass of scotch.

The moment Sam entered the vast room she, too, felt the waves of tension. On the surface everyone seemed to be enjoying the evening, but the tight faces on many said otherwise. She looked around uncertainly and caught her brother's eye. About to offer a tentative smile, the olive branch of peace after their many arguments about Pat's development schemes, she tightened her lips instead as he averted his face quickly and continued his conversation with Richard Farwell and several strangers in pinstripe suits. By the frown on Pat's face, she gathered the conversation was unsettling. Richard Farwell was slumped in a chair, saying little and looking very unhappy.

Liz Mallory, in diamond-studded black suede, prowled around the room like a hungry panther, stopping to chat briefly with friends, then continued her nervous stalking.

Sam felt as if she'd accidentally walked into the first act of a Verdi opera. All the characters were in place and waiting for the inevitable tragedy to unfold.

There was no doubt that the Mallory family was suffering from a *crise de nerfs*. Pat was as touchy as a porcupine. Liz looked like she was ready to explode. And Sophie had not been herself since Sam stepped into her apartment and voiced her incredulity over the desecration of the West End and her brother's part in it. Sam knew her mother was upset, because she'd overheard her make lethal threats to some recalcitrant caterers and florists. Such language from her mother! The consummate diplomat, the iron fist in the velvet glove could sound like that? What was happening to all of them? It was as though some strange disease had gotten into the drinking water.

When Sam saw Rosie Sukert arrive with her long-time escort, friend, and silent appendage, Bill Pugh, she was relieved to see familiar faces and rushed over to welcome them.

They made a strange couple. Rosie with her shape-less body and pipe-stem legs, Bill with his small paunch and skinny legs in tight jeans. Behind their back everyone referred to them as "Tweedledum and Tweedledee." They had been together so long that no one wondered what the initial attraction had been anymore.

It was a glittering crowd, even though they were mostly Sophie's friends—her cronies from the Historical Society as well as Les Dames, the guiding lights of practically every major Aspen event. Barbie Benton and her husband, Annie and John Denver, although not together, Robert Wagner and Jill St. John, local artist Sue Gurrentz and her husband Mort, Bill Stirling, the mayor, with his wife Katherine Thalberg, whose father had been the legendary Irving of MGM in the glory days of the thirties and whose mother was the actress, Norma Shearer, were all gathered at this heady event. There were a handful of Planning Commissioners, Leon and Jill Uris, Goldie Hawn and Kurt Russel, Anna and Rupert Murdoch, Mort and Lita Heller.

Although the invitation had read Aspen Informal, the designation was loosely interpreted. There were the usual number of jeans, boots, and tweed jackets rubbing shoulders with cashmere, flannel, and pinstripes. Women in fanciful Smith leather costumes dotted the vast room like bright spring flowers against the dark Ralph Lauren and Calvin Klein cocktail crepes. Melanie had been right: people were dressing this year.

Sam had ignored her purchases from Melanie's boutique and chosen instead to wear a black suede smoking jacket with quilted lapels, matching pants, and a black cashmere shell. Her Indian black hair, clinging to her shoulders like a shadowy shawl, gleamed like silk. She wore Sophie's pearls around her neck, fingering them unconsciously.

With Sophie regally attired in gray silk pants and a sequined top, she made the rounds of the guests, meeting new people, being reintroduced to those she'd not seen in years.

"Dear," Sophie whispered. "I've invited one of the hotel guests tonight. She's a writer. Rachel Fulton? Perhaps you've heard of her. She's written two very fine books on the West, and she's here researching for a third. I thought this might be a good opportunity for her to meet a lot of our friends. She's very anxious to talk to them about their remembrances of the past. I hope you don't mind."

"No, of course not. One more guest shouldn't matter."

"She's quite nice. Oh . . . there's Louis Breton. You remember him? Alex's father."

"Of course, Mother. You act as if I'd been gone for a hundred years."

How could anyone forget Louis Breton, the king of high culture in Aspen? As director of the Wheeler Opera House, he had been responsible for introducing a dazzling array of talent to the Aspen scene. From the Budapest String Quartet to Bruce Springsteen, musicians of every persuasion had come to the elegantly restored old opera house and played to full and appreciative houses. Even the most esoteric and intellectually rigorous performers were wildly applauded. Louis knew his friends well. Even though they might prefer to stay home and watch television after a long day of skiing, or go to Gordon's for a sumptuous meal, they felt the eyes of the world upon their sybaritic lives and proved that they were seriously culture-minded by turning out in droves for Louis's events.

Referred to as Prince Louis behind his back because of his resemblance to Queen Elizabeth's consort, he was even more princely in his manner. A tall man with the sharply ascetic features of a medieval monk and sardonic eyes, he was nevertheless the epitome of the man of fashion. He wore his faded blond hair short and combed cleverly to conceal a receding hairline.

As he saw Sophie approach with Sam in tow, he put on his most charming smile and extended his hand. He remembered the first time he'd seen Sam. He had persuaded Leonard Bernstein, in Denver with the New York Philharmonic, to make a detour to Aspen, then went to a great deal of trouble to fill his opera house with Aspen's most socially prominent children. Sophie had dragged Sam kicking and screaming to the concert.

Sam was apparently remembering the incident, too, for there was a devilish smile on her lovely face. Yes, she'd grown up a great deal since that time. He remembered the particularly malevolent look on her face when he'd personally ushered the Mallorys to their seats. Aspen kids were far more interested in hockey and slaloms than Haydn and sonatas.

"Tell me," he said in a rich bemused voice as he continued to hold her hand, "have you finally learned to love Mozart?"

She nodded and then added in a tone to match his, "And Mahler, and Stravinsky, too."

"Imagine!" He chuckled. "I hope I had some small part in putting you on the right track. And how fortunate you've been to live in New York these last few years. So much there to experience. Such a culturally rich city."

"An embarrassment of riches, I agree." She gently extricated her hand.

"Well," Sophie said, "you two have a lot to talk about. If you'll excuse me, I see Vivienne. I must talk to her about the Valentine luncheon."

"Mother, it isn't even Thanksgiving yet."

"I know, darling. But these things take planning."

They watched her swirl off in a cloud of silk, leaving behind the lingering scent of some delicately flowery perfume.

"She's quite extraordinary, isn't she? Pity she never married again. Such a handsome woman."

Sam nodded absentmindedly. Sophie was still in her early fifties and looked ten years younger. She had many male friends, bachelors and widowers who escorted her to the endless round of festivities, charming men who had not been above bribing Sam to put in a good word with her mother. But when Sam asked pointed questions about the steady stream of good-looking, gray-haired men, Sophie would turn her away with a smile and a vague answer.

Sam forced her attention back to Louis, who was talking about the winter program at the Wheeler, "which I hope you will be around long enough to enjoy."

"I think I plan to stay this time."

"That's good news," he smiled, "good news indeed. Your mother tells me you have artistic talent. You know I'm on the board of advisors for the Aspen Art Museum now."

"Are you?"

As Louis went on to describe in great detail what he hoped to accomplish, Sam saw Alex Breton arrive with Paul Emerson. Dear Alex. He was like a beloved teddy bear. She couldn't help smiling when he bumped into the door, then swung about to apologize before he realized the door was not a person. He was as awkward on his feet as he was graceful on skis. She waved at him.

"Ah, I see my progeny has arrived." Louis put his hands into his jacket pockets and sternly watched his son.

Sam was about to excuse herself when Louis caught her by the arm. "Samantha, I have to warn you about Alex. I know you and he were good friends when you were younger, and I was most grateful for your steadying influence. But he's changed. No one can say a thing to him anymore."

"He always had an independent spirit," she said loyally.

"Encouraged by me, I assure you. But since his mother deserted us, he's had a lot of problems. Poor boy! He was in a revolving door of prep schools before he came back and finished school here. I got him into Yale by giving the drama school a very generous check. I hoped with his good looks he might find acting amusing, but he rarely went to a class. You know what his greatest accomplishment at New Haven was?"

"He told me he'd written a pizza cookbook, that New Haven has some really serious pizza places. Wasn't it successful?"

"Mildly, I guess. I thought perhaps he had a penchant for cuisine, but when I suggested hotel school or a year in France working with the great chefs, he wasn't interested."

"He just hasn't discovered his life's work," suggested Sam.

"Oh, I think he has. It's driving his father to an early grave."

"Louis, I am sorry. Let me see what I can do. I don't know how much influence I have with him anymore. It's been a long time."

"I have every confidence in you."

"Then let me go say hello."

Sam walked over to Alex and was enveloped in a hug. He kissed her loudly on the mouth. Paul smiled. "Do I rate one of those?"

"'Fraid not, ole buddy, she doesn't kiss navy Aussies." Alex kept a protective arm around Sam's shoulders.

"Spoilsport. Pay him no mind, Sam, he's just a sore loser."

"What this time, Lexy?"

"Rugby," said Paul before Alex could answer.

"Hold on a sec." Alex turned to Sam. "This big lout comes blowing in one day for a couple of weeks skiing. The next thing I know there's a whole village of these big ugly brutes and they're putting together a rugby team. Gentlemen of Aspen, they call themselves. Well, look at him. Is that a gentleman, I ask you?"

"So I suggested," Paul interrupted smoothly, "that he put together a team of preppies, maybe invite Vail and Steamboat to come in to sweeten the wagers."

"Which I did. Willingly."

"So what happened?"

Paul chortled as he flung his arm over Alex's shoulder. "We beat the bloody cleats off them."

"You guys are practically professional," Alex protested. "Let me get a basketball league going and you'll see what hot stuff you are."

Though Sam was smiling at their byplay, she was reminded of Louis's words. Was this what he meant? Alex had always had a sense of play. Was Louis mistaking it for immaturity?

"So tell me, Sam, how did a lovely girl like you ever get mixed up with this churlish fellow?"

"We were partners in crime." Alex twirled an invisible moustache.

"In a manner of speaking." She ruffled his hair. "I met him out at Hank Campbell's ranch when we were kids. We used to go riding together." She thought back to those days after Joe Ferris had suddenly left town, how, although he was younger by four years, Alex filled the void left by him. They'd often played hooky from school to go off exploring or riding in the hills. Then she'd been sent away to school and later she'd gone to New York. No matter how short a time she spent in Aspen, they always managed to see one another, even if it was only for a cup of coffee.

As Alex went into giggling detail, recounting some of their more hair-raising schemes, she got a sudden jarring feeling. Alex's laughter was a little hysterical, his voice strident, his manner forced. He seemed to be wound tighter than a spring. Unconsciously she slipped her arm around his waist and leaned her head against his shoulder as if her presence might calm him. Then she was struck by a disturbing thought. He's on drugs and he needs a hit. That's what Louis was intimating.

A sudden flurry of excitement and noise made them turn toward the door.

"Don't look now, but Miss Scarlett's just arrived," said Paul with a half smile.

Melanie, in a short red satin miniskirt and red lace strapless top, paused and surveyed the crowd. Her escort was another one of those bland, good-looking men in his thirties that she had in ample abundance. Decidedly East Coast, in his Armani flannels and tweed jacket, he had the look of a sleek, well-cared-for cat. Sam had the feeling he had arranged the smile on his face several hours before arrival.

"Christ, she looks gorgeous," Alex moaned. "Who's the creep with her?"

"Sam, darling!" Melanie teetered over on perilously high heels to bestow an air kiss on both cheeks. "Hi, Alex, Paul." Then turning to her escort who stood several paces behind her, she held out her hand and pulled him into the circle. "David, come meet my absolutely best friend in the whole world, Samantha Mallory. It's her homecoming party. Sam, sweetie, this is David Fleming from New York. He's with Morgan Stanley. Sam just came from New York, didn't you, darling? Maybe you know some of the same people. Sam, tell David what you were doing. He knows just everybody."

Sam took her arm from around Alex's waist and gave it to David with a weak smile.

Melanie had noticed Alex and Sam wrapped around each other the moment she walked in and wondered if anything was going on between them. She knew that they had been friends for a long time, but that affectionate look that passed between them bespoke more than friendship. Her eyes narrowed. Alex was good-looking, probably the best-looking boy in Aspen, a lot younger than she liked her men, but David Fleming was turning into such a bore, she was sorry she'd encouraged him to come out and visit. Still, he had all that money. But Alex was rich, too. To Paul Emerson she barely gave a thought. He was fun to flirt with, but poor and an Aussie chauvinist to boot.

She turned the full force of her sapphire-blue eyes on Alex. Taking his arm, she snuggled into him, making sure he felt the soft swell of her breasts. "Alex, you look good enough to eat tonight." The heavy double meaning was not lost on him. His face turned scarlet, but he was not about to let her weasel away. He put his arm around her waist and caught her against his thigh. "I hope you have an appetite," he nuzzled into her hair.

Melanie turned big eyes to Sam. "Be a darling and introduce David to some of our friends, won't you? It's your party and I'm just dying to talk to Alex about those new skis I'm thinking of buying. Right, Alex?"

"Whatever you say, Melanie."

Paul watched Melanie go to work on Alex. The technique was familiar. He hoped Alex realized that nothing would come of it. But by the avid look on his face, he could see that Alex had swallowed the bait. "Anyone need a refill?" he asked. Receiving no answer, he slipped away to find Sam and save her from David Fleming.

She was making the rounds of the room, introducing David to various people, finally leaving him to talk to some brokers from San Francisco. But when he saw her join up with the ladies from the club he changed directions. Women in groups made Paul nervous.

"I thought you liked Alex," said Rosie.

"I do."

"Then go rescue him from the man-eater."

"He's a big boy."

"She couldn't care less about him. She thinks you want him."

"Relax, Rosie. Stop being such a bitch." Sam turned to Bill Pugh, silently drinking at her elbow. "Can't you do anything with her?"

He shrugged and took a swallow of his drink.

"Hey, I didn't deserve that!"

"Yes, you did. No one is less crazy about Melanie than I am, but she's basically harmless."

"Harmless?" Rosie bellowed. "Like a barracuda, she's harmless."

"You see the worst in everybody, Rosie. If I'm willing to give her the benefit of the doubt, why can't you?"

"I think New York has softened your brain. C'mon, Bill, I need a drink."

As they walked away, Sam had the oddest feeling that she was standing at the wrong end of a telescope, that everything and everyone was receding from her, leaving her standing totally alone. Then, seeing Gianfranco di Lucca walk in with an attractive woman with short dark hair, she made her way toward them.

Pat Mallory happened to look up as the newcomers entered the room. His eyes slid away from the man and concentrated on the woman. She was a delicate elfin creature with intense dark eyes that seemed to occupy a great deal of her oval face. Her nose was small and broad, her mouth sweet and generous. As the man introduced her to Sam, her face was suddenly lit by a smile of such warmth, he could feel it cross the room to where he sat.

He rose and approached his sister. "Hi, Sam," he

said, but his eyes were on the other woman. She barely came to his shoulder, so he could look down on her black curls and see the white scalp beneath the silky profusion. A pale blue vein beat steadily in the creamy skin of her temple. Not waiting for the introduction, he extended his hand. "Hello, I'm Pat Mallory, Sam's brother."

"Rachel Fulton," she said in a soft voice with thrillingly husky undertones. It was unexpected coming from this fey creature. He recognized the name from his mother.

"And this is Count Gianfranco di Lucca," Sam said. The two men shook hands as Sam quickly looked from Pat to Rachel. Recognizing the immediate attraction spring up between them, she frowned.

"We are guests at your family's inn," Gianni explained, "and your sister, whom I met recently, was kind enough to invite us to her party."

"Are you . . . ," Pat stammered and turned red.

But Rachel knew exactly what he wanted to know and smoothly answered the unasked question. "Gianni and I met in the lobby while we were both checking in."

"Yes." Gianni was quick to ratify.

"Why don't you come over and meet some friends?" Pat asked, quickly regaining his poise. Then, leaving Sam to Gianni, he tucked Rachel's hand into his arm. "Mother tells me you're a writer."

"Yes. I'm doing research for a book about the region."

"You'll have to tell me all about it over lunch."

Rachel stiffened. They'd known each other exactly three minutes, and he was already moving in on her.

As Sam dragged them around making introductions, Gianni smiled professionally, his mind cataloguing faces, names, and titles. So this is Richard Farwell, he thought, when the craggy CEO of Silver Mountain Corporation rose to greet him. The group made polite conversation for a while as Gianni tried to recede into the background. He hadn't come to this party to talk, but to listen.

Soon his presence was forgotten. Sam took Rachel off to meet some people, leaving Pat with Gianni. The conversation returned to the gloom and doom of before.

"At least it was a good summer," said one of the board members.

"It's winter I worry about," said Richard. "One more bad snow year and we're going to be in serious trouble."

"What do you mean going to be? We are already," said Monty Garbish, another board member. "We have to raise the cost of the lift ticket."

"But we're already the most expensive in the country," Pat protested.

"Well, we're the best mountain. We should be the most expensive," countered Richard. "Besides, the insurance rates are horrendous. Skiers refuse to be responsible for what happens to them when they ski. Good Lord, they sue for a hangnail these days. Or lie about accidents. Look at what happened last year with that skier who sued us because we didn't mark a road that he'd skied a dozen times. If witnesses hadn't come forth, we'd have been forced to pay him several million dollars. A couple of accidents like that could make insurance rates prohibitive for us."

"I'm more worried about the new resorts opening closer to Denver and the major expansions in Utah. You know how skiers are, they always want to try someplace new."

"And cheaper," reminded Ron Reeves, a major developer.

"I'm not interested in those kind of skiers," said Marvin Mayer. "They don't buy the kind of real estate I sell."

"But the mountain can't exist on those kind of people," Pat countered. "Most of them have Foundation passes and let their friends use them when they're not around. That doesn't sell a ticket. We need tours and groups and special deals."

"You want us to turn into another Sun Valley?" Marvin had left the glamorous ski resort when he found it crowded with developers.

"That'll never happen. We've got plenty of room. Why, Starwood still has plenty of empty space. And with the zoning, we don't have to worry. I don't know about business on the mountain, but I can tell you we've sold more million-dollar properties this month than in all of last year," said Ron.

Gianni listened as they talked of the need for greater development on and off the mountain, the importance of sharp marketing techniques to attract new skiers. One owner of some major commercial properties was bemoaning the space going unrented and how much it was costing him. "I tell you we're living in a fool's paradise. We toss millions of dollars around as if it were Monopoly money. The bubble's going to burst. The place is just too damned expensive. I can tell you I don't want to see another junky T-shirt or jewelry shop open here, but they're the only ones who seem to generate enough volume to stay in business."

"I think we have to adopt a wait-and-see attitude," Richard counseled. "If we have a good winter, this conversation will be academic. But I don't want to commit a lot of money to new development in a bad year. Besides," he said grudgingly, "the banks are not thrilled about risking their money right now."

"And I say we raise the money out of state," said Pat. "There's property going begging, property the county is dying to sell off. If we don't get it, someone is going to come into the valley and whip it right out from under our noses. We need more beds, more housing, more decent short-term rentals if we want to attract more people here. Forget the people who already live on Red and in the West End. That's our captive audience. Forget this boom-or-bust mentality.

If we don't build Aspen the way we want it, someone will do it their way." Pat's face flushed with passion.

"Your mother is our biggest stumbling block," Ron Reeves reminded softly. "Don't get me wrong, Pat, I think Sophie is one of the finest women in the world, but she is absolutely a tiger over what she calls the exploitation of Aspen."

"You leave Sophie to me," said Pat through tight lips. "It's Richard who needs convincing."

Gianni's mind worked like a computer filing and cross-matching information. Sophie Mallory was obviously at the head of an outspoken local group who were in favor of zero growth and cautious development. Pat Mallory and Richard Farwell were obviously in favor of controlled growth, but differed on what controlled really meant. And then there were the others, the hyenas who were waiting in the wings ready to make a killing whichever way they could.

Richard Farwell listened to Pat's impassioned speech, his own face expressionless. Though he had known Sophie Mallory for over twenty years, it was only recently that they had found themselves at the center of the two opposing camps. Suddenly he had become aware of her as a passionate defender of a cause while Sophie evidently looked upon him as a money-hungry vulture ready to sweep down on a helpless town and destroy everything that made it unique.

It was ironic. The fact was that it was her son who had come down with an epidemic case of build-itis. Unfortunately, their close partnership and special relationship lumped them together ideologically as well.

About the man who'd been her husband, Richard knew very little, only that for years Sam Mallory had remained in the shadow of his dynamic, outspoken wife.

But with Richard's own marriage a disaster, he found himself seeing Sophie with different eyes. She was a beautiful and spirited woman, dogmatic in the extreme, opinionated and persuasive. Despite her fragile appearance, he knew she was made of steel, had in fact watched her perform at local rodeos, knew she was a tireless rider to the hounds and still finished in the top five of the annual senior ski events in Aspen.

She had always been an exciting and creative opponent. Suddenly he had a fierce longing to spend a quiet evening talking to her without her family or his business associates around. He excused himself in the middle of one of Ron Reeves's house descriptions and set out to find her.

Louis Breton had once again caught up with Sam and was holding her captive in a corner as he discussed her future with her. She was looking up at him with rapt eyes as he charmed, amused, excited, and seduced her with words and wit that made her think of a sweeter, kinder Greg Francis. When she had been an impressionable teenager, she—along with most of her friends—had had a crush on the sophisticated Louis Breton. She and her friends made up wildly romantic stories about him: that he was an illegitimate son of a famous painter, an aristocrat, a royal prince in disguise; that he had a locked library of forbidden books; that he was an unfrocked monk. Every day produced another set of giggly stories.

What they didn't know was that Louis Breton had a Pygmalion complex. Ever on the lookout for raw clay to form, he had been without a major project for too long. Aspen had either ceased producing lovely raw talent, or he had grown too old and jaded to recognize it. But the moment Sam Mallory had returned and he'd seen her loveliness, her uncertainty, and her longing to express herself, he knew fortune had been kind again.

"So, Samantha, you see it can be—" Louis was suddenly aware he'd lost Sam's undivided attention. Turning in the direction of Sam's eyes, he saw Joe Ferris pause in the doorway and look around with those mocking liquid eyes that gave Louis the feeling he was staring into the glittering gaze of a snake about to strike.

Sam felt her face flame. So he had decided to come after all! Look at him standing there. So sure of himself. Like he was better than anyone else in the room. Her heart tripped the breath in her throat.

Just as Louis put his hands to her face and directed her attention back to him, Joe looked her way. Seeing Louis's proprietary gesture, Joe unbuttoned his jacket and, stuffing his hands into his trousers, walked languorously over to where they stood.

"Louis." He nodded, and then gently but firmly he took Sam's elbow and extricated her from Louis's encirclement. "Excuse us, please."

Louis tried to protest, but Joe cut him off with an icy look.

As Joe led her across the room, Sam pulled her arm from his grasp. "What do you think you're doing? Where are you taking me?"

Joe swept her into his arms and said, "We're going to dance."

"I don't want to dance with you."

"Yes, you do."

Music had been playing over an elaborate system all evening. Tired of the same boring conversation, people had begun to dance. There was a slow romantic tune from the forties playing.

"How come you changed your mind and decided to come?" she asked coldly.

"I didn't change my mind. I never made the decision until a few hours ago."

Joe Ferris was aware that his late arrival had produced the desired effect. Everyone was looking at them, and Sophie Mallory's affront at his appearance was written all over her lovely face. Liz Mallory followed their progression around the floor through lowered lids, but the intense red of her cheeks did not come from cosmetics.

Joe pulled Sam tighter to him, feeling her against his length. Now that he had achieved what he'd set out to do, which was to disrupt the Mallory party, the game had lost its savor.

Sam stared at him, a look of pained questioning on her face.

"Why, Joe? We were such good friends once. What happened?"

"We grew up," he said.

"That's no answer."

"That's all I have to give you."

"Why did you leave so suddenly?"

"Ask your mother."

"I did."

"And what did she say?"

"Nothing that made sense. But you went away and never said a word."

"There was nothing to say."

"Not even good-bye?" she prompted softly.

He didn't answer. The tempo switched to a beguine and he swept her through its sensuous rhythms. They were so tightly clasped she could feel the muscles of his back and thigh flex with their movement and for an instant remembered how he had looked that day in the spa. He danced as he did everything—with a sinuous grace and style that made every other man on the floor look spastic. She let her hand leave its place around his neck and touch his cheek. He made a small strangled sound in his throat and put his hand under her hair, bringing her temple close to his lips. As he sang the words softly against her hair, his breath stirred tendrils. She felt a fleeting touch of his lips against her temple.

For the first time in months, she felt desire stir.

"Joe?" Her voice sounded strange in her ears.

"No," he said gruffly and twirled her around until she was breathless. When the music stopped, he bent to kiss her hand, then left as swiftly as he had arrived.

She stared at the empty archway through which he

had departed. Pat materialized at her side. "What was that all about?"

"I haven't the vaguest idea."

Liz Mallory watched Joe Ferris's departure, furious that he hadn't even bothered to say hello.

Pat, who had also been watching, wanted to warn his sister about Joe when his wife appeared at his elbow and growled, "Take me home this instant!"

Sophie Mallory, who had seen something on those two faces that neither Sam nor Joe was aware of, felt misgivings. Richard Farwell took advantage of the moment to ask her if she would have dinner with him next week. Looking at him as if he were an annoying bee, she turned on him and said impatiently, "Don't you have anyone else to bother?" then walked off in a huff.

Louis walked up to Sam and slipped a warm hand under her elbow. "I think this party has passed its prime. Why don't we go over to the Jerome and have a nightcap and listen to some jazz?" His voice was as soothing as honey in hot tea.

"I'd like that, Louis." She felt off balance, strange, an alien surrounded by faces that were familiar but whose behavior was bizarre. To top off the evening, she had seen Alex Breton in a hall leading to one of the service kitchens, smoking crack, melting into the shadows before he could spot her. She wondered if she should tell Louis.

No, it wasn't her affair. Louis obviously had some inkling about his son's activities, else why would he have mentioned it to her?

"Shall we walk?" Louis's voice broke in.

She gave him a grateful smile. Only Louis Breton was behaving like a responsible adult. She felt some of the tension leave her as they struck out in the direction of the Hotel Jerome. Looking up at the sky, she saw one steady unblinking star staring down at her.

CHAPTER SEVEN

Pat Mallory surveyed the huge model of the Ute City project which occupied almost an entire wall of his office. It was complete in every detail down to the plantings and the fountains which were represented by strands of colored cellophane. It was one of the best design concepts he'd seen in fifteen years in real estate, and once again it had been rejected. The excuses were nebulous, a detailed report promised in the very near future. Meanwhile, that was another $100,000 down the tubes.

Pat detected his mother's fine hand in the latest rejection. She had been extremely vocal about her dislike of the project that was to wrap itself around the base of Aspen and Shadow mountains. In open forum and outspoken letters to the *Aspen Times*, she'd called it "too monumental, too ambitious." "We're losing our smallness" had been another complaint. He'd been so sure that this design would be accepted. It had strong architectural and aesthetic values, even Sophie had to admit that. Why was she doing this to him?

From his office he could see the mountain, could visualize what it could, what it should look like. Such valuable real estate, and presently it was full of decrepit trash. Is that what his mother wanted to save? "Damn!" He kicked the wall.

He poured himself a cup of coffee from the pot kept fresh by his secretary and returned to his desk to tackle the piles of paperwork in front of him. Well, Richard had warned him.

As he turned on his computer, the phone rang. He flipped the intercom. "Who?"

Betty Radley, accustomed to her boss's verbal shorthand, announced, "A Count Gianfranco di Lucca?"

Pat stared at the phone console. Who the hell was he? "Does he have an appointment?"

There was a pause, then Betty returned, "He says you met at Sam's party. He'd like to come over and talk to you about buying a house."

Pat looked at his watch. It was almost time for lunch. "Ask him if he can meet me at The Grill for lunch in a half hour."

He could. Pat shifted some paper from one pile to another, then threw his pen down in disgust. The forms were driving him crazy. Every new design had to be accompanied by forms. Maybe Count di Lucca was just what the doctor ordered. House-hunting, was he? He'd give the man a bird's-eye tour in his helicopter. Once he was in the air he usually felt a thousand times better.

Pat left his office and walked over to the Mill Street Mall and The Grill. He was given his favorite table and brought a Corona with a slice of lime stuck on the end of a pick. Absently he sucked the lime then took a swig from the bottle before pouring the pale icy liquid into the glass.

He recognized Gianni the moment he walked in. He stood out from the locals like a Porsche from a pickup. Pat had to smile at the appearance of the tall Italian. He was a Milanese tailor's idea of the well-dressed cowboy, perfect in every fashion detail from his Armani suede jacket and Locke boots to his turquoise-studded belt and Stetson.

The waitress brought him to Pat's table and waited for Gianni's order, a Campari and soda. After the men shook hands, Pat suggested they choose their food before the hordes descended. Gianni asked for recommendations, and Pat took care of ordering.

Over the goat-cheese salad and a shared barbecued chicken, the two men became acquainted with one other. Gianni told Pat essentially the same story he'd told Sam, discreetly emphasizing his wealth. It was important that Pat not think he was typical European nobility, flaunting titles and living like charming parasites off everyone they met.

"So you think you might like to live here?" asked Pat.

"My kind of work requires only a phone," said Gianni modestly.

"May I ask what you do?"

Gianni picked delicately at a wing of chicken. "I am what you call . . . an entrepreneur."

"Any specific interests?"

"At the present, real estate. I thought perhaps I might buy a house. If I decide Aspen is not to my liking, I can always sell it, no? Aspen real estate is always in demand."

"In certain areas you have to take a number."

Gianni gave him a quizzical look.

"Stand in line with hundreds of others who want what you want," Pat explained. "I think perhaps the best way to give you an idea of what's available is to give you an overview."

"An overview?"

"In my helicopter. That's the way I usually show real estate to good clients. You have no problems with helicopters, do you?"

"Only in the hands of poor flyers."

"I assure you I am a very good pilot. In fact, I was almost a test pilot."

Gianni smiled. "I hope it wasn't a crash which deterred you."

"No, I'm afraid it was my mother." The smiling waitress waited silently until Pat finished talking, then offered dessert.

"The hot-fudge sundae with Häagen-Dazs ice cream is a must."

"No, I have had quite enough. Just espresso for me."

Gianni expressed his admiration for Pat's appetite and the fact that he didn't seem to have to worry about weight.

"Nervous energy," explained Pat, suddenly tired of making small talk.

The silence stretched between them a shade too long. Gianni watched the younger man from under slitted eyes. Though his face revealed little, his body spoke volumes. He was obviously distracted about something. All of a sudden, he was like a sulking schoolboy on a warm spring day who found himself confined to a classroom with a dull teacher when he wanted to be out playing soccer.

The moment Gianni finished his coffee, Pat leaped to his feet and called for the check, tapping his foot impatiently when it wasn't immediately forthcoming.

As the two men walked back to Pat's office to get the car, Pat pointed out some of the Victorian landmark houses to Gianni. "My mother's much better at this than I am," said Pat wryly. "She's head of the Aspen Historical Society."

"That, too?" marveled Gianni. "She is a most accomplished woman. She runs a fine hotel, perhaps one of the best I have ever stayed in in your country."

"Yes, there's very little Mother can't do when she sets her mind to it."

And she's obviously set her mind to something that makes you unhappy, thought Gianni. Or is it the reverse? Have you set your mind on something she doesn't approve of? "Yes, I have enjoyed staying there, but I think it is time for something a little more permanent."

Pat's car, a sensible Subaru with four-wheel-drive, came as a surprise to Gianni. There was something perverse about these Aspen rich. You could tell who really had the money by what they *didn't* wear or drive. Yet to anyone who knew—as Gianni did—Pat's well-worn khaki trousers did not come from the Sears catalog. And the tweed jacket with the suede patches might have a rent in its lining, but it bore the hallmark of good English tailoring.

At the airport Pat's Bell 206L-3 Long Ranger III was waiting for them.

Tom Landon, the ops man, strolled by and stopped for a minute to chat. "Going up for a spin, Pat?"

"Yeah, I want to show a client some of the property around."

"Got some bad weather coming in later." Tom squinted downvalley.

"I probably won't be up for more than an hour."

Tom saluted. Then as Pat walked off, he shouted after him, "Do me a favor, will you?"

"Name it."

"Keep away from United's three-ten from Denver?" He laughed.

"That's a promise."

Gianni looked worried. "Is that a problem in such a small field? I remember when I arrived in Aspen, there was some crazy pilot who was making . . ." He made a waving motion with his hand. "All the glasses fell down, and many people thought there would be a collision."

At Pat's laugh, Gianni looked at him in surprise.

Then as the realization dawned, he asked nervously, "That was you?"

"I'm afraid so. I was welcoming my sister back."

"You have a strange way of saying hello." Gianni's footsteps lagged. It was clear he was not eager to trust his life to such a maniac.

Pat took him by the shoulder. "C'mon, I promise to fly straight and slow."

Despite the warning of bad weather, it was still a beautiful day for flying. A herd of fluffy lamb clouds made their way gently across the blue meadows of sky. As Pat's copter gained altitude, the entire range of mountains spread before them, the high peaks like double dips of vanilla ice cream on the dark cones of pine trees. Pat banked sharply and headed down-valley. Like a sinuous white body the earth seemed to stretch up and embrace the craft, trying to pluck it from the air. But Pat leveled out and followed the Roaring Fork River down toward Red Butte, a lonely projection in the middle of the valley which protected the exclusive Starwood development from prying eyes.

"That's Starwood," shouted Pat above the roar of the rotors.

"Why is it called Starwood?"

Pat laughed. "Maybe because so many stars live there."

"And houses are how much?"

"We just sold one completely furnished down to the wine cellar for six-five."

Gianni presumed that meant million. He nodded. "I don't think I would be interested in a place where celebrities live, nor a house already furnished."

"No problem."

Pat turned again and headed upvalley. On Cemetery Lane he dipped down to show Gianni a ranch sitting on a highland surrounded by gullies so sharp it appeared as if nature had cut them with a knife. He circled another beautiful piece of land with a multi-roofed house with distinctly Oriental lines. Sleek horses pawed at the snow to graze on the green grasses beneath. Directly beneath them was Pitkin Green, a newer development of spectacular homes nestled into the undulating hills above the Roaring Fork River. To the right the neat, grid-patterned blocks of town stretched out like a giant's chessboard.

As Pat flew by the West End with its treasure of Victorian houses, Gianni saw ultramodern additions of glass and stone, gardens and pools hiding behind the facades of gingerbread scrollwork. To a man accustomed to the look of the grandiose Italian palazzo, these funny cramped houses were of no interest.

"That's the house my sister wants to buy." Pat pointed to a corner lot.

"I think I would prefer something with a view," said Gianni.

Pat kicked the copter into a steep ascent and flew over Red Mountain to give Gianni a look at the view. Below them Red Mountain Road climbed to the summit in a series of tortuous switchbacks. Along its flanks lay huge A-frame chalets and extraordinary cantilevered moderns that spread out glass arms to catch the last dying rays of the sun. Pat pointed out a few of the houses he knew were for sale.

"They're big, perfect for entertaining. Maybe too big for one person, but there are no small houses up here."

"Size is no problem."

Gianni was impressed with Pat Mallory. His skill with the helicopter was only gloss to his obvious talents as a real-estate man. Gianni wondered what the young man really wanted from life, if Pat was happy just running the biggest and most successful real-estate and development company in the West. That much he had already discovered about Pat.

It was time to get to the point. Casually, he asked, "You are friends of Richard Farwell?"

"Yes. And we're business associates as well. Why do you ask?"

"I couldn't help overhearing at your sister's party. He seems to be in some kind of financial trouble."

"Not really. Richard's a very rich man. But the corporation has had a couple of poor years and has a cash-flow problem."

"Ah, yes, he is the CEO. But surely if the winter is a good one? . . ."

"It'll help, of course. The big problem is that our five-year development plan is on the back burner. And there are some people who think it's Richard's fault. Which is utterly ridiculous."

"Why?"

"You have to understand Richard. He's not your typical slap-'em-on-the-back westerner. He doesn't buy beers for the boys at the Jerome Bar and he doesn't laugh easily. His family is one of the richest in the West; he's eastern and English-educated. He's a reticent man. Mysterious in a way, because he doesn't talk about himself much. So people here tend to be put off by him."

"He seemed quite charming to me," said Gianni.

"Richard knows he's a prickly kind of guy. He's also caught between a rock and a hard place. He's trying not to offend the two main factions that run this town."

"And not succeeding with either, if what you say is true."

Pat shrugged. "One of the factions is headed by my mother."

"That must make it difficult for you."

"You don't know the half of it. Let me show you something."

Pat turned the helicopter toward Aspen Mountain and followed its base to Shadow Mountain, then turned right and flew along Castle Creek toward Ashcroft. The late-afternoon light turned the white cone visible in front of them to a pale rose. "That's

Hayden Peak. Once that might have been the greatest ski mountain around. But people think it's too far from the action. I'm thinking very long range. From the base of Aspen Mountain to here is where our future lies."

"Farwell agrees?"

"He doesn't even want to talk about it. At least not until we see how the winter goes. He wants to upgrade the existing mountain first. I want to build some first-rate hotels and condos so we have more beds to offer, mount an aggressive marketing plan to attract new skiers, and then start discussing some long-term possibilities."

"Your mother is aware of your plans?"

"Not only aware, but committed to see me go down in flames over them. Mother thinks that Castle Creek should not be developed. And she has a lot of support."

"In the long run, she will lose the battle. They always do."

Pat agreed. But he knew the battle wouldn't be over quickly, and might, in the process, ruin him. "Don't ever say that in front of her."

"So the only thing that stands between you and your dream is a great deal of money."

"That and the Planning and Zoning Commission."

"More difficult, I'm sure, than raising the money. What do you estimate?"

Pat Mallory's spirits took off like a thermometer on an August day. Was it possible that he had lucked into an angel? Trying to contain his excitement, he said casually, "There's another possibility which has more short-term potential." Once again he flew down along Castle Creek until he was perpendicular to the Highlands Bowl with its steep and deep snowfield.

As the copter hovered over it, Gianni's breath caught in his throat. "It looks like an Alpine snowfield," he gasped. "Is there more to it?"

Pat swung the copter in an arc and pointed out the

Highland trails to Gianni. "The locals love skiing here. It's a little less polished and less expensive than Aspen. And look!" He pointed below him as he dropped the copter down to a small paradise nestled behind the mountain. Here amidst virgin woods, meandering streams, and gentle meadows sat a ramshackle ranch house.

"I have never seen anything in nature so exquisite," breathed Gianni.

"The Highlands are for sale."

"And the ranch?"

Pat shook his head. "It belongs to an old fellow named Hank Campbell. His granddaddy came to this valley and filed a claim for several of the great and richest veins around Ashcroft. He lost them in a poker game to my great-great-grandfather, Gerald MacNeal. Granddaddy did so well, he gave old Jeb Campbell a chance to win himself a parcel of land. It was supposed to be done with a single pick of a card. Apparently word got around real fast and the next thing you know some enterprising bastard is not only selling tickets to watch the game but taking bets and laying odds on who would win."

"And?"

"It was the last time Jeb Campbell ever held a card in his hand again. He picked a king."

"And your great-grandfather?" Gianni, despite himself, was wrapped up in the story.

"He picked the three. He drew up the deed and there's been a Campbell there ever since. Hank worked the mines until they closed down. Then he tried his hand at ranching. He had a way with horses. Sam and I used to go out and ride in those meadows when we were kids. But the winters were really rough on him. Now he's got bad arthritis and chronic bronchitis. Sunshine, his daughter, owns the health-food store in town, so he doesn't lack for care."

"What have you offered the man?"

"His piece is right in the middle of the two-thousand-acre parcel I want. I've offered him a million dollars." Pat's voice trembled for a minute.

"And he turned it down?"

"Flat."

"Where do things stand at this moment?"

"I have some big money interested, but they're getting a little 'antsy' because I can't get the project on stream. They're about to pull out if I can't promise them some action, and I can't. I could swing this myself except for one problem."

"Your mother."

"Yes, and now my sister, too. It's two against one."

"It is a great pity. Even I can see that the project has great possibilities. I don't know whether your Ashcroft is as feasible. But certainly this . . . " He nodded his head, his eyes glittering.

"If you like the deal, maybe I can be persuaded to let you in on it. As my silent partner," Pat tried to joke. Only he was deadly serious. His mind raced ahead. What kind of deal can I offer him? What kind of deal will he accept?

Gianni seemed wrapped in thought. This wasn't what he bargained for, but Guillermo Santos, his boss, hadn't told him how far he could go. He'd simply said: "Do whatever it takes."

"If you're interested, I'd like to show you the prospective plan."

"My first priority is to find a home. But it certainly can't do any harm to look. Yes, show me your prospective plan. I don't make any promises. . . ."

Pat, with the face of a poker player about to draw to an inside straight, merely shrugged. Wanting to believe he was a breath away from success, he said, "None expected." And kicking the copter into a sharp 180-degree turn, headed back to the airport.

Gianni smiled to himself. Pat Mallory wanted this project more than anything else in his life. The fruit was almost ripe for the plucking.

* * *

"It's just a question of time . . . I don't know. Perhaps not until spring. Much depends on how good the season will be. Don't worry. We can make many things happen that can ruin even a good season. . . . The point is that I have met Pat Mallory. He's the key. Just make sure the money is deposited in my name at the Pitkin County Bank. Oh, yes, be sure you write in my full name: Count Gianfranco di Lucca."

"Pat, I've got to have this house. It's perfect." Sam was touring the rooms of the Victorian on Hallam for the fifth time. "I can move right in. Nothing really has to be done."

"I hope not. The last owner spent a fortune on those bathrooms and the new kitchen. There's a new roof, too."

After the party Sam and Pat had behaved like strangers to one another. But the links of family and their own love for one another were too strong. She had extended the olive branch, saying, "We never agreed on anything when we were growing up. Why should it be different now?"

But Pat would not allow himself to be caught up in a temporary euphoria. He knew it was just a question of time before the Mallory Debating Society would be off and running again. Maybe he'd won this latest round, but she was way ahead on moral points.

"Can we make an offer?"

"The asking price is eight-fifty."

"What do you think?"

"You can probably get it for eight. We'll offer seven-fifty and take it from there. Gives everyone a little bargaining room."

"Whatever you say."

"I never trust you when you're so amenable," Pat said, putting his arm around her and leading her from the house. "What do you say to some lunch and then we'll go back to the office and I'll make a few phone calls."

"Where do you want to go?"

"How about Poppycock's? It's quick and it's good. And you'll probably see all your cronies there."

He was right on all counts. Over coffee she said idly, "I see Joe Ferris has really come up in the world."

He gave her a sharp look. "What do you mean?"

"I mean manager of the Silver Mountain Corp."

"It's not as grand as it sounds. He manages the resort division. Sort of a glorified super, you might say."

"You never cared much for Joe, did you?"

"He was not the most lovable guy in the world."

"You never gave him a chance. Your crowd always called him 'the greaser.' You know his great-great-grandfather was a Spanish grandee."

"Is that what he told you?" Pat's laugh was cynical.

Sam ignored the laugh. "I always liked him. He was a wonderful teacher. Until mother put a stop to it."

"Maybe she was afraid of what he would teach you next."

"I was only ten years old!"

"What does that mean to a—" He clamped his mouth shut.

"What a rotten thing to suggest!" Sam's amiability disappeared in a puff of moral indignation. "You're a bigot. Under all that philanthropy is a bigot paying for his guilt."

"And under all that rhetoric is a girl who's ashamed to be wealthy."

"That's nonsense. Anyway, we were talking about Joe."

"*You* were talking about Joe."

"I guess he isn't married," she said.

"I guess not. He's too busy trying out all the beds in Aspen. You could call him the half-breed Goldilocks. You know, this blonde is too small, this one's too narrow. . . ."

"Oh, stop it! I hate it when you sound off like this. Get the check and let's get out of here."

Pat obliged. Sam's long-standing interest in Joe Ferris still worried him. He knew a few things about Joe's mysterious disappearance that he didn't ever want Sam to know.

He had to hand it to Joe. He'd returned to Aspen with money in his pocket and a good reputation from running several resorts. He now owned several prime pieces of real estate and ran the resort end of the business faultlessly. Yet despite the fact that he contributed to the town's most beloved causes, he still had not been able to win more than secondary status among the town's elite. And what's more, Joe was painfully aware that certain doors would always be closed to him.

While Pat phoned Coates, Reid to discuss the co-broke and Sam's offer, she prowled around his office. By the looks of the clutter, Pat seemed to have his hand in everything. Acrylic cases contained models of houses and developments whose placards informed her they were Pat's own rather than his clients'. There were some interesting single houses and a couple of cluster developments which bore such names as Hunter Creek, Independence, and Hallam Hills.

Her attention suddenly was drawn to the largest of all the cases, where an entire topological miniature of Aspen and Shadow mountains rose in complete and stunning detail. She could see the blue meandering ribbon of Castle Creek as well. Clinging to the entire edge of the two mountains was what appeared to be a city!

Pat hung up the phone. "Well, it looks pretty good. I think . . ." He saw Sam's face as she peered at the model in stunned surprise. "What do you think?" he asked nervously. "That's our Ute City model."

"Ute City was Aspen's old name," she said automatically.

"Right. That's why we want to . . ."

"You're going to build a whole city at the base of the mountain? Tear everything down?"

"We'd like to. That's valuable real estate. What's there now is mostly trash. We'll have every amenity you can think of. What do you think?"

Her green-blue eyes turned dark as the winter Atlantic as she stared at him in disbelief. "I hate it! I hate the whole idea! Why do you want this monster development? Aspen should be small and human-sized. Why do you want to change everything?"

"I just told you. It's prime real estate loaded with trash."

"I can understand a hotel. I can understand inns. Even houses. But a whole city?"

"We're not trying to tear down landmark buildings. They'll always be protected. We'll move whatever's designated landmark to the West End or Main Street, if we have to."

"And create a historical ghetto? Is that what we have to do in the name of progress?"

"Damn it, Sam! You're beginning to sound just like Mother. You refuse to understand anything. You both try to make me out to be some kind of dragon. *I'm* for preservation. *I'm* for environmental protection. But we can't close our eyes to what's needed here. If Aspen doesn't grow past its winter-sports image, it won't grow at all."

"Is that so terrible? Where is it written that every city has to get big or die?"

"Sam, let's face it. Right now we're a one-industry town. Do you want to go back to the old days when silver was queen? Look what happened when the country turned to gold. Aspen almost died."

"But it didn't. It survived. Besides, it's not the same. People will always ski and hike and ride bicycles."

"But we're losing out to the other areas. I'm trying to attract new blood to the area."

"There's nothing wrong with that. I can think of

loads of things we can offer to summer visitors. But does it have to be at the expense of everything that makes Aspen unique?"

Pat hit the desk with his fist, sending the last of his morning coffee flying over a bunch of contracts awaiting his signature. "I just can't talk about this with you anymore. Maybe you'd better deal with Coates, Reid on your house."

"Maybe I better," she said, one step from tears as she stormed out of his office.

It started to snow that night. Huge flakes, flakes as big as angel's wings, manna to a small group of skiers who refused to ski anything but fresh, fluffy powder. The temperature dropped, making every falling flake bone dry, almost weightless as it settled like the lightest kiss on the back bowls of Ajax Mountain.

Pat Mallory slid open the glass doors that ran the length of his huge house on Red Mountain and stepped onto the balcony. It was a brilliant, windless day. He looked down on the silent town crouching in the shadows, waiting for the sun's first warming rays. Picking up a handful of snow, he made a ball and threw it into the air. It was so dry, it splintered into a million facets of pure light, as ephemeral as the foundations of his life.

He shrugged and smiled at his dark thoughts. It was the first real smile to cross his handsome face in almost a week. "Perfect," he said aloud. "Just what the doctor ordered."

He returned to the living room, ignoring his wife's tasteful decor and his own rather sizable art collection, and went to his study. A few phone calls later, he was dressed for skiing and writing a note to let his family know where he'd be for the day. With a pang he thought of the kids. He'd promised to spend Sunday with them. But Tooey would understand and Mandy probably wouldn't care. Maybe Sam would come by and see them. Then again, why should she?

They hadn't parted on very good terms, and she detested Liz too much to pay a friendly visit.

He fired up his Jeep and went to pick up Richard Farwell and Tony Frantz, Silver Mountain's leading ski pro. In the past the three of them had taken some exciting trips to Europe and the Canadian Rockies. Today they would go to Little Annie. Though Tony was a friend, he was also a professional teacher and guide, and Richard Farwell, who liked to have his own ski pro with him at all times, paid Tony a yearly retainer. Little Annie Basin was not ferociously difficult or steep terrain, but there was always danger of avalanches in the backcountry. Tony, a licensed guide, thoroughly trained in survival techniques and mountaineering, not only kept them away from avalanche danger, but knew where to go for the best skiing, which runs would be free from wind slab, which should be skied before the sun hit them, where to turn in the trees.

When he was young, Pat was a willful, arrogant skier who liked to sneak away at every opportunity to ski the out of bounds. Then one day he started a small avalanche. If it hadn't been for Tony and his father, also a ski pro, he would have drowned in the heavy snow. From that point on, he and Tony were friends. Even a rivalry that pitted them against one another for one berth on the Olympic ski team hadn't destroyed their friendship. A broken femur took care of that. Pat dropped out, and Tony had taken two golds and gone on to race professionally.

At the top of his career, Tony was in an automobile accident that almost cost him his life. After a year in traction and another in therapy, he had returned to racing. Even as he grew older, he could still ski better than anyone Pat knew, and he was the best teacher he'd ever met. He also became deaf and mute when the conversation between Richard and Pat turned to anything that concerned the workings of the Ski Corp. Pat and Richard had grown accustomed to his silent presence even when they spoke openly of things that should have been kept behind closed doors.

"You met di Lucca at Sam's party. What did you think of him?" Pat asked, his breath a cloud of white. The snow cat which was conveying them up the mountain made it difficult to speak softly.

"Nothing special. He barely said a word. Why?"

"I think he plans to stay around for a while. He's interested in buying a house."

"Nothing unusual about that." Richard removed a silver flask from his fanny pack and took a jolt of Cognac. He offered it to Pat, who shook his head.

"I showed him the Ute City development, which didn't interest him much. But when I told him about the Highlands and showed him Hank Campbell's spread, I saw a glimmer of interest in his eyes."

"Meaning?" Richard tried to conceal his impatience. Pat Mallory was a man obsessed, determined to have at least one of his projects off the boards and in the works no matter how foolhardy it was.

"The man is not just a good-looking Italian playboy count. He asked some rather pointed questions that led me to believe he's a serious player. He seems to have no trouble with money. I showed him a million-dollar house on Red Mountain and he didn't blink an eye."

"Sure, Pat. How many times has some slick-looking dude rode into town, looked at every piece of expensive real estate you could show him, then left without a word?"

"This guy is different. I know it. I got his entire pedigree. I even spoke to Midge Morris at the bank. He has a huge line of credit."

Richard smiled bitterly. "Which is more than I have at the moment."

"I think he could be our angel. I intend to play out the scenario and see what happens."

As Pat carried on enthusiastically about Gianni, Richard shook his head in denial, leading Pat to say bad-temperedly, "God, I hate it when you're stubborn."

"I'm not being stubborn, I'm being cautious. Look, Pat, you're young and enthusiastic and that's a good thing. That's why I like having you on the board and as my friend. You keep doors open that I might be inclined to shut. But the country is going through tough financial times at the moment. I don't want to make big commitments before I get some positive feedback or good feeling that the golden bubble is indeed still floating."

"But what if di Lucca is interested?"

"It depends on what he wants in return. You don't think he's going to give you all that money as a gift because he likes your dimples. By the way, is he straight?" Richard asked half-seriously. "I never thought about that possibility."

"Man, your mind is absolutely Draconian. He's perfectly straight. And no, I don't expect him to hand over money with a smile and an admonition not to spend it all in one place. I don't know what kind of deal he would want. But I'm willing to find out. I just don't want you to have a closed mind. This could be important to us."

"Your mother wouldn't object to the Highlands development, would she?"

"Knowing my mother, she could object if you mowed your lawn the wrong way," Pat said with a rueful smile.

At the top of the run, Richard watched Pat as he stepped into his skis. Pat's enthusiasm sometimes ran away with his judgment. But Richard had to admit the younger man had an extraordinary aptitude for raising money. There was something so boyish and honest about him, he probably could have had a lucrative life in crime without ever raising suspicion.

On the debit side, Pat sometimes had difficulty in reading people. True, he'd never been taken in for long by fast patter and even fancier footwork, but he liked living and working on the edge. The last thing Richard could afford to do was drive Pat away by being too negative. Richard knew there was talk of unseating him as CEO of Silver Mountain Corp. He needed Pat and his support if he was going to survive any palace coup.

Richard Farwell's father had spent his entire life adding to the family's fortune, instilling his son with the Farwell philosophy, which was essentially imperialistic in nature. Power vested in the hands of one strong and honest man, the development of a loyal cadre, and rich rewards for that loyalty. "To have power, you must bestow power," his father had said, "but never give enough to put yours in jeopardy."

As part of his training, Richard, like Demosthenes, was taught to speak with pebbles in his mouth to improve his oratory. The best gurus of the East were hired to improve his powers of concentration, to teach him the art of relaxation and the sublimation of pain. Every time young Richard had expressed a desire for something—a bicycle, a sailboat, a new pair of skis—the father had extracted a price. Thus he had set the pattern for Richard Farwell's fierce will to succeed.

Starting at the bottom, he had worked his way up and through every branch of the Farwell Corporation. He became wealthy in his own right by the time the old man finally died, and to everyone's shock but his, left the bulk of his estate to dubious charities and a mistress of long standing. After probating the will Richard had ended up with one-third, which was—up to the market crash—worth several hundred million dollars.

Richard had never really known the warmth of a loving family. With an alcoholic mother and coldly indifferent father, it was not extraordinary that he had married a woman very much like his mother and was well on the way to becoming a man like his father. That was until he met Pat Mallory and bestowed on him all the paternal feelings he couldn't give to his daughter, that mother-shadow with the silent accusing eyes.

God, Pat, don't desert me now. I need you more than I can say.

Putting aside these dreary thoughts, he pushed off with his poles and followed the rooster tails of powder that curled from Tony's and Pat's skis.

CHAPTER EIGHT

THANKSGIVING CAME AND WENT. FOR A FEW DAYS THE Mallory clan forgot their differences and remembered what they liked about each other. Only Liz Mallory remained distant, preoccupied to the point where she did not once correct Mandy's table manners. Sophie Mallory, who had for years invited her "orphans" (those who couldn't go home for the holidays), asked Rachel Fulton to join them. The writer proved to be a perfect buffer between all the warring factions.

Then Sophie was off to Denver for a garden-club charity event of which she was co-chairperson. When she told Sam she would probably spend the weekend in San Francisco, her daughter asked, "What's in San Francisco?"

Sophie had replied blithely, "My lover," but Sam had only laughed and said, "I wish."

By the first of December Sam moved into her Hallam house and was busily decorating it from the

Mallory storehouse of antique furniture, carelessly mixing them with her own modern pieces from New York. The result was a charmingly eclectic hodge-podge. She happily settled into its clutter, finding old-maidendom rather relaxing.

Aspen had a history of wonderful old maids who had come out as teachers and nurses and become beloved curiosities. When Sam was little, she used to dream of getting old and moving to a small town where she would run a small business, see a few friends, and sing in the church choir. By the time she was twelve, she had other ideas.

Now she was home. There was snow on the mountain, and she realized how much a part of her life this place was. It was the part of her life she wanted to express in her painting. Louis Breton had promised to work with her as soon as the Christmas holidays were over and he had returned from Cabo St. Lucas. Which meant that Alex would obviously not be spending the holiday with his father. She'd ask Sophie to include him in their plans. No doubt one of Sophie's cronies would be giving a big New Year's Eve bash and she would be invited if she wanted to come.

Every night it snowed. Every morning the sun came out. The town started to fill up. Expensively furred and jeweled women with crocodile bags from Hermès came to town. They were tanned and California blond even when their accents were from somewhere else. They roamed the small streets in elegant bands, filling the air with their high bell-like voices gargling and gurgling over the glottal stops and trills of their language.

At Stefan Kaelin, they took five or six of the most expensive outfits from Bogner, Steinebronn, Descente, Progress of Finland, and Sportiva. Smith's sold their quantities of their $2,000 embroidered blanket coat as if it were disposable. They discovered antique Tiffany and Rolex watches at Second Time

Around and bought enough for four arms, and they cleaned Pierre/Famille of their rare estate jewelry. They destocked Ralph Lauren's shop in minutes, descending like locusts to snap up polos, shetland, and cashmere sweaters, paisley sheets and ruffled pillow shams. The oil glut and weakened world economic outlook did not prevent them from buying Jane Smith's cactus sweater, silver belt buckles from Curious George, silver and gold necklaces from Antony/Williams, or furs from Revillon. They filled up the best restaurants and hired the most famous of Aspen's ski professionals to teach them to ski.

And then came the Japanese, arriving in tight masculine battalions, spending vast quantities of yen on equipment and snowcats, looking for the most dangerous ways to kill themselves and those unfortunate enough to be on the slope when they took off on one of their kamikaze blitzes.

Business boomed. There was a shortage of help everywhere. Those who would have come to work in Aspen for the winter didn't because they couldn't find housing they could afford, except many miles downvalley. Shop owners, many in business for the fun of it, were forced to wait on customers instead of meeting friends at Bonnie's or High Alpine for lunch and a day of skiing.

The day of the ski bum was over. The locals who could have worked were long gone from the valley, their homes bought up by strangers who offered more money for them than they'd seen in a lifetime.

For Hank Campbell, living on his isolated ranch in the middle of the Highlands, December was the hardest of more Decembers than he wanted to count. The cold weather worsened his arthritis, and the wood smoke from the potbelly stove filled the room instead of going up the chimney, aggravating his emphysema.

His best brood mare had upped and died on him, and his few milk cows had developed some virus and had to be put down. It would take thousands of dollars to get everything back to rights. Although his daughter had offered to help him out, he turned her down flat. She worked hard for what money she had. Let her keep it. He hadn't told Sunshine yet about Pat's offer. If he had, she would have been convinced he'd gone senile, lost his marbles, called him a stubborn old hardhead and probably would have called the funny farm to take him away. But sell out to a Mallory! He'd die first.

On his way to the office, Pat Mallory passed The Grainery, Sunshine Campbell's health-food restaurant on the shady side of the Hyman Avenue Mall. Seeing that Sunshine was there, he played a hunch and went in.

"Hi, Pat. You alone or expecting someone?" Sunshine approached him with a stack of menus in her hand.

"Alone today, Sunshine." He straddled a stool with his long legs and parked his elbows on the counter. "What's good today?"

"Everything," they both said at the same time and grinned at each other. Sunshine was a couple of years older than Pat, but she was starting to develop the perennially tired look of a rancher's wife. Though still a handsome woman, she tended to look like a toy that'd been left out in the sun and rain too long. Nothing that a day at Elizabeth Arden's couldn't rectify.

He scanned the menu and then ordered his usual: turkey and sprouts on seven-grain bread with tomatoes and jalapeño jelly.

"Herb tea or Soho seltzer?"

"Both."

Pat looked around. It was still early, so the place was fairly empty. In the summer and on winter weekends, Sunshine's restaurant attracted the college kids and

Aspen's more down-to-earth artists and musicians. Most of them were too young to have even heard of Woodstock or the Beatles, but they were the inheritors of the dream. Still trying desperately to be cool and laid back, to go with the flow, they found establishment work a bummer, espoused the most radical of causes, enjoyed their tangerine-colored purple-cloud drug dreams, and thought yuppies should be thrown back into the creeks until they got bigger. They had a sympathetic earth mother and camp counselor in Sunshine who'd done it all.

"Sit down." He patted the stool next to him. "Have a cup of tea with me."

"Okay. Place is pretty quiet." She called out to a young girl with long hair who was hunched over a copy of *Rolling Stone* magazine. "Venus, keep an eye on the paying customers."

"Venus?" Pat mouthed.

Sunshine smiled. "A rose by any other name, et cetera."

They chatted about mutual friends for a while. Then Pat, without lifting his eyes from his sandwich, slipped in the question as though it were just another query about the weather. "Hank mention my offer to him?"

Sunshine was instantly alert. "What offer?"

"Then he didn't." Pat frowned and looked as if he didn't want to say more.

Sunshine shifted nervously and raised her eyebrows negligently. "Haven't seen a whole lot of him in the last few days. Been busy."

They both knew it was a lie. He waited.

"What offer?"

Pat put down the sandwich and turned to her. "I want to buy the ranch."

"The whole ranch?"

"All two thousand acres. Most of it is forest."

"Loaded with deer, elk, hare, squirrel, ptarmigan, grouse, and muskrat," she reminded.

"Right in the middle of a projected development that could mean a lot of jobs to Aspen."

"I'm afraid Hank doesn't give a hoot about that. Pat, you know he loves that piece of land! Better than anything in the whole world. It's his home, for the love of God!"

"I know that. I'm not going to turn him out on the street. We'll give him a nice condo over by Shadow Mountain. He'll be close to you and when he wants to come into town, he can walk, instead of driving that wreck of his on the highway."

Pat knew he had pushed one button. Sunshine hated when Hank, fortified with a couple of beers and maybe a shot of whiskey after a night at the Hickory House, made his unsteady way home. It wasn't Hank she worried so much about as the real drunk punks and rednecks on that dark ribbon of asphalt everyone called Killer 82. "Think you might talk some sense into him?"

"Don't count on it. He may be an old man, but he can still raise the roof with that voice of his."

Sunshine flung the red-and-white-checked tablecloth over the pine table and smoothed out the wrinkles. She took two white plates and cups from the open cupboard and opened the drawer of the chest that housed her mother's silverplate. She gave a quick count. Every time she came over, there were pieces missing.

"Hank, are you still throwin' away the silver when you clean off your plates into the garbage?"

"Don't be a fool, Val." Sunshine's real name was Valerie, but Hank had always called her Val because "what kind of highfalutin name is Valerie?"

"Well, there are some pieces missing."

"Maybe I was robbed."

"There's nothing here worth taking."

"That's what you think," he said darkly.

Sunshine stirred the rabbit stew as it sizzled in the

old iron skillet, poured a few drops of red wine into it, took a taste, and then seasoned it vigorously with salt and pepper. The smell of coffee filled the room as it came to a boil in the big blue-and-white-spattered coffeepot which had been in the Campbell family since the days of the silver strikes.

The fried potatoes sputtered and turned golden brown. She was about to sprinkle some chopped parsley on them when Hank seized her hand and wheezed, "Don't put none of that grass on my spuds. Save it for your freaks at the restaurant."

"Hank, you are truly a fat pain in the you-know-what."

"Say it, daughter, I heerd them words before."

"C'mon, old man," she said wearily, untying the apron and tossing it over a chair. "Sit down and eat your supper."

He sat and tied a napkin around his neck. Looking up at her coyly like a shy lover, he winked. "What's for dessert?"

"Apple pie."

"Your homemade pie?" She nodded. "Bring some ice cream?"

"No."

"Why in tarnation not?" He flung his fork on the table.

"Wipe your mouth. You got gravy running down into your beard."

"I don't give a hoot where it's runnin'. How come no ice cream?"

" 'Cause the doctor says you shouldn't have it."

He was about to protest again when she interrupted, "I'm not interested in what you have to say."

Hank grumbled his way through the rest of dinner. When he was on his second cup of dark burnt coffee, she said casually, "How come you didn't tell me, Hank?"

"Tell you what, honey." Hank was feeling mellow

after his meal. Val was just like her mother: the girl could cook rings around anyone. Though he never admitted it to her, he looked forward to the days she came out to the ranch to prepare a meal for him.

"Pat Mallory wants to buy the ranch. Why didn't you tell me?"

"Not sellin'."

"How much did he offer?"

"Last offer was," he stopped to think a moment, "think it was about a million. Yeah, that was it."

"Are you crazy? A million dollars. And you turned it down? Hank, you hardly have a pot to pee in."

"I still have my pride, and I'm not sellin' out to a Mallory even if my last pair of boots was fallin' off my feet. I tell you the boy won't leave me alone. He keeps after me like I was a sixteen-year-old virgin with a liquor store."

Her lips started to twitch. She quickly covered the smile and tried to look stern. Hank's similes were as colorful as they were farfetched.

"You know what he wants to do with our land, don't you? He wants to fill it up with hotels and condos and convenience stores and God knows what all. God didn't mean for that land to be anything more or less than what it is." His voice grew reverent. "All's I ever did to it was cut down a few trees to build the ranch. Otherwise it's been exactly the same for a hunnert years, maybe even more before me. The animals live there peaceful, knowin' that come November no one's gonna come out and shoot them. Tell me how anyone with an ounce of religion could shoot one of them sweet mule deers. What'll happen to my steelheads and my brook trout if them 'dozers come in and mess up their water? And them woods is full of grouse and quail and partridge. Where would they go?"

"Oh, Dad." Sunshine stood up abruptly and rushed to hug him.

He tried to push her away, but he liked the feel of

her strong, young arms around him. "Stop making such a fuss."

Gruff, stubborn old Hank Campbell. He was the true ecologist, a one-man environmental protection agency. As long as he felt so strongly, then she would, too. Pat Mallory would just have to find himself another place to develop. Even if it took her last cent, she'd make sure that Hank kept his land.

Gianfranco di Lucca signed his name with a flourish. He had just bought a million-dollar house on Red Mountain.

"Congratulations," said Pat. He went to the bar in his office and pulled a bottle of Taitinger champagne from the fridge. He popped the cork and poured the pale sparkling liquid into two flutes and handed one to Gianni.

The dry bubbles pricked his throat as Gianni declaimed, "*Delicioso*. The French can do one thing well, can't they?"

"We can probably close on this the end of next week. The former owners are anxious to get into their new house as soon as possible."

"So if you give me a set of the plans, I will take them to the decorator, and we can get started. By the way, can you recommend someone who is very good?"

Pat could, but whether he wanted to was another question. His wife was highly thought of. It was one of the things she was really good at.

"Well?"

"This is a little embarrassing. You see, Liz, my wife, is one of the best in town. But I hesitate to recommend her."

"Why? If she is good . . ."

"Oh, she is, she is. It's just that we . . . that is, she . . . we seem to be making a lot of money off you."

Gianni laughed. "Don't tell me you worry about nepotism. I can see you have no Italian blood in you. In Italy we would recommend anyone in the family, even the cousins by marriage for a job. So don't worry."

Gianni was delighted at the turn of events. Pat Mallory was an honorable man who liked to pay back obligations. Gianni would bank on that later.

"So how are things going in your attempt to acquire the rancher's land?"

"Do you believe the old codger just turned down a million and a half for it?" Pat had gone back to Hank with a new offer.

"No!" Gianni went to pour himself another glass. He stood for a moment, staring into the bubbles as if they were tea leaves, and the future was clearly indicated. "I have an idea. Let me try to feel him out."

"How are you going to manage that?"

"Trust me to find a way."

Gianni drove the black Corvette up the twisting Castle Creek Road as if he were doing the Mille Miglia. He kept an eye peeled for the ranch that Pat had pointed out for him earlier. Slowing down, he continued on past the ranch, made a U-turn, looking carefully around to make sure no one would see him when he deliberately drove the car into the culvert. About a hundred feet before Hank Campbell's place, he went off the road.

Getting out, he checked the damage. He hated to do anything so unkind to such a beautiful car, but extraordinary problems deserved extraordinary solutions, and the more favors he did for Pat Mallory, the more indebted he would be.

Arranging his face to mirror his distress, he walked up the road to the ranch. The path was slippery and icy. Hank had tried to clear it after the first snowfall, then gave up in disgust as every night brought more and more of the white stuff.

As Gianni knocked on the front door, he had a sudden vision of the old man appearing at the door with a shotgun and an attack dog.

When the door opened he was unprepared for Hank. Expecting a skinny, bow-legged wizened old man, he found instead a man who topped him by many inches. He had a full head of iron-gray curls and matching pewter eyes that seemed to be no more than small pinpoints of light, so overwhelmed were they by the ditch-deep wrinkles that surrounded them.

Hank had apparently been washing up, because all he wore was a pair of baggy Levis. Suspenders dangled from his waist. His face above the white-as-milk body was the color of a walnut.

"Yeah, what you want?"

"I am so sorry to disturb you." Gianni, in a pair of leather pants and a coyote jacket, was aware how he must look to this simple man. "But I have had an accident with my car. If I could be permitted to use the phone . . ."

"Well, sure. C'mon in. Help yourself. Phone's right there." He pointed to an old wall phone which surely must have been one of the first of its kind.

Gianni gave it a dubious look.

"It works," said Hank. "Best you call Frank Begley. That there's the number." He pointed to a pad with a string of numbers on it. "Tell him you're at Hank Campbell's place, so's he knows where to find you."

Gianni did as Hank advised, then hung up the receiver. "He says it will be at least a half hour."

"Which means an hour. So why don't you take the load off and set yourself down? Got some coffee on the stove if you care for it. Help yourself while I finish cleanin' up. There's a cup on the drainboard."

Gianni poured a cup and took a sip. It was the strongest coffee he'd ever tasted, making Italy's espresso taste like mother's milk by comparison.

Hank came back into the living room, buttoning up a faded flannel shirt. "You a tourist?"

"Not exactly. I just bought a house here."

"Whereabouts?"

"In town."

"I can see by your duds you don't have any money problems. Good thing, town's expensive."

"You, I take it, have lived here all your life?"

"That's correct. My daddy before me. And his daddy before him. Yep, the Campbells came in with the first silver families. We was miners back then. First in California, then up in Washoe, Nevada. You probably heard tell of the Comstock Lode. Took out about three hundred million dollars in gold and silver between eighteen sixty and eighteen eighty. Trouble was the money men bought up the best claims from the early prospectors. They had to move on. But there was always a new strike somewheres else. And they surely loved adventure."

"It must have been a most interesting time."

"I reckon. Comin' over from Leadville in those days was no easy trip. Maybe it was only forty miles away, but they was some of the highest mountain passes on the whole continent."

"But your family obviously made it."

"That they did. My granpappy had a claim they said was sure to produce the highest-grade silver in the area. Trouble was he spent every last dime gettin' here."

"What did he do?"

"Tried to raise himself a grubstake. My gramma and pappy were back in Leadville just waiting for him to send the word."

"So everything worked out for the best."

"It did not. Granpappy had to sign a piece of paper over giving an interest in his claim. They told him it was only for twenty-five percent. But when the mine started producing, he found out he had signed over seventy-five percent. They cheated him right out of his claim. He couldn't do nothin'. He'd signed the paper."

"Didn't he read the agreement?"

Hank blushed and looked at his feet. "He couldn't read," he said softly.

"By that time, the rest of the family had arrived. They was livin' in a shack up near the Enterprise mine. Got hisself in a card game and lost everythin'. The old boy started to spread word around town that he'd been cheated. To quiet him down, they give him a piece of land way out of town and some livestock to start a small ranch. They warned him not to step foot in town again."

"Who were these despicable people?"

"That would be the MacNeals. Sophie Mallory's kin."

"The woman who runs the Silver Leaf Inn?"

"One and the same. And don't you know history is repeatin' itself?"

"How so?"

"Pat Mallory, the great-grandson of the man who cheated my granpappy, is tryin' to get me off my land."

"No! Why on earth is he doing that?"

"Wants to put up a big development, I hear."

"Has he made you any kind of offer?"

"Sure. The more I say no, the higher it gets."

"Surely you're not trying to blackmail him to raise the price?"

"Do I look like that kind of a s.o.b? I don't want to sell my land. I tell you even if they burn the place down, I'm not gonna sell. And that's final."

Hank paced around the room. His agitation was so extreme that Gianni was afraid he might collapse in front of him.

Where was that damn mechanic? I want to get out of here. Aloud he said soothingly, "Mr. Campbell, just calm yourself. There's no need to get so exercised."

"Sorry about that. Didn't mean to pop off like that to a total stranger. Guess I needed to blow off steam."

Hearing a noise, Hank went to peer out the window. "There's Frank now." As Gianni got ready to leave,

Hank stuck out a hand full of veins. Gianni shook it. It was like shaking hands with a powerful snake. "Nice to have met you, Mr. . . . uh, Mr. . . . ?"

"Gianni. Just call me Gianni."

"Okay, Johnny, you take care now, you here?"

"Thank you, Mr. Campbell . . . for everything."

CHAPTER NINE

DECEMBER BROUGHT HEAVY SNOWS AND HUGE CROWDS.
The sleepy streets became choked with muddy pick-
ups from Arizona and New Mexico, BMWs and Audis
from California and Nevada, Subarus and Saabs from
Illinois and Massachusetts.

Hungry skiers formed patient lines as they waited
for tables at the Aspen Mine Co., The Cantina,
Eastern Winds, or Little Annie's. Reservations at
Gordon's, Abetone, and Syzygy were advised to be
made at least three weeks in advance. Chez
Grandmere in Snowmass had been booked for Christmas week a year in advance.

The week before Christmas there were over 400
private planes parked at Sardy Field.

At night, the Cooper, Hyman, and Mill Street malls
were clogged with fur-clad couples window-shopping
or enjoying hot chocolate on the benches which lined
the bricked pedestrian thoroughfares. Benetton brats
in layers of lollipop colors giggled and bopped as they

licked concoctions of ice cream, sprinkles, and sauce while their parents shivered.

Aspen in December was like being let loose in a candy shop. There were temptations at every step. Money flowed like champagne into the coffers of the dozens of boutiques which sold everything from five-dollar Aspen pins to stratospherically priced sables. Perhaps the goods did not have quite the prestigious European pedigree of St. Moritz, but then again St. Moritz was minor league in the sheer number of shopping opportunities. Hardly a person strolling the malls was without a colorful shopping bag.

Flashbulbs popped like firecrackers as dozens of cameras photographed the Christmas scene of snow-covered Aspen. Lights twinkled like stars from the cottonwood and pine trees all over town. Skaters turned every pond and lake into a Currier and Ives Christmas card. Dogs, illegally off leashes, frolicked in the snow and chased snowballs in Wagner Park. The voices of carolers rang out like clear bells, soaring upward to hang suspended in the crisp mountain air. For most, it was the prettiest, happiest time of the year in the Roaring Fork Valley. For some it was a season to get through with as little attention paid to it as possible.

At Andre's and the Ute City Banque, pretty girls sat together over beers or white wine and looked for eligible men on the street or tried to pick them out from the new arrivals in the restaurant. Many were new divorcées, recently arrived from large and small towns in the Midwest, attracted to Aspen by the life-style, the skiing, and the possibilities. In most cases, instead of eligible men they found other women like themselves and good friendships sprung up over-night. Misery loved company and a shoulder to cry on. All dressed in the latest Aspen style, displaying far more creativity than cash in their purchases, they were rail thin, not because they particularly wanted to be, but because they were too tired to cook, and it was too expensive to eat out every night. After a few years, most developed hard lines and brittle laughs. Whatever male relationships they formed lasted only as long as the visitor's vacation. Out-of-towners saw them walking arm in arm or sitting in bars and envied them their vitality and sparkle, their dashing way of wearing clothes, their perpetual tans. And in democratic Aspen they were often invited to some of the posher parties; thus their conversations were peppered with the names of celebrities. They worked in the posh boutiques or hostessed at the restaurants, sometimes both. It was one of the few ways they could afford to live, if not right in town, at least close enough to get home alone if they didn't score a dinner date.

There was a party every night, sometimes two. Inveterate hostesses, always searching for a new personality, a new theme, a new menu to enliven the social scene, lived on Valium and black coffee. Creative efforts grew feverish as the holiday peaked, for no hostess worth her salt wanted her affair to be "just another party." She wanted to be remembered for her genius, to be spoken of months after the snow had melted. "Remember Barbi's Masquerade . . . Sophie Mallory's rodeo . . . Roger Standish's Mississippi Riverboat Gambling Party . . . Pat Mallory's Aspen Olympics?" That was fame in Aspen.

Donald Trump, Barbara Walters, Jane Fonda, and Oprah Winfrey came to town. Don Johnson and Barbra Streisand gave big parties. Mobs followed Arnold Schwarzenegger and rode the lifts with assorted Kennedys. Photographers tried to take a picture of Oprah as she skied on Buttermilk, but had no luck. Cornering the most celebrities for a function became serious warfare. Although most came to Aspen because the locals respected their privacy, they were still as desirable as smoked salmon and caviar at a party.

But the one man who made every list and accepted

every party invitation was the dazzling, newest face in town: Count Gianfranco di Lucca.

Once more he became the subject of conversation over lunch at The Grainery. Rosie, who had taken a break from writing her column for the newspaper, was sharing a pot of tea with Sunshine when Sam, laden down with shopping bags, came in and plopped into a chair.

"God, I hate Christmas."

"So would I if I were you," said Rosie. "What do you get the family that has everything? Rhode Island?"

"Actually I was trying to buy Pat one of the Bahamas, but he already has one." Sam slipped out of her down vest and windbreaker. "Who are we roasting today?"

"Gimme a break," pleaded Rosie. "We were talking about the most eligible bachelor in town, and I don't mean Don Johnson or Robert Wagner."

"Count di Lucca," said Sunshine. "Everyone thinks because he has a title he must be rich."

"Who cares?" Sam shrugged, turning in relief to welcome the waitress bearing the salad specials she knew the group usually ate. "God, I'm starving."

"Spending money does that to me, too," said Rosie. She was determined to answer Sam's previous rhetorical question. "Who cares? The West Coast divorcées do." She enumerated a string of wealthy women in their midforties who were squabbling over the right to escort Gianni to the best parties in town. "I was invited to Buffy Prentice's the other night, and who was there as the extra man? Himself."

"Were you able to control yourself?"

Rosie made a face. "I even hear the 'starlets' are rolling dice to see who's going to be the first to sleep with him." "The starlets" was a nickname given to a group of small-time, no-longer-dewy actresses who lived in Aspen and who appeared periodically in low-budget "slasher" flicks or made-for-TV movies, and who kept their bodies ready for action with daily trips to the spa.

"Well, from what I understand, they're going to have to slug it out with Lola Koppelman," Sam, not above sharing gossip, confided. Lola was a six-feet-four former Vegas showgirl who'd married David Koppelman, the diminutive powerhouse who owned Worldwide Pictures. Lola lived in Aspen, David in L.A. She was as well known for her sexual appetite as she was for her height. "At Mother's party for the hospital drive, Lola took one look at Gianni and started salivating from every orifice. She's made it very clear that she wants him to be her exclusive property," she added.

"Poor Gianni. Whatever Lola wants, Lola gets," sighed Sunshine.

"It's the curse of the upper classes."

"And a schlong I hear that looks like an Italian salami. I hear he's a perfect match for her in the kinky department," smirked Rosie.

"There she goes again. Do you think she did graduate work in a locker room?" asked Sunshine of Sam.

"They didn't have locker rooms when I was born," said Rosie, who described her age as somewhere between forty and death.

"I don't know anything about his sexual prowess, but my mother thinks he's better than Santa Claus," said Sam. "He has endeared himself to her for life. He contributed over one hundred thousand dollars to be used at her discretion for whatever charity or good work she sees fit."

"Maybe he has hot pants for your mother," suggested Rosie.

"Maybe he wants to be guaranteed a seat on the right side of God," said Sunshine.

"What's that supposed to mean?" asked Sam, a hostile note creeping into her voice.

"Well, say a guy comes to town. He is or he isn't

what he says. It's a small town. A lot of very wealthy people live here. That's no secret. Maybe he has a scam. Maybe he just wants to marry a very wealthy woman. He's not interested in some has-been film star. He wants real money. The best way to find out who's who in town is to snuggle up to the powerhouses in that town. Pat Mallory, Sophie Mallory . . ."

"Are you saying he's using us?" Sam asked in surprise.

Sunshine shrugged. "I'm not saying anything. It's just a for-instance."

"Why are you so suspicious? You, of all people?"

"Yeah, Little Mary Sunshine. I guess putting my trust in so many wrong places has made me a little wary. I just have bad karma about this guy."

Sam thought for a moment. It was true. Sophie had brought the dashing Italian into her inner circle, where he was welcomed for his wit and charm by the women and his shrewd approach to business by the men.

Pat was deliberately cultivating him for his possible financial investment and introducing him to the other members of the Silver Mountain board. And the proof of Gianni's acceptance in town was that the out-of-town powerhouses were inviting him to their exclusive soirées. He was among the thirty couples invited to hear Gordon Getty's operatic work in progress for next summer's music festival. Evelyn Lauder invited him to the housewarming of her art-filled aerie with its wall-to-wall view of the mountains. Rupert Murdoch invited him to join a ski party of publishers. Only Robin Leach had managed to miss him, which, in many people's minds, was a blessing.

What Sam didn't know was that Gianni's ingratiating manner, his continental elegance and charm, covered up a subtle Machiavellian mind. He might have been born in the slums, but his intelligence was worthy of *The Prince*. Working on the more influential members of the Silver Mountain Corporation, Gianni had begun to cast doubt upon Richard Farwell's ability to run the Corp. It was surprisingly easy. Farwell was not beloved. His business acumen might be admired, but his personality, his arrogance, and his absolutism were not. He rarely socialized, and when he did make an appearance, it was usually alone and not for long.

The women of Aspen, married and divorced, had— in the beginning—found Richard's lean, lanky body and Gregory Peck awkwardness very appealing. They yearned to feel those big hands all over them, that sensuous mouth on theirs, that muscular body crushing the breath from them. But Richard had either danced away from their imploring arms or pretended ignorance of what they offered. So in time they, too, had turned against him, hoping that one day some woman would give him his comeuppance. They didn't know how close they were to getting their wish.

Meanwhile Gianfranco di Lucca was basking in adoration, fulfilling a long-buried need of the women in Aspen.

Mallory Interiors was housed in a sleek, modern office on Main Street. Designed for Liz by Massimo and Lelia Vignelli in high Milan minimalism, it was considered a perfect example of the Mallory look. The colors were pale: gray, cream, celadon, blush. The use of such utilitarian materials as particle board and galvanized steel, sand-blasted glass and aluminum grids gave the space a raw power, a grandeur against which the tools of her trade stood out in stark relief.

Now up to her arms in swatch books and rug samples, Liz was trying to prepare a concept for a Japanese architect's new house in Starwood that would show everyone that she was the best interior designer in the country. But the design wouldn't coalesce. She threw down her drawing pen and cursed. How could she concentrate when there were so many other things on her mind?

Her mother-in-law had requested them to attend the International Wine and Food Society's annual Christmas gala at Redstone Castle. The theme was "A Charles Dickens Christmas." Liz was bored to tears by Charles Dickens. About to say bah humbug and turn it down with the excuse that she had made plans to go to a spa in Mexico, she had changed her mind when Pat had taken her in the bedroom and promised to beat her black and blue if she persisted with that idea. He didn't care what she did after the holiday, she could drown herself for all he cared, but the children were not to be deprived of an evening they looked forward to each year.

The children were another thorn in her side. Tooey was impossible, a miniature Pat Mallory in every way. Mandy, generally docile, had suddenly turned into a small monster, questioning every command, refusing stubbornly to obey her. School had called several times to inform her that her daughter was becoming a discipline problem. The latest call had really caused a fuss. Mandy had been accused of stealing an expensive doll from a playmate. When confronted, she had denied the accusation. Two days later, Carlotta, the housekeeper, had discovered it in the hamper of a seldom-used guest bathroom, wrapped in a towel. Liz had grilled her daughter to no avail. Mandy refused to say a word. Liz had decided not to tell Pat. She was sure he would blame her.

To add insult to injury, Joe Ferris had suddenly started acting coolly toward her. She had waited for him at his house on several occasions only to leave after an hour when he failed to appear. Determined not to call him, her anger had grown out of all proportion so that when she finally did see him, she beat at him with her fists and called him every evil name she knew. He had treated her with amused contempt, toyed with her, then brought her to such a fever of wanting, she melted at his first touch. Under his relentless attack, she suddenly had a sick image of herself: the proud Elizabeth Mallory groveling before a goddamn half-breed. She cried hot, angry tears even as she moaned for him to never stop.

The sound of the door chimes brought her back to reality. She looked up in annoyance at the interruption, saw a tall figure silhouetted in the door, and went to open it.

"We're closed for . . ."

The tall figure stepped in. "I'm so sorry to interrupt. I could come back at a more better time," he said awkwardly. "Your husband suggested . . ." Her face tightened at the mention of her husband. "Perhaps you remember me, Count Gianfranco di Lucca? We have met several times, I believe?"

"Of course!" Immediately she was all smiles. "Forgive me for not recognizing you. Please, do come in. How can I help you?"

He pulled a set of plans from his Gucci case. "I have just bought a house through your husband. He tells me you are considered the best decorator in town."

Her eyes arched in surprise. Pat had said that?

He spread his arms in charming supplication. "I have grave need of your services."

Liz took the plan from his hand. As she spread it out, he took the opportunity to study her. She wore an expensive beige gabardine suit with a short skirt, beige opaque stockings that gave her elegant legs a satiny glow, and beige pumps from St. Laurent with very high heels. Her blond hair was held away from her face by a tortoiseshell band. She was the quintessential blond Americano.

Leaning provocatively on one hip, she stared at the plan. He approached her softly, coming so close that he startled her when he spoke. "What do you think?"

"I can think of several things we might do. But first, I'd like to show you some houses I've done in the past so you can decide if you like my style."

"I can already tell you that." His voice had a slight smolder to it.

"Really?" Her own voice lowered. Well, help does come from the most unexpected sources, she thought. Brown eyes extended an invitation to dark ones. There was a flicker, then a flame of unspoken complicity.

"Come." She led him by the arm to a low-slung couch with soft down cushions. She gave him a portfolio of her work. As he turned the pages slowly, she leaned into him, pressing her heavy breasts into his arm to make a point.

When he finished, he closed the book carefully and put it on the slab of granite which served as a table and turned to her. "What is our next step?"

"I need to know much more about you. I'd like to be able to give you just what you want."

The entendres were weighty. Too weighty? Liz wondered. It was the kind of vampy dialogue that sent people into gales of laughter at movies of the thirties.

"Mrs. Mallory, I have every confidence in you. When would you like to start?"

It had worked. "Is immediately too soon?"

Her rendezvous with Joe Ferris that afternoon was forgotten. How easy this was going to be! An affair with the handsome Italian was just what the doctor ordered. She'd simply tell everyone that she was doing his new house. That in itself would score her brownie points. There would be so many opportunities to be together, she wouldn't have to invent them. It was just a question of time, and Liz had the feeling it wouldn't take too long. When she had leaned over to point out a particular design, she'd accidentally brushed his crotch with her hand and felt him instantly harden.

Gianni listened seriously, loving the dangerous game they were about to play. It was not an unusual one in his adopted social milieu: husbands, wives, and friends sleeping together or with each other. What really appealed to him was that on any given day he might spend the morning discussing a deal with Pat, and the afternoon in bed with the beautiful barracuda who was his wife. He could taste her already. Sexual need poured from her like sweat from a ditch digger. When she'd touched him so casually, he knew—had he given her opportunity—she would have immediately opened his fly and begun to explore him with her long, sensuous fingers. There was no hurry. He could afford to take his time.

"Do I need to sign anything?" he asked.

"Not just yet. Why don't you just begin telling me about yourself?" Suddenly warm, she took off her jacket and settled herself in a corner of the couch.

"I am a man with a great appetite for beauty . . . ," he began.

Sam drove slowly through the crowded streets of town, keeping an eye out for the throngs haphazardly crossing the street on their way to early supper or late cocktails. They looked like cardboard cutouts against the sharp, snowy white, an interesting subject for a painting.

The old streetlamps sent out bright pinpoints of light to blend with the carriage lights of the old Victorian houses. With the black-green of the mountains above the Christmas lights and decorations below, the town seemed like a giant's Christmas tree.

She drove past the Hotel Jerome and turned down Monarch, then into Hallam, and made a U-turn to park in front of her house. Her house! The first one she'd ever owned. She sat in the car and studied it. It was the only one on the block that lacked Christmas decorations. She'd been too busy painting to get around to it.

In the pale glimmer of the streetlight she could see it loom substantially, its pale gray paint luminous against the snow, the long front windows half-hidden by the tangled bare branches of shrubbery.

Suddenly chilled, she realized she'd been sitting in the car with the engine turned off. Aspen days could be warm and pleasant in the winter, but at night the thermometer hovered near zero, and, despite the dry air, it was amazing how quickly the cold penetrated to fingers and toes.

She started the car again and parked in the driveway. Alighting, she paused at the marble stoop to fumble for her key, waiting for that tremble of excitement to overtake her. The house had come to represent something far more than walls and floors and ownership. It was her coming-of-age, her assuming of responsibility, her intention of setting down roots. No matter what changed in her life, the house would be an anchor.

She stepped into the hall and searched for the light switch.

The ceiling fixture was one of the old Tiffany Favrille glass ones, tulip shaped and pink. It would come down and be replaced by something more contemporary. The beautiful, gleaming parquet floors had already been refinished, but the walls were still badly stained. Once they might have been a warm cream, but now they were the color of tobacco juice. There were scuff marks along the baseboards as though a willful child had kicked them.

She walked through the house, turning on lights as she went. The living room was only partially furnished and would remain so until the painters left. The formal dining room, newly papered in a dramatic black oriental paper, the wood baseboards, and ceiling frieze painted a shiny black were completed. Her mother's Spanish refectory table had been sanded and stained to a pale fruitwood tone. There were a pair of Spanish benches with arms on each side and two big armchairs upholstered in sueded buffalo at head and foot. Above the table hung a many-antlered horn chandelier with taper lights.

The library, its denuded shelves awaiting the books which were still in their boxes on the floor, seemed a cold and empty place, so she passed it without a second glance and returned to the entryway. She switched on the upstairs hall light and walked up to her bedroom. This room faced away from the street. Here she had placed the brass bed she had slept in as a girl. It was piled high with pillows in pretty, flounced shams. A rare and beautiful blue-and-white lovebird quilt was folded at the foot.

A chaise which sat near the garden window had been covered in an antique flowered quilt. Deeply piled carpets of pale blue covered the random oak boards of the floor.

The master bath, her favorite room upstairs, contained the best of both worlds. The footed Victorian tub sat along one wall, completely fitted with old brass faucets and hardware. On the other wall, wrapped in a glass bubble, was a modern shower, its walls made of river rock and tile. A huge Victorian sink on a gainly Corinthian pedestal occupied the other wall. The commode was enclosed in its own closet to conceal it from the rest of the room.

In her studio, skylights faced north, giving her a view of the mountain, while south-facing windows looked to Red Mountain. Snow had given them the illusion of closeness. The light at this hour was impressionistic, a palette of pastel colors, misting, changing, merging, finally disappearing into that deep purple that always seemed lit from within.

The snow had blunted all the edges, turning trees into whipped cream and sharp gates into ruffles of white. Now snow was falling again, and the bright colors of the Victorians seemed like pale ghosts in the afterglow. She loved the snow. It made magic of reality. Buildings shifted like insubstantial images. People were no more than vague, moving shadows. Snow made the mountains disappear and left you alone in a swirl of white. Alone, but not afraid. Happy to be in your own silent house, warmed by the crackling fire in the fireplace and the drink in your hand. In New York, snow had meant isolation. In Aspen it was a friend.

She went to the bathroom, drew the water for a tub, and slowly undressed, kicking the worn clothes into a corner to be gathered later and thrown into the hamper. She braided her long hair and pinned it up and out of the way.

Testing the water, she added some more cool water and poured a handful of pale blue hyacinth crystals into the bath.

Gingerly she stepped into the tub and settled herself against the foam pillow with a long, satisfied "ahh" as the soothing water reached up to enfold her.

Suddenly she remembered Joe Ferris emerging from the pool at the spa. She had been walking by on her way to a late-afternoon aerobics class. He had not seen her. She'd stopped to watch him, struck once again by the sleek beauty of his body. He bore no more resemblance to the Greek ideal than she. He was better: leaner, trimmer, smoother. What would Michelangelo have done with that one, she wondered?

Joe Ferris emerged from the Olympic pool of the Silver Leaf Spa and shook the water from his sleek head. He slipped into the white terry robe which lay on a chaise nearby and summoned a waiter with a snap of his fingers.

"Straight tequila, Mr. Ferris?"

Joe nodded. It would take him years, if not forever, to get used to hearing himself referred to as Mr. Ferris. Funny thing, that wasn't his name at all. His name was José Fernando. But the name had been changed to Ferris when his father died a few months before his birth.

His grandmother, who lived with them in the tumbledown ranch up toward Independence Pass, had understood the reasons but could not find it in her heart to forgive such cowardice on the part of her son.

Besides, they would always look like what they were no matter how many times the name was changed. The grandfather was silent.

But as he grew up, the old man regaled Joe with the stories of his family. "Never forget, my son, you have nothing to feel shame for. You come from a family of Spanish grandees dating back to the days of Cortez. Gold was ours, and riches, too."

Don Miguel, Joe's great-great-grandfather, had left his family's hacienda in Mexico and the fine ranch to seek his fortune, first in the California goldfields, then in the silver mines of Colorado. Here he had fallen in love and married Little Silver Deer. He had run out of money and, like so many others, sold his claims to Gerald MacNeal for a grubstake.

It was Little Silver Deer and her Indian land which had saved his life, but he had lost that, too, when the gringos began driving the Indians from the land and onto reservations. Gerald MacNeal, taking pity on Don Miguel's plight and his half-breed children, had sold him a small homestead and hired him to work on his vast ranch for a pittance. A sullen hatred had been born at that moment, and hatred for the MacNeals had simmered in its own passion for all those years and been handed full strength to the youngster. Joe had grown up with it. It was as much a part of his emotional baggage as his mixed blood. The town's fear and loathing of the half-breed family had risen and declined with the times. They were hard workers; intelligent and proud. The Fernandos had always managed to survive, but Joe's dream was to restore them to a position as respected members of society.

For a while they'd been forgotten. The town had other things on its mind. In the era of McCarthy, many Hollywood people who vacationed in Aspen lived under a cloud of suspicion. Then came the sixties with flower children, drop-outs, marijuana, LSD, civil-rights disturbances, and the famous assassinations that rocked the world. By then Aspen had gone from one extreme to the other. As Peggy Clifford had written: "Once it was Camelot and Dodge City. Now it was neither: It was Palm Beach in the Rockies."

As Joe Ferris grew up, he was only peripherally aware of life outside the valley, living as he did in relative peace and harmony with horses, dogs, and nature. But Sophie Mallory had changed all that. Catching him with her daughter, she had turned an innocent outing into something dark and ugly.

Shortly afterward his mother said they were leaving the valley. He remembered the night as if it were yesterday. His mother had packed their clothes, stowing them in the battered Ford pickup, and then they had set out wordlessly for California. As they drove, stars bloomed in the black desert sky like wildflowers on a spring meadow. The sharp, biting smell of piñon filled the air. A soft breeze came in the window and tossed his hair about with a loving hand. He hated leaving the mountains and all the secret Ute places his grandfather had showed him. Hated leaving the imperious little girl with her turquoise eyes and Indian straight hair whose curiosity about the Indians far outreached his ability to teach her.

East Los Angeles had been dirty, noisy, and dangerous. Conchito, his mother, was a black-shrouded figure who spent most of her time praying and the rest of it murmuring dark imprecations against the gringo.

Early on, Joe had learned to use his fists. Sickened by his poverty, he had run with a tough Chicano gang because he was dying of loneliness and the need for companions. And eventually his inherent entrepreneurial spirit surfaced. He wanted money. He needed money. If his dream was to return to Aspen as a respected citizen, he would obviously have to do illegal things to realize it. To a kid with his background, that meant drugs.

Drugs brought him to the attention of Angel Espinosa, one of Santos's enforcers. Santos was one of the biggest drug suppliers in the Western hemisphere. And it was Santos's drugs which put Joe through Stanford University. Stanford gained him his first job, but it was dealing in the dangerous, complex drug world that taught Joe how to survive, how to manage difficult men, and how to guard his tongue. The rest had been easy.

Finally Joe was ready to return to Aspen. After his stints at Tahoe and Heavenly Valley, his credentials were impeccable enough for Richard Farwell to hire him as assistant to the manager of Silver Mountain Corp.

His drug dealing continued but only on a very high level. He had set high standards for himself: He refused to sell to kids, and he refused to deal in anything stronger than coke. Joe dealt only with high society and he worked in total anonymity. He had a network of dealers. Although there was a certain amount of conjecture, no one knew for certain that he was the supplier. When the harsh light of the press turned on the notorious drug scene in Aspen and the "accidental" deaths increased, Joe decided he had paid his debt to Santos, and it was time to put a lid on the entire operation. With the pressure on, Santos had allowed Joe to stop.

Joe himself had never been a user; it was his own peculiar morality. Now he was relieved of a burden and a fear that had lived within him since he was eighteen years old. The sudden freedom was intoxicating. And in the last few years he had come closer to realizing his dream of becoming an ordinary—albeit wealthy and powerful—citizen. He had proved his mettle on several occasions. Once just before the beginning of the season, the pro shop had burned to the ground. Joe had suspected another dealer in town of deliberately setting the fire, but the Pitkin County sheriff had called it an electrical fire. By working all night, Joe had devised a makeshift shop, stocked it with borrowed rental equipment so it was ready to go on opening day, and offered a complimentary buffet of hot coffee and delicious croissants and pastry from Pour La France for those who might be inconvenienced by the wait. Richard Farwell had been impressed.

He'd also been impressed when Joe had ordered tons of snow trucked in from the woods to prepare a slalom course for a big professional race after an early thaw had turned the mountain to slop.

Even being a half-breed no longer had the stigma it once had; in fact, lately it was proving to be a distinct advantage. Women found him irresistible. Yes, Joe Ferris at thirty-five was ready to sit back and enjoy life. Then Samantha Mallory had wrecked his peace by returning to Aspen.

Though he was sure he had not revealed it, he had been shaken the day she materialized in front of him at the spa. Eighteen years had melted away. All was forgotten, even his long-standing, smoldering feelings about the Mallory family. He smiled in amusement when he remembered her stamping her foot in anger at his deliberate rudeness, at her hastily extended and just as hastily withdrawn invitation to her homecoming party. Why had he gone after all? And why had he been so shocked at his reaction to her when they danced? For a moment he could feel that tight muscular body against him. It had stirred him far more than the lush curves of Liz Mallory.

He took a deep drink of the tequila and stared with unseeing eyes at a girl with no more than three inches of fabric covering her breasts and pubes.

Then a male voice interrupted his thoughts. "Excuse me, you are Joe Ferris, are you not?"

The man in the white spa robe looked vaguely familiar. "I am. Who are you?"

The man smoothed his dark, wet hair back with the palms of his hands and introduced himself. "I have a small problem which I think you might be able to help me with," said Gianfranco di Lucca.

"What makes you think I can help?"

Gianni snapped his fingers for a waiter. He had decided he didn't like Joe Ferris. Too cool. Too arrogant. He would never be dependable. Except, of course, Gianni had the magic persuader on his side. "Campari and soda," he ordered. Then leisurely turning to Joe, he said, "Santos says so."

Gianni was pleased to see Joe visibly pale at the utterance of the name.

"Santos?"

"He speaks very highly of you. That is, he spoke very highly of you."

"I'm out of the drug business," said Joe tightly.

"Santos is much aware of that. He understands your reasons. Pity. You were one of his best dealers, I understand."

Joe's eyes turned bleak, his hands clenched into fists.

"What he can't understand is why you refuse to help some of the younger . . . uh . . . trainees. Where is your sense of loyalty?"

Joe ignored the question. "What exactly do you want?"

Gianni sipped his drink and made a face. "I don't know why I insist on drinking this. I dislike it intensely. Uh, you were saying? Ah, yes, what do I want? Tell me, Joe . . . I may call you Joe?"

Joe nodded tersely. "Get to it," he said softly from behind tight lips.

"Tell me something. Could you see yourself one day in charge of the entire Silver Mountain Corporation?"

Joe laughed without mirth. "I'd say that was as likely as your being elected president of the United States."

Gianni tsked. "I heard you were a man of many resources. Unfortunate, isn't it, that an act of birth—even in this great democratic country—confers only secondary status?"

"What are you driving at?"

"Joe, I understand your problem. In fact, I share it. Oh, in my case, in my country, it hardly matters. There are ways to overcome such things. But here in this small town there is no hiding, is there? Everyone knows who you are. And changing one's name does not alter the fact of who your family is. Of course, in my case, no one stole my wealth. You must despise the Mallorys."

"What makes you say that?"

Gianni smiled. Would Joe Ferris be amused to know that Gianni was now involved with his former companion, Liz Mallory? And that Liz loved talking after sex? That she was a bottomless source of amusing stories?

"I know, too, that Richard Farwell only tolerates you because you're good at your job and he needs you."

"You seem to know a great deal." Joe's voice was deadly calm, a trick he'd learned to disguise dangerous anger. He stood up.

Gianni watched him struggle to control himself. "Sit down, please, I haven't finished talking."

"You have, as far as I'm concerned."

"Really, Ferris, you are being quite tiresome. I don't understand why our Colombian friend is so taken with you."

Joe sat on the edge of his seat, poised to spring.

"That's better." Gianni smiled, ignoring the belligerent pose. "Now, what if I told you I have a plan that—if you cooperate—can get us what we both want."

"And what's that?"

"The collapse of Richard Farwell and his empire."

Joe stared at the dapper man opposite him. "What did Richard Farwell ever do to you?"

Gianni leaned forward, sincerity oozing from him like honey from a hive. "I assure you, nothing at all. In fact, I rather like the man. He displays a ruthlessness I find most appealing. Oh no, I have nothing personal

against Richard Farwell. But Señor Santos is very
interested in going into the resort business."

"Why Aspen?"

"Why not? It has charm, reputation, cachet. It is
unique, beautiful, and a great deal of cash flows in and
out. Am I making myself clear?"

"He wants a place to launder money?"

Gianni turned over his palms like a teacher with a
student who has just made a successful breakthrough.

"And what have the Mallorys to do with it?"

"Originally, nothing. But they have much power
here, and under the circumstances and to ensure your
cooperation, I guarantee that whatever happens to
Farwell will rub off on them. Unfortunately, I don't
think we can force the Mallorys out of Aspen, but we
could cause them a great deal of embarrassment. A
woman like Sophie Mallory would not care for that."

"No, she wouldn't. Exactly what do you have in
mind, and how do I fit in?"

"I see that Santos is a shrewd judge of character.
Here is my idea. You must admit it is clever, legal, and
foolproof."

CHAPTER TEN

AFTER CHRISTMAS AN UNEASY PEACE SETTLED UPON THE Mallory clan. Pat spent more time on the mountain than in his office. He continued in his efforts to find an acceptable design for the Ute City project, quietly bemoaning the quantities of money he was pouring into it without any guarantee of a return.

At the same time, several foreclosures that he was interested in mysteriously slipped from his hands as a nameless corporation outbid him. And every time he called Hank Campbell to make another offer, the old man hung up on him as soon as he recognized his voice. Anxious to do something and souring on the entire Campbell property, he seriously considered reopening negotiations for the Little Annie Basin in back of Aspen Mountain. Little Annie, where he and Richard had skied together recently, was presently reachable only by snowcat. It was basically intermediate terrain, which would make it an attractive addition to the Aspen complex with its plethora of expert

191

runs. It also was blessed with deep, plentiful snow. If the land and permits could be acquired, it could be connected to Aspen Mountain by a complex and expensive network of lifts. Yet when he mentioned this project to Richard, the older man threw up his hands in desperation.

"What is this obsession to build and change?" he asked.

"Richard, we've discussed these things a million times. Why are you suddenly surprised?"

"We're in no position to tackle anything that major. The stockholders are screaming as it is." Ten years ago, in order to raise a great deal of money, Richard, against his better judgment, had offered a small percentage of shares for sale.

"Who cares? They aren't in control of the corporation's decisions, you are. Jesus, Richard, you're getting as bad as my mother! At least I know what her problem is."

"My problem is your timing. It's bad." Richard took his down coat from the closet and, declaring their meeting over, left the office.

One night as Pat and Gianni sat in the Jerome bar having a drink, Pat had a sudden flash of genius.

"I don't know why I never thought of this before." Pat leaned forward, shielding his mouth. The bar was jammed with skiers, mostly male. Their damp parkas piled on chairs near the fireplace had given the room a humid tropical atmosphere.

There was the usual after-ski conversation, tales of terrible accidents cleverly avoided, falls that would have destroyed an ordinary person, the killer moguls on the ridge, the horrendous conditions on Walsh's, the gorgeous girls at Bonnie's. Raucous laughter mixed with the sound of bottles being opened and telephones ringing. Waitresses apologized as they tried to get through the pack of bodies. The hubbub was a perfect curtain to conceal serious conversation.

"And what is that, my friend?" Gianni had just spent the afternoon with Liz Mallory. The day after their first meeting they had wasted little time in formalities and gone straight to bed. Liz had been like a starving animal. In all his life he had never been so devoured by a woman. For a moment he was afraid she would mark him for life. She was intense, passionate, direct, expert, but under the excitement was such anger, he had to wonder what put it there. Had Pat ever experienced his wife quite the way he, Gianni, had? Liz Mallory used sex like other women used the confessional or a psychiatrist.

"I was thinking of the way Bill Janss got Snowmass."

"And who is this Janss?"

"He was an ex-Olympic skier from California. He and his brother headed a land and cattle combine that their grandfather founded. Christ, they owned the whole Coachella Valley feed lot and developed half of L.A."

"In other words, they were wealthy."

"They were diabolically clever." Pat popped a couple of peanuts in his mouth and munched. "One day they were up on the Sundeck for lunch. The place was jammed. Bill said it was time to develop a new ski area. A friend of his, a ski instructor who came from big money, but never seemed to have any visible signs of it other than a bunch of planes and cars, went out looking on the Front Range but didn't find anything promising. Then one day he was working on his ranch in Woody Creek. Kept staring at this big mountain looming up over Brush Creek. So he got in his plane and flew over it, studied a U.S. Geological Survey map and compared it in size with Aspen and the Highlands. He went up on skis a couple of times and looked it over."

"This is what became Snowmass?"

"Right."

"I don't see the connection."

"If they wanted the property to be profitable they had to make sure that Janss could get his hands on *all* the land."

"You are drawing an analogy with the Campbell property, aren't you?"

"That I am. Janss had to keep quiet about his plans or the land would skyrocket in price. This is where you come in."

"I am afraid I don't see the connection."

"He got a broker to buy the key ranch at the base of the mountain. Even went to the trouble of bringing in cattle from the California feed lot so no one would suspect what they were up to. Those old ranchers were delighted to sell out to him. Got decent prices, too. But not anywhere what they would have got if they thought he was going to develop the properties into a ski resort."

"I'm beginning to understand. . . ."

"It's too late for me. Hank knows me, my voice, and what I want to do. And he's such a stubborn cuss, he might sell to you just to spite me. I tell you, Gianni, this is inspired. He really doesn't know you. Just saw you that one time. I bet he doesn't even remember you. But if he does, so what? You could buy the property from him. Tell him you've always wanted to live on a ranch. I don't know what you tell him. Anything that makes sense and convinces him to sell. What do you say?"

Gianni rubbed his chin thoughtfully. "Maybe. Maybe it could work. I must give it some thought."

"You do that. The more I think of it, the better I like it. Angie?" he called. "A couple of Coronas here." Pat leaned back in the club chair, a satisfied smile on his face. "By the way, I'm going up to the Canadian Rockies for some heli-skiing. Interested?"

"How long do you intend to be gone?"

"Maybe a week?"

Gianni looked contrite. "I'm afraid not. I have to be

in San Diego on Tuesday. Besides, I am not in the . . . how do you say . . . same ballpark as you on the skis."

"You mean 'league' . . . you're not in the same league. But Sam tells me you ski very well."

"Well enough. I am with skiing as I am with everything: a dilettante." With Pat away, Gianni could spend an interrupted week with the hungry Liz. He sighed at the thought.

"You okay? Not sick or anything?"

"Oh, no. Just fatigued. For such a relaxing town, there are too many things to do."

"So I hear. Sam tells me you're the wet dream of every unattached woman in Aspen."

"And a few attached as well," Gianni joked.

"We're famous for those," Pat said wryly, thinking of his own beautiful wife and the whispered comments that seemed to accompany her wherever she went. Pat didn't really care what she did anymore, but he didn't like his friends' knowing about it. If they were living in a large city, it would be easy to ignore. But in Aspen, where everyone knew everyone else's business . . . The last thing Pat wanted was to be laughed at. If he ever heard the name of his wife's current lover mentioned in the same breath with her, he'd kill the bastard.

Sam Mallory squeezed ochre directly onto her brush and placed squiggles of dense pigment on top of the white strokes in the lower quadrant of her canvas. Then she stood back to look. The light was fading rapidly. Wiping her paint-stained hand on her jeans, she decided to quit and give the canvas a better look tomorrow when she had the light.

She stretched up luxuriously, wiggling the kinks from her neck and shoulders. She had a terrible posture when she painted, she knew. She barely sat on a too-tall stool, one foot hooked into the bottom rung, her upper body hunched over the canvas, her neck slumping into her shoulders. No wonder she was a mass of kinks when she finished at the end of the day.

Three canvases sat on the floor drying. Two more were on easels. That was five altogether. She was still shocked that she had actually dared to be a painter with her slim talent. Was she any good? Would anyone else like them?

She had refused to show them to her mother. Sophie, with her schooled eye, would nevertheless be disinclined to tell her the truth out of love and loyalty. Pat, too, had a good eye, but not, she knew, a critical one toward his sister. Only Louis Breton could tell her the truth.

Much against Louis's advice, she had insisted on doing these first paintings without benefit of his input. Actually, she was embarrassed to have him see her work, afraid that it would not meet his high standards. As the town's cultural arbiter, Louis's approval was very important to her.

Rather than waste the morning light, Sam had switched her exercise schedule at the spa and, despite the crowds, went after work. After hours of being hunched over canvases, an aerobics class, fifteen minutes with the free weights, and fifty laps in the pool made her feel wonderful again. Without deluding herself, she admitted that she had changed her hours because Joe Ferris apparently had, too.

She had not seen him for several weeks. In a town as small as Aspen, it was almost unheard of not to run into people you knew, if not on the street, at least at the usual hangouts. Either he wasn't being invited to the same parties or he was deliberately avoiding her.

On one dazzling day after a particularly big snowfall, she let Alex seduce her into joining him for an early morning of powder skiing. In the strong winter sunlight, Alex looked tired and gray under the tan that stopped at the top of his turtleneck. His eyes held a strange glitter, and his normally soft, slow speech had given way to a rapid-fire delivery of words and snatches of sentences. He talked as if he were constantly out of breath.

But her concern evaporated when they were on the slopes. He was still the most graceful skier on the mountain. On the Ridge of Bell, he seemed to float, his ankles switching direction effortlessly on the chopped-off, steeply banked moguls as if he were on springs. There were many good skiers on the trail that morning, thumping and bumping down the mountain, grunting and groaning with effort. Their faces were wet with sweat or from the many falls they had taken in the soft fluff.

But Alex skied softly and silently, his airborne flights growing longer and longer. No matter how quickly she followed him, he was always ahead and waiting for her patiently at Grand Junction where Copper, the Ridge, and Spar Gulch met.

On the chair lift she said casually, "I never see Joe Ferris around. Is he skiing these days?"

Alex shrugged. "Beats me. He's pretty busy now that the season is off and running. I understand there's been some problem with the quad on Gentlemen's."

"Still?" Sam knew that problems with the new lifts continued to plague the Corporation. Sophie had told her about the terrible accident on the newly rebuilt Bell Mountain lift where a patrolman had been tossed from the chair when it crashed against a tower in a high wind.

"Some kind of mechanical failure. They have to run it so slowly people don't want to ski over there."

"It's a shame. It has some good skiing."

He nodded absently. As if stillness was a curse, he continued to clack his skis together in a ceaseless rhythm which set her teeth on edge. Then he seemed to remember that she was sitting next to him and turned to ask, "So how's the great artist?"

She made a little face. "I get the feeling I should be painting Hallmark greeting cards. You know, the corny ones, with plump little girls in pinafores and puppies? Anyway, I'm enjoying it," which was only partially true, "and since I go to the spa after work, I'm out of range of the local gossip."

"What's the matter? Did Rosie forget how to use the phone?"

"You're so bad. Why do you play such naughty tricks on her all the time?"

"She loves it." For a moment Alex was his old cheerful self again. His skin glowed from the crisp air and thrill of speed.

Sam decided it was time to take the bull by the horns. "I don't understand you, Breton. You're the best, most natural athlete I know. You're the living example of what Aspen's all about, you take such good care of your body . . . Tell me, why in God's name are you using?"

The cheerful countenance disappeared. It was replaced with the sulky little-boy's face she knew well, the one that said: fuck off, mind your own business. He ducked his head. "Get off my case, Mallory."

"Alex . . ."

"I mean it, Sam." He leaned forward in the lift, refusing to meet her eyes, staring down at the antlike figures on Copper Bowl. "What could you possibly know about it? You're a Mallory, you were the apple of your daddy's eye. Try being Louis Breton's son. See if you can pull that off without being either drunk, stoned, or dead."

"Oh, Alex, that's no excuse for destroying yourself."

"Don't 'oh, Alex' me. I'm telling you, Sam, he's a monster. Everyone thinks he's so suave, so erudite, so charming. Ask my mother or my dead brother." He turned to her, eyes dark with some unfathomable memory. "Sam, I know he's interested in you. . . ."

"My painting . . . ," she corrected.

"Yeah, whatever. Please, Sam, be careful of him.

He's clever and tricky. Before you know it . . . " He trailed off.

"Before I know what?"

But he refused to continue. They skied one more run together, then he loped off, saying lamely, "Gotta get back to the shop."

Alex had neatly sidestepped two subjects: his drug habit and the warning about his father.

She decided to continue skiing rather than go back to her studio. She should not have brought up the subject with Alex. The regret lasted about the same amount of time it took her to cruise Copper from top to bottom.

At Bonnie's she found the usual crew lunching outside in the sunshine on bowls of Bonnie's famous chicken chowder and hunks of homemade French bread. Bill Pugh, who refused to worry about his weight or his cholesterol, was laying waste to a flaky apple strudel slathered with real whipped cream.

Sam spent the rest of the day trying to keep up with them. After an afternoon of skiing only the superexpert trails, she felt as though her body had been used for a punching bag. New York had not prepared her for skiing with the tireless crew of Pugh, Sukert, and Campbell.

Too tired to walk home, she hailed a cruising cab and settled back with a groan. The cab driver exchanged pleasantries, told her his name and that he'd been a stockbroker until he came out west seventeen years ago to live. He had a small TV set, a two-way radio, a small collection of books, and an electronic backgammon set neatly arranged on the front seat. Sam thought he was the first really happy person she'd met in a long time.

Once home, she pulled off her ski clothes and replaced them with her leotard and a pair of sweats. She slipped her feet into fur-lined boots and grabbed her curly lamb jacket.

She was really too tired to take a class, but the thought of a swim in the warm outdoor pool followed by the hot tub was inviting.

The clear dome which covered the pool had been rolled back. The idea of an outdoor pool in the winter had always seemed an aberration to her, but since they had become so popular in Sun Valley years ago, most western ski resorts had installed them. Still there was something bizarre about swimming in a hot steaming pool when the temperature above you was a chilly twenty degrees or less.

Steam rose in such dense clouds it was almost impossible to see who was in the pool let alone the lane in which you swam. It was inevitable that she should bump into another body.

"Oh, I'm so sorry. I didn't see you," she apologized the moment her descending arm came down heavily on a hard body.

"No damage," said a familiar voice.

She peered through the mist.

"Hello, Sam. So nice to run into you. Or rather, it's so nice being run into. It's Joe."

"Joe?" She'd been thinking about him so much lately, it was embarrassing to find him suddenly materialize in front of her. She laughed nervously. "I was just talking about you. To Alex. We went skiing today. I happened to mention your name and that I hadn't seen you around town for a while." Please, say something. Don't just let me ramble on like some kind of an idiot.

"It's been pretty busy around here. We had a very big December. The equipment took a bit of a beating. And there've been a few problems. There always are," he said meaningfully.

"I was going to swim a few laps and then sit in the hot tub for a while," she said inanely.

"Would you like company?"

"If you'd like . . . " She shrugged.

"No," he insisted. "If you like."

"I'd like." Her voice was soft. She shivered.

He was quick to notice. "Are you cold?" Without waiting for her to answer, he put his hands on her shoulder and pushed her gently down into the comforting warm water. As they bobbed like two corks, her legs tangled with his momentarily, forcing him to shift his hands from her shoulders to her waist. The effect was electric. Blue eyes stared into black ones for a long moment. Bodies turned into dangerous live wires. He expected to see a path of blazing electricity go surging down the lane of the pool, ready to incinerate anyone it came in contact with.

Gently, unwillingly, she pried his hands away and climbed out of the pool. She ran the length of the pool and lowered herself into the hot tub.

For an instant he saw the young girl that she had once been, all long coltish legs and flying wings of hair. In the high-cut skin-toned leotard, she appeared almost nude. He could see the tight buds of her nipples as her small round breasts pushed against the fabric, see the rounded mound at the vee of her legs and felt an answering response in himself.

The desire that gripped him surprised him with its intensity. He fought for control, not daring to leave the pool until he won it. When he approached her he could feel her eyes stroking him like a caress.

She stared openly at his dark skin against the brief dark bikini that left nothing about him to the imagination. His body reminded her of the diver, Greg Louganis. It was almost perfect. Her head filled with romantic nonsense and unspoken yearnings, and as they sat in the hot tub she behaved like a silly teenager.

But it had been the beginning.

Now they met, as though by chance, almost every afternoon to swim. Occasionally, they would go off somewhere and have a quiet supper. After the first awkward stabs at conversation, it had become easier. Their shared early years gave them the foundation, and the old comradeship brought them closer in many ways, building trust and affection. But no matter how close they seemed, some subjects remained taboo. She never told him about Greg Francis, and he never discussed his years in Los Angeles.

Their friendship remained pure and innocent, as though she were still ten and he seventeen. Although they both yearned for something more, what it was remained unspoken as if they both knew the wrong step would change everything. Fighting the burgeoning feelings, they set up invisible barriers which they silently agreed not to trespass.

But all that changed the night she fell ill.

She had been feeling achy all day. Louis stopped by to take her to lunch, but she said no, that she had things to attend to. He disappeared and arrived a half hour later with a picnic basket.

As she nibbled at the rich paté, he laid slices of an exquisitely pink salmon across triangles of dark pumpernickel. He squeezed a bit of lemon on and popped it in his mouth. "People," he intoned, "make a dreadful mistake with salmon—or caviar, for that matter. Somehow they feel it necessary to gussy it up with chopped onion, or bits of egg and dill or some sickening sweet sauce. People like that should have their tongues cut out."

She made a gagging sound. He looked at her sharply. "My dear, are you feeling ill?"

"I don't know if it's your graphic description or something else." She sighed.

"I'll make you some good strong tea."

"No, really. I think I'll just lie down for a while."

"I hope you're not coming down with flu. There's a particularly nasty one running around lately. The House was only half full last night."

She sighed deeply. He laid a cool hand to her forehead. "You're warm. I hate to leave you like this." His fine aristocratic face wore a worried frown.

"Really, I'm sure I'll be fine after I have some aspirin and a rest. If not, I'll call Mother and she'll come and fetch me."

She almost had to push him out the door. And it was true. The moment she closed the door on him, she did feel better. Wrinkling her nose at the remains of lunch, she picked up the dish of paté to throw it away. At the liverish smell, she felt her stomach heave and dropped it in the sink where it smashed into pieces. The sight was almost as unbearable as the smell.

She left the mess and ran to her room. Lying down on the chaise, she pulled a quilt over her and went instantly to sleep. When she awoke several hours later, she was disoriented and thirsty. She got up gingerly and touched her head. It seemed cool.

The room was clothed in gray shadows as the sun dipped below the mountain. She turned on a light, and the reassuring glow sent the shadows chasing.

Should she go to the spa? By tacit understanding, neither she nor Joe ever called each other. They continued to pretend that they met by accident at the Silver Leaf Spa and like two old friends would go off for a drink or a bite to eat before going their separate ways. She looked forward to these meetings, considering them in the nature of a reward for her diligence and attention to work.

She couldn't bear to miss a single one.

She brushed her teeth and quickly braided her hair. When she pulled off her jeans and work shirt, she shivered, then felt hot. She had almost convinced herself not to go, when she felt suddenly better. Before anything could change her mind, she pulled on a pale blue, backless leotard and matching sweats.

Once outside the crisp, cold air revived her, and she set off in the direction of the Inn, glad that she had not given in to her momentary weakness.

Joe was already in the pool, swimming lazy laps. When she knelt at the edge, he turned onto his back and looked up at her with a smile. "Hello, Pocahontas," he said softly, yanking her braid. "I was afraid you weren't coming."

She pulled the long hank of hair from his hand and hit him softly. "I almost didn't."

"Are you coming in or do you want to be dragged in?"

She stepped away from his threatening hand but he captured her ankle, releasing it unwillingly when she gently kicked out at him. His hand was like a caress.

"I'm coming in. Just don't rush me."

She walked to the other side and stepped gingerly into the water. Joe knew there was something wrong immediately. Usually she dove into the pool at the deep end. In a few long strokes he was by her side. She looked pale.

He shook his head. "I don't like the way you look."

"I'm not crazy about the way I feel." Her eyes were like a protesting child's.

"Let's get out of here. Hurry up, go get dressed. I'm taking you home."

She offered no resistance, suddenly happy to put herself in his capable hands.

He was dressed and waiting by the time she came out. "Did you drive?" he asked.

"No."

"Good, I have my car."

In a few minutes, he was half-carrying her up the walk of her house and inside.

"Bedroom upstairs?"

She nodded.

When she seemed to stumble at the step, he picked her up in his arms and carried her up the stairs and into the room she pointed to. She turned on the light from her perch in his arms, and he took her to her bed and deposited her gently upon it.

No sooner had she begun to relax than she felt her stomach heave and rumble. She dashed across the room and into the bathroom. Kneeling, she vomited into the bowl. Waves of nausea rolled over her. She felt weak and dizzy and then she felt cool hands on her forehead and neck and a soothing voice telling her everything would be all right.

When her stomach grew calm, he helped her sit down. She brushed her teeth and he washed her face and hands, then again picked her up and took her to her bed.

"Nightgown?"

She gestured to a drawer. He opened it and plucked out a long-sleeved challis gown trimmed in pale blue ribbons. The garment looked infinitely fragile in his long brown fingers.

She did not protest when he pulled her shoes off. She closed her eyes when he removed the sweat pants and shirt. He paused a moment to look at her nude and vulnerable under his eyes. She was even more beautiful than he thought.

Cursing himself for a fool, he quickly pulled the gown over her head, lifting her to settle it down over her ankles. She opened her eyes and smiled weakly. "Sorry," she mumbled.

He pulled down the covers on the opposite side, and she rolled over to it gratefully. "Mmm." She smiled as she felt the cool sheets enfold her.

He touched her forehead with his hands. She felt cool. Maybe it was a touch of food poisoning or one of those quick intense stomach viruses. He was about to pull his hand away when she caught it. "Don't go yet. Stay with me for a while. Tell me the story of the beautiful Indian maiden and the elegant Spaniard."

He smiled. She remembered! Seventeen years ago he had turned the meeting of his great-great-grandparents into a story and told it to her one day after a riding lesson. Her blue eyes had grown as large as moons. He sat down on the bed and drew her into the circle of his arms where she snuggled happily. He was filled with irony as the two sides of his nature warred for supremacy. She was a MacNeal-Mallory and his family had hated the MacNeals and Mallorys for generations. But he didn't hate Sam. She was warm and sweet and generous. She had never looked at him as anything but her special friend. She was different. He didn't hate her . . . he . . . what were his feelings?

He felt her body grow heavy with sleep. Reassured by her deep breathing, he settled her into the pillows and drew the covers up to her chin. She murmured a complaint and stirred restlessly. He felt her head. She was warm again. He went to the bathroom and drenched a washcloth in cool water to put on her forehead. If he were home he would have made her one of the old elixirs handed down by the Indian side of his family to break fevers.

As she slept, his eyes never left her face. Thoughts, elusive as mist, ran through his mind. Finally assured that she was resting peacefully, he got up and prepared to leave. He looked down at her sleeping body, saw the tiny smile on her face, the fan of thick lashes under the heavy, smudged brows, and knew he would worry about her all night. So he took off his jacket again and lay down beside her, determined to be long gone by the time she awakened the next morning.

Sometime in the night he stripped down to his shorts and undershirt and got under the covers. Just before his eyes closed in sleep, he felt her roll toward him. Her body was like a warm furnace in the chill of the room. He lay beside her stiffly, afraid his breath would wake her, but the urge was too irresistible. He pulled her into his arms.

In the gray penumbra of predawn, Sam fought against wakefulness. But there was something different in the room. Convinced she was still in a dream state, she lay on her back staring at the ceiling. Then she heard the soft breathing next to her and tried to remember the night before. She turned her head and saw Joe Ferris staring at her. Somehow she wasn't surprised.

"You were sick last night. I was afraid to leave you."

"Oh," she said as if his presence beside her made all the sense in the world.

"How are you feeling?" He got up and leaned on an elbow. His tanned shoulders gleamed in the pale light.

"Much better. Joe?" She reached out her hand and touched his face.

He caught her fingers in his and held them. She turned toward him, then fell back heavily, her black hair tangled on the pillow.

He plucked a strand and played with it.

"You undressed me and put me to bed," she said matter-of-factly.

"You don't remember? You were awake, but I guess you were feeling feverish."

"You took care of me." Somehow those words gave her satisfaction, and she nestled deep into her pillows.

"Let me get you some breakfast." He started to get up, but she turned to him and stayed him with her hand.

"No, not yet. I'm not hungry."

It was a different kind of hunger she was experiencing. All she knew was that by some strange accident of fate, he was in her bed and they were alone. All the daydreams and night dreams she'd had since she was ten years old had included a shadowy figure on horseback who galloped endlessly toward her without ever arriving. Now she recognized him; the dark, muscular arms; the chest with its finely articulated muscles; the dark, straight hair and mocking eyes.

"It's you!" she said in a kind of wonder. "It's always been you."

Her words were both thrilling and frightening. He should get up and go, but those strange blue eyes held him pinned. He murmured some nonsense about fever playing strange tricks on the imagination.

But she wasn't listening, she was staring at him, seeing him as is for the first time. She reached out her arms and circled his neck. Drawing him close to her, she whispered, "I want to see you and touch you and taste you."

He was trembling violently as he spoke. "You don't know what you're saying."

For an answer she drew the sheet away from him. His body was not a surprise to her, she had seen him with less on in the swimming pool. But against her pale blue sheets, he was like a piece of bronze sculpture. Her hand touched him lightly, then began to trace the ridges of his chest. The skin under her fingers rippled in response.

"You're the most beautiful man I have ever seen," she whispered.

With a muffled cry he caught her to him, spreading out his fingers on her back until he seemed to hold her cupped in the palm of his hand. He lost himself in the fragrant cloud of her hair. Lowering his head, he flicked his tongue against her ear. She heard the sea roar as his moist tongue explored its hidden chambers.

She reached for him, thrilled by the insistent feel of him swelling against her belly. Now her avid fingers wanted to touch the reality of him. She pushed the confining bit of cotton away in her urgent need and felt him spring into her hand, felt the soft, doughy cluster grow long and hard and smooth as satin.

With one hand he held her face and brought it to his lips. The kisses he scattered over her face were like a million floating butterfly wings. As he came to life in her hand, so did his mouth in hers. His tongue was everywhere, exploring the moist recesses, probing, beating like another heart in rhythm with that which she held in her hand.

She was overwhelmed by her need of him, feeling her own eager wetness as she guided him into her.

He hovered above her, leaning on his elbows to take the weight from her.

"No!" she said and fiercely pulled him down on her so she could feel him cover her from toe to mouth. His hands slipped under her buttocks and lifted them, caressing them as he drew her deeper and deeper to him.

She moaned softly and spread her legs wide as if she wanted to swallow him, then with a cry, wrapped them around his back. There was a feeling of heat, then ice. She felt her senses leave her and return.

She drew all her feelings into a small, tight ball deep in her core, barely hearing the sounds of their voices as they murmured and encouraged with words that excited and maddened. Then that tight white star inside of her burst with the brilliance of a million suns. She was on fire, crying out because she was afraid she would burn. Rising up, she saw his face, now so dear to her, and brought him to her mouth. They clung to each other with the strength of angels, then collapsed onto the pillow.

She closed her eyes and exhaled a sigh of satisfaction. Her skin was burning. She felt cool lips on her forehead, a gentle hand push the damp, tangled hair from her face. She felt lighter than air and wonderfully happy.

When she at last opened her eyes, she found him propped on his elbow looking at her. She couldn't read his expression.

"I can't believe that this has happened to us," she said, her voice husky with passion.

He didn't speak, just continued to look at her.

"We were good together, Joe."

"Yes," he said. "Too good."

"What's that supposed to mean?" She felt a chill come over her.

"Nothing, really." How could he tell her of the fear he felt? This should never have happened. Neither one would be content with this one time—and to go further was madness. There were chains he couldn't free himself from, and even if he could, his past would reach out and muddy her.

But how could he keep away from her? With a groan

he pulled her to him again. Her skin was cool and smoother than the fine, silky cotton sheet that covered her. That cloud of black hair he would never tire of touching seemed to reach out and ensnare his fingers. And her eyes! Never were they the same color: He'd seen them the blue of the Colorado sky when she was full of joy and dark as midnight when she was angry.

His mouth went to her breasts. Small perfect globes, the nipples were sweet as a peach. He made love to her again with agonizing slowness. Not a word passed their lips. Their bodies fit together like separate pieces of a puzzle. Like creatures about to be separated for eternity, they clung and strained toward one another, lost themselves in each other, unable to stop even when both were satisfied.

Sometime before nine he rose and went to her bathroom to take a shower. In the mirror his eyes stared back at him, two huge dark bruises in the wreck of his face. Dark stubble covered his jaw. He thought of an excuse to offer later when he walked into the office, looking like a man who had not slept that night. I'll tell them I'm growing a beard. Something to hide behind.

He came back into the bedroom. Sam lay in a tangle of pillows and sheets offering glimpses of a body he could never get tired of exploring no matter how familiar it became. But that would never happen. He kept his eyes averted as he finished dressing.

"This is never going to happen between us again, is it?"

He sat down to put on his shoes.

"Don't you give me that goddamn silent Indian treatment, Joe Ferris!" She leaped out of bed and came to him. "Look at me!" He kept his eyes downcast. "I said look at me!"

He looked at her and smiled a rueful smile. That tone of voice. He could still hear the imperious tones of the ten-year-old commanding him to teach her. "I'm looking."

"What do you see?"

"I see a beautiful woman, very desirable, very, very desirable," he repeated. "She doesn't need a half-breed for a lover."

She crumpled at his feet. Tears filled her eyes. "Why must you be so hard on yourself? On us? Didn't you want this to happen? If you say no, I'll call you a liar. I know you did. This thing has been hanging over us for years, only I never realized it."

He pulled her to him and held her close to his heart. Tough, cynical, criminal Joe Ferris had images of wind blowing through black hair and golden skin glowing under clear water, of a man and woman walking hand in hand through wildflowers and wrestling like young cubs in a fresh snowfall. His mind led him down the most clichéd romantic paths.

"I know," he whispered. "But, Sam, it's not going to work. It's wrong for you."

"You mean for you."

"All right for me. We can still be friends if you want. Your friendship has always meant a lot to me. But this other . . ."

She pulled away from him, suddenly aware that she was naked. She was about to cover herself with a sheet. Instead she stood up and said, "The hell with it. I'll never forgive you." She sounded like a small child who had just been refused an extra hour of television.

"I don't blame you." He took her reluctant hands in his and kissed the palm of one, then the other.

CHAPTER ELEVEN

"So the story went that she—and remember she's the most prestigious gallery owner in San Francisco—she said she'd give him a one-man show in exchange for certain favors." Louis Breton made a steeple with his long fingers and lifted his eyebrows archly above them.

"You don't mean? . . ."

"I do."

"So the shoe is on the other foot these days."

"Unfortunately," he said dryly. "I must say I find that kind of woman most unattractive." He wrinkled his nose for emphasis.

Sam speared a slice of smoked turkey and put it between the seven-grain bread. From a jar of Heinz sweet pickles she picked out three and laid them neatly on top.

"I don't understand how anyone as discriminating about food as you can stoop to eating that junk." Louis eyed the jar of pickles with distaste.

"It's not junk. Besides, I love them." At his disdainful sniff, she dangled one in front of his mouth and laughed when he pulled away in distaste. "Oh, Louis, you're a food snob."

And you are a slob, he wanted to say. "Among other things."

Every day he had begun to appear with a basket of goodies from Charcuterie and Cheese or Les Chefs d'Aspen. As she worked, he would set the table and lay out the food so appetizingly that she was tempted to remark, "Perhaps I should start painting Flemish still lives."

Louis had brought his own Villeroy & Bosch china, some Waterford goblets, and two place settings of Jensen silver. "I detest plastic," he'd said in explanation.

Louis could not understand how a woman like Sam, born to appreciate the appurtenances of wealth, could have developed such plebeian preference for the plastic "kitch" she kept in her cupboards.

She had told him that such things were of little importance to her. She could appreciate them, but she didn't necessarily have to live with them every day of her life. That had infuriated him.

But Louis Breton was a patient man—and a confident one. Gradually he would replace Sam's casual aesthetics with his own highly developed brand. So subtle was his technique she was hardly aware that she had begun taking their elegant little lunches for granted and was disappointed when business forced other plans.

"Now," he said, patting his mouth with the oversize napkins he'd bought for Sam at Bendel's on his last trip to New York. "It's time you show me what you've been up to. I want to mount a show in two months. As your sponsor I'd prefer there were no surprises."

"Two months, Louis?" she asked in disbelief.

"March will be a busy month. Everyone will be in town. A summer show would give you more time, but it would be an utter waste of time; no one comes to spend money. Timing is everything." Seeing her stricken face, he cajoled, "You told me you've quite a few paintings already. Show me!"

"All right, Louis." This was the moment she'd been dreading since she first agreed to allow Louis to sponsor her. "I hope you like them." She hesitated for a moment, remembering the fear and excitement she'd felt when she'd first shown her work to Greg and how quickly that had turned to disappointment. This was far more important. Her future might depend on it. Even though Louis's insistence of an early show gave her the feeling she was about to plunge into an abyss, she still wanted to make the leap. Fantasies of success and fulfillment filled her mind. Just how good was she?

There were ten paintings leaning against the wall. She took a deep breath. One by one she turned them toward Louis's imperious face. She didn't have the courage to look at him for his reactions.

Finally all ten paintings were facing him.

"Hmm . . . mmm . . . um . . ." Sam had no idea whether the sounds indicated approval, disapproval, or indifference. She still couldn't face him. Instead, she looked at the paintings. They had a realistic look, but not too realistic, closer to a personal vision of a realistic moment. She had mixed several styles in each canvas, giving her paintings a rather unique overview that borrowed from many schools without committing to one in particular.

The silence was deafening. She had to face Louis at some time. Taking a deep breath, she whirled around. "Well? What do you think?"

He coughed. "Frankly, my dear, I don't know. They are not what I expected. Not at all."

"What did you expect?" she asked defensively. "We never really discussed my style."

"That was at your request, not mine. The artist's prerogative, I think you called it." He shook his head.

Sam winced. "Are you saying these are not good?"

"Samantha, dear heart, of course not. They have an interesting . . . uh . . . point of view."

"But nothing you feel would make a good show."

"I'm afraid not. To be in the forefront of art, you have to be aware of what's happening. I do wish you'd let me take you to New York for the weekend. We can go to SoHo and see all the new shows. I have influential friends on Madison Avenue that you should meet. The point of all this, Samantha, is that your paintings lack violence. By that I mean, that collision of color with theme. I need to see a stronger statement of intent from you. There's no . . . no brinkmanship here."

Louis droned on and on about geometry of reason, perpendicularity of subject, juxtapositions of power, and mythology of color. Irretrievably lost in the syntax, Sam decided she'd better go to New York and find out just what the hell Louis was talking about.

Twilight still cast a lavender glow on the peaks as a crescent moon rose over Aspen Mountain. Wisps of clouds stained deep purple and midnight blue hung suspended in the clear, frigid air. From Pat Mallory's house the mountain scene unfolded like a painted stage backdrop.

Inside the high-vaulted living room, a fire blazed in the huge fireplace. Sam and Sophie, curled up on either side, seemed miles apart in the vastness of the pigskin sofas. Pat was making tequila sunrises at the copper-clad bar a few steps up and a football field away. Mandy and Tooey were drinking Shirley Temples and playing noisy video games in the adjacent game room.

As Pat approached with the drinks tray, Sophie said, "You say Liz had to go to San Francisco."

"Yes, she's working on di Lucca's new house. It's quite a big job."

"It must be. She never seems to be home these

days," said Sophie. "I'm very disappointed. I've asked her several times to serve on committees and she's always too busy."

"Well, you have a good substitute," said Sam.

"Who's that?" Pat asked.

"Rachel Fulton."

"The writer who was staying at the Inn?" Pat had a sudden vision of the small intense woman with the enormous dark eyes.

"Yes, I happened to mention needing a co-chairperson for the hospital benefit, and she said she'd do it."

"How nice for you, Mother. I really like her a lot. I'm glad she's decided to stay around," said Sam.

"I am, too. But she's working very hard. The hospital benefit is a good place for her to meet people. By the way, Pat, don't be surprised if she comes by to see you. She hates the apartment she's rented. I think she wants a house."

"She's already been by the office. I couldn't take care of her myself. But I put her in good hands."

"Good. By the way, Sam, are you free Saturday night? I'm having some people in for dinner. Collectors. I thought you might like to meet them. They're very interested in local artists."

"No good, Mother. I'm going to New York for the weekend. With Louis. He wants me to see what's happening in the art world. I don't think he likes my direction. Not violent enough, he said."

"What does that mean?"

"I'm not quite sure. He tends to talk like an art critic. And you know they're all incomprehensible."

"Do you like them?" asked Sophie, referring to the paintings.

Sam thought for a moment, then said, "Yes, but what do I know? I'm only the artist."

"What does Joe Ferris think about you going off to New York with Louis Breton?" asked Pat sarcastically.

"What? . . ." was the simultaneous response of both mother and daughter.

"What does Joe Ferris have to do with this?" asked Sophie.

"You mean Sam hasn't told you?"

"Told me what?"

Pat refused to look at his sister's face. The first time he'd seen them together he'd considered it an accidental meeting. Aspen was a small town. You couldn't help running into everyone you knew at one time or another. But he had seen them together several times now and in places that their crowd usually didn't go to.

"You mean you didn't know that Sam was seeing Joe Ferris?"

Sophie turned white. "Is it true, Sam?"

"Yes . . . I mean . . . we've run into each other a couple of times. So what?" Her eyes were angry blue flames. "Are you spying on me, Pat? Trying to save the family honor? I suggest you concern yourself with matters closer to home. But that's beside the point. What I do is no one's business."

"But, Sam, the man has a very questionable reputation," insisted Sophie. "Surely there are more appropriate men around for you."

"I agree with Mother."

"Do you? That must be a first." Sam tried to control an anger equally divided between the two of them.

"Children, stop it. Why is it that every time we're together we always end up quarreling?"

"Because no one in this family has learned to mind their own business," snapped Sam. "Joe Ferris was my friend years ago. I hope he will be for a long time. What upsets you so much? That he was poor? Or is it because he's part Indian? That's no crime. After all, I'm not marrying him." Sam had started off bravely but found her resolve weakening as she collided with her confused feelings for Joe.

"His Indian blood has nothing to do with it. It's . . .

that is . . . I hear he's mixed up with drugs." Sophie knew drugs were plentiful in Aspen. She'd been to enough parties where small groups would drift into dens and libraries to find the innocuous white stuff spooned out on individual trays for guests. It seemed that cocaine had taken the place of brandy and cigars.

"I don't believe that for a moment," Sam defended. She was about to mention Alex's name, then stopped. That wouldn't help anything.

"He's promiscuous," said Sophie, trying one more time.

"And how do you know that, Mother? Have you been to bed with him?"

"That's not even funny." Sophie looked nervously at the children who were happily oblivious to the adult conversation.

"There are rumors . . . ," Sophie said weakly, sorry that Pat had brought up the whole subject.

"No one in this family has ever liked him. I don't know why. You're all bigots," she hissed softly. Standing up, she looked at them with contempt. "I can't help how you feel. I like Joe. And I am going to see him. If he wants to see me," she finished lamely. Her family had nothing to worry about from Joe. He'd done the rejecting, not her.

Pat Mallory dialed Richard Reiber, his ace salesman, to find out if anything had happened with Rachel Fulton. The answer came back negative.

Glancing at his watch, he wondered if he should call her. He checked the Rolodex for her number and dialed it.

When she answered her voice took him by surprise. He'd forgotten how low and resonant it was.

"Hello, it's Pat Mallory. I just wanted to find out if you were having any luck with a house and apologize for not being able to take you out personally."

She was polite but wary. He told her that several

new things had become available, and he would be happy to show them to her himself. They made an appointment for later that afternoon.

Rachel spent the morning at the Pitkin County Library, but Pat Mallory's raffish face kept intruding upon her work. Finally, she gave up. It was almost lunchtime anyway. The best break in the day for her was her lunch at The Grainery. The regulars had come to know her, greeting her with a cheery hello when she walked in; the waitresses had learned her taste in food.

As she walked in she waved to the Lunch Bunch, as she called them now, and took her usual seat by the window where she liked to look out on the busy street, read, or just daydream.

Rosie, Sam, and Sally Burke were at their usual table having a bowl of soup when Sunshine Campbell walked in with storm clouds on her face. The normally affable woman was about to explode.

"You're not going to believe this one," she said angrily, pulling out a chair. "Sam, your brother is going too far. I know he wants Hank's land; he's offered him enough money. But now he's making threats."

Sam had never seen Sunshine so upset. She tried to placate her. "Pat may have a lot of things wrong with him, but he's not a louse. What's happened?"

"Phone calls in the middle of the night. Veiled threats. Hate mail. Dead cats on the doorstep. Graffiti obscenities scrawled on the barn."

"That doesn't sound like Pat," Sam defended. "It sounds like local kids."

"Well, maybe he's paid some kids to hassle Hank. I don't know. But it's a really shitty way to behave."

"I can't believe Pat would be involved in anything like that."

"I hope you're right," said Sunshine, cooling down a bit. "But if he is, you tell him he's going to get an assful of lead if he steps foot on Hank's property. He's walking it with a shotgun, and he's furious enough to hurt someone."

Rachel frowned. Like Sam, she couldn't believe Pat Mallory capable of such behavior. Even though she'd only spent a few minutes with him, she was sure he was an honorable man. Nevertheless, the conversation disturbed her.

When she arrived in his office a few minutes before her appointment, she was asked to wait and given a delicious cup of coffee and the *New York Times* to read. But the paper remained folded in her lap as she thought over Sunshine's angry words.

The longer she stayed in town, the more she heard about the Mallorys, the Farwells, the Bretons. The gossip that surrounded them was far more lively than the things she heard about the *People* magazine celebrities that showed up weekly in Aspen.

"Hello! Sorry to keep you waiting."

Nothing she heard could prepare her for the sheer dynamism of Pat Mallory himself. He wore his self-confidence like a custom suit. He looked like a man who never had to struggle for a thing. She wondered if anyone had ever said no to him in his life.

He was dressed with studied casualness in gabardine jeans and his patched tweed jacket. The brown snakeskin belt had an elegant silver buckle with a large hunk of turquoise in it. He looked like an English tailor's version of a wealthy rancher.

Once again her eyes dwelt on the scars that gleamed whitely against the tan of his face.

If he was aware of her scrutiny, he made no reference to it.

"So," he took her extended hand, "I hear my office is not doing right by you. Tell me what you've seen so far and what the problem is. I'm sure we can find something that's perfect for you." Looking around, he saw the empty cup and the unfolded newspaper. "I'm glad my staff at least made your wait pleasant."

He carried on a monologue of chitchat until she finally put her hand up in defense.

"Mr. Mallory," she said pleasantly, "you haven't given me a chance to even say thank you."

He blushed. A laugh crinkled his eyes, giving her a chance to slip away from their penetrating gaze. Even as he was speaking in those rapid explosions of sound, she'd been aware of his slow, lazy gaze.

"I apologize. I do have this awful habit of monopolizing conversations." He led her into his office, seated her, then sat down in a nearby chair and folded his hands demurely. "The floor is yours."

"Mr. Reiber was very nice, but I think he was told I was some kind of celebrity. He showed me some very beautiful houses, none of which cost less than a million dollars. It was a little rich for my blood."

"You should have said something to him immediately."

"I must confess I'm a voyeur when it comes to houses. You see, I've never been inside a million-dollar house before."

"But surely in your profession you must know . . ."

"Honestly, my friends and fellow writers are not in that class. I was born in an apartment on the Upper West Side of New York before it became chic and expensive. My husband and I lived in an old converted barn in Bucks County."

"Husband? You're married?" He couldn't conceal his disappointment. Though he barely knew her, he got the same feeling when he was with her that he got from one of his solitary hikes, when he took the time to sit quietly and let the natural order of things flow over him.

"Divorced," she corrected.

"How old are you?"

"Thirty-five," she answered directly, smiling at the sudden red which stained his face. "Is there a reason you want to know?"

"No. And I don't know why I asked you that. Forgive me. It's none of my business."

"It's perfectly all right. Age or aging is of no particular interest to me except in terms of my work."

"How so?"

"I have so many books I want to write. I just hope I live long enough to write them all."

"You have years and years ahead of you."

"I come from a family that dies young."

It was an odd conversation to be having with a virtual stranger and a man who probably never gave much thought to his own mortality. No, she thought, I'm wrong. He sees it every time he looks at himself in the mirror. Pat excused himself and returned a few moments later triumphantly brandishing a folder. The slick salesman took over. "In here is a house for you. Or a condo."

Later, as Pat led her through a maze of houses and condos, she remembered the first time she'd met him a month ago. He'd come on strong and fast. But after that first night she'd neither seen nor spoken to him. She knew he was married, had two children, and mysteriously disappeared from time to time on "trips."

Now listening to him talk, she realized strong and fast was the way he dealt with everything.

"You know Sam has a small coach house on her property. You might like that. Let me see if she would be interested in renting it. It would be convenient to town and your research. It . . ."

"No, Pat," she said firmly. He didn't question her further.

"How about Martina Navratilova's first house? Or I could show you a small apartment where this unknown writer did the book that won her fame and fortune. It's over a restaurant." His eyes were twinkling with mischief.

As she got back into his car two hours later she said, "I'm amazed you're still speaking to me."

He had just shown her a particularly dark apartment on Hopkins Street.

"Why?"

"I've wasted your whole afternoon."

"I wasn't doing anything important." He closed the door, then went around to the driver's side. As he put the key in the ignition, he hit his head with the palm of his hand. "What a dunce I am! I've got the ideal place and I completely forgot about it."

With that he kicked the car in gear and headed down Original Street to Main. On the fringe of Seventh Street near Meadows Road was a tiny house, a dollhouse in comparison with the huge, turreted Victorian that sprawled over several lots.

"What is it?" she asked as he pulled up to the curb.

"Do you like romantic ghost stories?"

"I don't know." She looked at him suspiciously.

He got out and came around to take her arm. "The big house," he began, "was owned by Josiah Pinkerton, one of the early silver barons. The little house was built for his young daughter as a play house. When she was sixteen, she fell in love with a Spaniard who dealt faro at the local house of joy."

"How on earth did they meet?"

"Easy. She was shopping for some female trinket, he was out walking with the madam. As she crossed the street, a buggy came at her out of control. He picked her up and swept her out of harm's way. I don't have to tell you the rest."

Rachel continued for him. "He brought her home in the madam's carriage and tried to explain what happened to her father. Old Josiah was apoplectic and warned the man if he ever caught him so much as looking sideways at his daughter, he would horsewhip him." She laughed. It was a rich, mellow sound that made his hands itch to touch her.

"Of course," Pat picked up the threads once more, "he didn't listen. The Spaniard fell in love with her. Transformed by the pure love of a beautiful young girl, he repented his past life and swore to live an exemplary one with her at his side."

"Oh, Pat, you're making it up. I thought I was supposed to be the writer."

"But it's true. Boy Scout's honor."

"You're a rogue. C'mon, show me the house."

"Wait! I'm not finished. Unbeknownst to her father, she was sneaking out and waiting for her lover in the play house. One night, during a bad storm, Poppa woke up. Afraid his darling would be frightened, he went to her room and found her missing. He searched all thirty rooms of the big house and finally found them together here."

"And? . . ."

"He killed the Spaniard."

"And did what with the body?"

"Rumor has it that he buried him in the cellar behind a brick wall."

She hit him lightly on the arm. "You've been reading too much Poe. And her? What happened to her?"

"She was stricken with a mysterious fever. She languished, wasting away in the bedroom, refusing to leave the little house. Then one day she died. She was seventeen."

The moment Rachel set foot on the threshold she knew the story was true and that she and the house were meant for each other. It was a doll's house, but it had everything! A small, cheerful study overlooking a snow-covered garden where she could write without disturbance, exquisite but worn furnishings of the late Victorian period; charming old gaslights which had been converted to electricity, and a bathroom which still contained the old footed tub and wide marble sink. Leaded windows with diamond-shaped inserts of colored glass threw shades of amber, red, and amethyst across the tiled floor.

Brocade draperies and lace curtains hung from the windows in all the downstairs rooms. Concessions had been made in the bedroom. It was still a virginal young girl's room with a tester bed draped in white organdy and a pale Turkey rug on the mahogany floor. In one corner stood an elaborate armoire, in the other a dressing table which held a monogrammed silver-backed brush, comb, and mirror set. Filmy organdy curtains hung under pale blue damask swags at the window.

"I want it. How much is it? How long can I stay?"

"Wait a minute, wait a minute! Don't rush me." Pat looked through his folder. "Ah, here we are." He ran his finger down, mumbling such important facts as the capacity of the hot-water tank, sewage, town water, washer-dryer, until he found the price. "Four hundred dollars a month. Not including heat."

"In Aspen? How can that be?"

"I told you there was a catch. The house is haunted."

Rachel had met two women in Aspen whom she liked a great deal. One was Samantha Mallory and the other was Rusty Harris. Rusty, a flamboyant redhead, owned a series of cosmetic shops in the Midwest which featured organic cosmetics of her own formulation. She was part of a group of Chicagoans who spent half their winter in Aspen. All of them were excellent skiers, impeccable hostesses, and collectors of "interesting" people.

That she was considered an "interesting" person amused Rachel. Ordinarily she would have eschewed such company but the Harrises themselves were interesting, too. Rusty was a voluptuous titian redhead married to a short, slender man who made up in energy what he lacked in height. They obviously adored one another, constantly bragging about each other's accomplishments. Hank Harris was the owner of Multi-Media, a communications conglomerate that owned newspapers, radio stations, and movie theaters in small towns all over the country.

Rusty had invited her to a party that night at her Red Mountain home. At precisely 6:30, thirty people dressed in the usual eclectic Aspen style climbed the tortuous curves of Red Mountain and parked their four-wheel drive vehicles in the long, curving driveway.

It was one of the newer multimillion-dollar houses with the by-now-familiar view. On a clear day you could see Mt. Sopris looming in solitary splendor. The house floated in a sea of light, more one vast open space than a series of confined rooms. The walls were adorned with classic modern paintings by Klee, Arp, Chagall, and an eclectic collection which included African tribal masks and sculpture, chunks of pyrite, amethyst quartz, pre-Columbian, Cycladic, and Senufo artifacts.

Rachel was properly impressed and congratulated Rusty on the brilliance of her collection.

As she steered her around the room, Rusty would relate a delicious piece of gossip, then introduce her. Rachel learned that the girl friend and wife of the handsome man in the corner were best friends, that the bloomingly pregnant young woman hanging adoringly on the arm of a septuagenarian husband was carrying another man's child, that the New York society girl who had recently married one of the golden Greeks was also pregnant, but by one of the Austrian ski instructors.

When Pat Mallory walked in alone Rusty stopped to give him an appraising look. "I never see them together anymore," she said.

"You mean Pat Mallory and his wife?"

"Yes, she'll show up a little later. I don't know with whom. She likes men who are beneath her socially. There was a rumor she was shacking up with some guy who worked for the mountain, but I'm not sure which one. Probably ran the lift. I think she's nuts. Pat Mallory is completely delicious; he could put his Tony

Lamas under my bed any day of the week. Have you met him yet?"

She was about to drag Rachel over, but Rachel hung back. "We've met."

"Don't you agree with me?"

"I haven't formed a judgment."

"Oh, there's Louis Breton and Sam. Excuse me, I see someone I simply must speak to. You don't mind?"

"No, of course not." Rachel waved at Sam, then began a circuit of the room, stopping to admire and savor the top-notch collection of art. She felt a bit out of place—everyone seemed to know everyone else, so she slipped away to take a tour of the exceptional house.

It had few rooms but a great deal of space. The Harrises were obviously childless, for there were only the master suite with a huge marble bath and dressing rooms, a guest suite, and a den cum media room. On the lower level was the requisite lapping pool—an Aegean blue reflecting the Grecian tiles which framed it—and the personal exercise room with bicycle and rowing machine, trampoline and free weights.

She returned to the huge living room to continue her appraisal of the art. As she stepped back to get a better look at a large Jasper Johns, she stepped on someone's foot.

"Oops . . . forgive me, I was just trying to . . ." Seeing who it was, Rachel smiled and extended her hand. "Sam. I saw you come in. It's nice to see you again."

"Rachel! What are you doing here?"

"Research. No, I'm joking. I was invited."

"I didn't know you knew the Harrises."

"I don't really. But mutual friends introduced us."

"How do you like this collection?"

"Very impressive. But you're the artist. What do you think?"

"Heavy on the modern for my taste. But I wouldn't turn it down if someone offered." She looked around at the clusters of people gesticulating and talking vivaciously. "They're amazing, aren't they? You wonder how they can find so much to say when they speak on the phone every day, ski with each other every day, and socialize with each other every day. What do you think of our little group?"

"They all look very happy and successful."

"Successful, yes. Happy?" She shrugged. "I wouldn't be too sure of that."

"The Harrises seem to adore one another."

"They do, but he can't resist young flesh. Watch him. See that young blond teenager, the one with hair down to her waist and the face of a Botticelli angel? She's his golf partner's oldest daughter. Watch closely. In a half hour he'll have her in a dark corner trying to feel her up."

"You can't be serious." Rachel was truly shocked. "Wouldn't she tell her father if his best friend did something like that?"

"Are you kidding? She can hardly wait for Hank to take her to bed."

"But she looks like a . . ."

"Baby Hooker is what they call her behind her back. She's been doing it since she was thirteen."

Rachel shook her head in wonder.

"See those two men talking to one another over there? The one on the left is Drake Peabody, married to the stunning blonde in the satin jumpsuit. The other is Biff Prentice. His wife is the cute butterball loading up her plate with shrimp. Drake used to be married to the butterball. About five years ago Biff and Drake fell in love."

"Oh, come on, you're making this all up." At Sam's unsmiling face, Rachel murmured, "You're not. Do the wives know?"

"If they do, they're not admitting it."

Rachel was saved from additional Aspen confidential when Liz Mallory made a late but dazzling appearance in an attention-riveting short red suede skirt and bolero jacket. Her shapely legs were sheathed in boots that came over her knees.

Rachel stared at her appraisingly. It was only the second time she'd actually seen Pat Mallory's wife. There was no question that she was a sexy and beautiful woman, but Rachel thought there was something mean and ungenerous in her expression. This was a willful woman accustomed to getting her way and furious when she did not.

A few minutes later Gianfranco di Lucca walked in and was immediately surrounded by a dozen admiring women, allowing Rachel to watch an expert go to work. In a few minutes Liz Mallory had Gianni to herself, and the two of them were deep in conversation, a scant inch separating their bodies.

"God, I despise her," Sam hissed.

"Why? She's your sister-in-law."

"Thank God it's not a blood relationship. I hate the way she flaunts her indiscretions in front of Pat."

"I couldn't help but overhear you, Sam." Pat suddenly appeared at Sam's right arm. "She can't help herself, you know. It's all surface. She's a tease. But she is amazing. I'm surprised that Gianni encourages her. After all, he and I are talking a business deal. But what the hell, at least he's classier than some of her others." Despite his knowledge of his wife's affairs, Pat didn't truly believe that she and Gianni were lovers. He was just another of her flirtations.

Rachel was so embarrassed by his frank talk about his wife, she wanted to leave. What an uncharitable thing to say! Especially in front of a stranger.

Seeing the frown on Rachel's face, Pat realized what she must be thinking. He gave her a tight smile that apologized for nothing. "What the hell? Who cares? Sorry for airing my dirty linen in front of you, Rachel."

"Actually I've been airing everyone's dirty laundry," Sam confessed. "After all, Rachel is a writer. I don't want her to get the wrong impression about Aspen. It's very deceiving. Just because everyone's out in the fresh air skiing like birds or working out in the spas doesn't mean *mens sana in corpore sano*."

"We sound very self-righteous, don't we?" Pat tried to keep the sting from his words as he gave his sister a penetrating look. He hadn't forgotten their last go-round over Joe Ferris. He had been sorry for that. She'd been right. It wasn't any of his business.

"Sam, forgive me for having such a big mouth. I am sorry." He put his arms around her and tried to hug her. At first she resisted, then leaned against her brother and gave him a hug.

"It hasn't been the first time. It probably won't be the last."

Pat looked around the room. His smiling face grew thoughtful. "Don't look now, but the beautiful Melanie has just arrived with . . . I'm not sure. There's Alex Breton and Joe Ferris the requisite two steps behind her."

Sam pretended not to have heard Pat and continued talking to Rachel. Despite what had happened to them, despite their unspoken agreement to never bring the subject up, despite the fact they were free to do as they pleased, and to see whomever they wanted, the thought of Joe and Melanie together made her feel physically ill.

But it was Alex, dragging Melanie by the hand, who came to greet her with a kiss. Sam made the introductions, relieved when Pat finally took Rachel and her all-seeing eyes off to the buffet table.

Sam talked about her recent trip to New York, the galleries, the theater, the restaurants, trying to keep her eyes from following Joe Ferris as he worked the room. She was frankly surprised to see him at this party. Seven years ago Joe would not have been invited to the Harrises. At some point, probably when he took over the management of Silver Mountain Resort, his status had changed. Eligible men were rare, and Joe was not only eligible, he was a dramatically exotic addition to any social scene.

"I never realized how incredibly attractive Joe Ferris is." Melanie gave them her famous barracuda look. "He looks very sexy tonight, don't you think?"

"Yeah," said Alex, "if you like hoods." Joe was wearing black corduroys and a black silk shirt with an expensive Armani tie which did indeed give him a dangerous look.

Suddenly aware they were staring at him, Joe caught Sam's eye. Before she had a chance to turn away, he nodded and started walking toward her. But Richard Farwell, who was making one of his rare social appearances, intercepted him to say something which elicited a frown on Joe's usually composed features. Richard then headed toward a group of men which included Hank Harris (who had finally torn himself away from the nymphet), Bob Floyd, a venture capitalist, and Phil Grantz, a tax lawyer, all members of the Illini group.

As if each move was being orchestrated by a master choreographer, the groups shifted and reformed, broke apart only to emerge in other parts of the room. The room filled with the tension of the search.

Richard Farwell's eyes rarely left Sophie Mallory, the stunning center of three attentive men, all younger than her son.

Pat Mallory's wife was totally oblivious to her husband as he followed Rachel Fulton at a safe distance, racking his brain for something he could say that would keep her by his side for more than a minute.

When Melanie saw Joe Ferris in serious conversation with Sam, her eyes grew avaricious. She interrupted Alex in midsentence, mumbling that she needed to ask Sam something and made her way toward them. Exercising one of her patented Melanie moves, she pushed Sam aside and put her arm through Joe's and led him away to the bar.

Alex, whose mouth was still opened in surprise, had a hurt-puppy look on his face. Sam made her way to his side and tried to divert him with a joke.

Once again the players had shifted to different positions on the board.

"I know you think you and I are on opposite sides of the fence," Richard Farwell, taking advantage of the sudden vacancy on the couch, said to Sophie Mallory. "But you'd be surprised how much we agree upon."

"I'm sure I would," was her wry answer.

"I'm serious. Will you give me a chance to explain over dinner?"

Sophie gave her head a little shake. "Now I know why you've become so successful. You simply don't take no for an answer."

"Can I assume that's an equivocal yes?"

"Shall I ask my secretary to make the reservation at Gordon's, or do you want yours to do it?"

"Mine can do it. Is eight o'clock satisfactory?" At her nod, he said, "I'll pick you up."

". . . Are you enjoying the house?" asked Pat Mallory, who had finally caught up with Rachel Fulton again.

"I love it. But you were right, there is a ghost."

"That's an old wive's tale."

"Oh, no. You were right. Late at night I hear her sobbing."

"You're pulling my leg."

"You'll just have to come by and hear it for yourself."

He was not about to let that opportunity slip by. "How about tomorrow after dinner?"

"I have . . . that is . . . I was . . ." Rachel bit her tongue. How could she have extended such an invitation? She couldn't think of a good reason to say no.

Then, to her surprise, she discovered she didn't want to.

"God, she's such a bitch," moaned Alex, watching Melanie press herself against Joe Ferris's arm. "I don't know why I put up with her."

"I don't, either," said Sam.

"I can't believe she'd pick Ferris over me. Christ, he's a lousy skier."

If Sam hadn't felt so bereft herself, she would have laughed. Why did she get the feeling that Joe was acting out this little charade with Melanie for her benefit?

"You know Melanie, Alex. It's all a big game to her. There's no one else around but you and Joe to play it with her."

"But I've been dating her. She let me believe we had something going. . . ."

"Ooh, Lexie, forget her." Sam tugged at his arm. "I have a terrific idea. Let's leave before they start serving the serious food and go to Shlomo's for a bowl of chicken soup. It'll make us feel better."

"What about my father?"

"What about him?"

"Didn't you come with him? He'll be shit-faced if you just walk out on him."

"Then I'll tell him."

She went in search of Louis and found him expounding one of his more complex creative theories to the husband-and-wife writing team who had recently come to Aspen and become part of the local celebrity scene. She smiled and apologized for interrupting, amused to see them move swiftly away the moment she started to talk to Louis.

Louis was not pleased, but she insisted that Alex was suffering the pangs of rejection, that she was tired, but that Louis shouldn't feel he had to leave because of her. She didn't give him a chance to argue with her.

But when she looked for Alex, he seemed to have disappeared.

Twenty minutes later she saw him in an animated discussion with Gianfranco di Lucca. His eyes were bright and unfocused. She'd never seen him quite so relaxed. Leaning against the wall, he seemed to be made of rubber. When she approached him and put her hand on his arm, he looked at her without recognition.

"Alex, remember? Chicken soup at Shlomo's?"

He hadn't the vaguest idea of what she was talking about.

With a sigh, she turned to leave and saw Joe Ferris and Melanie Rogers. Melanie was clinging to his arm like wet paper, and he was looking down at her with the same smoldering eyes that had enveloped her only a short time ago.

So much for Joe Ferris. If ever she needed the solace of chicken soup, this was it.

CHAPTER TWELVE

THE JANUARY VISITORS POURED IN TO TAKE ADVANTAGE OF
Aspen's special ski packages. Told the town was full of
celebrities, they set forth in grim pursuit. Last-minute
cancellations got them treasured reservations for early
sittings at Gordon's, too early to see anyone. The next
day they were chagrined to learn that Jane Fonda and
Rupert Murdoch had come for the nine o'clock seat-
ing.

The news that Don Johnson had been seen on
Ruthie's Run sent them to number eight lift to get a
glimpse of him. Upon arrival they found not the
stubbly-faced star of *Miami Vice,* but a long lift line.
That night there was a rumor that Bruce Willis was
going to The Paragon. The place filled early in hope,
but Bruce never came. The next day they found out he
had spent the evening at the Paradise Club and that he
had even gotten up and sung a few tunes.

Jack Nicholson skied in peaceful anonymity, a

pudgy figure in black with heavy, dark goggles concealing most of his face, an old duck-billed cap, the rest. Chris Evert, John McEnroe, and Martina Navratilova took to the slopes with the same avidity as they did to the courts. But they were surrounded with such a retinue of friends they were almost impossible to see.

Harper's Bazaar Ski Week proved once again that despite the straitened finances of the country, people would still pay $1,700 for ski outfits and $20,000 for fun furs.

An ice sculpture contest in Wagner Park was emcee'ed by John Denver and won by eight expert Japanese snow sculptors. An antique ski race brought out the old-timers, many of whom had first discovered Aspen when they were with the 10th Mountain Division training at Camp Hale and the only way up was a double toboggan-type ski lift which carried 200 skiers per hour up Aspen mountain for ten cents a head.

At the same time there were a number of freak accidents. The winner of the canine fashion show died mysteriously after eating his prize of a large, chocolate-covered bone. One of the youngsters in the Ankle Biter's Junior Cross Country Ski Race never finished and was discovered hours later wandering in the woods, dazed, and screaming that he had been attacked by bears. Half a dozen happy drunks complained of severe stomach pains after the Bartender's Drink Contest. A pair of snowboards shattered during the snowboard races, a hot-air balloon collapsed, seriously injuring its two occupants.

With the crowning of the Winter Queen, a conventionally pretty blond cocktail waitress from the Silver Leaf Inn, everyone breathed more easily until Josiah Woods, the sheriff of Pitkin County, found her in an alley behind the bakery where she had been beaten up and left bound from head to foot in a dumpster.

While most of Sophie Mallory's friends thrived on a

steady diet of gossip and innuendo, her concerns were directed toward a recalcitrant boiler and its paltry production of hot water, and her prize-winning chef who wanted to go to California and work for Wolfgang Puck. She was ready to run away from home. So Richard Farwell's frequent invitation to dinner came as a welcome reprieve. Though their differences still outnumbered the things they shared, she found herself enjoying whatever time they spent together.

Richard proved to be a reticent man in most things, but as they spent more time together, he gradually loosened up and spoke of his early youth, his ambition, and finally his marriage. When she asked why he had not divorced his wife, his cold-blooded answer shocked her. "Why bother, she'll be dead of cirrhosis in a year." He later modified his remarks, but to a woman accustomed to the generosity and kindness of Big Sam Mallory, Richard's cynicism was unsettling.

Still she could not deny the attraction growing between them.

That night she dressed with special care in a pale gray cashmere wrap sweater and wool gauze skirt that showed off her still elegant legs. Skiing several mornings a week had given her face a healthy glow. She rubbed some moisturizer on it and touched her lips with a light coral lipstick.

As she fastened a heavy gold Florentine chain around her throat, the bell to her private entrance sounded. When she opened it, Richard came in on a gust of icy cold air. Rubbing his hands, he strode to the fireplace to warm them. "Must be down to zero. I hope you're dressed warmly."

He wore a coyote greatcoat. Sheathed in the pale fur, with his fox-shaped eyes, he looked like a giant predator. She felt a thrill of fear run through her.

"I am. Would you like a drink before we leave?"

"No, everything's ready for us," he said cryptically. She handed her fisher coat to him. As he helped her don the luxurious fur coat, his hands lingered for a split second on her shoulders before he returned them to the pockets of his own coat.

Outside, it was so cold every breath seemed to freeze in her nose. Sophie looked up at the mountain and the solitary light moving slowly up Little Nell. "Ah, the lonely Snowcat driver."

"What?"

"That's what Sam used to say when she was little. When the cats went out to groom the mountains. 'Mommy,' she would ask, 'does the snowcat driver have a wife? And children? Where does he live? What does he do all night in the snowcat? Is he lonely?' Now when we're together and we see him, we still say, 'Ahh, the lonely Snowcat driver.' "

He smiled a rueful smile. "It's nice to have such pleasant memories of your children."

Richard helped her into the customized four-wheel-drive Subaru. Like many wealthy men, Richard Farwell had an obsession for cars, owning a garage full of rare and exotic specimens: a 1929 Peerless, a white 1934 Packard which had belonged to Jean Harlow, a 1920 Stutz Bearcat that had been owned by F. Scott Fitzgerald, and a 1933 Duesenberg Speedster. But for getting around in the deep snows and steep ruts of Red Mountain, he preferred his four-wheel-drive Subaru.

He turned the car north toward Red Mountain.

"Where are we going? Obviously not to The Grill."

"No," he said. "I thought it would be nice to have a pleasant evening alone with you. I'm suddenly tired of crowds. Do you mind? I have an excellent chef. He's preparing dinner for us. If that bothers you, I can call him right now and cancel it." He reached for the phone by his side.

"It's all right, Richard," she replied, staying his hand.

Strange that in the twenty-odd years she had casually known him, she'd never been in his home. Neither the old Victorian in the West End nor this new one, built a few years ago for a reputed six million dollars. She had seen it, of course, looming above all the others on Red Mountain, like a marvelous glass-and-stone bird about to take flight. Now, from the banks of uncovered windows, blazing lights turned the house into a giant sun in a black starless sky.

He parked in front of the circular drive and helped her out of the car. A fourteen-foot-high carved teak door opened noiselessly at the touch of his hand. She followed him in through a rosy, marbled foyer covered with a rare Persian carpet whose faded tones matched the marble.

A young Oriental man appeared to take her coat, then disappeared as noiselessly as he arrived.

Richard drew her to the fireplace, a three-sided affair that warmed the two living rooms as well as the adjacent game room. The ceilings soared to a Gothic arch, but any resemblance to that lofty architectural style was immediately removed by the slowly whirring ceiling fans that kept the warm air circulating throughout the house.

"Please, sit down. I'll make a drink," he said stiffly.

He's uncomfortable, she thought. He's not accustomed to entertaining women. She found that insight made him less formidable.

Turning her back to the fire, she admired the living room with its circular pale suede couches and hammered-brass-and-cobalt-enameled coffee table, at which ten could sit comfortably and casually dine.

He handed her the glass of Chablis Premier Cru she preferred. "It's a spectacular house," she said, accepting the drink.

"I'll show you the rest, if you like."

Carrying her glass, she followed him, listening attentively as he inventoried its contents. She smiled. He sounded like a real-estate salesman.

"I have the feeling you've done this before."

He sighed and raised his heavy brows. "More times

than I care to count. Shall we?" He gestured to the curving stairs with its hammered-brass banister. The carpeting was a pale powder, so thick and soft, she sank up to her ankles in it.

The first level housed the customary pool and mirrored weight room; there were also several guest suites, one done in sand marble and white, the other in burgundy and navy. There was a servant's apartment, grander than any suite Sophie could offer at the Inn.

To Sophie's compliments, Richard replied, "I don't know how much longer I want to keep this house. I'm the only one who spends any time in it. It's really too big for me. And I'm afraid I don't entertain enough to make it worthwhile. I much prefer your comfortable inn. If you remember, I stayed there while the house was being finished."

"Yes, you did, didn't you?"

He showed her the octagonal library, the clever caterer's kitchen and laundry room with its own entrance off the garage, the navy tiled kitchen that was larger than most restaurants', the sunny breakfast room, the circular dining room which could seat thirty at small, well-spaced tables, the smaller dining room in the temperature-controlled brick wine cellar, and the master bath and bedroom. The bedroom was hung in rare Gobelins, and the giant testered bed on its raised platform was covered with fur throws befitting a medieval king.

But it was the bathroom that intrigued Sophie. Made of natural river stone and marble with its twin showers set in a glade under a waterfall, its greenery, its chaises and floating tubs, its cedared closets and chests, it was the ultimate sybaritic expression.

"What fun. Why, it's like taking a shower under a waterfall in some tropical island." She clapped her hands.

"Maybe you'll have a chance to try it."

She raised an eyebrow.

His smile of embarrassment did much to mollify her. "That did sound a little heavy handed," he admitted.

After the tour they returned to the barroom and waited for Dak Kim to summon them for dinner.

"Richard, something's been on your mind all night. Would you like to talk about it?"

He shook his head. "Whatever I say, even the most innocent remark, is going to sound like paranoia to you."

Although Sophie was still wary of Richard's motives in promoting a relationship between them, it was plain to see that he was very troubled. Certainly not the attitude of a man set on seduction! "Richard?"

"I'm being sabotaged," he said bluntly.

His unexpected answer affected her strongly. She stifled an uncomfortable laugh. A vein trembled in the delicate skin of her temple. "You personally?"

"Me, the corporation, what does it matter? You probably don't know what's been going on." He tossed down the remains of his drink and got up to refill his glass. "We've had a plague of accidents. Oh, nothing really serious yet. A fire in a storeroom, a sudden rash of annoying lift slowdowns and stoppages, bus breakdowns, missing ski-patrol snowmobiles, thefts in the sports shops. The kind of thing that happens from time to time but not with such frequency."

"Why do you think it's sabotage?"

"This morning I got a phone call. The caller said if I didn't resign as chairman of SMC, they would poison the water supply."

"Crazies have been threatening to poison the water supply for as long as I can remember. Remember when they were building Centennial and someone threatened to poison the Paonia Reservoir?"

"Are you telling me I should ignore it?"

"No, of course not. I would certainly plan to have guards on duty and I would test the water every day."

"But they could get to it from almost any point. Our water comes from Maroon and Castle creeks."

"But it goes into holding tanks. You could test it right there in situ."

"Look, maybe I'm making too much of this. Maybe it's just another run of bad luck. I'm not superstitious, but I feel that somewhere I must have broken a mirror or walked under a ladder or . . ."

"Stop. You're only making things worse for yourself."

Fortunately, the conversation was interrupted by Dak Kim announcing dinner. Over the exquisite meal, they turned to lighter subjects: books read, the stock market's future, Aspen's future. But that subject brought back into focus their shallowly buried differences.

As she warmed to her righteous indignation, he suddenly covered her clenched fist with his hand. "Sophie, Sophie, save your fury for someone else. I'm not the ogre anymore. The financial position of the corporation simply won't permit us to get involved in uncontrolled development. Besides, Planning and Zoning won't let us. It's Pat, your son, who has, if I may borrow Sam's phrase, the 'edifice complex,' not me."

"Damn it, I know that. But he got his big ideas from you." She pulled her hand away.

"You are wrong, terribly wrong. He got them from some kind of neurotic need for your approval."

"My approval?" Sophie refused to accept that. "If that were true, he'd give up those ideas right now. He knows how I feel."

"Yes, he knows. But in some kind of twisted way, I believe he thinks that you'll come to love and respect him when he successfully pulls off this Ute City project. He really believes that by controlling its size and following the planning and zoning guidelines he can have everything he wants and still keep the environmental peace."

"If he believes that, he's a bigger fool than I thought. Oh, God, how joyfully I look back at those days when billboards were our only major villains. Why is this happening?"

"Because everybody wants a piece of paradise."

The question that Richard Farwell wanted to ask, had wanted to ask for a very long time and still had not found a way to ask, was why Sophie Mallory treated her son as if he were an enemy. It had to be more than just difference of opinion.

From that point on, the evening lost its savor. The silences grew longer. To Richard's dismay, Sophie, pleading a sudden headache, asked to be taken home early.

Pat Mallory was having his own problems. Over the last year he had made a list of properties destined for foreclosure and chosen those that he wanted to acquire for his various development plans.

The first foreclosure to fall due was a beat-up old hotel that had been slated for renovation by a local group who had run into problems when the initial estimates for the job were found to be grossly miscalculated. But when Pat went to file his bid, he was shocked to discover that someone had beaten him out by doubling his offer. Furious, he demanded to know who the buyer was and was informed that the transaction had been handled by lawyers for an unknown company. When Pat investigated he found it to be like one of those wooden Russian dolls. Each time he opened one, there was another and another and another inside. It was impossible to learn who the true owner was.

Pat mentioned the incident to Gianni and in his annoyance failed to notice a satisfied smile flit across di Lucca's face and swiftly disappear as he expressed his concern.

Gianfranco di Lucca had successfully initiated the first step in his grand plan to squeeze Richard Farwell out of the Silver Mountain Corp. and begin the implementation of a tri-mountain resort built on the profits from "white gold." How perfect, he thought, that Santos should build his next fortune on another variety of "snow."

But Pat had other worries besides his thwarted deals. He was not only the owner of Silver Mountain Real Estate, a company with annual gross sales now nearing fifty million dollars, but he was CEO of Mallory, Limited, overseeing the financial investments of the entire Mallory clan. Under Pat's creative management, and despite the disastrous behavior of the stock market, the company had flourished. It would have been simple enough for him to take those assets and invest them in his own projects if both his mother and sister were not so dead set against them. And Richard Farwell's newfound conservatism was not making him very happy.

Gianfranco di Lucca could be his lifesaver. He had seen the projects and was thoroughly impressed. Yet whenever Pat brought up the subject, Gianni found a reason to switch attention to the acquisition of the Highlands. When Pat reminded him of Hank Campbell's refusal to sell, Gianni insisted that it was just a question of time. Pat, however, thought that time was running out.

The sun was shining when Sophie left Denver. By the time she landed at San Francisco's airport on United's 10:25 flight, a light rain had begun to fall, turning the city and its bay to silver. From the sky she could see the great bridge, its feet buried in billows of fog. They should change its name, she thought idly. It was certainly not made of gold, and much of the time it was wrapped in a bank of silver.

She took a cab into the city and was let off at the Huntington Hotel on Nob Hill. For years it had been her home away from home. Choice of the titled and the celebrated, its guest list could just as easily number Luciano Pavarotti and Alistair Cooke as Sophie MacNeal Mallory.

Of all the smaller hotels in San Francisco it felt most like home, if home happened to include elegant English and Oriental antiques, original paintings, and fresh bouquets of flowers every day. Sophie would stay overnight in the suite she booked on a yearly basis and which was kept unoccupied for her unexpected last-minute arrivals.

Taking off her casual western garb, she changed to her city attire: a quilted black leather Chanel suit. In the kitchenette she found a pot of her favorite Blue Mountain Jamaican coffee waiting for her and poured a cup. Taking it with her to the elegant Louis XV escritoire, she sat down in the scarlet damask chair and dialed a number.

Dr. Marcus Feldman picked up his personal phone on the first ring.

"Hello, Marc, I've just arrived," said Sophie.

They chatted a few minutes; then she hung up with a tender smile on her face. Over the next few minutes she made phone calls, confirming reservations, canceling others, reminding friends of the various charitable events she was chairing and eliciting attendance and large contributions.

Her doorbell rang just as she finished her last call.

She rose to open it and was immediately swept into the arms of the man who had been her lover for the last several years.

Seven years younger than she, Marc Feldman had prematurely silver hair, a narrow, intelligent face, and the most gentle brown eyes she'd ever seen. They had met when he came to Aspen with a group of psychiatrists for a week-long seminar. They had been introduced by mutual friends at the Christmas Ball and spent a pleasant evening chatting at the black-tie affair in the Silver Queen Ballroom. He had looked particularly splendid that night with his glowing, freshly tanned face rising above his immaculately tailored dinner jacket.

He was a fine skier, having learned as a child at Stowe, polishing his technique on the Dartmouth ski team, and skiing every weekend he could at Tahoe or Sun Valley when he moved to the West. After his first trip to Aspen and his meeting with Sophie, he'd returned often.

From the very first, she knew he was married, that his wife was paralyzed from a skiing accident that he felt responsible for, that she assumed he would find his companionship elsewhere, but would never leave her. He had never concealed anything from her. And gradually they had fallen into their present relationship, accomplishing the impossible: keeping it a secret. Not because they were ashamed of it, but because Sophie preferred it that way and had no wish to inflict more pain on Marcus's wife.

They kissed and held each other tenderly. "I've missed you so much," he breathed in her ear, his voice as soothing as honey. "Are you well?"

"I'm fine," she said from the haven of his arms. "The children are at each other again. I'm tired and out of sorts most of the time. . . ."

"Well, then, let's get going. Peace and quiet await."

San Francisco in winter was full of fog and mist, so they decided to wallow in it by driving up the coast to Mendocino where the dripping redwoods and fog-shrouded headlands created a muted, otherworldly silence. It was nature at its most mysterious and primitive.

They planned to drive along the Russian River to Ukiah, where they would stay overnight at the Palace Hotel and then go on to Mendocino, a Cape Cod-like village with galleries, boutiques, and a sweeping rugged coastline of crashing waves and playful seals. They would then stay in Little River at the Heritage House, a collection of New England-style cottages surrounding a 105-year-old low-ceilinged farmhouse whose dining room was warm with brass and copper and filled with the glow of antique wood. It was noted for its fine cuisine and distinguished collection of California vintage wines.

Later, as they dined in the glow of a crackling fire, Sophie toyed with her wineglass and stared into the flames.

Marc laced his fingers through hers. "Sophie, you've been distracted since the moment you came to town."

"Have I?" she said absently.

He gave her a rueful smile. "Tell me. Is it us?"

That got her attention. "Us? What about us?"

He shrugged, unwilling to launch the subject they had tacitly agreed not to discuss anymore.

"You know how I hate sneaking around corners, darling. You deserve much more than a backstreet romance. If you really wanted to, I'm sure Susan . . ."

She covered his lips with her hand. "But if it doesn't matter to me, why should it to you?"

"Because I love you. I'm proud of you. I want my friends to know you."

"Some do."

"But most don't," he added swiftly. "There isn't a soul I know who would make you feel uncomfortable. They know the impossibility of my situation; they're the ones who encouraged me to form other relationships."

"Oh, Marc, dear, I don't even think about it anymore." Unlike most women finding themselves in such a situation, Sophie had never nagged Marc to change the ground rules. She didn't expect to see him on special holidays, didn't expect to take long vacations with him, did not berate him for not calling every night. She'd been perfectly happy to let things drift along. Marriage was of no great importance to her at this stage of her life. If anything it would be an encumbrance.

But the companionable evenings with Richard Farwell had made her aware of the pleasure of having an interesting man in close proximity. Richard and Marc had much in common. Both were unusually fine men trapped in impossible marriages. She ruefully considered that fact. Was that a deliberate choice on her part?

But whatever the similarities in situation, the two men couldn't be more different in character and temperament. Her relationship with Marc was calm and tranquil. She and Richard had violent arguments, yet they found many other things to agree upon. No matter how much she wanted to dislike Richard, his big, comforting presence, his lanky, awkward grace overcame all. And there was an excitement about him that spiced their evenings together.

"You can't tell me you like getting on a plane in the middle of winter to escape to some little hideaway with me for a weekend of illicit pleasures."

"Don't make it sound so sordid," she replied testily.

"Sorry, darling, I was just trying to make you smile."

She kissed the inside of his palm, feeling guilty for thinking of Richard Farwell in the presence of this very special man. "Forgive me. That's what happens when you get older, you get testy and argumentative."

Marcus's face tightened. She knew he hated being reminded of the differences in their ages, though it made little difference to her.

"If you must know," she finally said, "it's Pat."

"What has he done now?"

"It's not anything new. It's his stubborn insistence on going ahead with this obscene Ute City plan of his. That development thing that I hate. He's modified it somewhat, but it's still a monster. Even his sister, who is far more tolerant of him than I, is finding his greed unbearable." She paused at the startled look on Marc's face.

"Greed?"

"Well I don't know what else to call it," she flushed. "His insistence, his obsession. Does he do it just to aggravate me?"

"Do you do it just to aggravate him?" he inquired softly. "Sophie, you have to stop kidding yourself. You're taking out your hatred for his father on him. And he doesn't even know why."

Long before he and Sophie became lovers, Marc had met Pat in Aspen, had liked the young man, and spent an evening talking with him. Pat's intense desire for his mother's approval was most affecting. Marcus did not learn why it had been so difficult for her to give it until much later.

"Sophie, he's still part of you. You simply must let those true feelings surface."

"You make me sound like an ogre." The righter she knew he was, the angrier she became. "And stop playing Dr. Freud with me."

"Sophie, Sophie! You can be so exasperating at times."

Richard Farwell had said those same words to her only a week ago. "I know." She slipped her hand into his. "I wonder that you put up with me."

"I wonder myself. But then I think of all the women I know or have known and I say: 'Sophie Mallory is an exasperating, infuriating, complex, independent, beautiful, and intelligent woman' . . . and that says it all. I'm hopelessly ensnared."

She looked at him with huge eyes, blue flames from the fire reflecting in their pewter depths. Her voice was low, thrilling, and insistent. "Marc, take me to bed. Make love to me."

He rose unsteadily from the table and pulled her into the circle of his arm. "With the greatest of pleasure," he responded tenderly. Her intensity thrilled him. So why did he have this feeling of dread? He had the feeling this controlled woman was fighting some desperate kind of battle, and he knew she would never tell him what was torturing her.

Lying against the pillows of the big old-fashioned bed, he watched her undress. She was in splendid shape; lean, firm, and lightly tanned. Just watching her unconscious striptease made him grow hard and hungry with want. It was only when she raised her arms and he saw her breasts, grown rounder and heavier, that he was reminded that age was slowly making its inroads on her.

She pulled off the pale gray silk panties, folded them, and added them to the neat pile on the dresser. As she turned to reach for her nightgown, he admired her long, muscular back and narrow waist, her athletic legs. A shimmer of pale gray satin fell like a shade to cover her.

"I don't know why you're bothering with that. I have every intention of removing it the moment you come near this bed."

Sophie ran her fingers through her short silver hair, then picked up a Kleenex and wiped off her lipstick. In the flickering light from the fireplace she suddenly looked very young and vulnerable. He held out his arms to her.

She ran to him and together they leaned back into the pillows. She nestled against his warmth and gave a tiny sigh of contentment. The breath-catching sense of wonder she'd felt at the beginning had waned. In its place now was the reassurance of something familiar and comforting. Their bodies fit together smoothly like matching pieces, concave meeting convex, hard nestling into soft, curves into smooth muscle.

As Marc's mouth made warm wet circles on hers, Richard Farwell's face, like some ghostly apparition, rose in her mind. With a murmur of annoyance she banished it.

To Marc's surprise and pleasure, Sophie began to make passionate love to him. Usually the pursued, she became the pursuer; her hands and mouth were everywhere. When they came together it was with such stunning power that Marc was filled with an emotion that left him shaken and fearful.

Later, watching the sleeping woman next to him, hearing her measured breathing, feeling her hand in his, he couldn't possibly know that tomorrow she would leave him shaken to the core and concerned for the future of their relationship.

Sam Mallory stood at her easel and looked at the slashes of paint morosely. She'd been in Aspen for two months, two months that made her wonder if she'd done the right thing in returning home.

The weekend in New York had done it to her. She'd forgotten how the city pulsed with twenty-four-hour life. With the distinguished Louis Breton at her side, she'd childishly hoped she might run into Greg just so she could flaunt and ignore him. But despite haunting his usual galleries, they never saw him. She'd even made Louis take her to the Cafe des Artistes for dinner, a place that she and Greg had practically called home, but he was not there, not expected, and in fact, the maître d' had informed her, had not been there in almost a year.

So Sam had finally given up and tried to enjoy herself. Their suite at the Mayfair Regent had a fireplace and a view of Park Avenue, and the tiny Christmas lights were still glittering on the pine trees in the median. Louis had been a perfect gentleman, which piqued her curiosity even as it brought relief. He seemed more interested in dropping names like the King of Spain, the Fendis, and Sophia Loren, celebrities reputed to stay at the charming hostelry when in town. Louis took pleasure in pointing out the columns and marble arches, the palms in Oriental tubs, the silver bowl in the lobby filled with polished red apples. He admired the elevator operators in their spotless white gloves. There were orchids and over-sized bathrobes in the bathroom. When she asked him why he was telling her all this, he had airily replied, "You might mention it to your mother. It would be a unique touch at the Silver Leaf Inn."

She had gone to FAO Schwarz and bought Tooey a Nintendo, a video-game system that cost as much as a good pair of shoes and an antique doll for Mandy's collection. Louis upbraided her for her extravagance.

She longed to go ice-skating at Rockefeller Center and clubbing at Nell's, but she knew Louis would have no interest. On the other hand, he had insisted she buy a short black lace strapless pouff she'd seen at Bergdorf's so they could go dancing at Maxim's, the New York sibling of the worldly Belle Epoque Parisian version. And in truth, there seemed to be an invasion of French-speaking habitueés dining and dancing amid the flattering pink lamps, free-form mirrors, and art nouveau woodwork. As she knew he would be, Louis proved to be a fine dancer and soon had an appreciative audience applauding them as she blindly followed him through the steps of dances which were popular before she was born.

For a while she'd forgotten everything worrisome back home, losing herself in the cloaking anonymity of the city. What she hated about Aspen she also loved: the close friendships, the small-town security, the gossip, the concern. New York seemed dirtier to her, the street people more numerous, the buildings taller, the sidewalks narrower. She missed views of mountains and blue sky. But, she reminded herself, she could eat at a different restaurant every day and still not run out of good restaurants for years. There were dozens of movies to choose from, discount drugstores, three resident ballet companies, two opera companies, and music from Mabel Mercer to Mozart. Despite Louis Breton's commendable attempt to bring culture to Aspen and the Wheeler, it couldn't measure up to New York's resources.

She threw down her brushes in annoyance and put

the kettle up for tea. As she waited for it to boil, she flipped through the pages of the *Aspen Times*. It was filled with the usual news of the latest zoning battles, accidents, parking problems, high-school basketball scores, triumphs of the Motherpuckers, the local women's hockey team—all the comfortable trivia of a small town.

Alex Breton was wasted. In the last three days he'd gotten no more than seven or eight hours of sleep. A throwback to the sixties, Alex was smart and resourceful with not an ounce of ambition or drive to achieve anything in what he called "the straight world." Rather than take a full-time job with his father, he preferred his job at the ski shop. It gave him plenty of time to do what he wanted to do. And lately what he'd wanted was to find a reliable source of the cocaine that kept him going. With increasing frequency he was leaving the daily running of the Silver Mountain Ski Shop to his pal, Skip Knowlton.

Alex was everybody's buddy. With his all-American blond looks, his phenomenal athletic ability, charm that captivated both men and women, his acceptance at all social levels, he made a perfect cocaine hustler. But unlike most who were in it for the money, Alex, who already had money, did it for the excitement. The same kind of brinkmanship that would send him soaring off a cliff in a high dive or hunt cougar and bear with a bow and arrow found him bringing blow to parties the way some people brought flowers.

Alex rarely met his suppliers face to face. His middlemen were a dishwasher at Sunshine Campbell's and the bartender at The Bottomless Pit, where he liked to hang out after hours with his friends. Spending the nights snorting cocaine and jamming on the guitar, they could go through his entire supply in an evening. And if the guys couldn't pay, so what? He could. He had a trust fund. His father might manage it, but his allowance was generous and more than supplemented his small income from the pro shop.

Last night had been a rough one. He was picking up coke tabs as if they came from a soda machine. Now he was flat broke. For the last few nights, he'd been shacked up with one of the waitresses from the Pit.

A few weeks ago, his source of supply had suddenly dried up. At first he hadn't cared. He'd always bragged that he could kick coke anytime he wanted to. But as the days wore on, he became erratic, did crazy things. One night Melanie came into the place with Joe Ferris and Alex had gone slightly nuts. But street-smart Joe had decked him with a karate chop, making him feel like a complete jerk.

Now the cocaine was available again, and in one night he'd managed to spend all his money, which meant he had to face the ogre, his father. Alex parked his Jeep in front of the Breton house. It had just won the National Design Award for Architecture. Alex hated it. It was light years away from the big rambling Victorian he had grown up in. That house had once belonged to a bootlegger, and the basement was a honeycomb of secret passages. He and his brother had grown up in those tunnels playing Dungeons and Dragons.

This new house not only looked like a modern museum, it was filled with contemporary art that put Alex's teeth on edge. It was a controversial house which suited Louis Breton mightily. A combination of circles, spheres, and triangles formed from brick, stucco, wood, concrete, and steel, it was as if the architect couldn't make up his mind which to use and so used everything. The rooms wandered off as if they had minds of their own. Walls were at angles, there were staircases everywhere connecting floors at different elevations, windows were set at crazy oblique angles.

Yet there were other rooms that contained his father's collections. Rooms that had no bearing with the modern concept of the house. Alex wondered how his iconoclastic father explained that away.

He walked into the study where his father sat, telephone to his ear. Alex could hear the unanswered ringing at the other end, could see the black clouds gathering on his father's thin ascetic face.

"Hi, Pop." He slouched into the room. "I just came by to drop off the dirty laundry and borrow a couple of bucks until Saturday. I can come back later if you're busy."

His father pretended not to hear him. In the cluttered room it was difficult to see anything. But the slashed painting on the floor stood out like a bloody body.

The receiver crashed into the phone. "Bitch," Louis Breton swore.

Alex put two and two together. The painting was Sam's, ergo his father had been trying to reach Sam. But Alex knew that Sam and the rest of her crowd were waiting for him at The Sundeck for lunch and an afternoon of skiing.

Alex waited for the storm to blow over. He took a peek at his watch and tapped his foot nervously.

His father looked up in annoyance. His eyes were icy pools of muddy water. "Where have you been for the last three days?"

Alex shrugged and scuffed a sneaker on the floor like a small boy. "Around."

"Around where? At that filthy place . . . that pit! And where have you been sleeping, or don't you bother to sleep anymore? Have you looked at yourself in a mirror recently? No, of course you haven't. The sight would frighten even you."

"Pop . . ."

"Don't call me Pop," the voice thundered. "Pop is something that southerners drink from a bottle; pop is to cause to explode or burst open; it is a sharp, explosive sound, and in your case it is to take drugs orally or by injection. But it is not your father."

Alex flushed. He knew they'd get around to the drugs. "I'm not popping," he said lamely.

"Excuse me," his father said caustically. "My error. You are sniffing or perhaps snorting is the better word. Maybe you've even graduated to smoking. That would please me even more. I understand it's a certain way to kill yourself."

"Thanks a lot. Look, if you'd just lend me some money until Saturday, you can deduct it from my check and I'll get out of your sight."

"Alex, you are twenty-four years old, you have no career, you think no further than the next five minutes, you have no future. What is to become of you?"

"You can't keep me from having my money. When I'm twenty-five, I get it all."

"If you live that long."

"Get off my back!"

"Get out of my house!"

Alex looked at him uncertainly. Was he serious? He and the old man had had dozens of fights over the years, but never before had there been such a ring of finality.

"You're a disgrace to yourself and an embarrassment to me."

"You said that once before, if you remember. Or was it twice?"

Louis's eyes narrowed. "What is that supposed to mean?"

"You don't think I know why mother walked out on you? Or why Rob killed himself? You drove them to it. Nobody can ever be good enough to suit you. You have some kind of nutty idea of perfection that only you understand. What's really going on under that pinstriped suit?"

"Spare me the penny-dreadful psychologizing. You're not clever enough to know what you're talking about."

"You'd like to believe that, I know. But remember this: you might have gotten me into Yale, but I stayed there for three years. They didn't throw me out. I left."

"It was ever thus. You always ran away from responsibility."

"And what are *you* running away from?"

Louis rose from his seat and walked around the desk to confront his son. They were about the same height, though Louis outweighed the wiry Alex by about fifteen pounds. He stared at him for a split second, then with the palm of his open hand, he slapped Alex across the face.

Alex barely flinched, yet was surprised by his father's strength. "What do you want from me?"

"I want you to stop being an adolescent. I want you to stop taking drugs and staying out all night with trash. I want you to seriously reconsider where you're headed. I want you to stop embarrassing me."

"What's the alternative?"

"Do what I ask or leave this house."

Alex turned and walked out of the room. As he started to climb the steps, Louis came running from the study. "What are you doing?"

"I'm going upstairs to pack my things. Enjoy your award-winning house . . . Father."

As Alex had said to his father, he was no dummy. He'd taken enough psych classes to know an anal/obsessive when he saw one: the preternatural neatness, the need to control and manipulate, the hunger for power and obedience. People in Aspen admired Louis Breton's charm, his charisma, his brilliant creative instincts, his wit and erudition, his taste, his life-style. They should know Louis Breton as he did. Louis Breton was poisonous snakes and killer spiders, a vulture sitting on a high branch, ready to pick apart his prey, a clever predator, a dangerous enemy.

And then he remembered the sight of Sam's painting on the floor. He knew his father all too well. Pretending to be Sam's patron saint and friend. Friendship was not his father's goal. He had to find some way to warn her to watch her step, to not take Louis's single-minded obsession as mere friendly interest.

When Alex caught up with the group at last, they had already finished lunch and were putting on their skis, headed for the Bell Mountain runs. To his surprise he found Joe Ferris with them and a vaguely familiar woman who turned out to be Rachel Fulton.

"Alex, you're late! Where've you been?" asked Sam as he pulled to a stop in a spray of snow. "Did you have lunch?"

"Didn't have time. I got trapped by a mean cat. Hi, Joe, where's Melanie?"

"How should I know?"

Sam turned away quickly and stepped into her skis. She was not interested in the answer, she was just happy to see Joe again. When Joe Ferris had suddenly appeared at The Sundeck and come over to say hello, Rosie Sukert invited him to join them. As he bantered with her friends, she was aware of his dark eyes upon her. They seemed to be pleading with her. But she ignored him. She could tolerate him being with anyone but Melanie Rogers. You idiot, she wanted to say, you think Melanie wants you? She's only after you because she thinks I'm interested in you!

Men are so ridiculous, she thought. Even the smartest of them are weak as water in the hands of a clever woman. Still, the thought of Joe's dark, sleek body entwined with Melanie's pale lushness sent her into swift flight. The further away from Joe she got, the less painful the thought would be.

For the rest of the afternoon she managed to stay quite a bit ahead or quite a bit behind the group. In the gondola she tried to sit next to Rosie, but it didn't matter, for the quarters were too close for intimate conversation. So intent was she on avoiding anything but the most casual contact with Joe, she failed to notice that Alex was desperately trying to tell her something.

It wasn't until the end of the day as they took their separate paths that Alex was able to move her out of the earshot of the others.

"Look," he said, "don't ask any questions, because I don't really have the answers. But you've got to promise me something."

"Why are you being so mysterious?" she countered.

"I said no questions. And I really hate sounding like someone in a spy story. But please, please do me a favor."

Her heart skipped a beat. Alex never behaved like this. "Of course, anything. Tell me."

"Watch out for my father."

He walked swiftly away, then turned for a moment to look at her. He nodded his head and admonished her with a finger. "Promise," he called.

She could only stare at him with openmouthed surprise.

CHAPTER THIRTEEN

SAM LOCKED HER SKIS INTO THE RACK ON HER JEEP AND changed to after-ski boots. She was tired. Skiing with the "big guys" as they called themselves was serious business. There were no stops to catch breath or admire the scenery, no one to help you up if you took a spill. There were no recreational cruising runs, only black and double-black diamonds. And that meant Jackpot, the Silver Queen, and the Elevator Shaft. But mostly it meant Bell Mountain nonstop: the Ridge, the Face, and the narrow trails of the back, all steep with deep moguls. To ski with Alex's breathless speed took fabulous technique and legs of steel. Sally Burke kept up easily; she had been an instructor. But Rosie was the amazing one. Hurtling down the mountain, she looked like a cannonball on stilts, laughable, graceless, and inexorable, but always the first down.

The last rays of the sun dropped behind the mountains and the pale mauvey-gray of twilight descended.

The trees that lined the malls wore necklaces of tiny white light. One by one they came on, enhancing the unreality, the fantasy that was Aspen in winter. Though there were no lagoons, no palazzi, no gondolas, Aspen at night held the same mystical magic of Venice.

After-ski crowds choked the streets. Delicious smells of wood smoke, garlic, hot chocolate, and barbecue sauce filled the air as Sam walked to the Silver Leaf Inn. In the midst of the laughing crowds she felt alone, but not really lonely. She wondered if her mother was happy without a man in her life, if Pat could possibly be happy living with a wife who'd rather sleep with a stranger than her husband.

She wondered, too, how many unattached females had come to Aspen, dreaming of meeting Mr. Right and ending up with a Mr. Wrong, who had left Mrs. Wrong home with the children while he went skiing with the boys.

Sam walked through the elegant lobby of the Silver Leaf Inn and headed for the Prince Albert Bar to meet her mother. The cozy clublike atmosphere came partly from the dark wood paneling and green leather chairs and partly from its magnetic attraction for Aspen's most beautiful people.

Newspapers and magazines from all over the world were arranged on convenient tables around the room. The bar's polished brass foot and arm rail had been brought over from England, having once graced The Prince and The Pauper, a Bloomsbury pub, at the turn of the century.

Sam saw her mother talking to several men at a nearby table and waved. Sophie excused herself and went to meet her daughter.

They exchanged kisses. "How was the skiing today?" she asked.

"Fast, as usual."

"Did Alex find you?"

"Yes, why?"

"I saw him earlier. He didn't appear to be very happy. He said something about being late for your date."

"You say he seemed upset? Did he say why?"

"No, I didn't ask. Was it important?"

"I don't know. He said something very cryptic when we parted."

"Good afternoon, ladies. Are we having something from the bar today?" Sam recognized the young waiter as the piano player at The Copper Kettle's late-night bar. He was one of the many people who held down two or three jobs in order to live and ski in Aspen.

"Two hot mulled wines."

When the waiter walked away, Sophie leaned toward her daughter. "You were saying? About Alex?"

"He said something strange today. He said I should be careful of his father."

"Oh." Sophie leaned back, vastly relieved. "He and Louis probably had an argument or something. You know how they are."

Sam nodded absently. "This was different. Mother, do you remember Alex's mother?"

"Of course, dear. She was related to the Cowenhovens, one of Aspen's first families. Why do you ask?"

"Do you know why she left Louis and what ever happened to her?"

Sophie frowned. There had been rampant rumors when Clarise Breton suddenly disappeared, leaving her sons behind. Talk of infidelities, violence, abusive language. "There was talk, but that's all it was. I guess the marriage was bad and she wanted out."

"But divorce was no sin in those days. Why disappear? Why not just move out and divorce the man?"

"I really don't know, dear."

"And what about his brother? The one who committed suicide?"

"Why are you suddenly so interested in the Bretons?"

"Just trying to figure something out."

As the waiter delivered their steaming drinks, they heard a voice say, "Well, here they are. The two most attractive women in Aspen. Might a lonely bachelor join you?" Louis Breton, in suede brogues, a loden cape, and Alpine hat, looked down on them with a smile. He had apparently been sitting at the bar, for he held a drink in his hand.

"Hello, Louis, we were just talking about you."

"How flattering. May one inquire about what?"

Sam gave her mother a warning look.

"Why . . . uh . . . about how we were looking forward to Mischa Dichter's concert next Saturday."

"Are you coming? How nice. I've invited the Dichters for a late supper at Gordon's afterward. Perhaps you and Samantha would like to join us?"

Sam gave her mother a gentle kick under the table.

"I'll have to let you know, Louis. I seem to remember that Sam and I made plans." She smiled through the lie with apparent ease, not failing to notice Sam's sigh of relief. "And what have you been up to besides keeping an eye on my daughter's career?"

"I'm sure she told you of our trip to New York. It was quite fruitful, I think, don't you agree, Samantha? We have an entire new perspective and direction, haven't we?"

As Louis charged along, expounding on the dynamism of New York art and how one breathed in creativity along with the automobile exhaust, Sam listened for telltale cracks in the man's armor. He was strong, opinionated, often sarcastic, definitely impatient with the mediocre. But vicious, violent, harmful?

It made no sense. Louis Breton was—if not the most well-liked—certainly one of the most respected men in town. She had never really heard a breath of scandal about him. He appeared to have no romantic ties. Even the few times he had accompanied Sam to a gallery opening or museum show, he'd been the soul of discretion.

She pulled her attention away from Louis, who was still talking, and looked at her mother. Sophie was staring intently at Louis, clinging to his every word. But Sam knew better. That glazed look of attention said Sophie was a million miles away. But Louis, aware only of her fixed, unblinking gaze, was wildly flattered. There wasn't a man who had experienced that clinging gaze without feeling convinced that the fabulous Sophie Mallory had picked him for special favors.

"Sophie, you and I must talk. I have some wonderful ideas on how you can improve attendance at some of your large fund-raising events next summer. I insist that you put me in charge of one of your committees. But I warn you, I will accept only under the condition that I am in complete charge."

Yes, thought Sam, those would be Louis's conditions. She hoped Sophie would say yes. It would take some of the pressure off her mother, give Sophie a chance to get away for a little vacation. And then she was reminded that her mother had slipped away, and quite recently, too, without saying a word. She would have to remember to ask her about that!

Louis was still droning on, the subject now his summer plans. "It's going to be our best season ever. We're having a New York Theater Festival next summer. All the national companies of the best shows have agreed to play Aspen: *Cats, A Chorus Line*, Jackie Mason, *Broadway Bound*, and *Coastal Disturbances*. I'm also negotiating for a series of cabaret evenings. I have contacted Karen Akers and Julie Wilson; Kiri Ti Kanawa has expressed an interest, and there is a good chance that Blossom Dearie will also accept."

"Now if you could get Woody Allen and his jazz

band from Michael's Pub you'd have it made," joked Sam.

"I've called Woody often, but he says he gets nose-bleeds at altitude," was Louis's serious response.

Mother and daughter exchanged quick smiles.

"Have I said something amusing?" he inquired, annoyed that they might be making fun of him.

"No, no," the women replied in unison.

Louis turned his disapproving gaze on Sam. She still wore her ski clothes. Really, she was incredibly trying and willful. An attempt to control his annoyance only set off the tic in his left eye. Trying to sound offhanded, he raised an eyebrow and queried, "Ski clothes, Samantha?"

"It's hard to ski without them," she replied with an innocent smile.

"What about your painting?"

"What about it?"

"Are you working on new things?"

She drew her shoulders up in a defensive ball. Louis had been relentless that weekend in New York. They had whipped through the MOMA and the Whitney, the Madison Avenue galleries, and the SoHo and Tribeca ateliers. Louis was in his element, pointing out the monumentality of the work being done, telling her that she had to broaden her perspectives, unconfine herself, be heroic.

While her palette tended to few colors handled in an impressionistic style, the new artists worked in clashing primaries, acrylics, and enamels. To add textural interest, those painters added broken crockery and glass, nails, burlap, torn newspaper, anything that would break up those glossy mirrored surfaces. It made for a dynamic kind of dissonance that gave Sam both a headache and a sinking heart.

Louis was obviously right about her work. It was too soft, too regional, too female. She was not in the mainstream.

If she wanted to be a serious painter, he'd said, she'd have to stop being a "Sunday painter."

"Samantha," she heard her name being called sharply. "Where have you been? I asked you a question. Have you started to work on new things?"

"Certainly. I just took the day off. All my friends were free, so we went skiing. Alex, too."

At the mention of his son's name, Louis's face tightened with distaste. He was about to say something, but thinking better of it, snapped his mouth shut. He tossed the rest of his drink down, then said to Sam, "I have been giving it a great deal of thought, and I've come up with some new directional ideas for your work. But you don't have a lot of time," he warned. "I shall be at your studio tomorrow to discuss them with you."

"But, Louis . . . ," she tried to protest.

"No buts," he said firmly.

There was nothing Sam could say. The pattern had already been established. By giving him her gratitude for his help, she had also tacitly given him carte blanche to run her artistic career. In his commanding presence, she felt vulnerable and unsure of her talent.

At a sudden flurry of commotion, Louis looked up. "Ah, the prodigal returns."

The two women turned to the door to see Alex, surrounded by Rosie, Sukie Porter, Sally Burke, Bill Pugh, and Sunshine Campbell, walk through the bar on their way to the Grill Room.

Alex paused for an instant and looked around. When his eyes met his father's he flushed, but good manners dictated he say hello to Sophie Mallory.

He sauntered over and bent to kiss Sophie on the cheek.

"I'd be careful if I were you, Sophie. God knows where my son's lips have been in the last few nights," warned Louis in a voice that tried to sound light and amusing but was instead etched in acid.

"Louis!" Sophie was shocked.

"I'm sorry to appear so crass, but what would you surmise when your son doesn't come home for nights on end?"

"Jesus, Dad, do we have to discuss this in public?"

"Louis, he's twenty-four years old! Where he goes is his problem, not yours, I should think." As if to indicate where her sympathies lay, Sophie put her hand on Alex's and gave it a squeeze.

"Don't you think a son who still receives an allowance from his father, who wastes his time in frivolous pursuits with unimportant people, and who still behaves like an adolescent should be treated as such?"

"Really, Louis, I think that this is neither the time nor the place for this discussion."

As Sophie and Louis continued their embarrassing exchange, Alex's eyes never left Sam's. "Sam, I have to talk to you," he said softly, urgently.

"I don't think you have anything to say that could be of interest to her." Louis's sharp ears picked up his son's words.

Sam blanched. He was going too far. "I'm quite capable of talking to Alex without your interference," she answered tartly.

"Samantha, I implore you to listen to reason."

"I don't know what's going on between you two," said Sophie, "but that's your affair. If Sam wants to speak to Alex, I doubt if anything you have to say would stop her."

"Thank you, Mother."

"Very well, then." Louis rose stiffly. "I shall see you tomorrow, Samantha. At precisely ten A.M." He stalked from the room, a king grown tired of his unruly subjects.

Meanwhile at a table for six in the Grill Room, the conversation revolved around one of the group's good friends.

"Maggy is really a cunt," said Rosie. "She doesn't

let that poor husband of hers take a breath without her checking it out."

"Do we really have to talk about Maggy?" asked Stoney. "No one has a good word to say about her, but I notice we never turn down her invitations to a party."

"I'm worried about Sam." Sukie Porter offered up a new subject for group discussion.

"Why?"

"I don't think she's happy. I never see her with anyone these days except Louis Breton. Yeck! How can she stand that faggot?"

"He's not a faggot and you know it. He's just a creep," said Rosie.

"Alex told me he's left home for good."

"Where's he living?"

"I told him he could stay at my place," said Sukie.

"Our Lady of Perpetual Care," razzed Rosie.

"So what? I have enough room."

"Honey, you have enough room to put up the first and second team of the Denver Broncos."

"Well, I don't mind. It gets lonely in that big house."

"What's Mama got to say about that?"

"She's in Cuernavaca."

"Who's she with this time?"

"I'm not sure."

"What happened to the bullfighter?" asked Sally.

"Oh, you didn't hear? Mrs. Porter delivered the coup de grâce. He died with a smile on his face," reported Rosie.

"Oh, my heavenly stars and stripes," cried Sukie. "Look who just walked in! And alone. I can't believe my eyes!"

Six pairs of eyes swung about and watched Liz Mallory, in a white cashmere jumpsuit and white boots, enter the room, pause, and look around. She dragged a lynx coat behind her.

"Who's she looking for?" asked Sukie.

"Does it matter?" whispered Rosie.

"I thought they played 'Hail to the Chief' when she walked in," Bill mumbled.

"No," said Sunshine, "they save that for Pat."

The harassed maître d' rushed to Liz to show her to a small table overlooking the inside garden.

"I have to say one thing," said Bill Pugh. "She's a beautiful woman."

"You don't have to say that at all." Rosie gave him a poke in the ribs. "You don't even have to think it."

"I don't know how she lives with herself," said Sunshine.

"You mean you don't know how Pat lives with her."

"I'll tell you one thing, if I was doing my bedroom over, I'd go to her," said Sukie earnestly.

"Why? Because she's the best decorator in town?" asked Sunshine.

"No," Rosie cracked, "because she's got the most experience with bedrooms."

"Do you think Pat knew about her and Joe Ferris?"

"If he didn't, he was the only one in town."

"And it used to be the wife who was the last to know," sighed Sukie from the heart.

"Who cares about Pat Mallory?" said Sunshine. "He's getting what he deserves."

"Watch it, Sunshine. Sam's a good friend. And somebody should tell Pat about his wife," said Sukie.

"Late flash on Liz," interrupted Rosie. "Rumor has it that Count di Lucca is in. Literally."

"How do you find these things out, Rosie?"

"It's my job, ma'am."

Sunshine, who'd been staring at Liz, shook her head and gave a little laugh. "I just figured out why Liz Mallory likes this place."

"She eats for free?"

"No, the mirrors. She hasn't stopped looking at herself since she came in."

"Y'all can have your bitchy reasons for not liking her. The reason I think she's so hateful is 'cause she doesn't give one ounce of her time to a single charity. She's always too busy. I know it upsets Sophie, not that she's complained outright, but I can tell." Sukie, Texas-rich and lonely, volunteered to help with anything and everything. On Thanksgiving, she went to Denver and cooked for the homeless who flocked to the Salvation Army. Her house was a hospital for anything wounded, animal or human.

"Oh, oh, the plot thickens. Look who's just walked in!"

"Who? I don't dare turn around again," said Sukie.

"Joe Ferris!"

"Alone?"

"Alone."

"What's he doing, Bill? You're looking straight at him."

"He's waiting. Oh, he just caught sight of Liz. She sees him in the mirror."

"And . . ."

"She's waving to him. He's walking over to her. Looks like she's invited him to sit down."

"And you think this is just an accident?" Rosie smirked.

"Listen, if she's able to get Pat Mallory, Joe Ferris, and Gianfranco di Lucca in her bed, I have to hand it to her," said Bill in admiration.

The conversation grew raunchy as Rosie painted lurid pictures of Liz Mallory and her lovers in singles, pairs, and trios. There was a great deal of laughter, but much of it was forced.

When Sophie and Sam walked in a few minutes later for dinner, the laughter had changed to a slow conversational hum as the table settled down to enjoy the thick, grilled veal chops and wild rice that were specialties of the restaurant.

"What did Alex want, dear?" Sophie's corner table

allowed her a complete view of the room so she could observe the service without herself being observed.

"The same thing, Mother. Only he was really insistent."

"Did he go into detail?"

"No, he wouldn't. He just said his father was not to be trusted. I don't know what to do. There's something going on between Louis and Alex, and I seem to be caught in the middle. Maybe you're right about Alex only overreacting. I hope so. I guess I'll . . ." Sam looked up and stopped in midsentence when she saw Joe Ferris and Liz together.

"You guess you'll what, dear?"

Sam turned her attention back to her mother and asked abruptly, "Where's Pat tonight?"

Sophie shrugged. "I'm not sure. He usually takes the children to the movies on Tuesdays. Why?"

"Don't look now, but Liz is over there with Joe Ferris. What on earth would Liz be doing with Joe Ferris?"

That was a question Sophie had been asking herself ever since she'd first heard the rumors about her daughter-in-law and the manager of the Silver Mountain Resort. As much as Pat tried to cover it up, Sophie was only too aware of the deteriorating state of the Mallorys marriage. Was Joe Ferris one of the reasons? Or had he been just another of Liz's poisonous darts aimed at Pat? Why was Liz so hateful? A surprisingly fierce maternal need to protect Pat rushed through her.

Sam looked as if she were about to cry. And then Sophie remembered the night Pat told her he'd seen Sam and Joe together several times. What was going on? Was Joe Ferris trying to sleep with all the Mallory women? Sophie squelched a desire to go over to the table and just throw the man out.

What on earth would Liz be doing with Joe Ferris? Sam thought again. And what are they talking about?

The two women would have found the conversation surprising.

"To what do I owe the pleasure?" Joe asked with lazy insolence. "Have you run out of game?"

"You should know better than that, Joe. Are we just a wee bit jealous?"

"You have to care a great deal to be jealous. Let's face it, Liz, love is not what brought us together."

"What's bringing you and the malicious Melanie together?" Liz scratched his hand with a sharp red fingernail.

"I suppose the same thing that brought you and di Lucca together."

She withdrew her hand abruptly. "Don't be silly. I'm decorating a house for him, that's all."

"Liz, who are you kidding? Remember, I know your tricks. I know your car. I know your hours."

"Have you been spying on me?" Then she laughed. "Hell hath no fury like a—"

"—a woman scorned," Joe finished for her with a mocking smile. "Anyway, what do you want?" At her look of surprised innocence, he reminded, "You were the one who summoned me."

She abruptly switched tactics. "Joe, let's not quarrel. After all, we did have something between us not so long ago. It was pretty good. You have to admit that."

"I think you're confusing sex with intimacy again. What do you want?"

"Tell me . . . what's happening between Pat and Richard Farwell?"

"I couldn't begin to tell you."

"Couldn't or won't?"

"I have no idea if there's anything going on. Why do you want to know?"

"No special reason. Just curiosity," she said.

But Joe knew Liz Mallory better than that. She was after information. But what kind and for what purpose he couldn't begin to guess.

"Rumor has it that your lover and your husband have their heads together over some deal." He searched her face for some reaction to that fact. "Must give you a terrific high to be caught in the middle."

Liz's answer was to summon the waiter to bring her another drink. "Join me for dinner? For old time's sake?"

"Sorry. I see my date has just walked in. If you'll excuse me?" He was grossly polite. As he turned to join Melanie at the bar, he saw Sam sitting with her mother. The look of confused hurt on Sam's face was almost more than he could bear. Whatever he felt, however, lay hidden behind the hooded curtain of his eyes. Feigning indifference was the only way he knew to protect Sam from the consequences of his life. He had shut her out, treated her as if she were nothing more than a one-night stand. It had been a cruel thing to do, but he didn't know any other way to protect her. He nodded coolly in mother and daughter's direction, then went to greet Melanie.

Rachel Fulton had never had a close woman friend before. As a beloved only child of two intellectuals, she'd been raised in the company of adults. At age five she was reading at the level of an eight-year-old. Trilingual, able since childhood to prattle away in French, Italian, and English, her precocity won her a coveted place at the prestigious Hunter Day School where the competition was formidable and friendships were made with difficulty. Her best friends had been her parents until they both died within a year of one another, leaving her terrifyingly alone.

She married the first man who came into her adult life, a Columbia professor of mathematics, twenty years her senior. They were divorced a few years later.

Once again she was faced with picking up the pieces after an unbearable loss. A motherly female psychiatrist helped set her feet on the path that led her from a job as editor to the successful writer she now was.

Sam's offer of friendship had not only touched her but warmed her. *"Muy simpático,"* Sam had said, and the seven years' difference in their ages had proved insignificant. In many ways Sam was far more sophisticated than Rachel, yet strangely frightened and insecure about the direction her life was taking. It was a contradiction that Rachel found puzzling. If nothing else, Rachel knew that her own life was firmly tied to her writing. Nothing—including an unhappy love affair or an absence of romance in her life—could take that satisfaction away. Sam, too, had to find that in her painting.

Rachel's fascination with the Mallory family continued to grow as her researches uncovered more and more stories of the early MacNeals. Like the other famous robber barons of America: the Astors, the Goulds, and the Rockefellers, the MacNeal family had been first cursed and reviled, then hated and feared until time and philanthropy finally brought them respectability and veneration.

The little she knew about Pat Mallory led her to believe that he shared many of the characteristics of old Black Devil Gerald, as his ancestor had been called behind his back. Yet there was something else about Pat that she found provocative. Although she was not immune to his physical beauty, there was more to him than that. He had wit and humor, two qualities she found absolutely necessary in anyone, male or female.

Satisfying as it might be, her friendship with Sam carried another aspect: the unexpected delight of Pat's company. When Pat and Sam were not at war with each other, they were close and loving, dropping in often to see Rachel and share a cup of tea with her at day's end.

They'd both taken a great interest in her new book,

sending her off to talk or to read about someone who could give her work the authentic historical background that gave her novels such a feeling of immediacy.

One day had found her off to Leadville to speak to a great-grandson of Horace Tabor, the great silver baron and husband of the legendary Baby Doe. Another time she braved a snowstorm to drive to Basalt to talk to an old hard-rock miner in his nineties. He had a head full of dim, idealized memories and a sharp tongue. From him she learned that miners' clothes were called "diggers," that they "took the ski" to go underground to drill and "shoot" (loosen rock with explosives). He told her with pride that he'd never been a green "mucker" (a mere shoveler) but the "shifter" (the foreman), and he was proud to be a hard-rock miner instead of one of those "hayshakers" that worked on the surface.

Rachel had loved the colorful expressions as well as the fusty old boy himself. She trotted out a bottle of rye in appreciation. By the time he'd put away half of it, he deigned to show her his collection of fool's gold. The pyrite chunks of iron and sulphur seemed to have all the glitter of gold and she learned they might indeed even contain some, though it was unlikely. He took her into a small room off the parlor. It was empty save for a glass case filled with chunks of rocks.

"Don't look like nothin' much, do they?" he asked rhetorically. "Watch 'em." He turned off the light that illuminated the case. Suddenly out of the blackness the rocks came to glowing life, fluorescing purple, rose, yellow, white, and blue.

"A lot purtier than gold, ain't they?" he said softly.

Each experience became more and more treasured as she met these disappearing keepers of the legendary myths that America still found so compelling. No war, no glory, no feat of mind or body had ever filled a country's need for heroes the way the old West had.

England had its King Arthur, France its Napoleon, Germany its gods of the Ring, but America had its cowboys.

When Sunshine Campbell discovered from Sam what Rachel was working on, she'd discussed it with Hank and found him curious to meet a "gen-yew-ine" writer. After all, he'd been a miner and a rancher, too. He knew the legends and stories from both camps. So, through Sam, Rachel met Sunshine's father. The day of Rachel's first visit he'd put on his best blue corduroy pants, flannel shirt, and Sunday suspenders. His tangled pewter-gray curls lay wetly slicked back on his head. As the heat from the fireplace dried them, they popped out like broken springs from a mattress.

Every week Sam, Rachel, and Sunshine would pay Hank a visit, bringing him sugary doughnuts from Fry By Night and a six-pack of Bud. He couldn't abide Coors, saying it tasted like cow piss.

This Friday it was snowing lightly outside. The old potbelly stove hissed and crackled as Hank sat in his chair, smoking the cigarettes he couldn't give up. He was remembering the early forties and the days at Camp Hale; how dull and dreary it was even with the PXs and the movies. "It was a cold, smoggy, flat valley at the foot of Tennessee Pass. We usually ended up in Leadville or Glenwood. Glenwood was nice and neat. They had the springs there, you know. Could burn the bejeesus out of your butt, if you didn't handle it just right. Anyways, some of the boys wanted to try skiing over in Aspen. So I showed 'em the way. The road had more twists than a snake on a flat rock and wasn't paved worth a damn. And o' course we had the gas rationing. I tell you it weren't so pretty then. Oh, you could see where it might have been nice once. But there was a whole bunch of trashed, burnt-out buildings. The Hotel Jerome was still standin', though, and we all would head up there. They had a drink they called the Aspen Crud." He made a horrible face. "Kind of a bourbon milkshake. Dinner cost fifty cents, so did a bed.

"When I come back after the war, I bought me three vacant lots in the West End. Paid about thirty dollars each for 'em. The ranch had gone to rack and ruin with no one to take care of it." He remembered how disappointed he'd been. "You wasn't even born yet, Val. Anyway, I sold off my lots. You can guess who bought 'em," he said wryly.

"My mother," Sam guessed.

"Right you are, girl. Paid me a couple of hundred bucks. Shoulda been suspicious she gave me so much. She knew. She was a MacNeal. They always had a nose for business."

"Oh, Pa, do we have to hear the story again? Besides Sam's company, and she doesn't like what's going on in the valley any more than you do."

"Neither does my mother."

"Sure, she owns half of the town already. And what she doesn't, either your brother or Farwell does."

Sam flushed. "Hank, if it's any comfort, I'm dead set against my brother's development schemes."

"Mr. Campbell, excuse me," Rachel's honeyed voice interrupted. "I'd love to hear more of your old stories."

Hank's tough old face softened when he looked at Rachel. It was obvious that he felt great affection for the small woman with the big bright eyes who sat quietly on a stool like an enraptured child as he spun his yarns.

"Well," he began, "did I tell you the one about the drunk?"

"No," came the cries from three throats.

"There was this old miner, went by the name of Happy Jack. They called him that 'cause he was always drunker'n a skunk with a snootful. Damn old boy could rattle off poetry like a professor though. And the drunker he got, the better he recited. Used to

lean up against the bar of the old Abbey Saloon—
that's where the Wheeler Block is now—toss down
the drink and recite some Shakespeare or maybe some
Byron. Didn't matter, he knew 'em all even though
nobody else did. He was smarter'n a whip. Man was
educated, you see. One day ole Doc Sanders said,
'Smart man like you, Jack. Why don't you sober up?'
Ole Jack took off his Stetson, scratched his head a
mite, and said, 'I would, doc, but it'd take too durn
much time to get drunk again.'"

They roared. Hank who'd told the story a hundred
times told it better each time and got the same kick
out of it.

"Now, Rachel, I know you're keen on gettin' into
one of them mines that crisscross the mountains
round about. But I warn you, it's dangerous."

"Oh, I'd never go into an abandoned mine alone,"
she assured him.

"No, I don't mean that. I mean ghosts."

She smiled and got ready for another story.

"Mark my words." He lit his corncob pipe and
leaned back in his rocker. "My granddaddy was out
walking one day up yonder when he found an abandoned mine. Well, he climbed down Conundrum
Gulch at the side where it separates from Maroon
Gulch. And what does he see but this real big cavern.
Well, he looks around real nervous-like. Calls out, but
there's no answer. So he goes up a little closer. Then
he sees these sacks. Well, they was full of rich ore. And
the minute he touched one, it just fell apart in his
hand. So he staked a claim and took himself a hunk of
the ore to have assayed. He wondered who could have
abandoned the claim and why. When he got to town
he checked it out. Nobody had ever registered the
claim. He had the ore assayed, and it was almost
ninety-two-percent pure. So he hightailed it back to
the cave. When he got there, what do you think?"

They were like children—spellbound. Sunshine
knew but she kept her mouth shut.

"It was gone. Not a sack or crumb left. Just disappeared. Like that." He snapped his fingers and they awoke as though from a hypnotic sleep.

"Yeah, there be plenty of them stories. Some of 'em's funny. Most ain't. I mean, they sound funny now, but you can imagine back then what it was like. You heard me talk about the old Smuggler Mine? It poured silver like Niagara pours water. Well, once that claim belonged to a fella, can't remember his name. Anyways, he sold it for fifty dollars and a mule. Fifty dollars! And the mule died. So there he was sittin' on millions and couldn't do a damn thing about it. It's the story of my life."

Held in thrall until the sound of the coffeepot running over on the sizzling hot plate of the wood stove broke the spell, they all leaped at the same time to pull it off the fire.

Sunshine pulled mugs from the cupboard and was just about to fill them when there was a knock on the door. She went to answer it.

Pat Mallory, a frosting of snow on his blue parka, came in on a gust of frigid air. "It's really cold out there." He went to the wood stove and held his hands over it, rubbing and blowing them to get warm.

"Don't recollect you bein' invited, Mallory," Hank growled.

Pat smiled nervously. "I noticed Sam's car outside and thought I'd stop and say hello. Hello, everyone."

Then he saw Rachel, who'd returned to her stool and was now looking at him with an unfathomable expression. "Oh, Rachel, I didn't notice you sitting over there. How's your ghost?"

"Quiet," she smiled. "She must like writers."

"What's this about a ghost?" asked Sam.

Rachel and Pat, interrupting each other in their eagerness, told the story as Hank rocked furiously in his chair and harrumphed. Bad enough Pat Mallory had forced his way into the house, now he was spinnin' yarns, too!

Pat's warm smile included the old fellow, but Hank wasn't buying. "Sure would appreciate it if you just left. Less'n it was your sister you came to see. Know it wasn't my daughter."

"Actually, Hank, it was you I wanted to talk to. I have a deal for you."

"Not interested in none of your deals," he growled.

"Be that as it may, can I tell you what it is?" Pat was like a small boy who had memorized a poem for class and was determined to recite it even though the teacher wasn't calling on him.

"Sure, you can tell if you want, but I ain't listenin'. If you like the sound of your own voice, be my guest."

The old boy was really a classic, thought Pat. He wasn't sure how much was contrariness and how much was showing off for the ladies.

"Okay, Hank, here's the deal. If you sell me your land, I will give you—give you, I said—one of the best condominiums in Aspen free, and that includes all your utilities, your telephone, and a four-wheel-drive vehicle so you can get around."

"You call that a deal?" said Hank disdainfully, knowing it was.

"Yeah," said Pat. "A damn good one."

"Damn bribe is what it is. Not interested, Mallory."

"Now hold on, Hank," said Sunshine. "Maybe you ought to consider it." She knew what it was costing them to hold on to the property. Her father was a sick man and soon he'd be unable to do even the few chores he insisted on doing. Though she loved the meadows and mountains around it, she hated the idea of her father struggling alone on the ranch. Maybe fighting to preserve it was just foolish.

"Not you, too, daughter?" Hank's tired face collapsed into the familiar road map of grim lines. "I thought you was with me on this."

Sam and Rachel were surprised, too. Sunshine had been so vocal against Pat's relentless pursuit of the ranch. Now it appeared she was giving up.

"I don't know anymore, Hank. I just don't know. It's such a fight."

Hank stared into the fire. "Nothin's changed. The MacNeals are still out to get the Campbells. Seems like everything we have, they want."

There was an uncomfortable silence. Pat's face was tight and unreadable. Sam felt sad. Rachel knew that no writer's art could capture the reality of moments like these.

Rachel sighed and stood up. Going to Hank, she looked down at him for a moment, then bent down until her face touched his. "Thank you so much for everything, Mr. Campbell. I should be getting back."

Caught in some corner of his memory, he appeared not to hear her. She let her hand rest on his shoulder for a moment, then took her coat from a peg, said good-bye, and left.

The silence stretched between them.

"Sunshine," Pat was shocked at the pleading in his own voice.

She shrugged and shook her head.

Silently Sam and Pat gathered their things together and left. Sunshine went back to the sink to pour Hank a cup of coffee. There was a loud snap and a log burst into a shower of blue sparks before settling in the grate where it faded to gray ash.

Pat drove around aimlessly after he left the Castle Creek Road, feeling an acute frustration. He had tried everything he knew to get Hank's land from him legally and fairly. The only thing to do now was to see if there were liens against the property. Hank had been given the land outright, but the ranch had been totally rebuilt about thirty years ago. Was it possible that Hank still had a mortgage outstanding? Or maybe he had used it for collateral to make a loan for livestock. If it were true, and he could foreclose, he'd still offer the old man the free condo. The thought eased his guilt somewhat, but Pat wasn't heartless, and he also knew that anything done against the popular old rancher would set the town against him. How did it all get so complicated? If he didn't develop the land, no doubt some stranger would. At least, they could depend on him to put up something that was harmonious and environmentally practical. Why couldn't anyone see that? At least his mother and sister should recognize the sense of his reasoning—and trust him to do the right thing. Instead—they seemed to regard him as a villain.

Finding himself in the West End, he drove slowly up and down the silent, snowy streets. Christmas lights still glowed in windows, and wreaths still hung on doors. As far as Aspen was concerned, it would be the holiday season until the snow melted. The lights were on in Sam's house, but there was no sign of her car.

He shifted into first and continued his aimless wandering over the streets of the West End. Without being aware of it he found himself in front of the dark, gloomy Victorian property upon which sat Rachel's rented dollhouse. It was shrouded in darkness. Only the contrast of dark bulk against the silvery white of the snow indicated its presence. It had stopped snowing and the fine crystals lay upon the old snow like a careless scattering of diamonds.

Pat had always loved the freedom of living in Aspen. Of taking off on a weekday when the powder was lying deep and fluffy to carve lazy esses in the pristine white. Of riding the thermals in a glider on a flawless summer day. Of running slalom through the highest peaks in his plane. Of disappearing into the backcountry with a sleeping bag and spending the night night under the star-studded, high-desert sky.

Now he felt the mountains that bulked like pale walls on every side close in on him. He felt trapped. His marriage was a joke. His business was stymied. He and Sam were speaking again, but the gulf was still there and widening weekly. The golden boy was beginning to tarnish around the edges. He was tired and heartsick. He wanted to run away from home like a little kid, "eat worms and die and then you'll all be sorry" as the old refrain went.

Pat was too wrapped up in his own misery to realize that he wasn't trying to run away from something, but toward something.

CHAPTER FOURTEEN

PAT MALLORY SLIPPED HIS FAVORITE STANLEY JORDAN tape into the tape deck. The mellow guitar poured forth "The Lady in My Life," a moody, bluesy piece that showed the dexterity and musicality of the young musician. It was perfect driving music, so he headed in the direction of Basalt to find himself a dark bar where he could drink in solitary splendor among strangers.

But as lachrymose as his feelings might be, his basic practicality prevailed. Getting drunk and driving back on Killer 82 could easily end in an accident and, with his luck, he'd get by without a scratch while somebody else could be seriously hurt.

He turned the car around at Brush Creek Road and headed back toward Aspen. But he wasn't ready to go home to the big empty house on the mountain. The kids were at a hockey game at the Ice Palace and would be driven home by one of their friends' parents.

Liz was most likely out, and even if she were home, they had little to say to one another. A few weeks ago they'd declared a temporary truce, even gone out to a pleasant dinner at Syzygy where they'd shared a cassoulet of oysters and celery-root pancakes and a pair of perfectly prepared quail. Liz had shown the first interest in months in his plans, making insightful comments about Richard Farwell, asking tough questions about Gianfranco di Lucca. They'd even made love that night. Feeling cocky and protected by the sanctity of his marital bed, he'd confided his intent to purchase a handful of soon-to-be foreclosed properties. For a moment he felt they had returned to the good days. But as he held her he could feel her body tense, and shortly after she had rolled to the other side and fallen asleep. The next day the demilitarized zone had again been raised between them.

He supposed he could stop and visit his mother, but he had nothing to say to her, either. Their last few meetings had started promisingly enough but as usual deteriorated the minute the conversation turned to real estate. And in Aspen that's where it inevitably turned; although since the October crash the conversations had grown increasingly sober. There was a lot less braggadocio, millions of dollars were not being thrown around with quite the same pre-crash abandon, and the entire community was waiting to see how prices would be affected. The talk was that Vail had already posted a decline of 20 percent.

Pat knew they would weather the storm. Silver Mountain Corp. itself owned resorts in many parts of the world and was now selling franchises for its ski school and tennis camps; Silver Mountain Ski Shops were situated all over the country in major skiing cities as well as ski resorts; Silver Mountain Skiwear was a major brand and particularly hot in Europe. Long ago Pat had secured the family fortunes by keeping his outside investments as liquid as possible and by being basically conservative in his investment choices. His realty firm was the largest in the Roaring Fork, and even with a decline, he would not suffer.

To an outsider—even to his family—it would seem that Pat Mallory had things under control. Even when he felt most insecure, he gave off reassuring waves of self-confidence. He had learned at an early age to keep his problems and his anguish buried. The technique had worked well enough to get him through school and college and into business with a suitcase full of charm, a good-natured outlook, and an attractive kind of machoness that offended no one. But he was approaching his thirty-fifth birthday and he'd never felt so alone in his life.

As he swung around Seventh Street to Main, he noticed the inviting log-cabin atmosphere of The Hickory House. His mouth watered at the thought of a side of smoky barbecued ribs, fat, greasy french fries, and a tangy bowl of cole slaw. He pulled his vehicle into the curb and parked between two battered pick-ups.

Inside it was noisy and smoky. The bar was crowded with big, burly men in heavy plaid shirts and duck-billed hats, drinking beer and wolfing down pretzels. Almost every table was filled with young local families whose one night out always had to include the kids. Many of the women held sleeping babies in canvas slings as they ate, the rhythm of their breathing a surrogate rocking chair.

The place was as rustic as Aspen got, with bare floors and red-and-white oilcloth-covered tables containing red and yellow squeeze bottles of catsup and mustard, a dispenser of paper napkins and plastic salt and pepper shakers. Nobody complained when the catsup bottles got messy, they just wiped them off with a paper napkin.

Pat eased into the only remaining stool at the bar and looked around.

At a round table of grizzled old-timers he saw a

slender figure with short dark hair. At first he thought it might be someone's grandson, but the shoulders were too narrow, the whole body too delicate. The plaid shirt seemed familiar to him. Where had he seen it? Then he remembered Rachel Fulton, tucked into a corner of Hank Campbell's living room earlier. He could see her as clearly as if she were standing directly in front of him. The bright yellow turtleneck, the plaid shirt, the beige corduroy trousers held up by bright red suspenders. She'd looked like any one of the high-school students he saw every day.

The old boys were having a field day, each interrupting the other to be the first to tell a yarn or embellish another man's story with some little-known fact of his own, slyly winking in hope of gaining a smile and her approval. There was much laughter and goodwill around that table and Pat felt a pang as he watched. Never in a million years would he be able to enjoy that kind of camaraderie with those men. If he were to walk over there and say hello, they would politely invite him to join them, but the good-natured teasing would stop, the laughter would become restrained, the conversation forced and monosyllabic until one by one they would excuse themselves and drift away.

What was there about Rachel Fulton that prompted these tough, gnarled men with characters forged in the icy furnaces of high-mountain winters and drought-ridden summers to forget their gruff ways and turn into boys with slicked-down hair on a Saturday night dance? Were they hoping for a little immortality in one of her books? No, it was more than that, he knew. He'd sensed it right away. It was her gentle acceptance, her reticence, her utter lack of pretense and guile.

From his hidden perch he watched in fascination as she handled them, watched their respect and obvious affection for her display itself in a dozen surprising ways.

Finally she rose and told them she had to leave. There was a chorus of "oh, no" and "we wuz jus' gittin' warmed up." But with a warm smile that wreathed their own faces in broad smiles, she apologized and promised to be back next week for another go-round.

She shrugged into her sheepskin coat and headed for the door. Pat quickly threw some money on the bar, picked up his own sheepskin, and hurried out.

When he got outside he heard the sputtering sound of her car trying to kick over. It made that retching "ooga ooga" sound that meant last rites for a dying battery, and then it quietly went to its rest.

Rachel opened the door and stepped out. "Damn it, car, did you have to pick this minute to die?" She kicked at the wheels. He heard her say "ouch." As she turned to go back into the restaurant, he stepped into her path.

She was about to scream when she recognized him. "Pat Mallory. You almost frightened me to death. What are you doing here?"

"I came to rescue you from the dreaded dead-battery plague. Can I give you a lift home?"

"That's really nice of you, but I'm not going home."

The smile vanished from his face. Seeing his crestfallen look, she hastened to add, "I have to be at the high school. I'm giving a writer's workshop tonight."

"Then I'll drive you over."

"I hate to bother you."

"No bother at all. My Jeep's over here."

She went back to her own car and picked up a briefcase. "Short stories," she explained. "We're discussing them in class tonight."

He led her to his Jeep and helped her in.

Getting in on his side, he said, "Any undiscovered talent there?"

"You'd be surprised."

"I bet."

"You know Grace Carmody at your mother's inn?"

"Is she one of the waitresses in the Prince Albert?"

"No, the Mollie Gibson room. But it doesn't matter. She's got a beautiful feeling for poetic imagery."

"Really?"

"I'm always amused when people respond that way."

"What way?"

"As if the only people who can write are the ones that graduate from college with a degree in English. You'd be surprised how many really good writers didn't have those advantages. Take Grace. She's very ambitious, she went to the Mortimer Adler Great Books seminar one summer, and from that point on she was hooked on literature. She writes very movingly about this world around her. I'm planning to send some of her work on to my agent."

"You're that interested?"

"Of course. Why would I waste very valuable time teaching if I weren't?"

"There are a lot of writers who live here full time who wouldn't take the trouble."

She shrugged. "I guess that's their privilege."

He headed back on 82 and turned up toward the Maroon Creek Road. The high school, an award-winning design of Fritz Benedict, nestled comfortably into the undulating foothills.

As he came around to help her out, he stayed her with his hand. "Have dinner with me later?" His voice was casual but his eyes sent out a special plea.

She hesitated for the slightest moment, long enough to bring down a look of such bleakness on Pat's face, she felt her heart contract.

She smiled sympathetically. "Why don't you come to my house? About nine-thirty if that's not too late?"

"How will you get home?"

"I'm sure someone will give me a ride."

"Red wine or white?"

She was nonplussed for a moment. "Oh, whatever you like. It'll probably just be pasta and a salad."

"Give me the keys to your car. I'll take care of it and see you later."

Rachel filled a large pot with water and put it on the stove to boil. Opening the refrigerator, she gave a baleful look at her collection of salad greens. She missed her New York greengrocer; there she'd been able to find all the out-of-season greens she loved: mache, radicchio, arugula.

Arriving home only a few minutes earlier, she'd barely had enough time to shower and change into something a little more festive. Her hair, still wet from the shower, clung to her head in a crown of tangled ringlets. In the black sweater and velvet pants, with her bare face, she looked like a teenager.

A few minutes later, Pat arrived bearing a '78 Cotes-du-Rhône and an '83 Chablis Premier Cru, a chocolate gateau studded with fresh raspberries which he had bribed Gordon Naccarato to sell him, and a loaf of sourdough bread.

Rachel took the things from his arms as he divested himself of his coat and followed her into the kitchen. He carried two books in his hand. Seeing the array of ingredients, he offered his help, telling her that he made salads that were famous for miles around.

"You've done enough just attending to my car. Just sit down and talk to me. You might open the wine and pour me a glass." She fussed about, eyes averted, feeling suddenly nervous. When she looked up he was reading the flyleaf of a book; another sat on the counter. "What are you reading?"

He closed the book so she could see the cover.

"That's my book!"

"So's this."

"Where did you find them? *Brother Eagle* went into paperback a few years ago. I didn't think there were any hard covers left."

"The Unicorn found them for me."

"You haven't read them, I guess."

"Not yet, but I plan to."

"It's not required."

"I want to." He watched her nimble fingers at work. "You find it difficult to take a compliment, don't you?"

She blushed.

Sensing her discomfort and knowing his presence was its cause, he got up and strolled around the roomy kitchen. "You've really made this place yours."

"Oh, you can do a lot with a few cookbooks and some flowers."

"Don't be so modest."

He pulled the foil from the bottle and removed the cork. Pouring a finger into the wineglass she handed him, he sniffed, swirled, sniffed again, then took a mouthful. Closing his eyes, he chewed, savored, then pronounced it "eminently drinkable."

"You did that very well," she complimented and accepted her glass. "Mmm, lovely. I better hurry with dinner. One of these on an empty stomach and Lord knows what you'll get."

"I can't imagine you doing anything badly."

She pretended not to hear him. Turning to the vegetables on the chopping board, she proceeded to julienne red and yellow peppers as if she were a surgeon. Snow peas, carrots, and broccoli went under the same careful knife. She poured olive oil into a glass measuring cup, then held it up to the light to read the measure.

"Alas, poor Yorick, I knew him well . . . ," quipped Pat.

She burst into laughter. "Whatever do you mean?"

"Do you know who you look like in that black outfit with your hair lying in adorable ringlets all over your face? You look like Hamlet. Will you do the soliloquy for me later?"

His eyes on her were warm and teasing. She shook

her head as if trying to rid herself of some bothersome thought.

He was quick to respond. "I've upset you, haven't I?"

Suddenly she was at a loss for words. "I don't know if you make a habit out of this . . . this kind of . . . flattery, but I have to tell you I'm uncomfortable with it. I'm not a frivolous woman, Pat. I never had the time to learn how, nor have I ever wanted to be one."

"I assure you I never took you for one."

"I'm not skilled with making small talk," she persisted.

"Rachel, I saw you with those men at The Hickory House. You had them in the palm of your hand."

"That was different. Besides, it was I who was in the palm of their hand." She turned to her stove. Almost as an afterthought she added, "And none of them were young, attractive, rich men with beautiful wives at home."

"Ah, so that's what's bothering you!"

"In a way it is. I don't usually go out with married men."

"We're not out," Pat defended. "We're here."

"Is there a difference? We're here together. Only no one can see us."

She turned away from him impatiently. "I knew this was a mistake. Pat, I'm no match for you. I can't play these games with you."

"Is that what you think this is?"

"Isn't it? A game that usually ends up in bed?"

"Not altogether. I'd be a fool if I said otherwise. You're a very beautiful woman. . . ."

"Don't!" She stopped him before he could finish. "I know what I look like."

"That doesn't mean anything to me. You may not be a raving beauty like Liz, or an exotic type like my sister. You're much, much more. You know, some people are like forest fires, exciting to watch until they get out of control and then they're frightening. You're different. You're like water, Rachel. Calm, cool, deep. You don't pound the rocks to pieces. You just flow over them, making them smoother with time."

Hearing a new note in his voice, she had paused to listen to his words. Now a delicate pink stained her face. "That's a . . . a beautiful way of putting it, Pat."

"Maybe I should join your writing class?" He shed the seriousness and returned to a safer kind of teasing.

Her smile spread, slowly transforming her face, softening the strong jaw, giving her that elfin look he found so enchanting. His breath caught in his throat, and he reached for her hand. "I want us to be friends, Rachel." *I'm lying, I want us to be much more than that.*

"I should think you had more than you needed. You of all people."

"I had a friend once, and everyone said the same thing about *him*. The upshot of it all was that no one ever called him because they were sure he was busy. He was the loneliest man in the world."

"Is that you, Pat? Are you lonely?"

"I never thought so before, but suddenly. . . ." His voice trailed off. "My marriage is largely a matter of indifference to both of us. My mother and I are at loggerheads. My sister hates my guts. The few friends that I have are involved with their own problems. The rest are casual acquaintances who number in the hundreds. There you have the real Pat Mallory in a nutshell."

"Oh, I think there's much more to you than that."

But she did not go into detail. Instead she concentrated on stirring the vegetables for her pasta. Again she was struck by the two sides of this man. Which was the real Pat Mallory? Or was he a combination of the two? Rachel had not lied when she told him she was inexperienced. She was. In the seventies when having sex was as casual as having a drink, she'd been too busy getting her life back on track. The men she did know were dedicated writers, academics, or homosexual.

Pat Mallory frightened her. He was handsome, powerful, articulate, and sensuous. And he was drawing her into a net of emotion for which she was unprepared. The cliché of the married man attracted to the naive spinster occurred to her, but she knew it was more than that.

"I can't afford to complicate my life," she said aloud in answer to her thoughts. She covered his response by dumping the pot of pasta into a colander to drain. Then she poured the pasta into the vegetables, tossed it around, and dished it into plates. She brought a chunk of fresh Parmesan cheese and a grater to the table while he served up the salad.

They made small talk as they ate, but both were feeling the strain of the unspoken words that lay between them.

Over coffee and the very rich cake, they talked about Sam and her painting, Rachel and her work, Sophie and her charities, and then the conversation turned to Hank Campbell.

"I must admit I heard quite a few things about the way you do business before I actually met you."

He gave her a tight smile, then speared the remaining cake crumbs with the back of his fork. "The Mallorys have been a source of conversation for over a hundred years." He held out his cup for a refill of coffee. "And now that you've met me?"

"In the case of Hank Campbell, you're living up to your publicity. The man keeps on telling you he doesn't want to sell, yet you persist in harassing him."

"You call an offer of over a million dollars harassment?" His warm, pleasant voice turned cold and hostile.

Ah, she thought, that's the other Pat Mallory, defensive, ready to fight. "No, I call phone calls in the middle of the night and threats to burn him out or kill him harassment." Her tone grew equally cold.

"Hey, wait a minute. Are you accusing me of—"

"I'm not accusing you of anything."

"But you're telling me—"

"I merely mentioned what's been happening to him. He's an old, sick man and despite all that bravado and walking his property with a shotgun, he's terrified."

"I don't deny that I want that property. But I'm not a jackal. I like Hank Campbell." At her dubious expression, Pat began to feel desperate. What would it take to erase that look of distaste from her face? "Rachel, I promise you, it's not me. I swear on my children's head. That's not my style. That's something out of a bad western movie."

"If it isn't you, then who is it? Who else wants his land?"

Pat looked puzzled. Who, indeed? A thought popped into his head but he shook it away. No, it was ridiculous. Why would Gianni do something like that? He'd offered to talk to Hank but . . . no, the idea was ridiculous. "Maybe Hank's made a few enemies over the years. He's always been a crusty guy. A lot of people hate his guts."

She shook her head and sighed. Pat, unable to bear to see her expression of disbelief, got up and carried the dirty dishes to the sink, pausing to stare out the window.

Rachel came to him on silent feet. She barely reached his shoulder. She put up her hand and touched it. "I'm sorry, Pat. I didn't mean to accuse you . . ."

At her touch he whirled around and looked down into her huge, dark eyes. They were full of sympathy . . . and something else? "Oh, God, Rachel, don't look at me like that!" And he swept her into his arms, holding her against his heart, his lips at her temple.

He picked her up in his arms and carried her to the couch in the living room. Sitting down, he cradled her in his arms, burying his head in her neck, tangling his hand in her silky dark hair.

She trembled at his touch, squeezing her eyes shut as though she were expecting a blow and wanted to shield herself from it. But it was not pain that parted her lips, it was desire. His kiss, when it finally came, had a kind of wonder in it.

She tasted fruity like the wine and sweet from the cake. His tongue explored her as if he'd never kissed a woman before, trapping her breath in her throat. Unsteady hands slipped under her sweater and reached for her breast. He filled his palm with her, surprised to find that she was not as small as she appeared. And then she was struggling out of the sweater and he was helping her. When the cool air hit her bare flesh she broke out in goose flesh. He turned her until she was stretched out beneath his long length; his hot mouth covered one breast, his hand the other.

When he felt tears splash on his hand, he looked up at her. "Rachel, little love, don't cry. There's nothing to cry about. I promise you. I won't hurt you. Not for the world would I hurt you."

"I know." She gulped. "Pat, I don't want this to happen."

"But why?"

"Because it will change everything between us," she said cryptically.

"Rachel, I need you. My God, how I need you." His mouth cut off any more objections.

She could barely deny her own need. It had been so long since she'd felt the warmth and strength of a man's body. As her mind warred with her emotions, he began to stroke her, trailing kisses down the length of her, pulling off the remaining clothes that stood in his way until her body was unveiled before him.

Gently he opened her, touched her. She was wet and

trembling. "Mmm," he said, "you feel like satin." His mouth moved down to cover her. "No, like roses, and you taste like honey."

Had she ever experienced such a feeling in her life? Did she call out his name and beg him for his love? She couldn't remember anything except the pinwheels of pleasure when he finally entered her. She only knew that her hands had reached for him when he pulled out of her and poised teasingly above her. He was silk and satin and marble, hot and cold, and he made time stand still for her. When the orgasm came, she was unprepared for its intensity, caught up in the astounding waves of pleasure.

"Oh, Pat." She rose up in a kind of involuntary spasm. "I had no idea. I had no idea."

"My beautiful girl, my beautiful girl," he murmured, lips lost in her hair. He stiffened. Clinging to her, he let loose all the buried anger, fear, and bottled-up love in one stream, with a cry that wrenched her heart.

Later, as she soaked her love-bruised body in a hot tub, she thought of what had happened between them. In the cold light of reality, she realized she could not let it happen again. When he'd been inside her, she thought she would die from the intensity of her feeling for him, but now that he had gone and reason returned, she knew she needed her emotions undiluted and concentrated. Yet she wouldn't forget how tender he'd been after they'd made love, how he had carried her to her bed, folded down the quilt and, wrapping her in a warm robe like a child, put her down on the bed. He'd dressed quickly, then returned to kiss her good-night, promising to call in the morning.

A minute later she'd heard the door close softly.

Now she paced the floors of the small doll's house, thinking of her ghost's love affair with the wrong man and what she would say to Pat when next they met. Finally, she warmed some milk and poured a healthy tot of brandy and honey into it before returning to bed.

Unable to sleep, she got up again and started to read her research notes. As she turned the pages, she noticed a reminder she'd made to herself to try to find a particular diary that had been mentioned in some bibliographical notes. It could explain a great deal about the Mallorys.

February's social calendar was a killer. One charity function after another. The Angels for the Arts was a new group of younger women who had pleaded with Sam to join and lend her prestigious name to their good works. Finally, under Sophie's urgings she had given in, annoyed that she was doing just what she said she wouldn't do. It wasn't that Sam was unphilanthropic. It was that the endless planning meetings and luncheons often deteriorated into gossip sessions, eating away the entire afternoon when she should have been home working.

There was the annual Bump Run which Alex Breton and Tony Frantz took turns winning. And they had resurrected a baseball game that someone invented as an excuse for getting drunk, requiring players to drink their way around the bases. The drunker they got, the funnier the game became, especially in a foot of snow in Wagner Park.

And then there was the Valentine Ball. She had to go to that. Her mother was a co-chairperson. But who would she take? On impulse she called Joe Ferris.

"Hi, it's Sam."

"Hello, Sam," was his guarded response. She had never called him before. "How are you?"

They made small talk. Finally, she swallowed hard and the words tumbled out, colliding with one another. "You probably know Mother is chairing the Valentine Ball and I have to go. I mean, I'm her daughter . . . so she expects me. There's no one else I can think of so I was wondering if you'd be my escort . . . that is . . . if you're not busy or have another date. Do you have another date? If you do, just forget I asked. As a matter of fact . . . Joe, are you still there?"

There was a long silence on the other end. She was about to hang up when he finally said in an oddly husky voice, "I'm sorry, Sam, I can't do it."

"I understand. You have another date. I mean . . . you asked someone else. It's okay, Joe. I just thought . . . I mean . . . oh, forget it."

"I'm sorry, Sam. Really."

She stared blankly at the receiver. The dull hum irritated her senses. How could she have been so stupid?

"Now what?" she asked herself.

Her question was interrupted by the phone.

"Hello? Louis, I was just thinking of you. Yes, everything's just fine and dandy. Working my fingers to the bone. Louis, I have a favor to ask you. Would you be my escort at the Valentine Ball? You would? You were going to ask me yourself? How nice."

Sam methodically cleaned her brushes and put them in the Mason jar on her taboret table. Noticing that she was running low on some of the acrylics, she made a note to replace them.

So much for Joe Ferris. Good thing he had pulled away before she had allowed herself to feel anything more for him. Chalk up the first and last time for her. It was time to rid herself of adolescent longings. It was time to get serious about her painting. Maybe Louis was right. Maybe he could make her into a much-in-demand artist. Anyway Joe Ferris was so much water over the dam, her future was on canvas, not locked in a tower waiting for a prince to come. Even though she was uncertain about the direction in which Louis was pushing her, Sam felt a growing confidence in her ability.

Resolve made her hungry. She went into her bedroom and stretched out on the chaise. Reaching for the phone, she called her mother and asked her if she wanted to have dinner with her. But Sophie pleaded fatigue, saying she was just going to have tea and toast and go to bed.

"Good idea," said Sam.

She stripped off her jeans and stained work shirt and donned a baseball shirt that had belonged to Pat. It covered her knees. She pulled on a pair of gray ragg socks and went to the kitchen.

About fifteen minutes later, she was perched on a stool in front of the counter having a peanut-butter omelet, a Diet Coke, and a bag of Pecan Sandies. When she finished, she stacked the dishes in the dishwasher, rummaged through the freezer until she found what she wanted: a quart of Ben and Jerry's Heavenly Hash. Taking a clean spoon and the whole quart, she returned to the bedroom.

She pulled back the quilt, turned on her electric mattress cover, put on the MTV channel, and hunkered down with a collection of art magazines. Digging into the ice cream, she started turning pages. God, there were a lot of good artists in this world. Well, she decided, they better move over, she was on her way.

Sam burrowed into the nest of pillows, the down comforter pulled up to her nose. The room was cold as a grave. From within the dark cave of warmth, a telephone ringing was interrupting her sleep. "Go 'way," she mumbled. "No one here." She was trying desperately to hold on to the ribbons of a particularly lovely dream, but the ringing grew more insistent as she slowly came awake.

"Damn it." She tried to see the time in the dawn-gray room. Whoever was calling was not about to give up. She fumbled for the phone and brought it inside the blankets with her. "Yes, yes, I'm here. Who is it?"

"It's Pat," came the chipper voice on the end. "I hope I didn't wake you up."

"You did," she grumbled.

"Good, get dressed. I'm picking you up in twenty minutes. Ten inches fell last night. We're going to Snowmass."

"Twenty inches? You're joking!"

"Ten inches," he corrected. "Twenty minutes!"

She threw off the covers and ran to the window. Outside it was all diamonds and whipped cream. The sun was just sending rosy fingers across the silvery sky. She shivered in the chill air, then went to turn the thermostat up.

A quick shower warmed her and she dressed in the bathroom, pulling on the tights she preferred to long johns and a turtleneck. She tucked her feet into warm slippers and went downstairs to the kitchen where the automatic timer was putting the coffeemaker through its paces. She peeled a banana and ate while she waited.

When the bell chimed, she poured herself a mug and took it upstairs to drink while she finished dressing. Looking outside, she tried to guess at the weather. It could be zero when they left but up to fifty degrees by noon. She donned a comfortable one-piece white ripstop nylon suit with squiggles of bright blue, turquoise, and black. It looked like one of Matisse's famous paper collages. She braided her hair and pulled a bright blue headband over her ears.

She was outside and waiting by the time Pat arrived.

"You look like a neon sign." She laughed. He wore bright yellow stretch pants with patches of hot pink, white, blue, and green and a matching sweater.

"I don't want to get run over by the crazies."

"I know what you mean." A powder day like today went to everyone's head. The conditions were so ideal, even the most cautious skier considered himself Olympic material. "Well, I'm sure no one can miss either of us."

She shoved her skis in the back of his Jeep, threw her poles after them, and they were off. On Highway

82 they joined a long line of assorted four-wheel-drive vehicles apparently making the same trip.

At the entrance to the village most of the cars kept going while Pat and Sam veered to the right and headed for Campground. As they got out of the car, they could hear the mournful cry of Krabloonik's huskies. One bark set them all off like firecrackers, and the sound followed them as they skied down to the Campground lift.

Everything petty and annoying was forgotten as brother and sister—graceful as dancers—carved 8s in the untracked powder. Each intersecting turn sent a spray of powder into the air where it seemed to hang suspended, then turned into a mist of sparkling fairy dust before it returned to earth. The aspen trees shimmered in the light winds, standing tall as sentinels at attention.

As the sun turned warmer, the sky turned a deeper blue. The wide-open slopes of the Big Burn, so called after a major forest fire turned the densely treed slopes into a desert, were studded with skiers in brilliant neon colors. Against the white snow, they stood out like traffic lights.

Looking down from the lift, Sam remarked, "With all the color and glittering snow, it looks like nature's jewelry store."

"A remark worthy of our beloved Melanie," Pat teased. "By the way, where is she? I haven't seen her in days."

"Rosie says she's gone off to Hong Kong with some incredibly wealthy taipan with a huge yacht in the harbor and a string of priceless Oriental pearls which he's dangling in front of her avaricious little nose."

Pat shook his head. "She's really crazy, you know. These days, especially."

"Maybe most of it's just conjecture. Those uptight yuppies don't look very sexy to me. And frankly, I never got the impression that Melanie was as interested in sex per se as much as the game."

As they skied off the chair, they spotted a group of friends from Aspen and stopped to chat. When the Mallorys invited them to ski, they were told they skied too fast. As they headed for High Alpine, they saw Rachel Fulton on her way down.

"Oh, look, there's Rachel. We just missed her. Oh, I would have liked to ski with her a bit."

Pat had seen the slender figure in the black-and-white suit, a hot pink headband worn Indian style around her head, and deliberately dawdled so they would be out of synch with her. After their evening together, he had called her several times, but her answering machine had picked up. He'd left messages which she didn't return. Upset, although he understood where she was coming from, he was glad they had not run into her.

"You like her a lot, don't you?" Pat, like most infatuated lovers, was desirous to talk about her.

"Yes, don't you?"

"I don't know her too well." It was not quite a lie. He knew her body intimately, but her mind was like a tightly wrapped bud that had yet to open to him.

"Oh, Pat, she's almost like the sister I never had. I seem to be able to tell her anything, and I mean anything. She doesn't look at me as if I were crazy or stupid or willful. And she doesn't judge me." After Joe Ferris's rejection and his apparent preference for Melanie, Sam needed someone to talk to, and turning to Rachel, had found a good listener.

"What is it?" she'd asked Rachel. "Did everything change because Joe and I made love? Did I do something wrong?"

Apologizing for prying, Rachel had asked her some probing questions, then grew thoughtful after Sam answered. "I think—judging from everything that went on so long ago—he's afraid to let himself feel anything for you. He's afraid of rejection, of hurt."

"What about me?" Sam had cried. "What about my hurt? Even when I was just a kid, I defended him. To the kids, to my own brother and mother. Doesn't that count for anything?"

Rachel had shook her head. "I have the feeling it has to do with something else. Melanie's just a smoke screen. She doesn't require any explanations."

And then Rachel had seized her hands and said, "Paint, Sam! Let everything you're feeling come out on your canvas. That's what's really important." Rachel was right.

"So you two are thick as thieves," Pat commented. Then very casually he asked, "Did she mention that I ran into her at The Hickory House the other night?"

"No, she didn't." She turned to him with sparkling eyes. "Wouldn't it be wonderful, Pat, if you and she . . ."

"*Wha-a-t?* Sam, I'm surprised at you. What would Mother say?"

"She'd probably give you her blessing, if I know Mother. Liz is not high on her list these days."

"No kidding?" Pat laughed bitterly.

They looked at the trail leading to High Alpine's mogul field. Sam got a grip on her poles, then, before he knew what she was up to, pushed off, screaming over her shoulder, "Last one down pays for lunch."

Straight down the fall line she flew, her ankles and knees working like pistons as she hit a mogul, edged, changed direction, and went for the next one. She made it look deceptively easy, but Pat knew what kind of timing and lightning-fast reflexes it took to ski that effortlessly.

When Sam heard Pat gaining on her she grew more reckless, prejumping and landing on the downside of the moguls. Close to the bottom, she misjudged and was thrown into the air, seeming to hang there, fighting for control. Pat saw her land off balance on one ski, fighting for control as she hurtled toward a cluster of people off the slope putting on their skis. He stopped and covered his eyes, waiting to hear the crash. But when there was no sound of impact, no screams, he took his hands away and saw her standing upright with her skis in her hand looking for a place to park them.

He skied down to her. "How did you manage to pull out of that one?"

"Weren't you watching?" she asked in surprise.

"Couldn't bear to. Too busy framing the words to tell Sophie that you had exploded on contact. Jesus H., Sam. Don't ever do that to me again."

"I was in perfect control of the situation," she announced coolly.

In addition to an enormous gourmet cafeteria, High Alpine was also the home of Gwen's, a reservations-only dining room that served outstanding meals and wine to sophisticated skiers who, after years of skiing in Europe, found that they liked stopping for a leisurely lunch and—if the weather permitted—a bit of sunbathing.

Pat ordered a half-bottle of a good California Chardonnay, and they both chose Gwen's rich sea-food chowder to start, followed by Cobb salads.

The sudden shift of activity, the enforced intimacy of the tiny table, made conversation constrained. Everything that had been forgotten as they skied returned now and insisted on being faced.

"I don't like what's happening to us, Sam." Pat finally broke the ice.

"I don't, either."

The waiter brought bread and butter to the table. Sam tore off the heel and began to gnaw on it.

"Was it Rachel's idea for you to go to Hank's that day?" He tried to ask the question in the same tone of voice he'd use to inquire about the weather.

"I just wanted to get out of the house for a while. The painting wasn't going well. So I called her for lunch. Then she invited me to go with her."

"I didn't realize he had company."

"Pat?" She put her hand out. "What's happening to

you? Mother and I are so worried. This thing with Hank . . ."

"You told her about Hank?"

"It's no secret, is it?"

He brushed her hand away. "The whole thing's being pushed out of proportion."

"But someone's threatening him."

"It isn't me," he said hotly.

"I know it isn't you. That's not what worries me . . . us."

"Us?"

"Mother. And me. Mostly me. Something's happened to you. You used to love Aspen for the same reasons I did. You were the one . . . that is, you and Joe Ferris"—she winced at the need to speak his name—"who taught me the names of berries and trees and showed me the difference between igneous rocks and sedimentary rocks. You taught me the history of the valley. You knew who owned all the Victorian houses on Bullion Row. And now . . . now . . ."

"I want to tear it all down. Is that what you're trying to say?"

"Well, don't you?"

He put his spoon down and turned away from her. Crossing his legs, he looked out the window.

"Pat, is it because of Mother you're doing this?"

"What's that supposed to mean?"

"I don't know exactly. I always had the feeling you think they loved me better than you."

"Didn't they?"

Sam sighed. How could she have brought this painful subject up? It was almost as if she were bragging, or worse, apologizing because she hadn't done anything special to earn their love other than be born. While Pat wore himself out trying to please them.

"If Mother's approval means so much to you, why don't you ease up on some of these development schemes that make her so angry? Does the town have to have a front-row seat for another Mallory feud?"

"I'd hardly put buying Joe Ferris off to get him out of town in the same league."

Sam turned white. "Is that what happened?" She felt her throat go dry. "Mother paid him to leave? She actually gave him money?"

"You never knew?"

She shook her head. "What was she so afraid of?"

"His influence over you."

"I was ten years old."

"Ten-year-olds grow up."

"I don't want to discuss this anymore," she said, tearing her bread into tiny pieces and rolling them in her fingers until she had a row of little pumpernickel pills lined up in front of her salad.

"And I don't want to discuss my affairs, either."

"Let's change the subject, then."

He refilled her wineglass.

"I saw Liz come in the other night when mother and I were having dinner at the Inn. She was alone. He wondered where you were."

"I was driving Rachel Fulton to the high school."

Sam choked on her wine. "You were what?"

"I think you heard me correctly. I told you I had run into her at The Hickory House. She was having trouble starting her car, so I offered to drive her."

"So what was this Mr. Innocent part you were playing?" She imitated him: "Oh, I hardly know her, you two seem thick as thieves . . . oh, really, Pat."

"I wasn't lying. I don't really know her. That's not to say I wouldn't like to know her better. But I don't think she shares my enthusiasm. In any case, what about you and Joe Ferris?"

"What about us?"

"You've been seen together in a couple of out-of-the-way places. What are you hiding from?"

"Questions . . . like yours. And other people's curiosity."

"So you are embarrassed about being seen with Joe? I don't blame you. He's got a fairly unsavory reputation—"

"So do half the people we know," Sam cut him off. "Besides, Joe and I hardly see each other anymore. I'm too busy. But we're still friends. Do you have any problems with that?"

Pat reached across the table and grabbed Sam's hand. "Let's not fight anymore. We've had such a nice day so far. I'm sure there'll be plenty of things we'll do that the other doesn't approve of. That's inevitable. But I love you, Sam, and I think you love me. That shouldn't have to change."

He got up and came around the table to kiss her on the forehead. For a moment she clung to him. They were the golden Mallorys. People envied them for what they had. They were handsome, talented, rich. But their real lives left something to be desired. Sophie lived alone with her memories, dedicated to good works and the conservation of the past. Pat could find his way in and out of the intricacies of real estate, and Sam could turn tubes of colors into paintings of beauty, but the landscape of their emotions seemed fatally booby-trapped.

CHAPTER FIFTEEN

By mid-February the days had started to grow longer, the sun warmer, the crowds heavier. The town was filled with celebrity faces, often unrecognized, because without makeup and clothes they looked so ordinary.

Galleries and shops took delight in reporting the sale of a painting or an article of clothing, a particular flavor of ice cream or a dessert at Gordon's to a star. It was good for business. Smith's sold a glitter-studded suede shawl because Goldie Hawn was supposed to have bought one. Häagen-Dazs couldn't keep boysenberry sherbet in stock because it was reputed to be Robert Wagner's favorite flavor. It was the same in all the posh shops in town. Clothes got to be known by their purchasers: Jill St. John's sweater, Suzy Chaffee's body suit, Don Johnson's boots.

It was just this kind of notoriety that Louis Breton was counting on for his protégée, Samantha Mallory, and why he had insisted on having her opening during the busy Winternational Week. The town would be bursting at the seams with skiers and visitors. The Murdochs, the Kennedys, the Ziffs, the Pillsburys, the Hammeters, Leslie Wexner, Ralph Lauren would all be in town and all would be invited. They would be encouraged to be among the first to own the work of this outstanding new talent. He even convinced Sophie Mallory that they could not have the ordinary wine-and-cheese fare at Sam's opening, that they ought to make Sam's show unforgettable with magnificent food, a statement which prompted Sophie to say, "I thought the paintings were supposed to accomplish that."

But Louis wasn't listening. "We should have those tiny new potatoes with golden caviar and sour cream and gravlax and smoked trout, aquavit and vodka."

After the discussion, Sophie and Sam continued their own over a light supper in Sophie's comfortable ranch kitchen. Warm golden light poured from a punched silver chandelier which hung over the big scrubbed pine table. A pot of chili bubbled on the big black restaurant stove. The aroma of freshly baked sourdough bread filled the room. Sophie sliced chunks from the loaf and slathered butter on them before tucking them in the napkin-lined Navaho basket.

"Louis certainly gets carried away, doesn't he?" Sam said between mouthfuls of the fiery chili. "I wish he'd paint the paintings, too." She was feeling very nervous about her work; none of the paintings she'd done under Louis's directions seemed quite right, and she was too aware of the importance of the upcoming show. It was a trial before her peers.

"I love the way he's spending our money. Oh well, it's for a worthy cause."

"Speaking of worthy causes, Mother, I have an idea."

"Speak."

"I'd like to have an auction."

"What are you selling?"

"Art." Sam carried her bowl to the pot for a refill.

"Between us we must know every artist and potter in the valley, right?"

Sophie nodded.

"A gallery in Boston did this once and I thought it was a terrific idea. We'll ask each artist to contribute a work of theirs, more if they want. We'll put a floor price on it. Then we'll have an auction. Half the proceeds will go to that Navaho/Hopi group that's protesting relocation by the government. The other half will go to the artist."

"And what will you get out of it?"

"Satisfaction that I accomplished some good."

Sophie smiled at her daughter.

"What's wrong?" asked Sam.

"Still fighting for the underdogs, I see."

"I learned at your side. You still believe in justice for the Indians, don't you?"

"What's that supposed to mean?"

"Maybe it's the individual Indian you don't like."

Sam had planned to have this discussion at some later date. But she was so angry at her mother's interference, she couldn't stop herself.

Sophie colored at her daughter's contemptuous tone of voice. "What's got into you, Sam? Why are you saying these things?"

"Why did you do it, Mother?"

"Have you taken leave of your senses? I don't know what you're talking about."

"I'm talking about Joe Ferris, Mother. The boy you paid to leave town."

Sophie opened her mouth to protest, but Sam cut her off. "You're not going to deny it, are you?"

"Who told you? Pat?"

"It doesn't matter, but yes, Pat did tell me. I don't understand you. I was just a child."

"A well-developed child. And you were crazy about Joe. Talked about him all the time. Played hooky from school to spend as much time as you could with him."

"But I learned things from him and his family. His

grandfather was an absolute treasury of Indian lore. You can't imagine how complicated those rituals were and how interesting. I owe as much to Angel Fernandez as I do to you for my love of Indian crafts." She nodded as if this explanation would convince her mother that she had misunderstood a young girl's passion. "And that wonderful kachina doll? Joe's grandmother made that with her own hands for me. I remember how gnarled and twisted they were and how fascinated I was watching her. I couldn't believe those ugly hands could make something so beautiful. She made these incredible baskets, and I used to watch her. It was a rare education just being with them. What could you possibly be afraid of?"

"It wasn't you. It was them. It was Joe. I was afraid that . . . that . . ."

"So you sent him away. Where?"

"I don't know where they went. Away. I gave Conchita, Joe's mother, ten thousand dollars." At the expression of shock on Sam's face, Sophie filled with guilty anger, protested hotly. "It was the best thing that ever happened to him. If it weren't for me, he'd be driving a pickup and scrabbling for a living downvalley."

"You were afraid I'd grow up and fall in love with a half-breed, weren't you?"

"Don't be silly. In the old days there was plenty of that. Who cared?"

"So what was it?"

"He . . . they lived in squalor. Manuel, his father, never went past grade school and his mother was a housemaid."

"So it was because they were poor. Well, now that Joe has proven himself capable of running Richard Farwell's resort complex, that should put a different complexion on things, shouldn't it?"

"It should, but it doesn't."

"Why?"

"There are stories . . . rumors . . ."

"Now what?"

Sophie turned from her daughter. She knew Sam would be disinclined to believe anything that she might say. "Can't we just drop this whole conversation? Why is it that every time I'm with my children something ugly rears its head and the next thing you know we're arguing. Can't we just have a pleasant evening together? Pretend we're polite strangers."

"Sorry, Mother. I just found this out and it made me furious. The whole subject is academic anyway."

"What do you mean?"

"If I really had any feelings for Joe it wouldn't matter in the least to him. He's not interested. He's seeing Melanie."

Sophie wisely held her tongue. Melanie was just one in a long line of wealthy women who'd fallen under Joe Ferris's considerable charm. Another reason why she was glad that she had interrupted Sam's childhood idyll. After Greg Francis her daughter didn't need any more hurt.

The Aspen Art Museum was packed for Sam's opening. The culture crowd had been torn asunder by some rather controversial shows that winter, so it was with great pleasure that they came to toast one of their own.

Sam, with an automatic smile pasted on her face, moved among the glittering crowd, trying desperately to still the panic that she had been living with since she'd agreed to let Louis mount this show.

The social vultures had been the first to arrive, staying for the gossip and the wonderful food. When the next shift came, they, too, forgot to leave. The noise level grew with each passing minute, as did the temperature.

For some obscure reason Louis had insisted on filling the gallery with exotic white orchids and freesia. Their scents added another layer of olfactory assault to the perfumes of the fashionably dressed women. Obsession mixed with Poison, Tiffany clashed with Cartier, Opium overcame Diva, and Coco flirted with Bijan. Ten-ply cashmeres arrived arm in arm with blue denim; black suede rubbed shoulders with white leather. In one corner three men in turtlenecks and horn-rim glasses discussed tachyons and time-space while next to them their wives exchanged recipes for power-dressing.

More and more people packed in, making it impossible to sit and even more impossible to stand. Still no one left. Sam tried to concentrate on the people around her who were plying her with questions. On the oyster-white linen walls, the paintings hung, big, ungainly assaults of color. Louis had convinced her to invoke a kind of hyper-reality within the vernacular of modern art, the cabalistic shapes, the juxtaposition of perspectives, the flattening of forms. It might be interesting art, but it certainly wasn't hers. At least she'd proved one thing: she followed orders well. Louis had been ecstatic with the results. With a mixture of panic and relief Sam noted that nobody seemed to be paying attention to them at all. A few late arrivals had made an attempt to view them but soon gave up, finding the bar more accessible.

Conversation and laughter swirled and expanded in direct ratio to the amount of food and drink consumed.

Sam had been to many openings and remembered how difficult it was to view paintings in the crush. But all that was forgotten. This was her opening! These were her friends and acquaintances. She couldn't bear the thought of failing here, of seeing the sympathetic faces, of listening to the forced approval. There would be dinner-party chat about "poor Samantha's little show." Hadn't she heard that kind of talk after one of their own had written a bad book or given a poor concert?

She felt the perspiration pool across her back. These violent paintings had nothing to do with her. Only one painting, smaller than the rest, tucked into a corner, was really her vision. When Louis said it would unbalance the show, she knew he was right, but had stubbornly insisted it be included. It was from her BL (before Louis) period, one of those early paintings that Louis had not liked because they were "weak and feminine."

Convinced that everyone would go out of their way to look outrageous, Sam had chosen to wear white gabardine stretch pants tucked into soft black boots and a black cashmere turtleneck with a string of fat pearls. Her flowing black hair, wrapped in a length of black silk, disappeared into the night darkness of her sweater.

She straightened her shoulders, attempting again to drive away the depression she felt when she looked at her unobserved paintings. The hot, noisy room closed in on her, and she was afraid she would faint. As she made her way to the door for a breath of air, she quite literally ran into Melanie, newly returned from Hong Kong and flaunting the famous pearls.

"Pooh, what a crowd." Melanie stopped, stared, then smiled. "Very clever, Sam, very clever of you."

"What? That I'm leaving?"

Melanie's laugh tinkled. "Of course not, darling. Your clothes. Understated so as not to take away from the paintings. Speaking of which, where are they? The paintings, that is." Melanie, in a belted chinchilla jacket over a black velvet bustier and short skirt, craned her neck. She tried to light the cigarette jutting from a long ebony holder, but the room was too crowded with people so she clenched it in her mouth, Franklin D. Roosevelt style, and surveyed the assembled guests.

"Sam, you must be a brilliant painter. Everyone is here."

"Brilliance has nothing to do with it, as you well know. Are you alone, Melanie?"

Melanie looked around. "I thought I came in with

someone, but he seems to have disappeared. Oh, well," she said airily, "I'm sure he'll turn up somewhere. Is that caviar everyone's eating?" Melanie saw Bill Pugh, his hands laden with plates of hors d'oeuvres, make his way carefully through the throngs to Rosie. "'Scuse me, darling, you know what a weakness I have for caviar. I'll be right back."

"Don't hurry," Sam muttered.

Once in the foyer where it was cooler, she took great gulps of cool air. Dropping into a chair, she surveyed the activity. The Aspen regulars seemed to travel in packs. They did nothing alone or in couples. Safety in numbers, she thought. Either that or insurance against boredom.

She squinted and the crowds in their colorful clothes ran together like squirts of paint, making a more interesting abstract painting, she was forced to admit, than those wounds on the wall bearing names like *Nude in Red Hot with Iris*; arbitrary names that were Louis Breton's attempt to make her paintings seem more profound. Thanks to him, Sam realized, neither the show nor her paintings were any longer hers.

With a sudden burst of clarity, she realized she was no longer nervous about this show. If it was a failure, it would be Louis's. It hardly mattered whether people liked the work or not. No, that wasn't quite true. Even if Louis had had the grand scheme, she was still the one who had agreed to apply the paint. The paintings were her responsibility. No one had held a gun to her head and said, "Paint what I tell you." Her own temerity had let that happen.

She stood up and blindly pushed through the crowd and into the arms of Joe Ferris.

"Just arriving, Sam?" he asked with a mocking lift of his brows.

"That depends. Have I missed anything?" she countered.

"I don't know." He looked at the packed room.

"Alone, Joe? Did you lose Melanie somewhere in the crowd?"

"Perfect place for her."

She forced a smile. "Don't tell me it's over between you two already?"

"There never was a 'we two.'"

Sam quickly changed the subject. "What did you think of the show?"

He shrugged.

"That bad?" Her words were light, but her heart was pounding.

"I never pretended to understand modern art. Never had it explained properly, I guess." She noticed he avoided a direct answer to her question.

"What's to understand?" She lifted her shoulders dismissively as if she, too, had no idea what it was all about. "You just buy it because you like it. That is, unless you're a collector. Then you buy what you don't like because that's the canvas that's certain to be important."

He laughed. "Such cynicism. I'll remember that, teacher."

"It's the least I can do, considering all I've learned from you."

They faced each other, a few inches separating them. As people tried to get by them, they were pushed together in uncomfortable but tantalizing closeness, only to be separated by the same surges and ebbs. She hated the brittle words passing for conversation between them, hated the closed look on his face.

He stared at her intently, his dark eyes reflecting pinpricks of light from the chandeliers. His slender brown fingers stroked his silk tie. "Samantha . . ."

She touched a finger to his mouth, sealing it from speech. One word would be her undoing. She felt the flush, a dizzy spiral, a sudden intensity of pulse. Something irrational was happening to her.

"I've got to go," she stammered, pushing past him, trying to force her way through the unyielding crowd. With an animal moan of fear, she flung herself against the wave of humanity like a fox caught in a cul-de-sac by the hounds.

A wall of noise surrounded her, pressing against her, making her claustrophobic. And then there was an abrupt silence. For an instant the only sound she could hear was that of her own blood coursing through her body. Caught in the strange maze of her emotions without map or guide, she needed to be alone to deal with these alien feelings. Why didn't these people go home? Why wasn't there more air?

Strange hands touched her, pushed her away, familiar voices spoke words to which some other Sam responded. When the crowd parted, she attempted to move toward the opening. But the moment she took a step, they closed around her, trapping her once again.

"I can't breathe," she said desperately.

It was Melanie who came to her rescue. "Now, Sam, you must explain this painting to me."

Sam felt herself slowly return to normal and was thankful for Melanie's babble as she half-pulled, half-dragged her through the crowd to a painting that seemed to be hidden in shadows.

"Now what does this mean?"

Sam stared at it. Had she actually painted that? She remembered nothing but the hours of frenzied production and the sound of Louis's favorite music on the tape deck. That's what she'd done! She'd painted the music.

"Mean? It doesn't mean anything. It's music. Yes, it's my vision of Bartok's Music for Strings, Percussion and Celesta," she ad-libbed. Then she went into a great deal of boring detail as she described fugues and elegies and key changes and whatever she could think of that pertained to music.

Again she was stunned by her discovery. She had

painted the music! Stravinsky, Penderecki, Prokofiev, Schoenberg. Her paintings carried their dissonances, the same dark, thundering passages, the burst of fiery pyrotechnics. Why hadn't Louis been able to see that? She began to laugh.

"Are you making fun of me?" Melanie, who had been mumbling and nodding glassy eyed at her explanations, stopped and peered at her crossly.

Now, in an attempt to get away, Melanie was turning from side to side to find someone she was willing to talk to. She reminded Sam of a robin in a garden full of worms after a spring rain. She was obviously finding it difficult to listen to Sam as well as the conversation of a nearby group. "Very interesting. I had no idea you were such an intellectual."

"Neither did I," murmured Sam.

"Obviously, no one else did, either." Melanie craned her neck, then shook her head. "I don't know, darlin', I don't see too many of those little red dots. Don't they usually stick those things on when they sell a painting?"

"Yes, but I'm not worried." She lied. "You rarely sell at an opening."

"Oh?" Spotting a painting in the corner which held the red dot, she chirped, "Look! Over there. That small one? 'Pears you did sell one!"

"That's nice." Sam kept her voice deliberately indifferent. She was dying of curiosity to know who had bought that painting. Probably Sophie, to make her feel good.

Where was her mother? She hadn't seen her all evening. Suddenly she spotted her deep in conversation with Richard Farwell. Richard Farwell? How curious!

Sophie, in a long-sleeved black Galanos wool and diamond pendant, felt slightly underdressed in this crowd of nailheads, studs, and sequins. Richard Falwell, on the other hand, was impeccably tailored in a navy blazer with his family crest on the pocket. His face had that bronzed glow that separated the natives from the tourists.

"You've been avoiding me," he said, his voice so low, Sophie was forced to lean much closer to him than she thought wise. "And you smell delicious. That's not fair. I haven't seen you for days and here you are before me looking like you just stepped from the pages of *Vogue*, and I can't do a thing about it."

"I wish I could think of a coy response to such outrageous flattery. It would serve you right." She sipped from her glass of champagne. Then with smiling eyes she asked, "What would you like to do?"

"Oh, lady, lady. Don't tempt me! How about dinner for starters?"

Another married man with a bad marriage, she thought. But Richard was tougher than Marc; he didn't bruise as easily. She knew he'd never feel diminished by her own formidable strengths. Whereas she felt comfortable and secure with Marc, Richard made her feel off balance, excited, furious, tongue tied, alive. She had the feeling he was constantly measuring her. But it didn't bother her. She knew she measured up.

"I'm waiting for your answer," he prompted.

"You said for starters. Does that mean you have other things on your mind?"

"I always do where you're concerned. But I'm a patient man. I can think of several things that even you would approve of."

"For example?"

"For example, dinner at The Smuggler and then over to The Jerome to listen to music."

"To my competition?"

"We could always go to my place. Or yours."

"The Jerome is safer."

"You give me hope."

"I didn't mean to."

He laughed. "Touché! You're a tough opponent."

She hated to admit it, but she enjoyed their fencing matches. There had been little time in Sophie's life for these pleasant male-female games. Now, thanks to him, she was discovering just how good she was at them.

As they turned to leave, she caught sight of her daughter-in-law in intimate conversation with Gianfranco di Lucca. When Liz lifted her hand to straighten the man's impeccable tie, then brush his cheek intimately, Sophie frowned.

"Damn her," she muttered under her breath.

Richard, too, had seen the exchange. He wondered how much Sophie really knew about her daughter-in-law. Aspen was such a small town and the occasions for gossip so frequent, discretion was difficult.

"Am I imagining it or is there something going on between those two?" she asked.

Richard offered a weak explanation. "Liz is a bit of a flirt."

But Sophie wasn't fooled. A look of distaste marred her lovely features for an instant. "That is the understatement of the year."

"Looks like it's time to go," Richard said as people started to leave. "Do you want to just disappear or tell Sam that you're leaving?"

As Sophie went in search of her daughter, she found herself face-to-face with Liz.

"Sophie, dear, such a wonderful showing. You must be very proud." Liz leaned forward and kissed the air near her mother-in-law's left cheek. "You know Count di Lucca, don't you?"

"Of course." Sophie smiled brightly at him, then taking her daughter-in-law by the arm, said, "Liz, would you excuse yourself for a moment? I want a word with you."

Liz did as she was asked and with her arm about Sophie's waist took a few steps with her.

"Liz," Sophie's voice grew cold, "I really don't care what you do or with whom you do it, but for my son's sake, could you be a little more discreet?" Behind the fixed smile, her voice was trembling.

Liz was about to protest, but Sophie, without giving her a second glance, brushed past her, making her way to the lobby where she stopped to chat with some guests. By the time Richard caught up with her, she was having difficulty controlling her anger.

Sam stood by the door with Louis Breton accepting hugs, kisses, and compliments from her friends and guests.

At last everyone was gone. Once more the large gallery became just an empty space with mediocre pictures on the wall. The buffet table was a graveyard of stale bread and crumbled crackers, dirty glasses and crushed napkins. Ashes, crumbs, and cheese had been ground into the floor by hundreds of feet.

"Samantha, darling," purred a well-pleased Louis Breton, rubbing his hands together in satisfaction as he walked toward her. "What a coup! Everyone was here and they stayed on and on."

"I guess they loved the caviar and champagne. It certainly wasn't the paintings that kept them here. They barely looked at them."

"Now, now. Don't be silly, darling. No one buys on opening night. People come for the food, wine, and gossip. You know that."

"Not in New York they don't. I'm sure that Julian Schnabel is sold out before the doors open."

"Samantha, you are not Schnabel. Yet."

"How well I know." She cast her eyes around the room at her paintings. "Frankly, I'm not sure I want to be." Her glance caught the red dot next to the painting that Louis hadn't wanted to include. It was a dark, sensual work of a seated Indian woman hiding behind a dark, shadowy door.

She approached it. "This one's been sold. Imagine!"

Louis turned around impatiently. "What did you say, Samantha?" He saw her looking at the painting he had called *Nepenthe and Fugue in Mauve*. She was running her fingers up and down the painting, enjoying its texture.

"There's no accounting for taste," he sniffed.

"I like it," she defended.

"Well, good. It's sold. Although I can't imagine who would want it. It's so . . ." Then he stopped in embarrassment at the look of pain and surprise that crossed her face. "I didn't mean that the way it sounded. I meant that with all the other really outstanding ones . . ."

"It doesn't matter, Louis."

"Now, now, don't get depressed. Come on," he consulted his heavy gold Cartier watch, "we're going to be very late. Barbi and George are expecting us."

"I don't think I want to go. I have a terrific headache. You go ahead. Make some excuse for me. No one will really notice whether I'm there or not."

"Really, Samantha, you're being quite tiresome. I promised to bring you."

Sam hated it when Louis pulled this Clifton Webb act. She hadn't even known who Clifton Webb was until he showed her an old movie called *Laura* in which he had appeared. And then she'd been struck— not by a physical resemblance, but by their similar characters—obsessive and jealous. "I said I didn't want to go, Louis, and that's final."

A sharp retort was forming on Louis's lips, but he cut it off and sighed instead. Samantha Mallory was proving to be much more difficult to handle than he'd expected. Admittedly he'd been attracted by her spirit and beauty at first. Then, mistaking her acquiescence for weakness, he'd set about trying to force her closer to his idea of her and her work, but lately she'd fought him every step of the way and the entire experience was becoming exhausting.

He enjoyed pitting his will against hers, but not to the point that it might drive her from him. He hadn't devoted this much time and emotion only to have their relationship disintegrate before it actually got started. No, he wasn't ready to let Samantha Mallory go just yet. Besides, he reserved the right of rejection for himself.

He came to her and put on his most placating smile. "I'm sorry, dear, of course you're tired. You should go home and to bed if that's what you want. I'll take care of everything. Shall I drive you home?"

He helped her on with her coat, already plotting the next move in his mind. He would pull her weary body to him and then as she rested against him, grateful for his warmth and reassuring presence, he would slowly turn her into his arms and kiss her. Her breath would catch in her throat, and in a moment the supper party would be forgotten and they would repair to his house.

But Sam ignored the planned scenario. At the first touch of his hands on her shoulder, she slipped from his grasp and took two steps backward. "Thank you, Louis." There was no gratitude in her voice. "I think I can get home by myself. You go to the party and have a good time."

Louis bit his lip in chagrin. "Whatever you say, my dear." He slipped into his own coat and smoothed his hair with the palm of his hand. He was seething with anger but managed to conceal it behind his customary sophisticated charm. He straightened one of the pictures, then without looking at her, asked casually, "Shall I come by tomorrow and take you to lunch?"

"I think not, Louis. I think I want to spend the day alone if you don't mind."

"Whatever you say. I'll call you during the day." He dropped a paternal kiss on the top of her head.

Sam watched the tall figure in the fur-collared coat stride through the lobby and out the mahogany doors. Alex's words of warning came back to her, words that she hadn't really paid much heed to. Now they seemed to take on an ominous new life.

There'd been a subtle shift in the relationship. At first Louis had stayed pretty much in the background, offering a word of advice or suggestion only when she asked. Then he had begun to make her feel uncertain about her work. She had taken his suggestions almost desperately, thinking it was too late to cancel or reschedule the show. She had allowed Louis and his encyclopedic knowledge of art to overwhelm her into producing these phony SoHo-school paintings that she had begun to hate. She was disgusted with herself, with her weak will. How could she expect anyone to take her seriously as an artist if she couldn't herself?

"Margo!" she called to the assistant curator. "I'm leaving."

"Okay, Sam. Good show, I thought."

"By the way, I noticed a red dot on the Indian woman. Do you happen to know who bought it?"

"Yes, I do. He was so hush-hush about it, how could I forget? It was Joe Ferris."

Sam got in her car and drove to town. A sudden rush of tears blinded her and made the streetlights run together. Joe Ferris had bought one of her paintings. But he had been so cool to her, almost insulting at times. Why was he fighting this attraction so? She wondered where he would hang the painting and if she would ever see it in his home.

Suddenly the thought of going home was more than she could bear. It was still early, the streets and malls were crowded with people on their way to dinner. She parked her car on Durant Street and got out. Four men gave a cursory glance at the slender woman in the white ski pants and mink duffle coat.

She walked in the direction of the mountain, a stark, ghostly white monolith; the lonely snowcat with its single searchlight like a fallen star crawled away in the distance. From The Tippler came the sounds of the latest Kenny Loggins track and bursts of laughter. It would be crowded with young men and women still in their ski clothes, drinking Coors and Corona, forming couples and groups to go to Little Annie's for a hamburger or Andre's for thin-crust pizza.

Her stomach growled loudly, and she realized she hadn't eaten all day. When she saw the lights of Shlomo's Deli beckoning, she headed toward it without hesitation.

In New York she'd become friendly with a brilliant Jewish girl from Brooklyn who'd introduced her to the joys of Yiddish and chicken soup. Samantha had known Jewish people in Aspen, mostly from the Middle West and West Coast. They were like anyone else whose culture was based on money.

She'd been unprepared for Heidi Goldstein and her fierce curly red hair, her plump body, her adoring parents, her proud Jewishness. Heidi had taken her home for all the holidays with their ritualized feasts and close extended family of aunts, cousins, and grandparents.

Heidi's mother was from "the chicken soup cures everything" school of medicine, and Sam had become an instant convert.

Now as she took off her coat and straddled a stool at the counter, she thought of the warm, boisterous family with nostalgia and longed to be with them.

Gad, a handsome, curly-haired Israeli, wiped the counter and set out the cutlery along with a basket of rye bread and a tub of sour pickles.

"Need a menu?"

She took it and asked, "Have any chicken soup tonight?"

"Does the pope have red shoes? You want with noodles, with rice, or with matzoh balls?"

"Rice?"

"That's goyische. Rice you can get from a can of Campbell's."

"So why do you have it on the menu?"

"Do I know?"

"Okay, I'll take matzoh ball. But only one."

"And what else? A cup of tea? A nice pastrami on rye?"

"Just the soup."

"It's not enough."

"How do you know how hungry I am?"

"You I know, Sam. You could eat."

"Not tonight, Gad. Maybe some rye toast."

"Okay, I wouldn't force. You'll have a piece babka or maybe some rice pudding later."

"Maybe." She smiled.

By the time she finished the babka and tea she felt almost human. Gad came to the door with her and looked up at the sky. "Could snow maybe?"

"Could," she agreed.

She'd enjoyed her solitary meal in the surprisingly empty place. Gad was good company because he was silent company, confining his questions and observations to food and leaving her in peace.

After her dinner she retrieved her car and headed for home.

She had to admit the Planning Commission was trying hard to control growth, but it was happening anyway. Old neighborhoods were being obliterated to make room for low-rise lodges. Large neo-Victorians had squeezed out the rows of small houses. Where once there had been nothing between town and the mountain, now rings of condominiums rose as divisive as the wall that split Berlin. Once there had been views. Now there was clutter, kitch, ersatz Bauhaus, timber-and-stone monsters.

Still the town had somehow remained relatively clean, spacious, and sunny. Not too many towns and precious few cities could make that claim.

So what was all the fuss about? And why was she one of the fussers? It had to do with change. Not her own personal change which she knew was necessary for her growth. But with life so tenuous and a future clouded and uncertain, something had to hold. There had to be one place unchanged by the whims of time. Something to remind you of your attachment and connection to an innocent past.

*   *   *

For three days Sam avoided her studio and went skiing with Rosie and Sunshine instead. One day they rose at the crack of dawn and drove to Vail to ski the bowls, arriving home late that night, too tired to eat or talk. Sam slept a solid dozen hours and woke the next morning with a burst of energy and new resolve.

She put on jeans, an old work shirt, and her L.L. Bean boots and went to her studio. She had decided to start a series of western still lifes. Strong colors, sharp-edged paintings that would have the same clear-eyed geometry as the Indian crafts she loved.

She stapled a piece of white canvas on a frame and arranged her palette. A half hour later, the door opened and a blast of cold air blew in followed by her brother. Behind him was Rachel Fulton.

"Hi," they called. "Are we interrupting?"

"Yes. I'm starting a new painting," she answered ungraciously. "What are you two doing here?"

"You haven't been answering your phone," explained Rachel. "I was afraid something was wrong."

"So she called me," continued Pat. "Together we decided to check it out. Where have you been?"

"Skiing. Yesterday at Vail. I'm fine. Just needed some time off to take stock."

"And?"

"You are looking at the new Samantha Mallory."

"I kind of liked the old one," said Pat.

"No, you didn't."

"You mean this one has decided to get out of the real-estate business?"

"No." She smiled. "I'm still determined to make you see the errors of your ways. This has to do with me."

"Are you going to say anything else?"

"Leave her alone, Pat. I think I understand what she means," Rachel intervened.

"Good, you can explain it to me later."

"No, she won't," said Sam. "You want some coffee?" At their nods, she went to her electric coffeemaker and poured three cups. "Okay, I'll give you fifteen minutes and then you have to leave. I have work to do."

"Were you pleased with your show?" asked Pat.

"Yes and no," said Sam. She heard a scuffle on the floor and turned to see Rachel moving some of her old unframed canvases around. "What are you doing, Rachel?"

"Just looking. Sam, what are these?"

Sam tossed her hair over her shoulder. "Just some of the old stuff I used to do."

"They're really lovely. Why weren't they in the show?"

"Louis didn't care for them. He thought they were too soft."

"Louis? You mean Louis Breton?" Rachel asked, looking up. "What has he got to do with it?"

"He's been my sponsor. He's very knowledgeable about these things. He felt I was out of the mainstream."

"The mainstream," Pat repeated. "What exactly does that mean?"

"Rachel, explain it to him, will you? I haven't got the time."

Rachel continued to look at the canvases. Sam's paintings enchanted her. Her life studies were swift flashes of color, as if she were trying to capture a fleeting moment, a gust of wind, a blinking eye. Her work had a painful immediacy, a sad nostalgia for an elusive thought, a psychic presence that tugged at the deepest recesses of the unconscious. Her nature studies captured the vast reaches of the Southwest landscape with an occasional figure placed against a corner to show the crushing weight of a benign yet indifferent nature. To a writer like Rachel, each painting set the scene for stories that sprang to her mind, fully fleshed, part dream, part magic.

"I'm certainly no art expert, but I love these, Sam. They have grandeur, along with your very obvious attachment for this world."

"I like them, too. But Louis said they wouldn't make a coherent show, they're too idiosyncratic, too personal."

Pat's face grew bright with anger. He was about to say something when Rachel flashed him a warning look.

Later, at lunch, Rachel and he talked.

"Pat, we've got to do something."

"About what?"

"About Sam and her work. She's got to rid herself of Louis Breton's influence. I don't care how knowledge-able he claims to be, he's going to destroy Sam as an artist."

"Aren't you overreacting?"

"No," she said sharply, "I'm not. Look, I know that you and Sam have this little brushfire war going on between you . . ."

"That doesn't mean I don't care about what happens to her," he protested.

"I know that. But perhaps it's getting in the way of realizing what's happening here. Your sister is on very shaky ground with herself. That love affair in New York . . ." She acknowledged his surprise. "Yes, she told me. Anyway, that man destroyed her confidence in herself. Now, she's back home where she feels connected and loved. And here comes Louis Breton, another destructive and manipulative influence in her life."

"I didn't know you knew Louis."

"I don't, not really. But I know men like him. Men who are incapable of creating anything themselves, but very clever in manipulating other people. They love the ones that are insecure and unsure of themselves. They're artistic parasites with some kind of cockeyed vision they need to see realized."

"You sound as though you speak from experience."

"I do." But she offered no further enlightenment.

"And you think Louis Breton is that kind of person?"

"I get that feeling. Also, I've run across his name several times in old newspaper articles. And what I read I don't like. He sounds like a dangerous man to me."

"He's never killed anyone."

"No, he's done worse. From what I gather he's made other people so desperate that they did the job themselves."

"You mean the son that committed suicide?"

Rachel nodded. "And there was a music student that he was sponsoring who hung herself. They found her diary, and there were all sorts of nasty rumors. And then his wife disappeared. Isn't it strange that she never even tried to contact her son? If she's still alive, what is she afraid of? The point is, I'm much too fond of Sam to let anything happen to her."

"Believe me, Sam's a survivor. She's a strong person."

"But right now she's vulnerable."

"Can you talk to her, reason with her? She can be pretty stubborn—"

"I'm sure she can. But I don't think I can simply go to her and say that Louis Breton is dangerous. I have to find another way."

Despite the evidence, Pat couldn't take it very seriously. Perhaps because he couldn't believe a man so respected could really be a monster, and partly because he thought Sam was like Sophie—strong and indomitable.

"Listen, maybe we'll get lucky. Maybe Louis will just go a step too far and cook his own golden goose."

She shivered. "I hope it's soon. Men like Louis hate to be out of control."

* * *

When Liz Mallory heard her husband come in, she emerged from the bathroom wrapped in a large white towel. Her blond hair lay damply on her shoulders. "Where were you all day? I've been trying to find you."

"I had appointments and then I stopped in to see Sam."

"Were you alone?"

"Why do you ask?"

"Melanie thought she saw Rachel Fulton leave Sam's with you."

"Oh, don't tell me you're jealous."

"Don't flatter yourself. I could hardly be jealous of someone who looks like her."

Pat remembered how Liz looked at Sam's opening. Silver-studded red leather jacket and miniskirt, red tights and shoes. She had circulated around the room like hot fire. He felt a twinge of desire. He really disliked his wife, but her ability to inflame his body hadn't died yet.

It was true that Rachel, in her dark paisley skirt and velvet jacket, looked subdued by comparison.

"Your mother was very rude to me at the showing."

"Mother, rude?"

"Yes, your sainted mother was more than insulting, and in front of friends." Then, realizing that Pat's curiosity about the incident would only get her into trouble, she changed the subject. "I'm planning to go to New York next week. I can't find what I want. I hope you don't mind."

"Would it matter if I did?"

"No, but I worry about the children."

"That's new, too."

"Really, Pat." She let the large white bath towel slip from her body. "I'm not a complete ogre."

"I hadn't noticed."

She walked toward him. Her heavy breasts, like big, ripe pears, swung temptingly. She was at the peak of her lushness, like a Renoir bather. Pat slammed his hands into his pockets to avoid touching her.

"Look at me, Pat. I'm still your wife." She twined her arms around his neck.

"Why are you doing this, Liz? You stay away from me like I had the plague. Then all of a sudden you get horny. What do you want?"

"You ask too many questions." She pulled him close to her damp, fragrant body. With a groan, they fell to the carpeted floor. There was no foreplay, no tenderness, just the sounds of rutting animals.

Later he learned what the seduction scene was about.

"Your mother never gives up," she said, following him into the shower.

"What now?"

"She wants me to co-chair a fund-raising luncheon and house tour for the Aspen Ballet. I turned her down."

"Why do you do this all the time? Why can't you say yes once in a while? Do you realize what an embarrassment it is for me? My own wife is too busy to involve herself in community affairs. There are other women as busy as you who seem to find the time."

"It's boring. B-o-r-i-n-g," she spelled out. "The same people, the same gossip, the same disapproving long noses I have to put up with. I hate it."

Pat looked at her bleakly, cursing his hunger for her body and his hatred for her morals. "I'm sick of listening to this refrain. I don't know what you want, Liz. And I'm tired of these games you play with me. I can't take it anymore. I *won't* take it."

He flung himself from the shower.

Drying himself quickly, he pulled on his clothes. With one shoe on and the other in his hand, he started for the door.

"Where are you going?" she screamed. "I'm not finished talking to you."

"Well, I'm finished talking to you."

"Where are you going? I have a right to know!" Her lovely face grew crafty. "Rachel Fulton?"

He turned to her in anger.

"Ah, I've hit a tender spot, haven't I? So it's true about you and the little schoolmarm." Her laugh was harsh.

His hand, when it came in contact with her face, was a dull thud rather than the crisp sound he expected.

She looked at him with hate in her eyes. "You'll pay for that."

"I have. A million times over."

Pat knocked on the door of his mother's apartment.

"Pat?" She looked at her watch. "What time is it?"

"Late. I'm sorry to disturb you. But I just had a huge row with Liz."

"Come in, dear. I'm sorry about it, but I guess I'm not surprised." She pulled him into the living room, made him sit down, and poured a shot of Jameson's. "Do you want to spend the night here?"

"Do you mind?"

"Don't be silly. Do you want to tell me what happened?"

Tell his mother what? That once again his wife had made a fool of him? Had drugged him with her body and then tried to exact payment? "It was over nothing. Her refusal to work on the Aspen Ballet thing."

"That's not worth fighting over."

"Maybe not. But I simply don't understand her, Mother."

"If you told her that Baryshnikov was the guest of honor, she'd be there with bells on," said Sophie wryly. "I'm afraid your wife is only interested in making social appearances when somebody important is involved."

He hunched over his knees, the drink dangling from his fingertips. "It's amazing, isn't it? I seem to know how to make money, but when it comes to my private life, I'm a disaster. You're angry with me because we're on opposite sides of the development fence, Sam's angry with me because she thinks I interfere in her personal life, and Liz is just plain angry. Something's going to have to change."

Sophie's heart went out to her son. She went to him and in a rare gesture cradled his head in her arms.

"There's not much of a marriage left, Mother. I think we've got to get a divorce. I've put off asking for the children's sake. But I frankly can't see how staying together is going to help them."

"There isn't anyone else you're involved with?" At his silence, she took him by the shoulders and looked into his eyes. "Is there?"

"Of course not, Mother." He stood and walked to the fireplace. With his back to her, he said, "There've been other women. Nothing serious. One-night stands. I'm sorry if that offends you, but it's an unfortunate fact of life. Liz is not very generous with her favors. At least not to me. Except," he remembered, "when she wants something."

"I didn't mean that kind of woman."

"Who, then?"

"A Rachel Fulton kind of woman?"

"Who said anything about Rachel Fulton?"

"No one, dear, but Sam seemed to feel that there might . . ."

"Sam! And she accused me of meddling in her affairs? She had no right . . ."

"No right to what? She simply said that you two seemed to get along very well."

"What else did she say?" Pat paced about, anger robbing him of his usual ambling grace.

"Pat, you're getting upset over nothing."

"There is nothing between Rachel and me." That was the partial truth. They had put any kind of physical relationship on hold. "We're friends, that's all. You should applaud that friendship," he said bitterly. "She hates the despoiling of the West just as much as you."

"I'm aware of Rachel's feelings on the subject," his mother said coolly. "It's your feeling for her that has me worried. She's a lovely woman, Pat. I'd hate to think of you toying with her."

"Toying with her? Mother, how Victorian! You do realize that sexual mores have changed since you were a girl."

Sophie blushed. Why did she react to Pat like this? Her uncontrollable and misplaced desire for revenge against his real father always fell on his puzzled shoulders.

"Please, don't be angry."

"It's Sam I'm angry about. She betrayed a confidence."

"Did you swear her to secrecy?"

"Of course not. Don't be ridiculous. I haven't done anything wrong."

"So why are you overreacting?"

"Why indeed?"

But they both knew why. Skirting around the real issues for so many years, they had vented their frustrated feelings by creating outlets, or hitching their anger to minor misunderstandings. Both were loath to change the status quo, to venture into truths that in the long run might do more harm than good.

CHAPTER SIXTEEN

THE FIRST WEEK OF MARCH—RACE WEEK—WAS LIKE A
Mardi Gras. Ski racers from all over the world poured
into town for Winternational, a week of parties and
ski races, culminating with America's Downhill and
La Grande Affaire, a black-tie gala that brought out
even the most dedicated stay-at-homes. Not quite up
to New York or San Francisco standards in the
department of haute couture or legendary jewels, it
was nevertheless a more pleasant experience.

Each night, with flaming torches held high, the
Silver Mountain ski instructors and patrolmen gave a
lesson in precision skiing as they carved perfect esses
down Aspen Mountain. From afar they looked like a
troop of well-disciplined fireflies, their descent made
even more brilliant by the burst of red flares and
diamond sparklers which exploded in their wake. The
Aussies, in bright rugby shirts worn over sweaters and
turtlenecks, led a sing-along to Wagner Park where a
huge bonfire burned. All the local dogs raced about,

barking and leaping in joy at the noise, the crowds, and their unaccustomed freedom from confining leashes. Aspen's famous, leggy young girls were here in profusion, the orange flames of the fire turning their tanned faces and streaming blond hair into something wildly pagan. Here, too, were the young men, lean, broad shouldered, hardened by physical fitness into modern-day gods.

Beyond the mountains the world continued to decay; concepts of morality and ethics joined Latin and Greek on dusty, forgotten shelves. Big nations talked disarmament while dreaming of ultimate confrontations in space. There was talk of making Highway 82 a toll road, and the Pitkin County downvalley plan was as unpopular as ever, but Aspen remained golden. Only people with things worth stealing locked their front doors. There were no skyscrapers to cut off the sun, no factories spewing soot, and no honky-tonk billboards. There was only fun and games and a frenzied glitter that had less to do with the town itself and more to do with the marketing departments' attempts to fulfill the fantasies and expectations of their visitors. If Aspen had not existed, someone would have created it.

People came to experience Aspen for the same reasons they went on African safaris or treks to the Himalayas. Certain things in Aspen set one apart from the rest of the world: playing poker with a president or a famous actor, a lesson with Scooter Le Couter or Tony Frantz, the complimentary champagne at Gordon's, the amount of vertical downhill skied in the deep Canadian powder. Although it was considered bad taste to brag about such accomplishments, it was easy to let them slip out in casual conversation and satisfying to see the looks of envy on less-fortunate faces.

So to be in Aspen during race week was like being invited to a sumptuous buffet with the opportunity to taste it all.

There were, of course, ski races without end: the Invitational Challenge, the Subaru Press Challenge Race, the Super G Race, the Celebrity Challenge, and finally the prestigious World Cup Downhill.

There were parties and dinners, picnics, fiestas, and musicales. The rich, famous, and celebrated poured in. The resident diehard skiers left for Wyoming, Utah, or the Canadian Rockies where the mountains, streets, and restaurants were less crowded. Before skiing had become such big business, most of the racers had been ski bums, content to work as waiters or busboys for a pass and a couple of hours of skiing. But skiing—like tennis—had changed. It was big business now, and being a racer conferred instant celebrity. Willy Bogner, Susie Chaffee, Billy Kidd, the Mahre twins, all had been Olympic skiers. Now their names were linked with Kennedys and Fords. Bob Beattie, Martina Navratilova, Chris Evert, and John McEnroe had become more exciting to celebrity watchers than the usual Hollywood faces.

The Kennedys came: Ethel, Pat, Eunice, and Teddy with assorted children and cousins. And though most people didn't recognize them, many of the political pundits whose names had been household words in the sixties when Jack Kennedy was president came, too. They were tireless skiers and formidable competitors.

Visitors found themselves caught up in the nonstop carnival of activities, while life for the people who lived in Aspen moved at its own pace.

After the strange confrontation between Joe and Sam at the opening of her art show, they had, without comment or question, returned to a casual relationship that included skiing, spontaneous meetings at local hangouts, tennis parties, and group dinners. But wherever they went or whatever they did, they were never alone.

A deeply satisfying friendship continued to grow between Sam and Rachel. Both were involved in silent, solitary work. Both needed time alone to stay in touch with that inner world from which all creative effort springs. Their understanding of one another's needs was unspoken and respectful. And because they saw each other so often, Sam had begun to show Rachel work in progress. In turn, Rachel, who'd always been secretive about her work, afraid to talk it out of life, had begun to tell Sam what she was trying to accomplish with her new novel.

One night Rachel dropped in just as Sam was finishing for the day. She watched as Sam covered the half-finished canvas with a cloth. Even in its early state Rachel could see the vitality, the perception, the love represented on the canvas.

"It's amazing how good these are. . . ."

"In comparison to what?" asked Sam.

"Do we have to make comparisons?"

"Yes. But I know what you mean. You didn't like the paintings in the show. Nobody did. That is, nobody but Louis."

"That must tell you something." Rachel turned to look at several other paintings propped against the wall. "You know, there are some people who can paint or write to order. 'Send me a swatch of your living-room couch,'" she imitated one of those fast-talking TV hustlers, "'the size wall you want to cover, and we will send you back by return mail, absolutely guaranteed, a genuine authentic oil painting.'"

Sam laughed.

"That's not you, Sam. Nor me. Samantha Mallory has her own history, her own experiences, her own visions. And Louis Breton has his. Never are the twain to meet. Unfortunately, Louis can't paint."

"But he wants me to paint with his eyes."

"And your show was the result. Sam," her hand described an arc, encompassing the paintings that had remained at home like bad little pigs who couldn't go to market, "this is what you are, what you see. And it's wonderful. I can't tell you how moved I am by what I see here. Your love for this southwestern heritage, your respect and understanding of it . . . why, you make people feel what you feel."

Rachel's heartfelt word touched Sam in a way that she had never felt before. Coming from this very sensitive and fine writer, they both thrilled and frightened her. Perhaps for the first time she realized what being serious about her work meant. It meant taking risks, taking responsibility, it meant reaching deep inside herself and, most of all, it meant not being swayed by another's vision.

"Trust yourself," said Rachel softly. "Let your own voice be heard."

Sam put her arms around her friend and held her close. "Louis Breton could take lessons from you. Thank you, Rachel. I think I know where I want to go now."

"Good. For starters, how about to my house for dinner?"

"Terrific." As they left the house, Sam squeezed Rachel's hand. "For the first time since I got here, I'm starting to feel good in my own skin."

"I'm glad."

Later that evening as they watched the flames leap in the fireplace and sipped their wine, the peaceful moment was shattered by the sound of a mournful sigh wafting through the house like a chill wind. Sam froze. "What on earth was that?"

"It's my ghost. Didn't Pat ever tell you the story?"

"I think he made it up." Sam smiled. "It's just like him. It probably has something to do with the wind."

Rachel shook her head. "I thought so, too. But during my research I came across the story and then found some rather unghostly evidence. Other people who lived here have reported hearing the cries and whispers as well."

Sam shuddered. "Aren't you frightened?"

"Not really. I rather enjoy it. I think of her as my muse. I'm even convinced that she comes in the night sometimes to read what I've written."

"Rachel!"

"Seriously. I'm a very tidy person. I put everything in neat stacks when I'm finished at the end of the day. When she pays a nocturnal visit, I find the pages scattered all over the floor in the morning."

"I have to see this with my own eyes."

"Then you'll have to move in. I can't promise a manifestation at will. It's up to her."

Sam chuckled. "I'll have to take your word for it." She pulled a pillow from the couch and leaned back against it with a contented sigh. "Oh, if life could always be this pleasant."

Rachel looked at her friend fondly. The tight lines and tortured expression had begun to soften now that Sam had made her decision about the direction of her life. Gradually Sam had opened to her, telling her more of her relationship with Greg Francis and her confusion about men. Casually Rachel inquired, "Tell me, where does Joe Ferris fit into all this?"

"Nowhere. That is, he's a friend." Sam sat up. "Why do you ask?"

Rachel shrugged. "You seem to be on good terms again."

"I guess we are. After a fashion." Again she stared into the flames. "I'm worried about him though. There's something bothering him. He seems distracted. If I didn't know him better, I'd say he was afraid. Don't ask me of what, I haven't a clue."

"I have to admit the real lives of people who've lived here are more interesting than anything I've ever read in a book. Everyone's so intertwined. Perhaps it's a peculiarity of small, inaccessible towns."

"Speaking of which, I was rummaging through mother's storage room and found some old letters and diaries that you might find of interest. I don't know how they escaped getting into the Historical Society archives."

"Have you read them?"

"I'm embarrassed to say I haven't. No time. But if you find anything juicy, let me know."

The storeroom in the basement of the Inn had turned out to be a treasure house. Because of their friendship and her trust in the older woman, Sam had thought nothing of aiding in Rachel's research. She'd meant to tell her mother that she was giving some of the material to Rachel but had forgotten. It never occurred to her that she might be bringing to light things that were better left in the dark.

Despite the fact that she had just celebrated her fifty-fourth birthday, Sophie Mallory was still a strong and daring skier. By the time Sam appeared at the top of Little Nell, Sophie was already at the bottom and out of her skis and waiting.

Little Nell, referred to scornfully as "the baby slope," could be the most dangerous on the mountain. Icy, crowded, studded with deceptive and randomly carved moguls, it caught many a hotshot unaware as he stormed into the washboardlike runout of the slot only to find himself in the path of a slow-moving, terrified skier. More accidents happened there than any other place on the mountain.

Sophie watched her daughter dodge the human tenpins with pride. Even as a toddler, Sam had displayed an uncommon grace on skis. She remembered taking Sam up the chair lift in her lap, her tiny feet encased in the best boots money could buy and a pair of skis that an adult would envy.

Sophie would hold Sam between her legs and together they would ski Little Nell. When Sam got more proficient, Sophie took her all the way up so they could ski the many good intermediate slopes at the top. Before long, the little girl, her skinny legs in a limb-defying snowplow, was carving turns and crying at the top of her lungs, "Faster, Mommy, faster!"

The years away from daily winter skiing had slowed Sam down a bit, but the grace and good form still remained.

With hair streaming behind her like a black silk veil, the slender figure in the sleek, shiny turquoise racing pants and oversize white sweater had been gathering admiring looks all morning. Men materialized out of thin air and crashed lines to share the quad lift with them. For the most part they were delightful. Young, single, and excellent skiers, attractive and highly amusing in their approach. They were too immature for Sam to seriously consider, but just as she enjoyed the whistles of the burly construction workers and truck drivers, she enjoyed the flattery that was such a tonic to the ego. When they asked her to go out with them, she said no, telling them that she was a nun about to take her final vows, or that her boyfriend was a heavyweight fighter and very jealous. Once she said she'd be delighted if she could bring her three children along. Sophie breathed a sigh of relief. The Greg Francis episode was finally drifting into memory.

Sam skated to a stop in front of her mother. "So that's what you look like," Sam complimented. "That's a very becoming color on you."

"Sam, you've been skiing with me all morning. You're just noticing what I'm wearing?"

"You were going so fast, I never got a good look at you. There was this kindly old lady with silver hair who flashed by me. She was wearing something sexy in old rose. Was that you? I thought you looked familiar."

"Old lady? Very funny."

"You ski very fast for a woman of your age."

"Flattery will get you nowhere." Sophie looked at her watch. "Now, I have time for a little lunch and a quick run before I have to get back. What about you?"

Sam nodded. She ought to go back to work, too, but the morning was proving so pleasant she hated to see it end. She rarely had a chance to ski with her mother or spend such a relaxing time with her.

They took the gondola up and got off at The Sundeck. While Sam went in to the restaurant for food, Sophie looked for a place to sit in the sunshine. The deck was crowded, so she made a seat in the snow with her parka and leaned back to take the sun while she waited for her daughter. She, too, was filled with peace. To spend a day without quarreling was a rare delight.

Looking up contentedly, she spotted Sam with a tray in her hand and called out to her. Sam waved and carefully stepped over people sprawled all over the snow to get to her mother.

"It's like the beach up here," Sam commented, handing her mother the tray so she could take off her sweater.

As Sophie drank her soup from the plastic bowl, she said casually, "Richard Farwell's invited us to dinner tomorrow to watch the fireworks."

"Richard Farwell . . . the man you love to hate . . . has invited us to dinner? Since when have you and Richard Farwell gotten so chummy?"

"He's co-chairing the Silver Mountain Festival with me."

"You've been on committees with him before. . . ." She gave her mother a piercing look, delighted to see the color rise in her cheeks. "Has that sly old fox managed to melt the Virgin Sophie? How long has this been going on?"

"Nothing's been going on. Don't make this sound like *Romeo and Juliet* revisited. After all, Richard and your brother are involved in business. It's not un-al for us to get together socially."

"No, you're absolutely right." Sam filled her mouth with Caesar salad and mumbled something her mother couldn't hear. But she wondered. Sophie had always made her feelings about Richard Farwell very clear. No, that wasn't exactly true. She'd never made known her feelings about him personally, only about his practices. Had the mysterious and enigmatic CEO of Silver Mountain Corporation fallen for her feisty mother? Well, why not? Sophie was a prize catch and still a stunning, sexy woman. In a way she was glad. Sophie needed someone in her life. A more interesting question was what their relationship would do to the future course of development in Aspen.

"So who else is invited?"

"Pat, of course. You. Louis." Sam made a face. "I don't know who else. Will you come?"

"Do you think he'd mind if I brought Rachel? I think she'd get a kick out of seeing the fireworks from such a vantage point."

"Do you think that's a wise idea if Pat is coming?"

"Why should that matter?"

Sophie looked nonplussed. To avoid further discussion, she gathered the remains of their lunch, wiped off the tray with a napkin, and tucked the orange peels into her plastic coffee cup.

"Mother, what on earth? . . . Uh-oh!" Sam recognized her mother's ploy. She'd always gone through some elaborate nonsense when she didn't want to answer a question.

"Mother? You didn't answer me. About Rachel. Why should that matter?"

Sophie sighed. "I said something I shouldn't have."

"To whom?"

"Pat. He and Liz had a big fight the other night and he spent the night with me. We talked a little bit. He said something about divorce. I asked if Rachel had anything to do with it . . ."

"And he got mad. Oh, Mother, how could you? I told you about Rachel and Pat in strictest confidence. He must be furious with me. It's bad enough he knows we talk about everything as it is. Now, he'll never trust me again."

"I'm sorry, dear. It just slipped out."

"Sometimes I think you deliberately try to hurt him."

Sophie uttered a pained cry. "That's not true."

"What a family we are! Every day one of us is mad at the other. Today I'm on your side, tomorrow I'm on Pat's."

"My concerns were for Rachel," Sophie protested. "Pat's a married man. Even if he is unhappy. I don't think Rachel needs that kind of heartache." Sophie was thinking of herself and the early stages of her romance with Marc. How guilty she'd felt spending time with another woman's husband, a woman who couldn't fight back. And yet she had been glad that their relationship had no place to go. Marc was very much like Big Sam: loving, kind, gentle, self-sacrificing, easily hurt. That's what had attracted her to him in the first place.

But she was still Sophie Mallory. Strong, stubborn, selfish, opinionated. She would never forget Big Sam's condemning, wounded eyes before he died. She couldn't, wouldn't take the chance of doing that to a man again.

Then Richard Farwell's mocking eyes came to mind, and she understood why she had had to break things off with Marc. Much as she cared for him, she simply didn't love him enough to go on seeing him. She would miss his gentleness greatly.

"So will you come?"

"What about Rachel?" Sam's jaw jutted aggressively.

"When you call to accept Richard's invitation, ask him if he minds."

Richard Farwell was no more surprised than his guests at the idea of his throwing a party at his home. Generally he did his entertaining in the less personal atmosphere of one of Aspen's fine restaurants. He had built the huge house on Red Mountain because his wife hadn't enjoyed entertaining at the Silver Leaf Inn. And since he was spending more time in Aspen than in Denver, it seemed like a good idea.

But the moment the house was finished, Cynthia had refused to live in it or return to Aspen again. To all intents and purposes, they lived estranged.

Richard's Vietnamese couple unobtrusively cared for his needs with computerlike precision. Germaine, whose father was French, had received the best from both culinary worlds. When told there would be twelve for dinner, she'd immediately set about preparing a banquet of exquisite complexity. A clear golden soup studded with tiny bundles of jewel-toned vegetables and solitaires of fish mousse was followed by fiery hot game hens, bronzed with a gleaming glaze; and an entire carp, boned and reformed with scales of paper-thin cucumbers in a mirror-brilliant aspic and garnished with lemon grass, dill, and star fruit.

They dined at two round tables in the brick-walled wine cellar which permitted Richard easy access to the vintage wines he served with each course.

In addition to the Mallorys he had invited Louis Breton, Jill and Leon Uris, Gianfranco di Lucca and, at Sam's request, Rachel. When he discovered that Liz Mallory planned to come, too, he had needed an extra man. None was available, so as a last resort he had called Joe Ferris and asked him to join the party.

From the moment everyone arrived, the great living room was filled with a tension that built to unbearable intensity. By the time they sat down at the table, it hung as heavily as the threat of a summer storm. Richard had placed Rachel with the Urises, assuming they shared a common interest. Joe and Sam were also seated at the same table. Sophie, presiding over the table, kept the conversational ball rolling. It was due only to her spirited comments and breezy wit that the entire evening did not turn into a disaster.

Louis glowered at the other table—most particularly at Sam—throughout the evening. When a burst of laughter broke through one of the brief silences, both Liz and Pat turned to look at the other table with obvious envy.

In most socially sophisticated cities, the Richard Farwells and their wives would be aware of the vendettas and feuds of their friends. A recently estranged wife and her new boyfriend would not be invited to the same small dinner party as the outraged husband and rejected wife. Only at large balls could all patently ignore one another.

Like most men, Richard Farwell was not interested in gossip. He knew that Liz Mallory slept around. But he didn't know about Joe Ferris and Gianfranco di Lucca's relationship with both Mallorys. And he certainly didn't know of Louis Breton's obsession for Samantha Mallory—or of Pat's interest in Rachel.

After an interminable time, Richard finally moved his guests into the game room where a large buffet table was set with fresh fruit, sorbets, tiny buttery almond cookies, and a pot of aromatic coffee.

The meal had been carefully orchestrated to finish just as the fireworks began. Richard was about to turn off the lights so they could sit comfortably and watch the pyrotechnic display in the dark when Sam decided that she'd rather watch from the deck. Joe Ferris joined Sam on the balcony. She was shivering in the cold air. He took off his jacket and put it over her shoulders.

The Urises, too, decided to watch from the deck and soon everyone was outside. The deck was a huge wraparound affair, built to hold over 200 people. Six couples could easily speak in total privacy.

Joe led Samantha to a corner away from the rest and leaned casually on the railing. The night, though cold and bright, held a hint of approaching spring. A soft breeze blew strands of Sam's long hair in Joe's face, caressing it like silken fingers.

"Smell the sea?" asked Joe.

"It's twelve hundred miles away."

"I know, but sometimes you get the distinct scent of seaweed and salt water."

"Did you live near the sea?"

"What do you mean?"

"It's all right, Joe. Mother admitted all. She told me about giving your mother money so you would go away."

"Did she tell you why?" His face in the moonlight seemed carved from some dark marble.

"She was afraid we were getting too close."

"Yeah," he said laconically. "I bet."

"Did you live in California? Near the water?"

"Not very near the water."

"I know you got a scholarship to Stanford. But what did you do before that? I mean . . ."

"I know what you mean. What I did I'd just as soon forget. Nothing I'm very proud of."

"You were in a street gang?"

"Something like that. The barrios are the same in every big city. You join a gang if you want to survive."

"But what do they do? You didn't get into fights or kill one another, did you?"

Joe saw her eyes widen with curiosity and laughed without mirth. She sounded like a rich kid whose knowledge of poverty came from what she saw on television. How could he ever tell her what it was really like? He'd almost forgotten himself. Everything but the smell. The garlic and rancid oil, the stale wine and unwashed bodies. The steamy rooms and dark, vermin-littered stairways. The pretty teenage boys who sold themselves to buy drugs. The adolescents who went to school with swollen bellies. The young kids who hustled dope and picked pockets.

Conchita Lopez Fernando Ferris had done only one wrong thing in her life and that was taking money from Sophie Mallory. Tired of being an outcast, her reasons had made sense at the time.

At least in Los Angeles there were people like themselves and opportunity. Wasn't the proof in Joe himself? Joe had gone to Stanford on a full scholarship. Conchita Lopez Ferris had never questioned the divinity that had provided such opportunity. If she had she would have been horrified and spent the rest of her life on her knees begging for absolution.

Joe remembered one thing about his mother. Her blazing black eyes piercing him like needles, the entreaty that became a litany. "Joe, you never take drugs. You hear? Never. You do, and I cut you up in small pieces when you sleep." And she'd meant it, too.

He never did take drugs. What he did was worse. Much worse. He sold them. It was the Faustian agreement he'd made with his own personal devil to get the scholarship. And he'd paid his benefactor back a million times over. At the time he hadn't really considered the morality of what he was doing, only his survival. Through eight steaming, fear-ridden years he had dreamed of icy air and high mountains, of blue skies like endless seas and all his old haunts in the hidden woods. Finally he'd come back to Aspen. With his Stanford degree and a fine reputation earned at other resorts, it was easy to win the right job. He'd made all the right moves, kept his mouth shut and his hatreds concealed.

Then the long Colombian arm reached out and plucked him to its bosom again. "Just a little more, Joe. For old time's sake. You're the best we have. There's big money to be had in Aspen. Really big."

The tone had been cajoling but the meaning unmistakable. Do it . . . or else. And now Gianfranco di Lucca appeared.

He looked over Sam's shoulder. There he was, the slimy bastard! Joe's eyes narrowed when he saw Liz Mallory pull di Lucca into the shadows. He couldn't hear what they were saying, but there was no mistaking the provocative tone of Gianni's voice. He's fucking her with words, he thought. She might as well be lying underneath him. He recognized the whole routine. Liz Mallory and Gianfranco di Lucca; they deserved each other. He wondered if Pat Mallory knew about it. Or even cared.

"Joe, where have you been? I asked you a question and you just took a trip."

"Whaa . . . ? Hey, I'm sorry. What were you saying?"

"Never mind. It's none of my business anyway. Oh, look, there they go!"

Bursts of color lit up the sky like high noon—pinwheels of blue fire, starbursts of green and gold, a rainbow of colors. The flag appeared in a streak of blue and white, a shatter of red stars. Joe's fingers beat a nervous tattoo.

Sam put her hand on his face and turned it to hers. In a shower of bright blue and white flares, she could see the confused, tormented expression. "Joe," she said softly. "You're in some kind of trouble, aren't you?"

He shook his head savagely, the touch of her warm hand going through him like a bolt of electricity.

"Tell me. I'm your friend."

"I can't tell you anything. Don't ask me. Look, it's a mistake us being here."

"But we're not doing anything!" she protested.

"It doesn't matter."

"Joe, doesn't that night mean anything to you at all? We were good together. Why can't you see that?"

"Why? Why? You're still like that little kid. Always asking questions. Damn it, Sam, let it go. Forget that night. It can't happen again." Joe took her arms in a crushing grip, but his voice was low and pleading. "Please, Sam, you've got to forget it." Then he turned abruptly and went inside. A few minutes later, she saw Gianni take him roughly by the arm and pull him to the other side of the room. From the look on their faces, the exchange of words was angry. How odd that should happen between two relative strangers.

A few minutes later, Joe made his apologies and under the pretext of unfinished business, took his leave. The statement brought a fleeting smile to Gianni's face and a frown to Richard Farwell's.

"Pat, I need to talk to you," said Richard a few minutes later. "Perhaps someone else could see Liz home. I'm sure Lee Uris won't mind dropping her."

"I'll be happy to drop Mrs. Mallory," said Gianni in a voice as smooth as extra-virgin olive oil. "It's on my way."

Liz gave him a winning smile, then turned to her husband with a purr of concern. "How long do you think you'll be, darling? You need your rest, you know."

Pat winced at the unexpected sound of the endearment, then realized it was said for Rachel's benefit. Only Rachel was busily talking to the Urises, so Liz's effort was wasted.

"A half hour at most," Richard promised. "Certainly no more than forty-five minutes."

"Hurry home, darling," said Liz sweetly before she turned and put her hand through Gianni's arm.

Germaine came in silently to straighten the room. Richard took Pat into the large octagonal library. They sat down on the deeply tufted green leather couch. Richard poured an aged Armagnac into two balloon snifters and offered his box of Havana's finest.

The two men settled back, contented for a few minutes to watch the smoke rise lazily into the air of the two-story room. A full moon bathed the mountains in ghostly silver light. It was a deceptively peaceful scene, timeless and perfect.

"We've had a pretty good season," said Richard. "Good crowds, plenty of sunshine."

"Not to mention snow almost every night."

"I think we could have a season in the black."

"Good. My business has never been better. We've closed a record number of deals the last couple of months."

"All the other Silver Mountain resorts are reporting pretty much the same increase."

"I know. It's great news."

"So why am I still hearing rumbles that the board is dissatisfied with me?"

"Are you?"

"Don't try to spare my feelings, Pat. You're a member. Surely they've come to you. Who's trying to get rid of me?"

"I swear no one's approached me. Why would they? They know I'm your biggest supporter."

Richard looked at his young associate sharply. There was no reason for Pat to lie to him. He was the heir apparent to the throne and he knew it. Yet he couldn't deny that something was amiss and that Pat had been more preoccupied and impatient than usual. Was he impatient to take over now? Richard hadn't been completely cooperative with Pat's development plans; maybe Pat thought he would be better off without him? Nothing would surprise him.

But Pat's insistence and genuine outrage finally convinced Richard that he had nothing to fear from Pat's side.

"Someone wants me out badly. Badly enough to use influence with the banks to make sure that I don't get that line of credit I want. They are really giving me the runaround."

"Caution because of market uncertainty?" Pat suggested.

Richard shrugged. "Who knows? The market crash hurt us all, but my personal losses were minor."

"So? You're leading up to something, aren't you?"

"I've had a couple of conversations with di Lucca. His offer is very sweet. There's only one problem. If Silver Mountain Corp. defaults on the interest payments on the bonds, or the balance sheet shows insufficient coverage of the debt, di Lucca has the right to convert his bonds to stock and get two voting seats on the board. I worry about losing that control."

"Aren't you being a little paranoid? What could

possibly happen? The bottom line looks pretty good. There's still another six weeks of spring skiing. March is always a great month. What could happen?"

"That's what worries me. We've had a lot of freaky lift accidents this season. Thank God no one's been hurt. And the damage has not been extreme. But it takes time to repair. And it's annoying, interrupts the smoothness of the operation. We're in bad enough odor as it is. No one's forgiven us for raising the lift prices and refusing to meet the ski patrol's demand for a benefits review."

"So what else is new?"

"Anyway, I've about decided to accept di Lucca's offer. I just wanted to touch base with you about it. What's your real opinion of the man?"

"Truthfully? I don't have one. He's tough to get a handle on. His charm makes it difficult. I can't help but wonder about a stranger who comes into town and suddenly turns into Santa Claus with no apparent ax to grind. Then I curse myself for being so cynical. After all, this isn't New York."

"New York doesn't have a lock on questionable deals. What's happening with your deal? Weren't you trying to buy that old parcel near Shadow?"

"There's a weird one for you. I'm going to court for a summary judgment."

The case in question was garnering a fair amount of notoriety. Pat had bid for a piece of property in foreclosure against a holding company. The holding company had won a tactical point and redeemed the property. Pat had then made a counterbid and filed a suit contesting the granting of the deed. The suit was based on the claim that the Savings and Trust Bank which held the title did not have a recorded lien on the total acreage. Included was the ten acres on which Pat wanted to put up a new hotel. And though he had delivered a check to the public trustee for 18 million dollars, it was rejected and the holding company's considerably higher redemption won it the entire parcel. Pat was contending the process was faulty and wanted the courts to decide on who really owned the land.

"Have you been able to find out who's behind the holding company?"

"Only that they're not American."

"Arab? I can't believe that Pitkin County would let Arabs own property here."

Pat laughed. "Remember the last one who tried? He wanted to build a mosque near Independence Pass."

"Maybe if they'd agreed to make it look like an old Victorian . . ."

The two men laughed. Pat allowed Richard to give him another tot of brandy. They chatted desultorily for a few more minutes. Then Pat left.

Pat had been unable to talk to Rachel all evening. Somehow having her so near and yet not being able to talk to her or touch her was more than he could bear. The memory of her soft pliant body, the sweet surprise of her own pleasure made him give in to impulse and turn the car around and head toward her house.

He parked deep in the trees and ran lightly around to the back door. It was open. He let himself in and looked around.

At the foot of the stairs he looked up and saw the light in her bedroom. Taking the stairs two at a time, he stopped abruptly at her open bedroom door. She had apparently been reading, then dozed off, propped up against her nest of pillows, her glasses perched on her nose, the open book still in her hands. She looked like a slender child in the pink-and-white flowered granny gown she wore.

His breath caught in his throat. In a single step he was across the room. Carefully, he sat on the edge of the bed and lifted her glasses from her nose. She brushed at his hand as though he were an annoying fly.

"Rachel, sweetheart. Rachel, it's Patrick."

She murmured a little complaint and tossed her head.

"Rachel." He touched her where the long lashes lay like dark fans against the rosy cheeks.

Her eyes fluttered open, then widened with fright. She was about to scream, but he gathered her into his arms. Her body under the flannel gown was warm with sleep.

"Pat! What are you doing here? How did you get in? I didn't hear you . . ."

"Shh, I didn't mean to frighten you. Your door was open, so I came in."

She pulled away from his arms and looked over his shoulder at the clock. "What time is it?"

"It's late, very late. But I needed to see you. They monopolized you all evening. Suddenly it was very important."

"What was very important?"

"That I come by and give you a good-night kiss."

"I don't know what to say." She gave an embarrassed laugh. "I'm not used to having gentlemen callers at this hour of the night." Or any hour, she thought.

"I'm glad I could be a first." He took her gentle heart-shaped face in his hands. "You look about sixteen in this silly thing you're wearing."

"I wish I were," she said with a rueful smile.

"No, you don't. Oh, Rachel." He bent his head and touched her lips gently with his.

A pure white flame anchored itself in her belly as his lips moved to her neck and then to the V of her nightdress. She felt him tremble and then suddenly she was struggling to free herself from the long flannel gown. He shed his clothes hurriedly and gathered her warm body against his nakedness.

"Your toes are cold." She wiggled against him.

He rolled her over on top of her and rubbed his feet against her thighs. "You feel like a nice warm oven."

Their kisses, at first gentle, grew in intensity. They

explored each other feverishly, hands, mouth, skin, nose, ears, all senses tuned to the hidden music of a beloved body.

When they surfaced, she tried to cover up her shaken senses with a joke. "Do all real-estate developers have this highly developed sexuality?"

"Do all writers ask such difficult questions?"

She touched the hard planes of his chest with her finger. And then her fingers went to his face and the livid scars that stood out like tiny ropes. "They're very romantic, these things. Like something out of a Viennese operetta."

"Getting them was not romantic."

"Were you trying to kill yourself or just prove that you were immortal?"

He rolled over on his back. "A little of both, I guess."

She shivered.

"Cold?" He scooped her up against him and drew the quilt over them.

In the warm cocoon their individual scents twined around each other and merged into one. Pat felt a blanket of peace descend upon him.

"You are so good for me." He felt his eyes grow heavy and languid. "I want to be good for you."

His arms around her loosened, his breathing grew even. Lying beside him, listening to the sounds of his sleep, Rachel decided to let him rest for a while. Then she would wake him and send him home. She curved her body against him and put her arm around his waist. Her hand dropped against his flaccid penis, sending a volt of warmth surging through her. It trembled in her hand, but he didn't wake.

At some point she, too, fell asleep.

When she awoke, the sun was pouring in through the window. Pat was sprawled across her, his head on her chest, his arms around her waist.

"Pat, Pat! Wake up!"

She jostled him. He groaned and opened one eye.

"Good morning." He rubbed his eyes with his fists and made smacking sounds with his lips. "Yuck, I taste cigars and brandy. What time is it?"

"Late. I meant to wake you hours ago, but I must have fallen asleep. I'm sorry. I hope this won't be difficult for you."

"Why should it be difficult?"

"I mean Liz."

"Please," he groaned, "don't ruin my morning."

She rolled out of bed.

"Where are you going?" He grabbed her leg. "Come back here. Don't think you're getting off so easy."

"I'm going to make coffee. Aren't you hungry?"

"Yes, but not for food. Don't we have some unfinished business?"

"Pat, about last night . . ."

"It's morning now. Sunshine outside. See?" He turned her head toward the window and put his tongue in her ear.

She squirmed and tried to push him away. And then his hands clasped her waist and she could feel herself disappear into his hands' demanding explorations.

Gently, he pushed her back against the pillows. Staring at her unabashedly he said, "I love the look of you. In clothes you look like you don't want anyone to notice you. But without them . . ."

She'd never felt sure of her body, never paid much attention to it. She kept fit and watched what she ate, but she was not a freak about it. In New York she'd joined one of the health clubs but never went. Instead she took long walks and played a little tennis when she visited friends in the country.

Now, a prime example of the Aspen fitness species was looking at her with eyes that seemed to take pleasure in what they saw.

He cupped one of her breasts in the palm of his hand. "Juicy," he said, bending his mouth to kiss her. Her hands tangled in his hair. She closed her eyes and let her feelings float to the surface. A man like Pat

Mallory was easy to love. Without guile or pretense, he had a sweetness to him that took nothing away from his obvious masculinity. But there was a desperation about him, too. He wanted something very much, but it seemed to elude his reach. With her writer's sensitivity, she felt the pain of a scared child whistling in the dark to keep the ghosts away.

When he bent his head to kiss her inner thighs, she shivered with shock at the incredible pleasure his invading mouth brought her.

"Oh," she cried aloud. And again, "Oh!" But the explosive vowels turned into pleasurable moans as his tongue went deeper and deeper into her.

When she thought she couldn't stand it for another moment, he covered her body with his, entering her slowly.

She clung to him, never wanting the sensation to end. The sun rose higher in the sky. The room grew unaccountably warm. Somewhere a sleeping fly had come to lazy life and she could hear it buzz. She opened her eyes and saw it, trying to climb the slippery glass bowl of the lamp. It would make some progress then slide down where it seemed to grow dizzy and confused before attempting the climb again. She understood its problem. And then lost herself in the incredible feeling of Pat's mouth on hers, his body against her, his hands holding hers above her head as he rhythmically pulsed inside her. Release came like an explosion.

He held her against him until his breathing became more regular.

"I'll take that coffee now," he said in a ragged voice a few minutes later.

CHAPTER SEVENTEEN

GIANFRANCO DI LUCCA STRETCHED LUXURIOUSLY AS THE late-morning sun poured into the glass-enclosed breakfast room. He nodded approvingly at the decor. Liz Mallory had done a fine job so far. As decorator, lover, and unknowing pawn in his plans, she had turned out to be a gold mine.

Last night he'd discovered her fascination with danger when he'd taken her home from Farwell's party. They'd no sooner stepped in the door of her house than she was at him like a hungry tiger. Stripping off his clothes, she'd pulled him into her bedroom and literally laid waste to him. After an hour of feverish lovemaking that had left him exhausted, she made love to him again, slowly, as he leaned against the pillows and watched her. There was something mechanical in her frantic suckings and pullings. Yet it excited him even as it disgusted him. And despite his distaste, he still needed her. She was the conduit to the business affairs of her husband. Just before he exploded in her mouth, he reminded himself to tell her that she had to be nicer to Pat.

When the ivory clock on her night table struck the hour, he tried to warn her that Pat might walk in the door at any moment. But she had laughed and kept on going. Even though he was exhausted his stupid cock had ignored his brain and continued with a mind of its own.

At the sudden sound of a door slamming he had gone soft. Holding his breath, he waited for the inevitable footsteps, trying to think of what he could possibly say. But when the house remained silent, he realized that it had only been a gust of wind.

"I think we should stop now," he'd said. But again she'd laughed. She was ready to continue, but his own self-preservation dictated a slightly modified version of the old adage: "He who fights and runs away lives to fight another day." And then he stumbled home to sleep surprisingly well.

He made himself a cup of espresso and took it to the unusual table Liz had had created from poured concrete and oxidized steel. Although secretly in love with the heavy, rich furnishings of the Renaissance, Gianni had nevertheless allowed Liz to talk him into the more appropriate decor of the modernists from Milan.

Everything was going according to plan, although slower than he would have liked.

Picking up the phone, he dialed a number. Without wasting time on pleasantries he got straight to the point and gave his progress report.

"Things are going slowly but well. We have created a number of . . . incidents which are not making the board happy. I have planted the seed of doubt in two of the board members. They have never cared much for Farwell, but as long as the corporation was making money, they kept silent. Farwell has at last agreed to accept our financial help. It's just a question of time before he will find himself unable to pay the interest on my loan. And then I shall have two seats on the board. I am working on Mallory. He's still the cipher. Sometimes it appears that he, too, is becoming disenchanted with Farwell. But if it comes to—how do you say?—a showdown, I'm not sure whether I can count on him. Yes, I agree. I'm working on it."

He hung up the phone. He had to think of something: What could he use against Pat Mallory to ensure his vote? Exposure of his relationship to Pat's wife? No, from all appearances he couldn't care less. Blackmail? He really had nothing worth using against him. Lengthy investigations had revealed that Pat had never done anything illegal and his indiscretions were worth nothing.

As far as the Colombian drug czars were concerned, Gianni's greatest asset was his ability to take care of enemies and opposition with almost Machiavellian cunning. Gianni never left a trail of blood and—like Caesar's wife—always remained above suspicion. He could take the most minor information and turn it into a monumental threat. But if that avenue were no longer open, he would be considered useless and—possibly—dead.

A dazzling smile suddenly creased his face. Of course! How stupid of him not to have thought of it sooner. It was simplicity itself. With the solution at hand, he felt no rush to finish his breakfast. He poured himself another cup of the dark aromatic espresso, spread raspberry jam on a flaky warm croissant, and sat back to savor every bite.

Finally content, he reached for the phone and made the long-distance call to New York. As he waited he looked out over the panoramic view, admiring the clarity of the sky, the soaring snow-covered mountains. A feeling of reverence, very similar to that which he felt in the great churches of Tuscany, stole over him.

When he heard the voice on the other end, he said

crisply, "Sophie MacNeal Mallory and her daughter, Samantha. Find out everything you can about them." He spelled out their names. Hanging up the phone, he leaned back. That should do it. Gianni knew that no matter what their disagreements, Pat would not allow anything to hurt his mother and sister.

Rachel Fulton had often pondered the issues of honesty. Was there ever a time when a lie was better than the truth? Looking at the documents scattered over the dining table she used as a desk, she came to a decision.

Several days ago Sam had given her the old dust-covered letters and diaries of the MacNeal family. Some of them had crumbled in Rachel's hands as she took them from the box in which they'd been resting for decades. Picking a few at random she had quickly scanned them and found nothing of interest. Finally she'd turned to a batch of letters whose dates were closer to the present and begun to read. The contents shocked her. They were letters exchanged between Sophie and Big Sam and they revealed that Big Sam Mallory was not Patrick's father. To avoid bringing disgrace on her family, Sophie had married Sam without loving him. In the fifties it was probably the only choice a well-brought-up young woman could make. The identity of Pat's real father was not revealed in the letters.

Did Pat know? Did Sam know? Rachel wondered. How did you ask a man you cared for such a question? Yet Rachel sensed that the knowledge held the key to Pat's relationship with his mother, a relationship that filled him with such love and anguish.

The clock struck the half hour. Hurriedly gathering the material together, she shoved it back in the box. Pat had gotten into the habit of stopping by her house late in the afternoon for a drink and a chat. Though neither discussed the obvious feelings growing between them, they did nothing to prevent them. Rachel

was still uncomfortable in her role as "other woman."
And he knew it. They talked of everything but themselves, masking the words they wanted to say. It gave
their conversation a kind of suspended foreplay.

"Did you ski today?" *Did I ever tell you that your
face makes me think of the wood sprites in Sam's
nursery books?*

"No, I'm working on my outline." *It's not fair that a
man should be so physically blessed.*

"How's it going?" *I want to make love to you this
instant!*

"Not as easily as I would like." *I can't think when
you look at me like that.*

"I wish I could help. But I won't even offer. I'm a
dolt when it comes to anything literary." *Ridiculous!
You couldn't be a dolt at anything.*

Gradually through their brief meetings they came
to know one another as friends do. The dialogue of
lovers remained for the most part silent.

It was at one of these visits that Rachel decided to
broach the subject of Pat's birth.

Pat came over directly from the airport, having just
flown back from a meeting in Denver. When she
opened the door, she barely recognized him.

"Well, are you going to let me in?"

"I'm not sure I know this Pat Mallory. You look
so . . . so . . ."

"The writer at a loss for words? Is *citified* what
you're looking for?"

"That's as good as any."

"Banks hate it when I dress like a cowboy."

"No cowboy dresses like you." She laughed, pulling
him in and shutting the door. He hung up his coat in
the closet and, rubbing his hands, strode into the tiny
living room.

"Is this place getting smaller or am I still growing?"

"A little of both, I think."

"Let's go into the sunroom."

"Where there's no sun."

He shrugged and followed her into the glassed-in room which she had furnished with comfortable secondhand wicker and fluffy pillows. She disappeared and returned a few minutes later with a tray that contained her pot of tea and his bourbon.

He folded his big frame into a chair and accepted his drink. "It's amazing how comfortable I feel here."

"You have that huge house to move around in and you feel comfortable in a room that can't possibly measure more than ten by six?"

"Ten by ten," he corrected.

"Excuse me. I forgot I was talking to the expert."

"On practically everything." Pat smiled. "Except spelling."

They bantered back and forth, pleased to be with one another. Though he had not kissed her nor given her more than a casual touch, the warmth that enveloped them was palpable.

To get him talking about his early memories, Rachel deliberately set the stage by recounting a story about her youth and her discovery of how much older her parents were than the parents of other kids her age.

"I was sure they had adopted me. I even made up this elaborate and tragic story of how they lost a child when they were young and then how Mother discovered she couldn't have any more children . . . you know, the usual." She took a sip of tea and looked out at the soft vaporous light that clung to the mountains and asked softly, "Did you ever think you were adopted?"

"Are you kidding? What kid hasn't? I remember asking my mother if she was my real mother. She said, 'Of course!' And then I asked her if Sam was my real father."

Rachel's breath caught in her throat. "And she said?"

" 'Don't be silly.' "

A perfectly camouflaged answer! So it was true, and Pat didn't know.

He went on to talk of the feelings of alienation he'd experienced growing up. How he'd always felt that Sam received far more attention and love than he had.

"And that didn't affect your relationship with her?"

"Not really. I was crazy about her from the moment she was born. She was such a beautiful little thing. Of course, every time I got near her, Mother would snatch her away. I don't think she trusted me. But when Sam started walking, it was big brother she came to first."

"And now?"

"She's my worst critic. I know she hates what I'm doing. But I think underneath it all, she loves me a great deal. As I do her."

She put her hand against his face. "I'm glad."

He turned his face until his lips found her palm. He kissed it gently. "You are, aren't you?"

It was the first time Samantha Mallory had been in Louis's house. She sat in a remarkably uncomfortable chair whose back was formed of interlocking stag antlers and stared in openmouthed disbelief at his study, so unlike the rest of his modern, uncluttered house.

Never had she seen so many things on walls, on tables, on shelves, on the floor. He seemed to collect everything: Meissen leopards, exotic shells, ivory cane handles, anything in Derbyshire blue, miniature cabinets once used by makers as samples, Battersea and Bilston boxes, animal figures, fans, Victorian snuff boxes, silver pillboxes . . . it was like being in Uriah Heep's, the idiosyncratic store in Aspen that had a little bit of everything from everyplace in the world.

Louis seemed keyed up. He was rambling on about how little he'd paid for most of the pieces in his collections, applauding his superior knowledge of the rare and arcane in the face of the know-nothings who were happy to sell.

"I like buying things from gullible people. I once

paid one hundred twenty dollars for a Picasso etching. And the blue spar over there which is so rare now came from a peddler in the Camden Arcade."

He triumphantly pointed to a sketch of himself drawn as a shoe. "Andy Warhol. The poor darling boy. Such an unfortunate way to die. He was once an illustrator of shoes. Did you know that? He did that drawing as a joke. I paid him seventy-five dollars. Of course, he himself was an incredible collector."

Louis's collectibles were dizzying and so was his ceaseless cataloguing. Sam's mind sought escape, drifting to the painting she was now working on and which she called *The Sacred Lands*. Louis would probably call it poor Georgia O'Keeffe, but it didn't matter; she knew it was good. Still, Sam didn't want to alienate him; his patronage could be important.

Suddenly she started to sneeze uncontrollably. He stared at her in annoyance.

"Dust," she offered in explanation between the *achoos!*

When she finally stopped, she gave him a tentative smile and asked, "Louis, this is all most interesting, but why am I here?"

"For lunch and chitchat, of course, my darling. Come."

He offered his hand. She took it although she had a sudden aversion to touching him. Under the dry, papery skin his palm was damp. He wore a strong patchouli cologne that seemed to get stronger with every step and which was obviously the cause of her sneezing.

Even though he tended to go on monotonously, he was an erudite and fascinating man. Many women found him extraordinarily handsome. And he was. But rather than finding his attention flattering she was embarrassed by it, and quickly developing an aversion to his physical presence. Even the most casual touch from him made her flesh crawl.

When he put his hand on the nape of her neck, she jumped. He's sweating, she thought, as her flesh rippled in protest. There's something not right here.

He led her to a small Empire-style dining room; its saffron enameled walls hung with a profusion of eclectic modern paintings. Bright red carnations in a black ormulu and marble sphynx sat on a heavy glass table with a base of burnished steel and brass.

"I'm serving you myself today. I gave Theresa the day off."

The first warning bell sounded. She was alone with Louis, a prospect that didn't fill her with pleasure.

"But you've gone to so much trouble . . . ," she protested weakly.

"Nonsense, my dear. I feel I owe you something."

"For what?"

"Your patience. I know I've been a relentless taskmaster."

"Don't be silly."

He pulled out a chair and seated her. Against the wall stood an elaborate carytid table laden with a collection of silver warmers. Louis removed the top of a tureen and ladled out an aromatic seafood bisque. "I had the fish flown in especially for our lunch."

"How nice," she said woodenly. Perhaps she could survive this meal through mechanical politeness.

They ate the soup which she had to admit was delicious, as was the warm chicken salad on a bed of wild rice and chopped arugala. He poured a superb Chassagne Montrachet into the slender Baccarat glasses. Dessert was fresh raspberries with *crème fraîche* and petit fours. After the demi-tasse, he offered a brandy which she refused.

Louis Breton, exquisite host and elegant man-about-town was complimenting himself. Not for the lunch which he knew was superb, but for the almost superhuman control he'd maintained over himself today. No one could possibly guess at the anger that had been eating at him since the night of Farwell's party when he had watched that slime Joe Ferris monopolize Sam all evening.

The next day he began to plan his assault. He was not about to see that worm, with his seductive hands and talk, destroy all his plans.

That was the trouble with most young men. They had no finesse. They didn't know how to woo a woman, how to ingratiate oneself, how to become a total necessity in a woman's life. If Sam couldn't see that he—Louis—was the only man who could help her, he would have to point it out.

Louis led Sam back to the sitting room and a small elegantly striped satin loveseat.

"Samantha, I've come to know and treasure you over the last few months. You are a beautiful woman with a burgeoning talent. Maybe even a great one if you don't squander it."

Sam stared at Louis's face, seeing for the first time its forbidding lines. He looked like one of El Greco's lugubrious cardinals. Though his words made her want to run in terror, his handsome face remained expressionless, closed tightly as the shutters of a cloister.

What on earth was he driving at? "Squander it? I don't understand."

"To be a great artist means to be single-minded about your work. Samantha, do you want to be as great as I think you can be?"

"Well," she waffled, "of course, what artist wouldn't?"

Louis leaned closer, and Sam had to stop herself from inching backward. "I have influence, as you probably know. There are galleries in New York, London, Paris, and San Francisco who will go to great lengths to please me."

She was surprised. She knew Louis was influential, but that influential? "I'm impressed," she said.

"I hope you're not being flip, my dear," he said severely.

"No, of course not. Forgive me. But, Louis, do get to the point. If you'll excuse me, you have said this to me before. I have the feeling you mean something else."

"I do. I want you to put yourself solely in my hands."

"I don't think I understand."

"Those friends of yours waste your time. And Joe Ferris—"

"What's Joe got to do with any of this?" Sam interrupted.

"There were rumors that you might marry him."

"That's utter nonsense." Sam blushed.

"I'm relieved to hear that." Louis paused, before concluding dramatically. "Because marriage would be a horrible mistake for you."

She looked genuinely puzzled. "Even though I have no intentions of marrying anyone, what would marriage have to do with my painting?"

Louis, ignoring her question, poured himself another brandy. This was going to be so easy, he thought.

"Nothing must stand in our way." He took her hand and put his lips to her palm. Like his hand they had a dry, papery feel.

Our way? What did he mean by that? A crippling wave of anxiety swept over Sam. Louis was certainly behaving most peculiarly. And why did he have such a death grip on her hand?

As he lifted his head to look at her, she felt she was looking into the hooded eyes of a cobra.

"Louis?" Her voice was soft, pleading. And when she saw the look of triumph come over his face, she knew he had misunderstood her tone. He lunged, violently shoving her back against the couch and kissing her. The stiff arm of the couch dug into her back. She arched in protest, a movement he mistook for passion. Immediately his hands reached for her breast and she could feel his fumbling under her sweater.

"Louis," she cried, truly frightened. He was much stronger than she expected. "Stop it, you're hurting me!"

"Samantha, you must know how I feel." In the heat of his desire he seized her hand and put it over the burning hardness of his groin.

"No, no, leave me alone. For God's sake, Louis. Stop!"

But he was a man caught in a frenzy of passion fueled by anger and long denial. "Don't deny me, Samantha. I want you. I've waited a long time for you." His hands were cruel as they rushed over her body, pulling away at her clothes.

In terror, she realized that Louis was going to rape her. He was completely crazed, and his strength seemed almost demonic. With his weight crushing her, his mouth firmly sealed on hers she felt as if she would suffocate. Alex's words came thundering back. *Be careful, Sam. He's a dangerous man.* Dangerous! Just the sound of the word was enough to terrify her.

At last, he eased up a bit, allowing her to look into his eyes. Stunned, Sam lay still, hearing his words as if they came from the end of a long tunnel. "Samantha, I adore you. You're my bright angel. My beautiful ivory doll."

My God, Sam thought, the man is talking to me as though I were a part of his collection! She tried to sit up, but he used the time to pull up her sweater, pinning her back with both hands holding her breast as his mouth sucked at her. Wildly she looked around, and her eyes fastened on a malachite candlestick. She stopped struggling, allowing her body to go limp. Mistaking her sudden stillness for acquiescence, he eased up his painful hold on her, as one hand reached down to remove her pants.

Pretending to arch toward him, she fumbled for the candlestick, almost knocking it over in her haste to lay hands upon it. It was heavy, but her anger and outrage gave her strength. Fastening her hand around it, she picked it up and, with a fury that surprised her, brought it down across Louis's back.

The sound—somewhere between a thud and a snap—sickened her. He let out a scream and, clutching his back, rolled to the floor.

She leaped up and stared at his strangely quiet body. Without bothering to see if he was breathing, she rushed out of the house.

On legs shaking so badly they barely could support her, she walked on to her own house nearby. Opening the door, she managed to get to the living room before collapsing on the couch in sobs. It was an hour before the trembling stopped. Then she went upstairs and took off her clothes. Bundling them up, she threw them into a wastebasket. Finally she stood under a hot shower until she felt she had washed away every vestige of Louis Breton's hands and mouth.

Then she called Rachel Fulton.

"You've got to call the police," insisted Rachel.

"I can't. Besides, nothing really happened."

"Except that he assaulted you, and you could have killed him."

"I don't think so. Oh, Rachel, if Mother finds out, it will kill her. You know how she feels about the Mallory name and reputation."

A tight smile formed on Rachel's lips. She knew a great deal about Sophie, and a lot of it she didn't like. "Well, I can't force you to do anything. But you realize if Louis decides to press charges and there's a trial, I'll be forced to tell them about our conversation."

"Don't worry. I'm sure Louis will never breathe a word."

The news of the attack on Louis Breton spread through town faster than brush fire. It was the topic of conversation at The Hickory House as well as Gordon's. Louis was a well-known, though not beloved, figure. Some who mistook his asceticism for homosexuality whispered that it was probably the attack of a male lover. Most people thought it was an intruder, though nothing appeared to have been stolen.

It never occurred to anyone that Louis's attacker might have been a woman.

Despite her assurance to Rachel, Sam waited for the Pitkin County sheriff to pull her in for questioning. But as the days went by and nothing happened, she began to believe that a man of Louis's pride and ego would never admit the truth.

As the days passed Rachel began to feel like the caretaker of the Mallory clan. After the attack Sam drew even closer to Rachel, the surrogate mother, bemoaning her guilt for making Rachel keep silent on the Breton affair. And partly to take Sam's mind off her own problems and partly because Rachel felt Sam ought to know, she told Sam about Pat's parentage. Even Sophie had taken Rachel into her confidence, telling her of her very real concerns for both her children's happiness. She said that Sam had suddenly started avoiding her, and she didn't know why. So desperately unhappy was Sophie about this latest rift in the relationship with her daughter that it had been on Rachel's tongue a hundred times to talk about what she knew.

"I'm sorry I ever told you about your brother," Rachel said one day while they were having lunch at Sam's studio.

"Why?"

"Because your coldness is making your mother miserable."

"Did you show it to her?" Sam's voice was sharp.

"Of course not."

"I'll never forgive her for what she's done to Pat."

"Put yourself in Sophie's shoes. And remember her age and the times. For a woman to sleep with a man she wasn't married to was bad enough. To get pregnant was a disaster. Things like that didn't happen to high-born young women. Knowing that, would you have told your firstborn son that the man he worshiped as his father was not his father?"

Sam agonized. "I don't know. But it's been perfectly obvious all these years that mother has been torn between love and hate when it comes to Pat. And though he never says much about it, he is what he is today because of her lifelong inability to give him unqualified love."

"Is he such a terrible man?" asked Rachel softly.

"No, of course not. But that marriage of his . . ."

"Is not our business," said Rachel firmly.

"Mother should tell him," insisted Sam stubbornly.

"What good would it do now? I think it would drive a wedge between the two of them that could never be repaired. You don't want that, do you?"

"I feel like Solomon. I'm damned if I do and damned if I don't."

"I know how you feel. I would feel the same way. But so much time has passed, I don't think it would serve any purpose or good whatsoever to tell Pat. Unless you want to feel particularly self-righteous."

"No, of course not. the awful thing is that I've been on Pat's case, too. I've taken Mother's side against him on all these development issues."

"But, Sam, one thing has nothing to do with the other. You can't possibly think your mother's behavior toward Pat's development schemes has anything to do with her feelings against his real father."

"No, I guess not. But who knows? Mother can be clever and devious. Did you know that she and Richard Farwell have been seeing one another? It's like the Hatfields discovering that they'd made a mistake and that it wasn't the McCoys they'd hated all those years, but some other clan."

Rachel laughed. "Maybe she'll have some influence on his decisions."

"I never thought of it that way. You always manage to find the end of the rainbow, don't you?"

Rachel's smile was rueful. If she was so good, where was hers?

Richard Farwell pulled on his sheepskin coat and strode through the house to the garage. As he walked, thunderclouds gathered on his face. His faded blue eyes took on the color of the threatening weather outside.

Women were as unpredictable as the March weather. Yesterday it was sunny and warm. Today the snowclouds lay low and heavy over the valley. He didn't mind the weather behaving that way, but he did mind Sophie MacNeal Mallory running hot and cold.

Richard knew that any relationship between them was bound to come under terrific pressures. Sometimes it seemed their differences were far greater than what they shared. Although the last few weeks had brought them closer together, last night had returned them to square one. After a delightful dinner at the Grill Room, they had gone back to her apartment for coffee and conversation.

One of them—he didn't remember who—had brought up the plan he'd submitted for the development of the Little Annie basin. From that point on, it had been all-out war.

Sophie had made all the familiar arguments against it. He had voiced the same tired clichés for it. He had hoped for an evening that would put their relationship on a new, more intimate plane; instead the contretemps set them back twenty years. He was furious. And mixed in with the fury was sadness.

His marriage was becoming more and more impossible, and Richard didn't look forward to a future as an eligible—although older—man. He knew he was desirable. Even if he were homely, his money would ensure his eligibility. But that was not what he wanted. He wanted Sophie Mallory.

Sophie was not only a worthy opponent, she was

also a spirited and beautiful woman. He'd found himself looking forward to spring and long horseback rides in the mountains with her. He wanted to take her up to his cabin in Canada and show her the matchless splendor of those Rockies. He wanted to go to New York on a theater binge with her. Maybe even to London. She would be a marvelous companion anywhere.

It was all academic. She'd told him to get the hell out; he had.

He slammed his Jeep down the snaking road that led from Red Mountain, crossed over the Roaring Fork River and into town. The weather, far from scaring off skiers, had brought them out in force. As he neared the foot of the mountain, he could see long lines at the gondola. He calculated how quickly they would be whisked to the top of the mountain and knew that although there would be grumbling at the wait it would dissipate once they were on the high-speed lift. The gondola had made a huge difference in the amount of downhill skiing. Skiers no longer spent a great part of their day waiting in lines and sitting in the chair lifts. Even the local hotshots told him they were exhausted by the end of the day. Compliments were in such short supply for him, any kind word tended to ensure a good day.

He pulled into the parking spot reserved for him and mounted the steps of the gondola to watch the operation. The operators were young, attractive local boys. Pleasant and helpful. They joined in the teasing and joking; the loading and off-loading proceeded without a hitch.

Richard chatted with a few of them, took their good-natured teasing, and made a mental note to have someone from maintenance check gondola number twenty-five. As he turned to leave he happened to look up the mountain. Right in the middle of a newly planned extension, he saw some kind of construction.

Realizing he needed a closer look, he returned to his car and pulled out a pair of ski boots and skis which he kept in readiness.

He crashed the line, much to the dismay and cries of protest of people who had been waiting patiently, and smiled apologetically when the lift operator called out, "He's the boss!"

A skier sitting next to him tried to engage him in conversation. Richard mumbled a few words, but he was too busy trying to see what was going on on his mountain.

His descent from the top led him through some of the most difficult terrain on the mountain. He could hear the hammering before he could see what was being hammered.

To his horror he found the beginnings of a shack. He skied up to one of the construction workers and asked as any curious skier might, "Hey, what's going up here?"

"Cabin, mister."

"Someone building a house?"

"They're opening up one of the old mines, I hear."

Another man with nails in his mouth grinned. "Wait 'til old Richard Farwell hears about that!"

"Old" Richard Farwell gave the man a tight smile, did a kick turn, and skied straight down Little Nell, ignoring the terrified novice skiers making their tortured way down the gentle slope. At the sound of his skis clattering over the icy moguls, they began to fall like tenpins as he skied by them. Later they would report they had seen this man "who looked like he was late for an execution" come barreling down the mountain at sixty miles an hour, totally out of control.

Richard kicked off his skis and carried them back to his car. He pulled on his fleece-lined shoes and made haste to his office.

Without a word of greeting to his secretary, he bit out, "Get me Pat Mallory!" The sound of his slamming door reverberated throughout the office.

"What's wrong with him?" asked one of the typists.

Marge Cameron, his secretary of ten years, shrugged. "I think he just found out about the shack going up on the mountain."

When Marge buzzed him a few minutes later, Richard punched the button, and Pat Mallory's voice filled the office with warm bass tones.

"What the hell is going on, Pat?"

"Good morning, Richard." When Richard didn't respond, Pat answered for him. "Good morning, Pat. How are you? How's the family?"

"Cut the crap." Richard's angry voice overrode Pat's.

"Could I have the question again?" Pat asked, determined not to let Richard's rudeness annoy him.

"That shack going up. Near Little Nell."

"I don't know. Is there a shack going up? I haven't been around the mountain for a couple of days."

"Christ, you can't miss it. Anyway, find out and get back to me as soon as you can."

The phone went dead in his ear. Pat smiled. Richard was really furious. He was barking orders like the old marine colonel he once was. Pat knew why he was the designated hitter on this one. He had friends in high places. Like one of the Pitkin County commissioners. He made the call. After a few switched calls, he finally had the facts in hand.

When Pat called Richard back, he was put through immediately. He could imagine the usually imperturbable Richard Farwell pacing like a trapped fox as he waited for Pat to get back to him.

At the sound of Richard's strained voice, Pat decided it was not the time for humor or lighthearted teasing.

"What have you got?"

"Did you know that when Silver Mountain Corp. leased these lands from the National Park Service they leased the mining rights, too?"

"What do you mean? How would I know that? The

Corp.'s been in existence for over thirty years. I would assume that they bought out whatever claims there were long ago."

"Apparently not. You, or at least the Corp. has mining rights which have not been exercised. And as long as you don't make at least a token attempt, someone else can."

"You mean someone is going to start mining on Aspen Mountain?"

"That's the way it looks to me."

"But how did they know those rights existed? If I didn't know about it, who? . . . I mean, that's the kind of thing that stays buried in obscurity in dusty files."

"Until someone goes into those dusty files and finds it."

"Then find out who it is. Maybe we can make some kind of deal. We damn well better make some kind of deal. He's in the middle of a ten-million-dollar development plan."

"I'll get back to you."

It wasn't easy to find out. The secrecy that prevented Pat from learning the true identity of the company that had recently snatched so many foreclosed properties out from under him prevailed.

Finally, he called the U.S. Forest Service, who were happy to supply him with the requested information. When they mentioned the name, Pat froze.

Fingers trembling with anger, Pat called Richard back.

He didn't even wait for Richard to speak. "You'll never believe this one."

"Who is it?"

"Hank Campbell."

"Sunshine's father? The old boy who has the ranch on Castle Creek?"

"The very same."

"Pat you've got to talk to him, make him stop."

"I'm not one of his favorite people."

"You're the real-estate maven. There must be something."

"I could find out if he's following building regulations."

"What do you mean?"

"Well, I'm on really shaky grounds with this one. You see, even if he didn't ask for a county permit, it might not matter. The Forest Service requires that applicants follow local regulations, but the Constitution says that federal law prevails when there are conflicts with state and local law. Which means if the county tried to prohibit a building used for mining operations, the courts might say the county was overstepping its bounds."

"There's got to be some loophole we can wiggle through."

Pat thought a moment. "There's one possibility. If the shack is going up where you say it is, it could be a safety hazard."

"Then you get on the phone and tell your friend, the commissioner, that we have a potential safety problem."

"I'll do my best."

"It's going to take more than that. Look, if Hank is behind this, it's to get back at you. And you'd better do something about it." Richard hung up without a farewell.

Pat stared at the phone. He was angry at Richard's tone, but mostly he was disbelieving. Hank Campbell? The guy didn't have a pot to piss in. He turned down a bona fide offer of over a million dollars for his land and now he was about to reopen a mine? Who was putting up the bucks? And where did the information come from?

He ran over the likely players in this newest scenario. And could come up with only one. Sophie Mallory, his mother!

CHAPTER EIGHTEEN

IN AN ATTEMPT TO SMOOTH THINGS AMONG THE VOLATILE Mallorys, Sophie invited Pat, Liz, and Samantha to dinner. The atmosphere, however, was closer to that of three hostile countries meeting in a final, half-hearted attempt to avoid outright war.

It was not unusual for Sophie's relationship with Pat to follow a roller coaster in its swift shifts between love and anger; and despite Liz's infuriating lack of interest, she never stopped trying to include her daughter-in-law in her social life. But for Sam to walk about tight lipped and hostile was very unusual. It broke Sophie's heart, but she was loath to question Sam, afraid her daughter would tell her something she didn't want to hear.

In a sudden burst of intuition, Pat realized what his mother was trying to do. With a rush of love, he decided he would try to help her get through a most difficult evening.

382

Prepared for Liz's refusal to accompany him to dinner, she surprised Pat by accepting. And now it was Liz who was making animated conversation and Sam who stared blankly into space. Despite her marriage into a family of wealth, Liz still felt like an outsider. She peppered her conversation with the names of Aspen's big-money crowd, the mere mention of which seemed to give her a kind of confidence by association. Also the master of a kind of vitriol that passed as clever conversation in jet-set circles, Liz's deadly barbs were delivered with a humor and wit that superficially smoothed the sharp edges, but fooled no one. She was regaling them now with a story of decorating a new house for a well-known millionaire as well as one for his mistress of long standing and how she'd mixed up the plans.

"I wanted to sink through the pink marble floor in embarrassment."

Sophie was amused in spite of herself. "So what happened?"

"You had to admire the wife's sangfroid, Sophie. She didn't blink an eyelash. We just exchanged plans and continued. I don't know if there was a big discussion afterward, but his secretary called my office a few days later to cancel the job for the mistress."

"So you lost a big commission?" said Sam, suddenly coming alive in her corner.

Liz shrugged grandly. She looked gloriously savage in St. Laurent pants and green corduroy jacket splendidly embroidered in gold sequin arabesques. "Isn't it nice that I don't have to rely on them? One of the advantages of having a rich husband."

Pat's lips pulled up in a smile of distaste, but he said nothing.

There was a shocked silence which Sophie tried to fill by noisily taking drink orders.

"No, let me, Mother."

Pat took elaborate care refilling their glasses, using

the time to cool down and gather his thoughts, a process which Sophie interrupted by asking, "What's all this I hear about a shack going up in the middle of the mountain?"

Pat gave his mother a curious look. Either she was playing a clever game or she really had nothing to do with this latest attempt to harass Richard—and stop Pat's development plan. He brought the glasses back and handed them out, pointedly taking a seat as far from his wife as possible. "It seems that Hank Campbell is planning to reopen the Compromise mine. He's building a service shack, and the Corp. is screaming. Richard wants the county to close him down because he didn't submit building plans for approval. But Hank does have federal-lands approval, so I'm not sure it's going to work. Richard is ready to explode."

"How on earth could such a thing happen?" Sophie asked.

"Somebody very clever went to the trouble of doing some research and discovered that the Corp. had mining claims which, if not exercised, could be taken over by someone else."

"But the shack, the filing of the claim, all of that takes money. And Hank doesn't have a dime," reminded Sophie.

"I know," sighed Pat. "Someone's backing him. But I don't know who or why."

"Does it really matter?" asked Sam.

"Of course it does!" Pat bellowed, angrily slamming down his drink. "The damn thing's right in the middle of the mountain! It's dangerous. There are skiers all over the place." Remembering his desire to help his mother with the evening, he shut up.

"And, of course, it would interfere with your development plan for that side of the mountain, wouldn't it?" said Liz, who was delighted to support anything that would discomfit or discredit Richard Farwell or her husband.

"Can't you find out who's behind Hank?" Sophie insisted.

"We're trying. So far no luck." Pat tossed down the rest of his drink. "When's dinner, Mother? I'm starving."

"Oh, anytime we're ready."

As they ate Sophie's excellent venison ragout and drank an outstanding Margaux, Sam nurtured her secret knowledge with a niggling sense of guilt. She knew exactly where both the idea and the money to raise the shack had come from.

It had all started one night when she and Rachel were talking about Hank's war with her brother and Richard Farwell. Rachel, who proved to have a diabolical mind, had said, "We need to find something that Hank can hold over Richard and Pat. Something that he can trade to stop them from bothering him. I'm really concerned that one day we're going to go out there and find him dead."

Both women had developed a great fondness for the colorful old man. While he regaled them with tales of the old West, Sam would make sketches that would later become incorporated into paintings. But the stories were interwoven with fearful accountings of the latest harassment. Puzzled by the ceaseless barrage, Rachel and Sam had separately accused Pat, who once again denied his part in such activities. Both women believed him. That left Richard Farwell.

Shortly afterward, Rachel through her research in Aspen's history discovered that the Corp.'s mining claims were about to lapse. And it was Sam who had advanced Hank the money to get started on the shack. Their secret work made them feel like Don Quixote and Sancho Panza fighting the windmills, and they knew it was only a question of time before their scheme would be discovered. But for the moment they were enjoying the most supreme satisfaction.

"It's a classic confrontation, isn't it?" Sam leaned

her elbows on the table and smiled at her brother. "The gunslinger against the simon-pure sheriff. The rustlers against the rancher. The stuff of western myths."

"Sam, don't get carried away. This is not a movie."

"Could be, though. I wonder how it's going to end. . . ."

"The good guys don't win all the time anymore," reminded Liz with a sly smile.

"Leave it to you to remind us," said Sam in disgust.

"Let's drop the whole subject. I didn't bring us all together to argue." Sophie rose from the table. "Shall we go into the library for brandy?"

"Not for me, Mother. I have to fly down to Taos tomorrow."

"You didn't tell me you were going to Taos," accused Liz.

"Didn't I?" Pat's look was bland and innocent. "Sorry. I'm going to Taos."

"For how long?"

"As long as it takes."

At the murderous look in his wife's eyes, he relented. No sense in making a scene. That would be the capper for an already badly strained evening. "A couple of days," he said.

"Thank you," she said stiffly.

He pulled his sheepskin coat from the bleached antlers of an elk. "Are you coming, Liz?"

"I guess I'll go home, too," said Sam.

"But it's so early," Sophie protested. "Darling," she turned to her daughter and put an arm around her shoulder. "Surely you can stay a little while longer? I haven't had a chance to talk to you in days."

Sophie felt her daughter's resistance. With a sinking heart she dropped her hand and shook her head, trying to hold back the tears that threatened to fall.

Sam's heart immediately melted. "All right, Mother." She sat down on the couch and curled her feet under her. As Sophie saw her son and daughter-in-law out, Sam picked up a copy of one of the glossy decorating books and turned the pages idly.

Each room was a magnificent still life of objects and textures. She wondered if anyone really lived in the pristine order shown in those rooms. Certainly not her, or Rachel, or even her perfect mother. Their rooms were like their minds, overflowing with comfortable disorder. Only Liz's house had that curious bloodless perfection. But she was a decorator. No, it was something else. Liz's compulsive neatness was a cover-up for the total disorder of her life.

Sophie returned and set about puffing up pillows and picking up glasses. As she worked she made small talk. Her forced cheerfulness grated on Sam's nerves.

Suddenly Sophie stopped, straightened her shoulders, and looked at her daughter squarely. "What's wrong, Sam? You've been avoiding any conversation with me for days."

Sam averted her eyes. Her lips tightened in the same stubborn line she'd worn as a child.

"I know about it, Mother."

"Know what, darling?"

"About Pat," Sam repeated.

Sophie looked puzzled. "I don't understand."

In exasperation Sam threw down the pillow she'd been hugging to her. "I know that Dad was not Pat's father."

Sophie's face turned white. For a moment she felt as if she would faint. She stumbled to a chair and dropped into it. "How do you know that?" she asked in a voice cold as death.

"Does it matter?"

Sophie opened her hands in wordless plea.

"Why? Why have you let him believe all these years?"

"I couldn't tell him as a child. He worshiped Sam so I couldn't bear to tell him as he was growing up. And then it was too late."

"But he had the right to know!"

"Did he?"

"Do you know how difficult it's been for him his entire life?"

"What's been difficult?"

"You were so hard on him. Demanding something from him he couldn't give. Asking him to be something he could never be. Daddy's son. You've always treated him like it was his fault."

"That's not true," protested Sophie weakly, knowing it was completely true. "I love him."

"I'm sure you do. But not the way you love me. I always knew that. It was perfectly obvious."

That startled Sophie. "To him, too?"

"He's much more sensitive than you might believe."

"I do care for him," Sophie protested.

"I hope so, because the only thing he's ever wanted and worked to have was your love and your respect."

The tears poured unheeded from Sophie's eyes. "It was such an awful time. I wanted to die. But your father saved my life. When I discovered how much he meant to me, how much I loved him, Patrick was always there, a guilty reminder of my sin."

"You have to tell him," Sam said firmly.

"No!"

"He has a right to know."

"No, he doesn't. What good would it do now? Do you want him to really hate me? This is one time that honesty is not the best policy. Believe me, Sam, Pat would not thank me. And I don't want to hurt him anymore." She put her head back wearily. "In a way I'm glad it's out in the open. Between us, at least." She gave her daughter a pleading look. "Despite everything that's happened, despite the fact that Pat and I are on opposite sides more often than not, I'm very proud of him. He's turned into a good man. The only thing I wish is that he find some happiness before it's too late."

Sophie's anguish touched the deepest recesses of

Sam's heart. She knelt at her mother's feet and reached out her arms. Thinking of Rachel, she held her mother close and said softly, "He will. I promise you, he will."

Liz Mallory, her arms filled with plans, sample cases, and swatch books, told her assistant that she had a meeting with Count di Lucca. She put everything in her Volvo station wagon and headed up Red Mountain Road to Gianni's house.

Her design was slowly taking shape. Which was just fine with her. It gave her convenient excuses to see Gianni. Although lately he'd been so preoccupied, he was barely aware that she was there. When she asked where his mind was, she received the same vague answer and a dismissing wave of a hand.

As she stood in front of the fourteen-foot-high carved teak door, she felt that same breathless mixture of anxiety and desire. She'd never had a lover like him before. Half-convinced she was in love with him, she wondered what his feelings were for her.

He opened the door at her ring and bowed her in. Although he looked particularly stunning this morning in a Missoni sweater of shades of plum, black, and purple, she noticed his distraction, even his usually smooth hair was rumpled.

"Lizabetta." He smiled and bent to kiss her cheek. His Italian version of her name never ceased to thrill her. "How lovely you look today."

Knowing she would be spending the morning with him, she had taken great pains with her dress. She wore a short black leather skirt and tobacco-colored cashmere sweater with a wide alligator belt that pointed up her small waist and made her round hips swell invitingly.

"I have the plans for the downstairs bathroom." She brandished the drawing. "Lapis lazuli! It will be stunning, I promise."

She raced through the plans quickly, aware that he

was watching her. Finally she stopped and looked into his eyes. "What?" she asked softly.

"I'm sorry?" Despite his ardent gaze his mind was on neither her nor the plans.

"You're looking at me strangely."

"Not strangely, I assure you. Perhaps with longing?"

She shivered with delight.

He put a tanned hand on hers. "So tell me what is new and exciting in town?"

"Oh, wait until you hear this one. Pat told us at dinner last night. It's delicious." As she recounted the story of Hank Campbell's shack and his intention of reopening one of the mines on the mountain, she spiced the story with a few drolleries of her own. It had the desired effect, and Gianni joined her in uproarious laughter. But he was far from amused. That tattered old man was making fools of all of them. It was obviously time to stop fooling around and turn to more serious threats.

"Gianni?"

He brought his attention back to her.

"Pat's going to be in New Mexico for a few days."

"What about the children?" His smile displayed a concern he didn't feel. Lately Liz was getting more demanding, asking for accountings of his time away from her. She was expressing a growing disatisfaction with Pat and making threats of leaving him. He was getting weary of the little scenarios that seemed to begin with: Wouldn't it be wonderful if we could (1) go away together, (2) share the house, (3) take a trip to Italy and visit your family.

"Don't worry. The housekeeper is always there. And they're getting used to me being away from home almost as much as their father." She turned slowly to him and put her arms around him, nuzzling his head into her breasts. Hiking her skirt, she straddled his leg, riding it like a mechanical horse. "I'll be so happy when I can just come here without a sheaf of plans under my arms for protection."

"I, too," he murmured. God, he wanted to dump her! But he couldn't, not just yet. He wasn't finished with her.

A top professional in many disciplines, Gianni was extraordinarily able at making love convincingly. He simply put his brain on automatic and turned the trip over to his cock. Liz's mouth and greedy hands did the rest.

Later, as she dressed slowly, her aimless chatter almost drove him mad. He was impatient for her to leave so he could put in a phone call to Caracas where Santos was waiting for a progress report.

He gave her a final kiss at the door and promised to call her later for dinner. As soon as she was gone, he put in his call, waiting impatiently to clear the three layers of security before he was given permission to speak to Santos.

Gianni was prepared for Santos's annoyance at this new turn of events, but not for anger. With disgust he listened to the sound of his own voice, whining and pleading with a man who despised weakness of any sort. He offered excuses, valid ones, which were met with icy scorn. Santos's final words, "Make something happen or prepare to be replaced on the project," spurred Gianni to promise that he only needed another month. Hank Campbell would be stopped immediately, and it was just a question of time before Farwell was unseated and he could step in.

What Gianni didn't say was that he had become fond of Aspen. The skiing, the night life, the hungry women, the steady and interesting sex, the weather, and his role as the count. Thanks to Pat—though he didn't know about it—he'd already turned over one of the properties he'd surreptitiously stolen from under Pat's nose and made a tidy profit. Now he could return the "borrowed" money from the Santos Aspen account with no one the wiser. It was a particular kind of business that Gianni liked. Absolutely no risk and the generous use of someone else's money.

Nevertheless, the Mallorys had not been as easy to dispose of as he thought. And now he had to take care of the Hank Campbell problem.

Dawn came over the Roaring Fork Valley in a burst of lavender. As the sun rose, the sky blossomed into a vaporous pink, curled with cloud wisps of smoky gray. There was a smell of spring in the air. The sound of hounds barking in the distance cut the morning silence. To their howls was added the crowing of a hoarse rooster. The noises died away, only to be replaced by the hum of the various lifts as they carried the daily food supplies and the ski patrolmen up the mountain.

Suddenly a series of earth-shattering explosions split the air. Survivalists who had been preaching doom for the last forty years nodded with grim satisfaction. Even as old Gorby and Ronnie were signing treaties, they were setting off the bomb. Born-again Christians prepared to meet their maker. The Zen followers tranced out with mantras and got ready for the next stage of their existence.

But ordinary people threw on coats and ran outside to mill about like frightened sheep and ask questions.

Joe Ferris and Richard Farwell each pulled up in front of the gondola within a matter of minutes.

"What happened?" Joe asked the foreman.

"Big explosion in the old mine tunnel. Dynamite. Knocked out a side of the shack."

Richard groaned. "Anyone on the mountain when it happened?"

"No skiers. Too early. But some of the patrol guys were on their way up."

"C'mon." Joe pulled the man into one of the snowmobiles and the three of them went zooming up the mountain, slowing down when they drew abreast of the shack and gave it a cursory glance. The building had suffered only minor damage, so they crisscrossed the mountain looking for bodies. The force of the explosion had ripped a hole in the center of the beginner's slope which would have to be cordoned off before the lifts started taking up skiers.

Continuing up the mountain to survey the damage, it was Joe who first saw the crumpled body in a red parka and navy pants. The blood oozing from the patrolman's crushed head had stained the white snow an obscene dark red.

They pulled over, and Joe ran expert hands over the man's body, felt for a pulse, then got on the walkie talkie and called for immediate help. "Head wound," he reported crisply. "Nothing seems broken. Pulse rapid. Breath shallow. Shock. Hurry."

Within minutes, a snowmobile arrived with a doctor who'd picked up the call on his car CB as he was heading for Mountain Valley Hospital.

"Good diagnosis, Joe," he reported after a quick examination. "If he lives, he'll owe it all to you."

Richard and Joe continued surveying the damage and checking for bodies. Satisfied that the patrolman was the only one, they headed down the mountain, where they noticed that one of the gondola towers was leaning precariously. Getting out to check, Joe found that it had a large crack in it. He put his weight against it. It gave a groan. He got back into the snowmobile and for the first time all morning Joe and Richard looked at each other.

"It could have been worse," Joe offered lamely.

Richard dropped his head into his hands. His voice muffled, he asked, "Do you think it was an accident or deliberate?"

"I don't know. Dynamite explosions aren't usually accidents. Jake came down with the other snowmobile to call the sheriff." He looked up at tower number three. "But we can't run the gondola until that cracked tower is fixed."

"I know, I know. How long will that take? There's still a month of skiing left."

Joe shrugged. "I'll get on the horn and talk to the chief engineer and get back to you."

"Someone up there doesn't like me. Job was a happy, carefree man compared to me. Get back to me as soon as possible."

"I will." Joe was about to enter his office when he thought of something else. "Richard?"

Farwell turned.

"There's something else you probably should worry about."

"What else could there be?"

"A lawsuit. That patrolman might never be able to work again even if he does live."

Richard groaned.

It was only the beginning. When skiers arrived to find that the gondola was inoperative, there were screams of protest. That meant huge lines on the west side of the mountain and virtually no skiing on the east side unless skiers had no objection to cutting back to 1A or taking the Bell Mountain chair lift.

Richard Farwell had no alternative but to instruct the ticket office to cut the ticket price in half to compensate for the loss and inconvenience to the skiers. The patrolman's insurance would take care of his hospital costs, but the next day a lawyer informed Richard that a negligence suit would be brought against the mountain. Their only defense was that person or persons unknown were responsible for the blast and the Corp. was not guilty. It would be a tough and unpopular case for the Corp., but they had lawyers who were used to handling them. Depending on the outcome and the settlement, there was no doubt that the Corp.'s insurance rates would take another astronomical climb. This, on top of Richard's other problems, would seem to seal his fate as CEO of the Silver Mountain Corp.

The next morning Pitkin County Sheriff Carl Jarvis

questioned Joe Ferris about the accident. Jarvis had only been sheriff for two years, but his predecessor had passed down to him some of the rumors about Joe Ferris.

"Any ideas on this, Joe?"

"None."

"Who stands to gain from this?"

"Gain? What kind of gain if half the mountain is unskiable?"

"What about the other side of the coin? Who hates Richard Farwell or the Silver Mountain Corp.?"

Joe laughed. "Take a number. Neither one could win a popularity contest."

"So maybe we're looking for someone who has a grudge?"

"That's possible."

Carl eyed him thoughtfully, and then asked, "What about Hank Campbell?"

"Well, I know that Richard and Pat have been interested in getting their hands on Hank's ranch for future development. But the Corp.'s finances are a little stretched now, so I don't think that's a possibility."

"I think we should pull Hank in."

Two deputies brought Hank in to Jarvis's office. Joe was there but remained in the background as Jarvis gently questioned the old man.

After a half hour Hank exploded. "Jesus H. Christ, Carl! Why would I want to dynamite my own mine? Besides, I wasn't even around when it happened. I was in Denver seeing my doctor."

"You could have set it up for someone else to do it."

"Don't you gimme none of that crap, Carl. You been seein' too many cop things on the television. Besides, you don't think I'm gonna give money to some drifter to set off an explosion. Hell, I can hardly afford to buy gas for my pickup."

"Reopening the mine must have cost some."

Hank's face closed tight as a bar on Sunday. "That's not my money responsible for that."

"What do you think of Richard Farwell?"

"Not much." Seeing the interested smile on Carl's face, he corrected himself. "That is, I don't give him a hell of a lot of thought. Me and him don't travel in the same circles."

Sunshine verified that she had indeed taken her father to Denver and that the old man could not have had anything to do with the explosion. He had a big mouth but he was totally harmless, a fact known to everyone in the valley.

After Hank was released, Carl turned to Joe Ferris. "You say Richard was strapped for money?"

"I don't know about Richard personally. But the Corp.'s had a couple of bad years."

Carl rubbed his chin thoughtfully. "Maybe we're lookin' in the wrong place. Maybe Richard Farwell is our man."

Rachel stepped out of the quiet gloom of the Pitkin County Library into the bright, blazing sunshine. She had been in the archives reading some old family histories and run into an interesting feud that she thought might make a good story.

It concerned the MacNeals and a family known as the Fernandos. Don Miguel Fernando, one of the early Spaniards whose ancestors had come to the new world with Cortez, had gradually made his way from the California goldfields to Colorado's silver mines and been one of the unlucky ones who had to sell his claims to Gerald MacNeal. With his new wife, a beautiful Indian named Little Silver Deer who had saved his life, they'd moved onto Indian lands where Don Miguel tried his hand at ranching. Then the whites had appropriated the lands for themselves. Out of pity or guilt, Gerald MacNeal sold him a small homestead. A diary kept by Little Silver Deer had painstakingly described how she had paid MacNeal by allowing him to use her body.

From the letters and diaries that had come down

through the years, the MacNeal family's fate had once again intertwined with the Fernandos'. This time when Miguel, son of the first Don Miguel, married a beautiful silver baron's daughter. Dodge Blackwell was apparently a flirt and an empty head. Beautiful as a summer's day, she became enamored of the handsome half-breed. But life with him had proved hard, and she ran away. After an annulment of the marriage she'd married James MacNeal, Gerald MacNeal's son and Sophie's grandfather. Shortly after, she and her child had died in childbirth.

Miguel Fernando, however, produced a son, Angel, who had once again chosen to marry a beautiful Indian girl, a Navaho named Helen Whitecloud. And there Rachel lost the threads of the tale. But she'd found enough to encourage further research. Like most easterners she was fascinated by the myths of the West and the clash of cultures between the westward-moving settlers, the native-born Americans, and the old Spanish colonials who'd come in from Mexico to settle California, New Mexico, and parts of Texas.

Most of her research had been completed; the story was fairly clear in her mind now. The hard part would be writing the detailed outline and working out all the interconnecting relationships.

Today she decided to declare a holiday for herself. She would find a place to have lunch in the sunshine and perhaps take a hike up the road toward Castle Creek and say hello to Hank Campbell.

As she walked along Main Street toward town, she was stopped by the steady honk of a horn. Turning in annoyance at this break in the pleasant hum of the day, she saw Pat Mallory in a Saab convertible with its top down. In the backseat were two children she immediately knew were his.

"Rachel, hi!" he called, pulling over to the curb.

"Hi, yourself. I was about to bawl you out for disturbing the peace. What are you up to?"

"We just got back from a couple of days in Denver.

It's school break, you know. We're off to lunch. Want to join us?"

"I was hoping to find a place to sit in the sun."

"We'll go to Pinocchio's for pizza. Okay with you?"

"Okay."

"Hop in."

He introduced her to his children and told them she was a writer.

Tooey stared at her with fascination while Mandy pretended to be uninterested. But she was instinctively aware that her daddy and this lady with the pretty dark hair were special friends.

The minute they sat down, Tooey started to question her. "Do you write books about Indians?"

"Kind of," she replied with a smile.

"What kind of?"

"Well, my first book was about the Hopi Indians in Arizona and how their land was stolen from them. I wrote about their fierce attachment to the land and the beautiful things they could do with their hands."

Pat smiled. It was a slight oversimplification!

"Did you write about scalping and wars and things like that?"

"You bloodthirsty little tiger." Pat ruffled his son's hair, but Rachel could see his genuine concern. "There's a lot more to Indian life than war cries and scalping, Tooey," Pat gently admonished. "You should learn about them. They're a very important part of your heritage."

"Yessir." He suppressed his excitement and continued along gentler tones. "And what else did you write?"

"This is boring," piped in Amanda.

"Mandy!" The warning flashed out.

"Well, it is."

"I think if you spent more time listening to your teachers and people like Miss Fulton and less time on clothes and mirrors, we'd all be a great deal happier.

"Ohh, Daddy." The child's big blue eyes filled with tears at this scolding in front of a stranger.

"It's all right, Pat. We can talk of other things," Rachel said softly. She didn't want to be caught in the middle of a disciplinary lesson.

"No, it's not. Mandy has to learn once and for all that the world does not begin and end with her."

"But not here," Rachel pleaded softly.

Behind Pat's strong words lay his condemnation of his wife's influence on her daughter. Tooey had managed to escape it; perhaps being younger was a blessing. She sighed inwardly. With Mandy it was probably too late. She'd already been pressed into the mold of her mother. Children of wealth have it rougher than we know, she thought.

Tooey continued to ply her with questions. She discovered that he had a curious mind that absorbed information like a sponge. With his gentle prompts and occasional interjections, Pat displayed his overwhelming hands-on love for his child. Even Mandy had begun to lighten up, and although she contributed nothing to the conversation, Rachel caught the girl staring at her with curious eyes when she spoke.

"Miss Fulton has pretty eyes, doesn't she, Daddy?" This surprising remark came out of Mandy while they were waiting for their dessert.

Pat turned to look. The one thing that had struck him from the first was Rachel's eyes. They had the silvery glitter of a stream in sunlight as it ran over the rocks. "Yes, she does." His look of warmth had the same power of a physical caress.

She lowered her lids and immediately gave Mandy a compliment in return which wreathed her lovely face in smiles.

Rachel clutched her trembling hands in her lap. This pleasurable scene was filling her with a deep longing. Here they were: a man, a woman, and two children sitting in the sun, laughing and talking, the perfect picture of a happy family. Only she was not the wife nor the mother, only a stranger who had happened upon them and been allowed to enter their charmed circle for a brief moment.

Her growing feelings for Pat frightened her. There was no place in her life for a man right now, certainly not a married one. Falling in love was full of pitfalls at best, falling in love with him could be disastrous. Although she'd always fought against the concept, she was aware that a caste system existed in the democratic United States. More than money separated the well-born from the rest; in Rachel's case, the differences were cultural as well as social.

She turned the conversation to their visit to Denver. Here Mandy took over, describing their dinners and their visit to the museums, the ballet which Tooey didn't care for but which she loved, a stop at Colorado Springs to see the Air Force Academy, and a side trip to Cripple Creek.

"Did you know that they called themselves 'the World's Greatest Gold Camp'?"

"No!" said Rachel in mock surprise.

As Mandy went into tedious detail, Pat watched their byplay with a happy smile on his face. He wanted his children to like Rachel.

"By the way, Pat, did you hear about the explosion?" Rachel asked when there was a lull in the conversation.

"What explosion?"

She told him of the day's events. Immediately the atmosphere changed from one of pleasant relaxation to tense alertness. "Look, kids, we've got to get you home. I have some things I have to take care of in a hurry." With a press of his hand on hers, he threw money on the table and steered the children away.

Rachel found his remark very strange.

CHAPTER NINETEEN

THE BOTTOMLESS PIT WAS A GOOD DESCRIPTION OF THE kind of after-hours spot that young Aspen seemed to prefer. It resembled one of Hopper's paintings of the thirties with pools of light in otherwise dark surroundings. High leather booths that once might have been bright red had been darkened by years of sweaty palms and thighs. There was a raised bandstand and a handkerchief-sized dance floor. What the bar lacked in decor it made up for in privacy. It was here that most of the valley consummated their drug deals. Although the police had long suspected the place as a base of operations, they had never been able to make a bust due to a strong communications network that seemed to start right in the sheriff's office. By the time an informer's tip got to them, it was useless.

Joe Ferris paused in the doorway and allowed his eyes a moment to adjust to the murk. It was fairly full for a Wednesday night. With the exception of himself everyone seemed to be in their twenties.

Soft, insinuating music floated over the couples. Since the film *Dirty Dancing,* the wild solo style had changed to one of vertical fornification as lean muscular bodies slid and squirmed on the floor in unselfconscious pornography. Wearing little bandeaus and tights or tiny skirts, hair streaming in electric shock disarray, the girls danced with closed eyes, switching partners at will. In a world frightened of AIDS, this substitute for sex seemed to hold more grace and promise than the real thing.

Joe went to the bar and ordered a Corona. Across the dance floor he saw Sam with Paul Emerson, Alex, Melanie, Rosie, and Bill. Melanie was obviously slumming, but Sam's appearance in the place came as a shock. He knew she hated these dark, steamy places.

At the other end of the bar near the bandstand, he spotted a group of Alex's cronies. They were the bad boys, the perennial troublemakers. As bored teenagers they used to shoot out streetlights and overturn garbage cans. They were habitual drunks, having conned older friends to buy them beer when they were underage. Their names appeared with boring regularity in the lists of DWIs. Then came the drugs.

Although they had plenty of money from overgenerous allowances, they found kicks and big bucks hustling on the street. Joe knew them well. He ought to. When he first came back to Aspen, he'd been their supplier. They didn't know it, because he was smart enough to work through a middleman—an expensive practice but one that protected his anonymity.

His mouth fell in the bitter lines that would never leave. As long as he remained in Aspen he would never be able to escape. Much as he wanted to he couldn't change anything that he'd had to do to get his family out of the pit of poverty.

A burst of applause came from the corner booth as Alex pushed his way to the stage. With a good-natured smile he picked up his guitar and ambled to the mike.

Joe's experienced eye told him that the boy had been probably using all night. He was giggly and unsteady, his voice and movements jerky. But he could play guitar!

Joe ordered another beer and hunkered down on his barstool to listen to Alex play and sing. His mouth twisted in a rueful smile. Alex was a seriously good musician wasting those talents just as he wasted all of his other talents. He watched a bar girl with pneumatic boobs and a short skirt bring a pitcher of beer and glasses to the band. Alex reached for one and toppled over the edge. As his cronies jeered and teased, he picked himself up, gave a sheepish smile, then allowed them to drag him back to his table.

Joe turned away in distaste and tossed down the dregs of his beer, then headed for the men's room. From behind the stall door, he heard a noisy group enter. Alex's voice cut through clear but unsteady.

"Sshh, you guys, everyone'll think the party's in here." He giggled. There was a sound of restless feet. "It's payday, boys."

Joe heard the rustle of a plastic bag, then the squeak of a razor blade on a mirror; Alex was cutting lines. There was a murmur of excited voices, then the snort that told him they were inhaling.

"Good stuff, man," said one.

"Hey, where are you getting it? I thought your old man had cut you off."

Alex giggled. "I have a friend."

"Yeah, I sure could use a friend like that."

"You've got me. It's the same things. Hey, thanks for the help, you guys," said Alex sincerely.

The teasing back and forth had a sophomoric edge to it. Joe was anxious to leave, but he didn't think making his presence known was wise.

"So what's the drill? How are you scoring?" asked one friend who obviously was on the outside of this charmed circle.

"I'm doing a few jobs for this guy."

"Need any assistants?" One of them laughed knowingly.

"I might," said Alex.

"So what kind of gig is it?"

Alex lowered his voice. "That explosion in the mine? I set it."

"No shit?" an unbelieving and respectful voice sounded.

"No shit!" said Alex.

"Boy, you were taking some chances!"

"Not really. It was early in the morning. There wasn't anyone around."

"Except that patrolman who got blasted."

"Yeah, but he's okay."

"How come they wanted you to do that?"

"I didn't ask. I didn't really care. I guess someone's trying to put a scare into Farwell. Couldn't happen to a nicer guy." Alex laughed.

Joe was surprised. What did Alex have against Richard Farwell? And then he heard Alex say, "C'mon, I gotta get back."

When he was sure that everyone had gone, Joe left his hiding place. He looked around the room. As he washed his hands, he saw the infinitesimal traces of the white powder.

It was obvious that Alex was doing Gianni's dirty work. He had to tell someone about this. But who? Whom could he trust? Even though Richard Farwell was his employer, they had never had a personal relationship. Quickly he went through his other possibilities. Whom could he tell? Patrick Mallory was definitely not a consideration. That left Sam. He could trust her, but did he want to involve her? Anyway she'd never believe him. Not in a million years. Alex was one of her dearest friends. They were part of the same social class.

As he returned to the noisy bar, he paused for an

instant at the bandstand to look at Alex. Lost in a cocaine cloud of euphoria, he was bringing forth an astonishing series of sounds from his guitar.

"Hey, sailor. Come here often?"

He turned abruptly to find Melanie at his elbow. She wore a short bright purple satin skirt and one of those $800 Aspen folkloric sweaters. His mouth twisted in a half smile. Eight hundred dollars for an angora mountain! Despite his distaste for her cavalier attitudes, he had to admit the outfit made her look very desirable.

"You've been avoiding me," she pouted.

"I've been busy."

She pushed her breasts against his arm. "You're not busy now."

"What do you have in mind?" He glanced over her shoulder and caught Sam's eyes on him. A faintly derisive smile curved her lips.

In answer Melanie took his elbow and steered him toward the door.

"Hey, what about Alex?" he protested.

"What about him?" She smiled and tugged him away.

Alex, who was deep in some mellow riff, finally opened his eyes in time to see her walking away, her skirt, like a bright beacon, flashing through the press of dancers on the murky floor.

"Melanie!" he moaned. "Hey, Mel, where you going?" He shook his head like a punished puppy and murmured to himself, "Where's she going?"

His guitar dropped to the floor with a dissonant protest of strings. Pushing himself into the booth next to Sam, he asked, "Where was Melanie going? The ladies' room's not in that direction."

"She left with Joe Ferris."

"Why?" he whined.

"Damn it, I don't know!"

"I don't trust that guy. I never did," said Alex. He

slumped against the leatherette. He made Olympic rings on the black table with a wet glass. Then he leaned forward. "You know it wouldn't surprise me at all that he's the guy responsible for all the accidents on the mountain."

"What are you saying, Alex?" Sam's face echoed the disbelief in her voice.

Alex gave her a crafty look. His voice sank to a whisper as he gleefully elucidated. "He certainly has the opportunity. He's got total freedom of movement all over the mountain. And," this said triumphantly in his best Perry Mason style, "he's got the motive, too."

"What motive?"

"If Farwell gets kicked out, he's gonna benefit."

Sam shook her head. "They're not going to make Joe the CEO."

"Shows you how much you know. There are two guys on the board that think Joe Ferris is a white knight. After all, he really runs the place. They wanted to make him president last year, but Pat and Farwell got the votes to nix the idea. Joe wasn't too happy about that."

"But—" Sam was about to protest.

Alex interrupted smoothly. "I'm not suggesting Joe's tried to kill anyone—but with his past anything's possible. He's probably just trying to embarrass them."

"What do you mean—with his past?"

"Ask him," Alex replied cryptically, then wandered off, leaving Sam openmouthed and trembling.

With a sinking heart, Sam had to concede that Alex made sense. But her instinctive feeling about the real man under Joe's icy exterior protested. This was the boy who had helped her pick pasqueflowers in the late-spring snow and gather kinnikinnick berries in late summer, whose grandfather had shown her how to use a divining rod to find water, who had taken her to a place that contained 3000-year-old arrowheads, who had helped her do her first Indian beadwork, who had encouraged her love and curiosity of all things Indian.

So his family was honorable. Since when did that have anything to do with reality? Joe had grown far away from his Indian integrity and sense of honor. And why would Alex say it, if he didn't believe it? He had certainly been right about his father. And Sam remembered Pat's warnings, referring to something unpleasant in Joe's background. Pat was probably right about him after all, she conceded with a heavy heart.

Richard Farwell paced the length of Sophie Mallory's living room.

"I'm at my wit's end, Sophie. This last thing has me reeling."

"You're talking about the explosion?"

Richard ran his hand through his ginger-colored hair. It stood up like a wet rooster's. In place of his usually immaculate appearance, he appeared rumpled and sleepless. "These so-called accidents are just too . . . too regular to be mere coincidence. I think there's a divine plan behind them."

"But who?"

He stopped and gave her a candid look. "Let's face it, Sophie, I would never win a Bill Cosby award for popularity."

Sophie smiled. "Yes, you can be a very difficult man."

"I hate agreeable women."

"Whom do you suspect?"

"That's it. I don't know. Your son? No, that's not Pat's style. Besides, he's not tempted by my job, he's got enough to deal with."

Sophie, aware of the large sum of money he had lent Richard, suggested Gianni.

"No, the man's been a lifesaver. He's put absolutely no pressure on me, and he knows our revenues are down because of the lift situation. Now they tell me it's going to be another week before we can run full capacity. Christ, the season's almost over! I tell you someone wants me out of the Silver Mountain Corp."

"But Richard, you've put a great deal of your personal fortune into the company."

"My stupid fault for considering it my own personal fiefdom. So I was foolish."

"I think you're anything but foolish," she said softly. She stopped him in midpace with a touch of her hand. Wearily he sunk into the couch next to her. He spread his legs and leaned his elbows on them, staring at the floor. When he turned his head to look at her, the rigid face softened. "Right now the only sane and sensible thing in my life is you." He took her hand. Turning it over, he kissed her palm. "Thanks for letting me back into yours." She touched his bowed head with her fingertips, then let her hand trail to his chin. She tilted it toward her and kissed him softly. It was meant to ease, not to suggest. But Richard, caught by a surge of emotion, caught her to him and turned the kiss into a demand for more.

"Sophie, don't make me wait. You know how I feel. Time's passing by too swiftly for us to play these silly games with each other."

"Richard, there's something you should know about me."

"I don't want to hear. If there's another man in your life, get rid of him. I won't ask questions. I'm not interested in confessions."

She had been about to tell him of her relationship with Marcus Feldman, and why, despite her disinterest in marriage, she was loath to rush into another dead-end affair. She wanted to add the bit about mistress and home-wrecker, but his refusal to hear anything negative stilled her. Ruefully, she considered making a long postponed appearance at confession just to share her secrets with someone.

"I've made lunch for us," she said softly, then laughed at the frustrated expression on his face.

"I'm making earth-shaking admissions and she's talking lunch. Give me strength!" He threw pleading hands to the sky.

"Come, Richard, be patient with me. Don't forget that I disliked you thoroughly for twenty years. You have to give me a chance to overcome that."

"Neither one of us is going to change, you know." She laughed. "Don't be too sure."

"Well, it won't be me," he insisted.

"Don't be too sure," she reiterated. Taking his hand, she pulled him up. "We can talk later. Now, I'm making *huevos rancheros*."

He followed her into the kitchen, once again admiring her lean, long-legged body in faded jeans tucked into the elaborately stitched boots.

"Christ, I completely forgot to tell you. I'm going to give a party. I want you to be my hostess. Here's what I want you to do."

As Richard outlined his needs she couldn't help smiling at his imperious tone. There was no changing Richard Farwell. He was accustomed to giving orders and having them obeyed immediately. Like her. She could just picture a life with him.

"Well, what do you say?"

"No," she said firmly. "I will not."

"But why?" His mouth compressed into a narrow, annoyed slash.

"Oh, Richard, be sensible. That would be an admission of a relationship that I'm not ready or willing to make public just yet. I'll be happy to come. But that's the extent of it."

"I have to accept your wishes, I guess."

"There's hope for you yet." She patted his hand.

Richard Farwell's house glowed with lights visible for miles around. Everyone knew his would be the party of the year and that the cream of society from both coasts would be there. Many were flying in on private jets for the evening. For those, Richard had booked suites at the Silver Leaf Inn and the Hotel Lenado. Many like Barbara Walters and Merv Adelman, the Murdochs, the Davises would stay at their own homes.

By the end of March, roads were clear enough to bring out the Jags, Ferraris, and BMWs. They choked Richard's huge parking area and curved around the driveway.

Three hundred people had been invited for a sumptuous buffet prepared by Larry McIntyre with desserts from Rebecca. Richard had flown in caviar from Petrossian and champagne from Moët in California. His friend, Peggy Lee, had come in from New York to entertain and Liza Minelli had promised to show up if she could sneak away from other commitments.

Despite its reputation for glamour and glitz, Aspen was a country mouse compared to such cities of excess as New York, Los Angeles, and Dallas. There had not been a single 30,000-dollar Lacroix pouff or 17,000-dollar St. Laurent embroidered jacket seen all winter. Aspen party dress tended toward the casual or the outrageous. Elegant women were aware of the Lacroix pouffs of Paris and the sequins and marabou of St. Laurent, but felt them inappropriate in a town whose streets and sidewalks were either choked with dust or snow. Those to whom these things were important saved their jewels and French couture clothes for visits to cities where that kind of power-dressing counted.

But from the very first, Farwell's party was different. Perhaps because winter's hold was weakening, perhaps because they were tired of ski clothes and bulky sweaters, perhaps for no reason at all, the fact remained that all of Aspen was dressing for this party.

Rosie Sukert, resplendent in red crepe, stood with Bill Pugh who had resurrected his dinner jacket from the back of the closet and, unmindful of its condition, had donned it, wrinkles and all. To her left, Sam, in a short black strapless dress and white jacket, was deep in conversation with Rachel.

A sudden flurry of excitement broke out as the huge mahogany doors opened dramatically and Melanie Rogers walked in with Tucker Thompson, the richest oil man in Texas, a man ten years older than her father.

"Oh, my God, it's Pocahontas in her wedding dress," stage-whispered Rosie. "Do you believe that outfit?"

Melanie wore white buckskin, fringed, beaded, and painted with a gold rattlesnake that twined from hem to shoulder. Her white boots were hand-tooled in gold as well. She had made a slim braid on one side of her hair from which dangled a gold feather and a shower of diamonds.

Before anyone could offer additional comment, Pat Mallory arrived with Liz trailing a step behind. Pat wore jeans, a black dinner jacket and white pleated shirt, a fur felt Stetson and ostrich skin boots. He looked devilishly handsome, a true son of the New West. Liz, donned in a short black lace dress from St. Angelo which was so tight she was forced to walk as if her feet were bound, had pulled back her blond hair severely and caught it with a black-and-silver cuff.

"I see they're still together." Rosie, claiming a reporter's privilege, had stationed herself near the front door so she would be sure not to miss an arriving guest or the opportunity for a comment.

Alex arrived with a waitress from The Bottomless Pit. Rosie clapped her hands over her almost flat chest and rolled her eyes. "Bill, don't look. You'll have a stroke." The girl was a Dolly Parton look-alike in more ways than one. "Those aren't real," she said, pointing to the globes that threatened to explode from her low-cut black sweater.

"How can you tell?"

"They don't move when she walks. And see how

shiny they are? Like big inflated balloons? Definitely silicone!"

"Whatever you say, Rosie," said the long-suffering escort.

Rachel, who was wearing an almost monastic white satin shirt with high-waisted trousers, said, "I didn't know people dressed up like this here."

Sam was about to give her another piece of Aspen social custom when Pat appeared. He kissed his sister, then said mysteriously, "Do you mind if I borrow Rachel for a moment? I want to talk to her."

Sam made a gesture with her hands and turned to find Joe Ferris watching her. She gave him a furious look and was about to turn away, but not before she realized that it was the first time she'd ever seen him in dinner clothes. Next to Pat he was without a doubt the most attractive man in the vast room.

"Wait." He caught her hand in his.

"For what?"

"We need to talk."

"About what?"

"A lot of things."

He was about to steer her away when they heard the sound of a loud voice. The once-beautiful Cynthia Farwell, a drink sloshing over her hand, was pointing a crimson finger at Sophie Mallory. Regal as a queen in a white crepe dinner suit and diamond earrings, her silver hair swept back in a smooth halo, Sophie was a vision of control in contrast to the other woman. Cynthia's face showed the ravages of drink and pills. Her heavy makeup gave it the grimacing look of a mask. A black sequined Norell dress, a size too large for her wasted body, hung from her bony shoulders, giving her the appearance of a glittering scarecrow.

"Don't think I don't know about you," she railed.

"Know what?" asked Sophie with icy calm.

"Never mind." Cynthia turned to the curious crowd that had surrounded the two women. "Hey, everyone! Guess what?" She turned and took an unsteady step toward Sophie. "There stands the uncrowned queen of the duchy of Aspen. Bow down, everyone. Did you know the queen is sleeping with my husband? Did you know that? Did you know he never sleeps with me anymore? Cunt," she said, almost conversationally. "Bitch."

Richard Farwell seized his wife around the waist. "Come along, Cynthia, you've had too much to drink."

"I always have too much to drink," she said.

Richard's daughter appeared at his elbow. "Take her away, anywhere," he whispered tightly. At his daughter's protest, he growled, "Just get her out of here."

His daughter steered the now malevolently laughing woman away as the crowd, realizing that they were witnessing what should have been a private quarrel, turned away in embarrassment and continued the business of partying as if nothing had happened.

Sophie stood as though cast in stone, her face as white as her gown. "I'm sorry, Sophie, that should never have happened," Richard turned to apologize.

"But it did," she whispered fiercely. "I had no idea she was coming. Why didn't you tell me? Why did she make those outlandish accusations? What have you told her about us?" The questions tumbled out in a flood.

"Nothing, I swear it. I asked her for a divorce. She must have seen us talking and realized . . . She's not a stupid woman, only a drunk. I guess she saw something . . . " He lifted his hands helplessly.

She turned from him abruptly.

"Sophie, where are you going?" He reached out to stop her.

She brushed him away with her hand, unwilling to make a scene of her own. Without a word to anyone, she retrieved her coat and left the party quietly. As far as she was concerned her relationship with Richard was over.

Sam's heart had gone out to her mother as she

watched that proud woman stand like a martyr under the flaying tongue of Richard's wife. She wanted to run to her rescue, but Joe Ferris restrained her.

When it was all over, Sam was furious. "How dare she!"

"She's a sick woman. Alcohol makes people do strange things."

"Then you must have been drunk the other night." She turned on him savagely.

Joe, who rarely drank more than a few beers, looked perplexed. "What other night?"

"The night you walked out with Melanie."

"We've got to talk." He looked at the crowded room, then took her hand and dragged her to the library.

"Don't say a word. You don't owe me any explanations. You can do what you want, but do you have to do it with Melanie? Of all people."

The familiar iron curtain fell over his face.

"Oh, Joe!" Her cry was so plaintive, he was seized with remorse. She looked so beautiful standing there in her stark black dress. The white satin jacket was shaped like a calla lily and curved up to contrast with her richly colored skin and black satin hair.

With a hoarse cry, he pulled her into his arms. "God, you're so beautiful."

At first she responded to him with eagerness, but then she dropped her arms to stand passively within the circle of his. "There's something that keeps pulling us together whether you like it or not."

"I know," he said fiercely.

"Then why do you resist it so?"

In answer his mouth crushed down on hers. She tasted as sweet as wild honey and he wanted never to leave her lips. But he forced himself to wrench his mouth away from hers. "Sam, we've got to talk."

"So talk," she said softly, her voice husky.

"Not here."

"Then come home with me."

"No! Not now."

She was surprised at his vehemence.

"Tomorrow. I'll come to your studio."

"What is it, Joe?"

"We'll talk tomorrow."

Louis Breton, arriving fashionably late, immediately set about looking for Sam. As his eyes darted from cluster to cluster, he saw her come out of the library with Joe Ferris. They were holding hands. Then he watched them part reluctantly, their hands remaining locked until the last moment before they separated. Bitch!

Louis started to walk in her direction, only to see her immediately snatched up by a group of handsome young men who whisked her away to the buffet table. He could feel the flames of anger scorch his eyes and burn his chest. He had refused to believe her attack on him had been deliberate. Convinced that he had frightened her by his unexpected move on her, he wanted to apologize and reestablish their relationship. Now he was half-crazed by frustration. No one treated him this way.

Lost in the coils of memory was his own treatment of her. Once again thwarted in his attempt to have her, he let his imagination play with unique tortures.

Sam slept late the next day. As she dressed in her work clothes, she considered calling her mother. But she knew Sophie. If she wanted to discuss the ugly scene between her and Cynthia Farwell, she would make the overtures. So she made a huge pot of coffee and carried it into her studio.

She eyed the new painting appraisingly, liking what she saw. It was of a rosy adobe pueblo against a flat blue sky. In the turquoise doorway sat an Indian woman grinding corn. The entire canvas, though flooded with brilliant color, had the flat look of certain Oriental paintings. Humming along with the soft rock music that was a constant presence in the studio, she began to prepare her palette.

She became so absorbed in her work that when the doorbell rang, she thought it was a fire alarm.

She looked at her watch. Joe hadn't said what time he was coming. She flung open the door. "Joe, since when—"

"Sorry," Louis Breton said icily. "It's not your lover."

"Louis! What are you doing here?" Sam took a step back, remembering how frightened she'd been when she'd left him lying on the floor of his study. Except for briefly at the party last night, she had not seen him. A flood of fear rooted her to the spot.

"I want to talk to you! I think I've earned the right by keeping silent about your attack on me." He brushed by her and before she could stop him, was striding past her and into the studio.

Pushing past her fear, she said angrily, "You can't just walk in here and . . ."

"Be still," he thundered. Then with a smile that made her blood congeal, he made a majestic turn as his eyes swept over her canvases like eager brooms. "So this is the direction your work is taking now. I see I have finally made an impression on you."

"What do you mean by that?"

"I mean you're following my directives."

"I don't know what you're talking about."

He stormed about the room. "This and this and this." Pointing to details with one of her long brushes, his voice grew shrill. "These details, these colors, this texture."

Forgetting everything, Sam felt a desire to laugh. "You're joking. What a colossal ego you have! These are the things you hated."

He looked down on her sadly. "So it's come to this, has it? You stab me in the back. I, who literally made your reputation."

"Almost ruined it, you mean." Her voice rose as she argued with him.

"Unscrupulous," he hissed. "Just like the rest of your family. You take advantage of everything and everyone."

"*I* take advantage?" Sam was stunned, almost speechless. Tears of rage made her incoherent. "Aren't you forgetting something?"

"If you mean what happened at my house. . . ."

"Among other things."

"You owe me, Samantha." He advanced closer to her. "I spent a great deal of my valuable time with you. I gave you the benefit of my knowledge and expertise. I introduced you to the right people in New York. I sponsored your showing. People came because they knew you were my protégée."

She was an artist, not Louis's protégée. Recently, she had come to believe in her talent. Now she had to believe in herself. And with a sense of wonder, Sam realized that she did. Somehow, somewhere, she had accomplished that which had most eluded her. She didn't owe him anything. The painter she was now had little to do with his efforts to mold her. Quietly she said, "That may be true, but the price you ask is much too high."

He took another step toward her and seized her arm. "You used me, Samantha. Now you want to throw me away for that disgusting half-breed. I will see you dead before I'll let him touch you." Louis's elegant face was mottled. So intense was his anger that he didn't hear the soft footsteps.

"I believe the lady made it quite clear that you offend her," Joe Ferris interrupted. His hand snaked out and fastened on Louis's arm. Black basalt eyes glittered dangerously, knuckles turned white as Joe's grip tightened. "I may be a half-breed, but I never force myself on a lady."

Louis, with the cry of a wounded lion and surprising strength, wrenched out of Joe's grasp. "I wish I could challenge you to a duel," he rasped. "You'd soon see who was the stronger."

"Sorry, I was never good with dueling pistols. A shootout at OK Corral maybe." He pulled Sam into the protective circle of his arm. "I believe you were just leaving, weren't you, Louis? Sam and I have a meeting scheduled."

Louis took out a clean pocket handkerchief and wiped his hands as though he'd touched something filthy. "I won't forget this, Ferris."

"I'm counting on it, Louis," Joe said.

Sam held her breath until she heard the slam of the front door. Then she turned to Joe and threw her arms around him.

Gently Joe pushed her away. "All right, Sam. Now we have to talk."

CHAPTER TWENTY

"You're making it up."

"I'm not."

"Why are you telling me now? Why not months ago?" Joe's revelations about his life in Los Angeles and his return to Aspen had left her speechless.

"Because months ago there was no reason."

"And now?"

"Now, there are . . . uh, feelings."

"Yours or mine?" she asked angrily.

"I don't blame you for being angry, Sam."

"Angry? I feel betrayed. I trusted you. I thought you were different. When everyone else was calling you—" she stopped.

"I know," he said softly. "Look, Sam. I've been trying to tell you. Every time we've been together. I told you that there were too many things that stood between us. That there never could be a relationship."

"Who said I wanted one with you?" Her anger took on the tones of the hurt ten-year-old.

Joe's face froze. "Then forgive me for misunderstanding. I thought . . . I mean it seemed . . . I'm sorry."

She wanted to cry out, to put her arms around him, ask him about all the things Alex had told her, and to have him assure her that they weren't true. She wanted to tell him that she loved him, had always loved him, but her Mallory pride wouldn't let her. Pride? No, it was fear. Joe was a dangerous man, a fact she'd chosen to ignore by clothing him in unromantic prince's raiment after he rescued her from Louis's unwanted attentions.

Joe picked up his jacket and folded it over his arm. He was loath to leave her feeling like this, glad he hadn't divulged more, hadn't told her about Gianni. He wondered why he hadn't. Maybe he was testing the waters. To see how much she could accept. If he'd told her the entire truth, he'd probably be in jail by now.

After Joe left, Sam tried to return to work, but the sound of his words echoed in her ears. How could she be so stupid? She had trusted two men since her return to Aspen—Louis and Joe. And they had both turned out to be something far different than she imagined. What was the matter with her? She kept giving her trust to people who betrayed it: Greg, Louis, Joe.

She called Rachel to ask her for lunch, but her answering machine said she'd gone to the historical society. So Sam went skiing instead. Alone. Needing the time to sort things out. Her mixed feelings for Joe. The significance of what he'd told her. His revelations and his strange behavior did more to convince her that Alex was telling the truth than Alex's own words.

Joe rubbed his eyes, waking slowly. When he opened the blinds of his bedroom, the sun exploded into the room as if it had been freed from a dark place. Surveying the rumpled sheets, he shook his head in mild distaste. The room contained a faint aroma from Melanie's perfume, which last night had been seductive but this morning hung as stale and heavy as an ashtray full of cigarette butts.

Joe was about to hit the showers when the phone rang. It was Gianfranco di Lucca.

Dispensing with small talk, he got right to business. "It's time to stop screwing around, Ferris. I need your help. Hank Campbell has got to be taken care of."

"Why, tell me? You seem to be doing all right without me."

"What do you mean?"

"One of your little elves has a big mouth. I know about the explosion and your part in it. Don't involve me in any of your plans."

Gianni's laugh was menacing. "You talk like a man with a clear conscience. Very big for a man who has quite a few secrets of his own."

"I don't care. What's past is past."

"The past is never past. Many people would be interested in yours."

Joe stubbornly continued to resist Gianni's threats.

"Well, if I can't persuade you, perhaps I can find someone who will?"

Joe was immediately suspicious. "Yeah, who?"

"I think if the lovely Samantha Mallory could be isolated for a few days, she might be able to persuade you."

"You fucking bastard!"

Gianni chuckled. How futile resistance was when he had the heavy artillery. "I'll be in touch."

Joe's hand was shaking as he replaced the receiver. The bastard! That was no idle threat. Gianni would think nothing of using Sam to get to him. It was all over. There was no fighting it. His past had marked his future. There was nothing he could do to escape it without putting those he loved in jeopardy.

* * *

As Sam was making a cup of tea for herself later that afternoon, Pat walked in.

"Hope I'm not disturbing anything. I saw your car and figured you were probably alone."

"Oh, Pat, I'm so glad to see you. This has been some day."

"Tell me about it," he said ruefully, taking a mug from the rack. When she finished with her tea bag, he put it in his cup and poured water over it.

"Have you spoken to Mother since the party?"

"We had some business to discuss, but if you're talking about the scene that Farwell's wife made, she refuses to discuss it or him. Sam, were they getting it on?"

"I haven't the vaguest idea. I know they were seeing each other."

"Will wonders never cease! I always thought they were bitter enemies."

"Maybe Mother decided she was using the wrong tactics."

"Maybe. You know, something very strange happened while I was there. At least, I thought it was strange."

Sam held her breath. Had Sophie finally decided to tell Pat about his real father?

"I was telling her I was going to change the scope of the Ute City project, make it a little more human. More green space, less buildings. I told her that you and she might have a point. That maybe we are trying too hard to change Aspen into something it was never meant to be. That if people come to Aspen for its history and uniqueness as well as its skiing, developers should take advantage of that."

"She must have been stunned. And thrilled."

"That's when it got strange. She came to me and put her arms around me and held me very tightly. She kissed me. Then she said, 'I love you very much, Patrick. You might not have thought so, but I do. I'm sorry your father never got a chance to see what a fine man you've become.'"

Cleverly put, Mother, she thought. Revelation inside an ordinary statement of praise. She was about to explain to Pat, then stopped herself. Mother was right. It didn't really matter. After all this time, only the cause of truth would have been served. And who said that was always the best?

"You did a wonderful thing to make her happy, Pat. As far as her love is concerned, I think you always had it. It just didn't come out quite the way you wanted it to."

The jarring ring of the phone intruded on unspoken thoughts.

"Hi . . . Sure . . . I'm here . . . Pat's with me."

She hung up the phone. "That was Rachel. I'd called her earlier and left a message on the machine."

A few minutes later Rachel bounded in. She'd been running. With her pink cheeks and elfin hair she looked to Pat like a pagan wood sprite who'd become trapped in the present.

"Sorry I missed you when you called," she said breathlessly. "What happened?"

Pat looked at Sam. "Something happen?"

"I got so involved in your thing I forgot to tell you. But since you're both here . . ."

Sam's story of Louis Breton's malevolent behavior brought a frown to Pat's face. But when Sam described Joe's timely intervention and the subsequent revelations, as well as Alex's beliefs that Joe was behind the trouble now, Pat's face grew stormy.

"In a way, Pat, I think the Mallorys were responsible for that," Rachel's quiet voice interrupted.

"You mean if Mother hadn't sent him away, none of that would have happened?"

"No, Sam. That feud dates way back. I don't think you realized how rich those diaries and letters you gave me were. But it was really the Fernando records that pulled the pieces together for me." And she told them what Joe had always known. About hatred that had taken root in the arid ground and blossomed through the years as the tale of loss and betrayal was nourished and handed down.

Pat shook his head in disbelief.

"I came across an interesting bit. Miguel Fernando, who worked on one of the MacNeal ranches and was apparently a very handsome man, eloped with Dodge Blackwell."

"Our Dodge Blackwell?" Sam asked. "Great-grandfather's first wife?"

"God, the Blackwells owned millions of acres of ranchland in those days!" Pat added.

"Dodge and Jamie MacNeal had been betrothed when she suddenly married Miguel. Apparently they had been trysting for months and she became pregnant. Several months later she gave birth to twins. I found her letter to Jamie asking for him to take her back along with her baby."

"Which he did?"

"Apparently."

"Wait a minute, you said twins. Now you say baby."

"Apparently, Miguel would not let her have the boy. So she took the girl."

"What happened to Miguel?"

"His body was found in an arroyo months later."

"Was he murdered?" Sam asked, fascinated.

Rachel shrugged. "No one knows for sure. The newspapers of the time said he had been drunk and fallen from his horse. The Fernandos accused the MacNeals of murder.

"In any case, Dodge was dead a year later. And the daughter, who was named Abigail, never married. She died in her thirties. But Angel Fernando, her twin brother, lived. He was Joe's grandfather."

"The grandfather who taught me all I know about Indian life and culture? He must have known who I was and never said a word." Sam was amazed.

"Well, from that point on, the intensity went out of their hatred and the two families more or less coexisted."

"Until you got involved with Joe," reminded Pat.

"I wasn't involved with him. Not like that. We were friends. But I can see why things happened the way they did. Obviously both families knew the history."

"I wonder when we were to be told," said Pat.

"Maybe your mother felt it was time to end the feud."

"Is that why she sent Joe away?" Now it was Sam's turn to be bitter.

Pat leaped up. "This is fascinating, but I think I should tell Richard about Joe's past associations."

"Wait!" said Rachel. "Joe's suffered a lot at the hands of the Mallorys. Sam's really the only one in your family who ever accepted him for what he was. I think her instincts are good and she should listen to them. After all, he did save her from Louis Breton."

"For which I'm grateful, but . . ."

"You think he's guilty of the things that are happening now?" asked Rachel.

"Oh, God, I don't want to," cried Sam.

"What am I supposed to do? If Alex is right, Richard should know about it. He could be in danger, not to mention what might happen on the mountain." Pat wanted to do the right thing, but when he saw the stormy faces of both Rachel and Sam, he wasn't sure what that was. He had finally found some peace with his family, and he didn't want to destroy it.

Rachel put her hand on his arm. "And what if Alex is lying?"

Pat grew thoughtful. "Joe's career here is over, no matter what happens. Sam, if you have any influence with him at all, tell him to come clean."

But when she called Joe's office, he would not take her phone calls. And no matter what time she appeared at the Silver Leaf Spa he was not there. She left messages on his machine at home. She could have tracked him down if she really wanted to, but she was afraid to learn the truth. As the days went on, her disappointment in him grew apace. Still she pleaded with Pat to wait.

One day as Sam, Rachel, and Sunshine sat in Hank's kitchen, looking out the window, enjoying the spectacular colors of the dying day, it seemed that peace had finally descended on the ranch. Hank puffed comfortably on his cob. Rachel closed her eyes and let the fragrance of damp earth and new hyacinths from the open window sweep over her. Sunshine was at the stove frying chicken.

Suddenly Sam sniffed the air. "I smell something burning."

"You smell chicken, honey."

"My cob don't always smell too good," added Hank.

Sam apologized for alarming them. But a few minutes later, she noticed heavy acrid smoke curling from under the door of a closet.

"Sunshine, what do you keep in that closet off the porch?"

"Junk, old rags, paint cans, I guess. You know, stuff you mean to throw away and don't. Why?"

Sam stood up and pointed. "There's smoke coming from there. I knew I smelled something!"

As everyone stared, motionless as pillars of salt, there was an explosion. The next few minutes were pandemonium. Hank, who'd been sitting with his back to the closet, was hurled across the room by the blast. The women were knocked to their knees. Suddenly the room was engulfed in flames and heavy black smoke.

Sam tore off a piece of her shirt and covered her nose. Dropping to her knees, she inched away from the searing heat, breathing the fresher air along the floor through her makeshift mask.

"Rachel! Sunshine!" she screamed. "Where are you?"

"We're here, Sam." She heard them between coughs. "Try to head for the door."

"I can't see it, the smoke's too heavy."

"We're gonna die if we don't get out of here. Try to head away from the heat. The door's got to be there someplace."

As the women clawed their way across the wooden floor, the door suddenly flew open, bringing with it a blast of cool air that drove the flames and smoke back. In that instant the three women found their direction. But the fresh supply of air only fanned the flames into greater intensity.

"Where's Hank?" came the clipped sound of a familiar voice.

"Joe, is that you? Oh, God, I don't know. In there somewhere. The blast knocked him down. Oh, God, I've got to go back and find him," cried Sunshine.

"No, you get out of here. I'll find him. Are you okay?" There was something reassuring in those clipped, masculine words. Someone was in control. "Go for help," he ordered. "Get the fire department. An ambulance. Move it!"

Coughing, tears pouring down their smoke-stained faces, the three women made it outside. They lay on the ground sucking in great gulps of fresh air as Joe Ferris went back into the blazing house again and again to find Hank Campbell. They tossed buckets of water from the trough on him each time he came out empty-handed, his clothes smoking.

Sam watched in agonized fascination at the leaping flames clawing their way up to the sky. It was impossible that anyone could still be alive in that holocaust.

Then like something out of an apocalyptic painting she saw the dark silhouette against the dancing orange light. Joe Ferris staggered out and ran to the far edge of the yard where the horse trough stood. Using his hands as a scoop, he doused Hank's smoking clothes. Then he sat back on his heels. Like an Indian from the past, he roared up at the sky.

By the time the fire trucks arrived, the ranch house was a smoking ruin and the barn charred beyond saving. Fortunately Hank's several horses were still in the field. Now they clustered at the fences, neighing and pawing the earth, eyes wide with fear at the smell of smoke.

When Joe was sure he could do no more for Hank, he came to Sam. She was still kneeling, frozen like a statue at the horror she'd just witnessed. At his touch, she came unglued and started to cry hysterically, pushing him away from her.

"No, don't touch me!"

"There, there, it's over." He patted her tenderly, not something that a man who'd just set a fire would do. Yet beneath her need for his comforting, reassuring touch lay niggling suspicion. How come Joe had been so close at hand when disaster struck?

His grip tightened, words and murmurs spoken convulsively, "God, I thought I'd lost you."

She lifted her eyes and looked at his grimy face, suspicion suspended as she touched the singed eyebrows. "You've lost your eyebrows," she said in a kind of stunned wonder. "Joe, your skin. You're burned."

"I'll be all right," he said with a grim smile.

Much later, when they'd both been released from the emergency room and sent home, Sam and Joe were in her kitchen, gingerly hugging mugs of hot coffee in their blistered hands. Sanity and movement had returned, if only momentarily. Sam found it hard to look him in the eye.

"Cream?"

"No."

"Sugar?"

"No."

"Anything?"

"No. Sam, look at me."

"I can't."

"You think I did it?"

"I didn't say that."

"But you thought it."

Sam shrugged. "You were there. Was it a coincidence?"

"No."

She looked up sharply. "No?" Her voice was a husk.

"I knew it was going to happen sooner or later."

"You knew?"

"Di Lucca wanted me to do it. He threatened to hurt you. And I was going to do whatever he wanted to protect you. But I couldn't. Not even for you. When I saw you outside, I . . ." He dropped to his knees and enfolded her in his arms. "Oh, God, Sam, I was so afraid for you.

"Di Lucca's behind everything that's happened here this winter. The accidents, the slow-downs, everything."

"Di Lucca?"

"You heard me. He even got Alex Breton in on it. Paid him in cocaine. Alex did it for kicks." He told her what he'd overheard that night in the men's room of The Pit and then he waited. For her scorn, her anger, her hatred. All of which he deserved.

Her words were neutral. She hadn't yet reached a decision. "We've got to tell Richard and Pat."

Richard Farwell, hands in his back pockets, paced up and down in front of the floor-to-ceiling windows of his office. From time to time he stopped to look out at the mountain. The snow had completely melted on Little Nell except for a strip about the size of a sidewalk. A handful of skiers made their way down cautiously. When the snow finally ran out, they took off their skis and walked down the rest of the way. But even these diehards couldn't help the resort now. Nothing but a large infusion of money could.

He turned abruptly. "That's it. I have to default to di Lucca. I can't make the payment."

"I could lend you the money," suggested Pat.

"Nope. No good. Then I owe it to you. If it comes to that, I could use my own money. But I'm tired of throwing it away. Di Lucca will get the seats he wants, and I'll get the boot." Richard paused for a last look. "Maybe it's for the best. This goddamn job has cost me too much, and I don't mean money alone."

Pat and Richard stared at each other, not knowing what to say when Sam and Joe burst into the room.

Richard turned to look at the younger man, noticing the cuts and burns on his face. "What is it, Joe? What's wrong?"

"Joe has something to tell you, Richard. You, too, Pat."

Joe folded his arms over his chest. With the proud stance and impassively handsome face, he looked more like a brave than ever. Her heart went out to him. And then Joe started to speak. He told essentially the same story that he had told Sam, only going into more detail. When he told of Alex's involvement, Richard interrupted him and went to the phone. Buzzing his secretary, he said, "Go to the ski shop and get Alex Breton. Bring him here even if you have to drag him yourself."

When the news of the fire came, Gianfranco di Lucca was lying on his stomach, a big nude Swedish girl massaging him. He rubbed his hands with satisfaction. He knew that Joe Ferris would be forced to set the fire after his threats against the Mallory girl.

He was feeling so good he even considered rolling over and having a quick fuck with the Swede. Her heavy breasts tickled his back. He would like to feel them on his chest.

When the phone rang, he snapped his fingers and she handed it to him silently. That was nice, too. Quiet. Not like Liz Mallory's busy gossipy tongue.

The moment he recognized the voice, he smiled. "So my man came through. Just as I told you. Now we ave the board meeting and . . . what? What's that ou say?" Gianni listened to the angry voice grow in ntensity, then stop abruptly. The bastard had hung ip!

He stared at the dead phone with a rapidly beating heart.

"Get out of here," he snarled.

"But? . . ." The Swedish girl said her first and last vords.

"I said get out of here. . . ." He raised his hand in a ist. The girl scurried away. Joe Ferris hadn't set the ire! The company had sent their own goons to take are of it because Gianni was dragging his feet. The oons were still here. He would be next. Gianni sat up bruptly. They would probably be watching the air-ort in Aspen. He would drive to Grand Junction and ly out of there. Gianfranco di Lucca ran upstairs and tarted to pack.

Alex, youthful charm personified with rumpled blond air and a peeling nose, breezed into Richard's office. "Hi, guys! What's up? Someone run off with the till?" Seeing Sam, he came over to hug her, but she pushed im away.

"Tell Richard, Alex."

"Tell him what, Sam?"

"Tell him about the explosion and the threat-:ning telephone call to poison the water supply and ill the other little nasties you did for Gianni di Lucca."

Alex's face tightened imperceptibly. He tried to brazen it out. Then Joe took him by the arm. He was shorter than Alex by several inches, but his grip was ounishing. "Tell them, Alex. You see, I was in the nen's room when you and your little friends were pragging about your 'dirty tricks.' They know every-hing." He gestured to Pat and Richard.

"Okay, okay, so I did it. I didn't mean to hur
anyone. He just wanted to throw a scare into you."

"Why?" asked Richard.

"I don't know. He never told me."

"But why you of all people?"

"I needed the money. He knew it."

"But you have plenty of money," said Pat.

"The old man tied up my trust. Said I was pissing i
away."

"And you were, weren't you? On drugs, among othe
things," said Sam.

Alex didn't answer. "But I didn't torch Hank'
house!"

All eyes turned to Joe. "Don't look at me. I didn't
either. I told you. Di Lucca threatened to expose me
to you, then he threatened to hurt Sam if I didn't do
what he wanted. I was going to, but even before I go
there, I knew I couldn't do it. I was going to warn
Hank, and then I saw Sam's car. Even if you think I
could have done it," he turned to Pat, "you must
know I wouldn't have hurt Sam. Anyway, someone
else did it. I saw them running away."

"Who?" By the way Richard and Pat were looking
at Joe, Sam knew they didn't believe him.

She had to say something. "But he saved our lives! I
it weren't for Joe, Hank would be dead!"

"I can only guess that Santos sent in some goons to
set the fires," said Joe, knowing how weak and uncon-
vincing he sounded.

Richard sat behind his desk. Without looking up, he
said, "There'll have to be an investigation. Ferris, in
return for letting this whole thing drop, I'll accept
your resignation from the Corp."

Sam gave Joe a heartstruck look.

"You'll have it this afternoon," Joe said quietly.

If Pat had ever hoped to see the relationship between Joe and Sam over, he knew that Richard's
request for Joe's resignation had put an end to that.

Sam, lover of lost causes, had found another worth her energy and emotions.

With a sigh, he turned. "I'm calling di Lucca."

"He won't be there," said Joe. "Santos doesn't like failure. Di Lucca's long out of town. I'd bet money on it."

"He doesn't know what's going on."

"Give it a try."

Joe was right.

Later, Pat called each member of the board to invite them to an extraordinary meeting.

That afternoon they assembled, grumbling and annoyed to be interrupted and called away from their "real" work.

"Jesus, Pat, there's a board meeting tomorrow. Couldn't this wait until then?"

"No, it can't," said Pat peremptorily. After making them sit, he told them of the events of the last few days, and Gianni's part in the things that happened over the winter.

"Do you expect us to believe that?" asked Ron Reeves, the other major developer beside Pat on the board.

"You better," warned Pat, "or you're in big trouble."

"Threats, Pat?" Monty Garbish asked from behind a cloud of cigar smoke.

"Look, all I ask is that you hold together and try to prevent di Lucca from taking over Silver Mountain."

"Now, see here, Pat—" blustered Ron.

"I don't know what di Lucca has promised you, but it's not going to happen. In fact, if he wants to be CEO, he might have to do it from the Pitkin County Jail."

Using his most convincing arguments and some velvet-glove threats, Pat finally got a grudging agreement from a majority of the board members.

After getting their word that Richard Farwell would

not be unseated as CEO, he dismissed them, then decided to drive up with Richard and see if Gianni was hiding in his own home. He couldn't believe Gianni would just leave a million-dollar house. But when he let himself in, he again realized he was wrong. Gianni not only could, but had left. His closets were empty.

"Sorry, Richard, I guess you're left holding the bag. You'll have to stay on."

"I will on one condition."

"I think I know what it is already. Mother finally got to you, I see."

"I didn't say a word."

When Richard returned to his office, he took a deep breath and dialed Sophie's number. "Sophie? Don't hang up on me. I'm coming over! You and I have things to talk about. And don't lock the door, because I'll break it down." He slammed the receiver and grabbed his jacket, then suddenly stopped. A rare smile wreathed his face. She hadn't uttered a word of protest.

Pat had one more errand to run before he went home, and that was to see Hank Campbell in the hospital.

He found the old man in a bright, sunny room staring out the window.

As Pat walked in, Hank gave him a cursory glance. "Gonna be spring real soon," he said without enthusiasm.

"Ranch house should be finished in a couple of months. Guess you can stay with Sunshine awhile, huh?" Pat matched his voice to Hank's.

"Whatcha sayin', boy?"

"You heard me."

"Ain't takin' no charity from no Mallory." He tried to rise up from his pillow. But Pat gently pushed him back.

"It's not charity. It's a deal. You forget about that

old mining claim on the mountain. It'll cost you more than you'll take out anyway. If you do, I promise no one will ever bother you again. For that you get the new house. It's a good deal, Hank.

"Give up my claim, huh?"

Pat nodded.

Hank smiled. "Alw'ys hated going into them tunnels. Okay, boy, yuh got yourself a deal." They shook hands on it. Then the old man gave him a smug smile. "And mebbe if I ever decide to sell out, I'll give yuh first crack."

"You better."

"Not making no promises, you unnerstan'."

The minute Pat Mallory stepped foot into his own house that evening, he knew something was different. The lights were on, seductive music poured through the house's sound system, and delicious smells issued from the kitchen.

When Liz appeared in a black dress that left nothing to the imagination, he was convinced. "What's going on, Liz?"

"Can't a woman do something nice for her husband once in a while?"

"Not when she's you."

"Come on, darling. Change into something comfortable and come down and have a drink. I sent the children to Sam's for dinner. It's just us."

Once that would have been tempting. Now he felt totally indifferent. As he showered, he wondered what Liz was up to. A pattern had developed over the years. Every time Liz dispensed with a lover or he with her, she'd returned to him for a brief night of reassuring sex.

Who was it this time? he wondered.

Piqued with curiosity, he began to nose around. Her wastebasket was filled with crumpled tissue and cigarette butts. He rummaged around in the bottom and felt a ball of crumpled paper. It was not tissue.

Smoothing it out, he read the brief message, saw the scrawled G, and the lightbulb went on.

As he entered the living room, she looked up with a melting smile and held up her arms to him.

"You must despise me." He ignored the outstretched arms.

"Pat!" she protested.

"Then you must think I'm very stupid." In place of himself, he thrust the letter at her.

At once her face grew sulky. "So?"

"So who's G? Let me guess."

"The bastard," she said in a low voice, as if she were speaking to herself. "I gave him everything he wanted and this is the way he treats me."

"What, Liz?" Pat bent forward. "What did you give him?"

"Nothing."

"Something besides your hot body?"

An ugly red stain mottled the perfect ivory skin. Was it possible? His mind flashed back, remembering bits of conversation, conversation that made no attempt at disguising his business dealings. She'd been the leak. Gianni had bought those properties out from under him because of information he'd unwittingly given his wife. One look at her face told him he had guessed correctly.

When he spoke, his voice was cold and menacing. "You poor bitch. He used you. God, do you think I care that he slept with you? Those things used to bother me. But no more. It's the fact that you tried to destroy this family, your own children included. What did Gianni give you for that information? You certainly didn't need money. Did he promise to marry you? To take you away from all this and live in some crumbling villa in Italy?" He came closer and closer until his face was inches from hers.

"Yes, yes," she screamed, trying to push him away. "I would have been a contessa. Away from here and your mother and your self-righteous sister. And you. But he lied to me. He's gone."

"Probably lied about the title, too. You pitiful woman. I'm leaving now. By the time I come back I don't want to see anything that even suggests you once lived here."

"What about the children?" she said as he turned to leave.

He looked at her. "Forget about the children. Out. I mean it."

He got into his car and headed down the mountain to Rachel's.

In the comfortable garden room, he watched her pour coffee. Every move, every nuance of her soft, quiet manner brought him pleasure. Even her compact little body in the old corduroys and shrunken sweater made him happy.

"I don't want you to say a word. Just listen." He told her about Liz. "She's gone. It's over. There's nothing to stand in my way. I want you to know that I have no intention of letting you out of my life. I'm probably in love with you already, but I want to be sure. And I want you to be sure, too."

Rachel held her hand over her heart as if to prevent it from leaping out of her chest.

"It won't work, Pat," she said. They were so different with different goals and philosophies. "Besides, I have to go back to New York."

"When?" he asked, tight lipped.

"Soon."

"But not this minute."

"No."

"Good." He came to her side and put his arms around her, turning her to face him. Then he picked her up and carried her to the couch. Looking lovingly at her delicate face with the too big eyes and long lashes, he lowered his head and put every ounce of his love into their kiss.

She sighed in his arms.

"When are you coming back?" he whispered into her ear.

"Soon," she said, tightening her grip on him. They both deserved the chance.

"You know I've loved you all my life," said Sam, turning to wrap her arms around Joe's chest. She nuzzled the hard paps on his chest.

"Foolish girl."

"You love me, too. Don't tell me otherwise."

"Ever since you were ten. Although I can't understand what I ever saw in a ten-year-old."

"I can."

"What?"

"Potential."

He laughed, but there was sadness in the sound. "This is going to be very difficult for us, Sam. Our percentages are lousy."

"Sshh." She closed his mouth with hers. "We have a lot to make up for. All those MacNeal and Fernando ghosts are hovering over us. Don't you see, Joe? We are connected. Fated. Surely an old Indian savant like you can see that."

"I've got a lot to live down."

"You saved me and Hank. You told some very tough truths to Richard and my brother. You've paid your debt as far as I'm concerned."

"What about your mother?"

"She knows everything."

He shrugged. "I rest my case."

"Good. Now, would you please make love to me?"

On an unseasonably hot day in late May, long after the snows had melted, a boy was wading in Castle Creek looking for cans. Instead he discovered a body and told his father.

When the sheriff and his men came, they saw a badly decomposed male body. An expensive gold watch with a florid engraved G dangled from the unrecognizable flesh. The shoes, though badly water-logged, were obviously expensive.

Spring had arrived with a vengeance. The meadows of Aspen were covered with wildflowers. Tender green aspen leaves trembled in the fresh breezes. Bikers sent their aching muscles to work on newly opened Independence Pass.

Pat Mallory, on a solitary hike up to Maroon Bells, stopped to listen to the sounds of the high mountains. A flock of nutcrackers hovered about him hoping for a handout. For the first time since he was a boy, he was beginning to feel what the women in his family had felt all along. This land he'd considered empty because there was nothing built on it was truly filled. With those treasures that calmed the heart and fed the brain. Rachel, his love; Sophie, his mother; Sam: The earth goddesses, as he thought of them, had always understood those things. Now he was beginning to see. It was up to him to help preserve them.

ABOUT THE AUTHOR

Writing under the name of Lorayne Ashton, Rita Picker Silton, a former advertising executive at BBD&O and J. Walter Thompson, is also the author of *Park Avenue, Show and Tell, Island Paradise,* and *When Lightning Strikes.* She is currently working on a sequel to Aspen and divides her time between Vermont, New York City, and Aspen.